ARTIFICIAL LIGHT

By: Nathan Wall

Congrats! Hope you love it as much as I enjoyed writing it.

Copyright © 2015 by Nathan Wall

All right reserved

This is a work of fiction. Names, characters, businesses, places, events and incidents are either the products of the author's imagination or used in a fictitious manner. Any resemblance to actual persons, living or dead, or actual events is purely coincidental.

The characters, events and world created in this Novel are the sole property of the author. No portion of this book may be reproduced, stored in a retrieval system, or transmitted in any form or by any means-electronic, mechanical, photocopy, recording, or any other-except for brief quotations in printed reviews, without the prior written permission of the copyright owner and author.

ISBN: 978-1-941714-05-8

DEDICATION

To my wife and children

For all you mean to me

My inspiration and purpose

Without you I am nothing

ii

EPIGRAPH

"I simply believe that some part of the human self or soul is not subject to the laws of space and time."

- Carl Jung

iv

Artificial Light is the 3rd book in the Evolution of Angels series.

It is the culmination of coinciding events in book 1 "Evolution of Angels" and book 2 "The Descendants."

Table of Contents

Prologue: Page 1

Chapter One— Jarrod I: Page 9

Chapter Two— Austin I: Page 17

Chapter Three— Lian I: Page 23

Chapter Four— Austin II: Page 27

Chapter Five— Set I: Page 35

Chapter Six— Horus I: Page 45

Chapter Seven— Madame Patricia I: Page 59

Chapter Eight— Lian II: Page 69

Chapter Nine— Jarrod II: Page 79

Chapter Ten— Isis I: Page 89

Chapter Eleven— Isis II: Page 97

Chapter Twelve— Anubis I: Page 105

Chapter Thirteen— Horus II: Page 111

Chapter Fourteen— The Observer: Page 121

Chapter Fifteen— Horus III: Page 137

Chapter Sixteen— Set II: Page 153

Chapter Seventeen— The Observer: Page 167

Chapter Eighteen— Lian III: Page 177

Chapter Nineteen— Austin III: Page 185

Chapter Twenty— Jarrod III: Page 195

Chapter Twenty-one— Jarrod IV: Page 201

Chapter Twenty-two— Lian IV: 209

Chapter Twenty-three— Anubis II: 217

Chapter Twenty-four— The Observer: 223

Chapter Twenty-five— Horus IV: 235

Chapter Twenty-six— Set III: 247

Chapter Twenty-seven— Austin IV: 257

Chapter Twenty-eight— Lian V: 265

Chapter Twenty-nine— Jarrod V: 271

Chapter Thirty— Jarrod VI: 281
Chapter Thirty-one— Lian VI: 291
Chapter Thirty-two— Set IV: 297
Chapter Thirty-three— Isis III: 305
Chapter Thirty-four— Anubis III: 313
Chapter Thirty-five— Madame Patricia II: 321
Chapter Thirty-six— Anubis IV: 333
Chapter Thirty-seven— Madame Patricia III: 345
Chapter Thirty-eight— Austin V: 355
Chapter Thirty-nine— Lian VII: 359
Chapter Forty— The Observer: 365
Chapter Forty-one— Jarrod VII: 383
Chapter Forty-two— Set V: 391
Chapter Forty-three— Austin VI: 395
Chapter Forty-four— Horus V: 401
Chapter Forty-five— Lian VIII: 409
Chapter Forty-six— Set VI: 415
Chapter Forty-seven— Jarrod VIII: 423
Chapter Forty-Eight— The Observer: 435
Epilogue: 439

Thank You: a
About the Author: c
After Credits: e

PROLOGUE

The Birth of a Prince

O siris barreled towards the large slate-grey sliding door, fleeing the scene of scattered debris and flames. His fortress of angelic alloy rattled as the methodical boom-boom of the ground quaking beneath his feet sent cracks slithering up the walls and dust falling from the ceiling. His left hand pressed firmly onto the side of his stomach, trying to stem the flow of blood oozing out of a knuckle-wide puncture. His vision was hazy, and he was barely able to see his beautiful pregnant wife standing in front of the flaming torches waiting for him. A pink light shimmered behind him.

"Turn around!" Isis screamed, hunching over. She removed her hand from a control pad and the blast door stopped lowering.

Osiris swiveled to face his hunter, manifesting a sword in his right hand. The blade deflected Raphael's attack. Their steel sparked in the shadow-enveloped corridor. The slicing of their colliding blades was enough to send a shiver down one's spine.

Isis fell to her knees. Her husband was losing his grip on the fight. Raphael was too fast – Osiris couldn't maneuver to deflect every blow.

An ache in her stomach caused her to hunch as the life inside kicked furiously on her ribcage. The cramp squeezed her chest, back, and abdomen. It was as if a horse-drawn sled was being dragged over her.

Raphael grabbed Osiris by the neck and slammed his head into the wall. His long sword shifted into a misericorde and he thrust it towards his enemy's heart. Osiris, leader of the Southern Corner, slid to the right. The blade missed, penetrating rock. Raphael elbowed Osiris' throat and backhanded his face. He pulled the blade from the wall, aiming it for the head. Isis intervened, blinding him with a flash of energy from her aurascales.

Osiris kneed Raphael in the gut. The sword in his hands morphed into a mallet. The weapon glanced off the side of Raphael's armored face, sending him to the ground. Osiris prepared to deliver a deathblow but his wife called out once more.

"The baby," she cried, snaring his attention. He turned to look at her, noticing her thighs and hands were wet. "He's coming now. We must escape to the other realm."

He looked down at Raphael. The angel's curly brown hair fell across his chocolate skin hiding his radiant green eyes, which glared in Osiris' direction. Osiris tempered his erratic breathing and nodded. The fight was over. Raphael lay still, bleeding subtly from his mouth. Osiris ran as best he could to be by Isis' side. The wall closed, sealing off the outside, keeping Michael's second-in-command at bay.

"W-where's Th-Thoth?" she stuttered, grinding her teeth together.

"Beheaded by Raphael," he replied, holding her hands firmly as he moved his free palm along her neck. His piece of the Forge hung from a golden necklace between her breasts. Her sun-kissed skin was clammy. She shuddered once more. "You must tell me how to do this."

"Nephthys," she whispered, short of breath.

She pointed towards another room where a young boy about three or four years of age stood looking in from the doorway. He was a pudgy child with an almost gray complexion and black hair. The boy smiled and his fat cheeks scrunched up over his dark eyes. Large dimples absorbed almost half of his face.

"Anubis," Osiris said, looking at the boy. "Please find your mother."

Anubis giggled and turned, running off to find his mom. The large white cloth around his waist and crotch slid from side-to-side. Isis moved her fingertips to Osiris' abdomen, touching his wound. He grimaced, and she gently stroked his tanned, rigid cheekbones with the back of her hand before curling her fingers around the jet-black hair that sprouted from his square chin.

She groaned again, scrunching forward. Beads of sweat ran down the side of her face as she dug her fingernails into his other hand. He continued to massage her with gentle circular motions along the small of her back. She wailed as she leaned down.

"You must go," she said, pleading with her eyes. "We can't open the rift and leave this plane without the power of your starstone."

"I'm not leaving your side," he said.

"If you don't go, they'll break through the barriers and kill our child. To them, he's an abomination. His life should not be."

"Yet here he is." Osiris shook his head, balling up his fist. He mumbled to himself. "Why must we be different?"

"How long has she been like this?" Nephthys asked, rushing to the side of the two lovers. Anubis meandered behind her and poked his head around his mother's legs to steal a glimpse of his aunt.

"A few minutes," Osiris replied, slowly standing. He looked at his wife, as if promising his return, and she nodded. "All will be taken care of."

A white light emanated from his palm and a starstone appeared in his hand. The little metal cubes shifted from the stone to his skin, changing in color. The fluid lime aurascales formed over him and silver armored plates jutted out over his shoulders, chest, neck and back. The armored plating ran across the bridge of his nose, over his forehead and along the back of his skull, elongating down his jaw line. The aurascales covered his face and cheeks with two slits in the helmet that allowed his amber eyes to glow through. Green aurascales sprouted from his back and formed wings.

Osiris flew through the corridors of his Armada cruiser. He arrived at a cylindrical chamber, soared to the top of the silo, and stepped onto a landing that looked out upon the numerous galaxies. His brother, Set, stood at the helm, waiting.

"I see you took the scenic route," Set joked, still typing away on a control panel made of pure white energy. In front of them, orbs and streaks of light manifested out of the dense black nothingness. An outline of the infinite cosmos took shape in holographic form. "Where should we establish our new realm?"

"There," Osiris replied, pointing through the infinite lights to a quickly spinning blue orb in the distance; one that barely glimmered at all when compared to the others. He swiped his hands to the side, wiping away all of the shining spheres of energy until only the one that he had selected was visible. His fingers spread and the orb enlarged. "We can live here. Far away from the troubles of this galaxy, and the shield of Michael which protects it, and the prodding sword of Lucifer which poisons it."

"Hardly a paradise." Set shook his head, not bothering to hide his distaste for the location. "Father isn't bound to keep his promise beyond the shores of this world. We should fight to the death."

"Those who stand in Father's way will perish, or worse." Osiris put a hand to his brother's shoulder, rubbing it. He laid his other hand out, palm up, and reformed the starstone in the center of his grasp. His aurascales peeled off into his starstone. "Let us flee and make a new life for ourselves elsewhere, as the other Corners will do—perhaps one day Father will accept us."

"What about our portion of the Forge?" Set asked. "Can we get the other pieces?"

"It still hangs around my wife's neck," Osiris replied. "When we align with Zeus, our pieces of the key will unite."

"I still can't believe you mean to mingle our kind with Zeus'," Set snickered, slowly taking Osiris' powerful Archangel starstone into his own grasp. "That pompous ass has always looked down his nose at us. What about Vishnu and his portion of the key?"

"Zeus has found a way to make his own people, who may prove useful in the years to come." Osiris hunched over the control panel, his wound aching. "The followers under his watch and those under ours have always had a strong bond. The marriage of his daughter to my son will ensure our legion's place among the rulers is safe. What Vishnu does is his own business."

"Your son." Set nodded, smirking. He went to place his brother's starstone into the center of the light in order to open a rift in space-time, but stopped. He pulled it back. "Anubis was the first. A new light just as much as your son. I see no reason why he shouldn't take Athena's hand."

"What?" Osiris shook his head, seeing triple. He struggled for breath, falling to his knees. The battle and the wound on his side were taking their toll. "I am the Archangel of our Corner. Set, you will do as instructed."

"I'm beginning to see in you what Cain saw in Abel." Set's facial armor formed over his face. Shimmering wings sprouted from his back. Three razor-sharp blades sprang forward from his wrist and around his hand. He drove the heel of his boot into Osiris' chest, casting his brother across the floor. "I don't want your planet, and I don't want to live under your son or the offspring of that rat, Zeus."

"Then where will you go?" Osiris gasped, trying to push himself up.

"I've got my own options." Set jumped onto Osiris' back, pinning him to the floor. The three blades stuck into Osiris' shoulder blade and twisted. "There's always Vishnu. He was quite perturbed by you and Zeus plotting all this without him."

"He'd never make an alliance with a lesser angel such as you," Osiris said, biting back the pain. He screamed as the blades were pulled out of his back. Set dropped him to the floor. Osiris choked on air. "He's just using you."

"I thought of that too, so I don't really like that option either. You Archangels always thought you were better than the rest of us. Maybe you are – that's why I arranged to become one."

"You can't..."

"But I can." Set smirked with satisfaction. "I cut a deal. A nice little plea bargain, if I do say so myself."

He typed a code into the control panel to his right. The top of the fortress opened and the infinite black of space gave way to the radiant light from Heaven. Osiris turned his gaze up, watching as Raphael and two others slowly descended upon them.

"No." Osiris lunged for Set. He slammed Set's head into the floor and reconnected with his starstone before leaping off the platform. His aurascales didn't respond, deeming him too frail for bonding. He crashed at the bottom of the silo, shattering his legs and a few ribs. His starstone bounced to Anubis' feet. He looked at his young nephew, barely able to mutter a word. "Go."

Anubis smiled innocently, picked up the stone and waved. He ran back towards his mother and aunt, towards the screams of his baby cousin. Nephthys removed the baby boy from between Isis' legs and placed the crying child in his mother's arms. She looked over to Anubis, curious as to what was in his hand.

"Anubis, what do you have?" she asked, reaching to take the stone from him, but briefly halted upon realizing what it was. "Oh my..."

"What is it, sister?" Isis smiled, rubbing her baby's chin. She gazed at Nephthys and the look of joy bled from her face. She motioned for the starstone, taking it from her sister. Her fingers rubbed the metal squares. "Osiris..."

"Is dead for his treason," Raphael interjected. Nephthys turned to face him, but she did not move quickly enough – his sword slashed through her neck and her body and head collapsed to the floor, separately. He crept towards Isis and the two young boys. "There is only one punishment for creating an Angel-born."

"I know." She took Anubis into her arms and squeezed the stone tightly. A bubble of light surrounded them. She merged Osiris' star with her own, forming an energy shield of lime green and aurora pink that Raphael couldn't penetrate. "But I don't accept it."

Like the quick flicker of a shooting star reflecting off Raphael's breast plate, light erupted from the fused starstones and opened an escape to the unknown. The pink glare pulsated once and vanished, taking Isis and the cousins with it.

8

CHAPTER ONE

Jarrod I

Jarrod clung to the sides of the toilet, heaving once again. Loud blasts, reminiscent of a child banging his arm across all the keys of a synthesizer, ran roughshod across his temples. Was insanity finally sinking in? After all, he was the only one who could hear the noise.

The sound hit him upside the head with all the subtlety of a baseball bat. His fingers curled and raked across the floor. A mirage of floating figures, cast about in blinding white light, entangled themselves with the physical world around him. Visions and sounds of the hazy silhouettes were gone as suddenly as they'd appeared, sucked back into the void. The color in his face returned, bleeding from an off shade of pearl into something a little more human-looking, but the whites of his eyes remained crimson.

He took hold of the washbasin, aching as he pulled himself to a standing position, and looked in the mirror. His black facial hair had grown long, to the point where it could no longer be considered scruff. His belly grumbled, yet food no longer appealed to his palate or agreed with his stomach. Oddly enough, his frame had never looked healthier.

Again, he retched into the toilet, finding it hard to believe that there was anything left in his stomach. The strained, raw taste at the back of his tongue taunted his insides and prodded at his throat.

It'll go away. He rubbed his eyes as the numbing sensation that plagued his intestines began to cease. *Nothing can last forever.*

He flushed the toilet and then splashed some hot water on his face. Leaning over the sink, he took deep breaths of the rising steam and dried himself with his sleeve before wiping the fog from the mirror. With one stroke, it was as if he'd pulled open the curtain to another dimension. His face stared back at him, snarling with a devilish grin. It wasn't him, though. At least, he didn't think so. He placed his fingers on his cheeks. It didn't feel like he was making the expression he saw in the mirror.

"I'm agitated," stated his reflection. The voice was clear as day, definitely his own although he hadn't said anything. The reflection spoke again, rolling its eyes and laughing. "You're pathetic. Just look at you. You're going to get them killed."

Jarrod knew who the reflection was talking about, but didn't want to acknowledge it. Somehow just thinking their names seemed to lend credence to the reflection's taunts.

"Are you listening to me?"

The figure in the mirror smashed its fist into the glass, causing a spider-web crack to slither across its surface. It punched again, this time breaking through, and grabbed Jarrod by the throat. Its fingers turned into spikes, piercing Jarrod's skin. Black goo frothed from the figure's mouth as it crawled out of the broken frame. Its eyes were pure blue energy, its face shifting into a ghoulish form with prominent black, skeletal features.

"You. Are. The. FAKE."

Thump. Thump. Thump.

The triplet of knocks jolted Jarrod awake. He drew a long, exaggerated breath, refreshed and ready to tackle anything that lay ahead, as if waking from a long night's rest. A quick glance at his surroundings and he realized it wasn't the same restroom as before.

It had happened again. His palms began to sweat as he thought about the things he might have done on autopilot.

"C'mon mate," said the muffled voice filtering through the door. "I've gotta drain me-self. I'm burstin' at me seams."

"Yeah, uh, just a second," Jarrod replied, running his fingertips along the smooth glass of the mirror before touching his own face. He smiled mechanically, just to make sure it was his own reflection.

"Naw, right now buddy." The man pounded the door again.

"I said SHUT UP," Jarrod yelled with a ferocious growl. He punched the door and a large indent appeared in the metal. The cracked skin on his knuckles quickly resealed, leaving only a small trickle of blood that was easily wiped away.

How can this keep happening? He stared at his wide-eyed reflection as his worried mind turned to his friends.

Jarrod tried to avoid people; especially those closest to him. He couldn't remember the last time he'd slept in the cabin with his friends. He was too scared of what might happen to them. Every soul now called out to him, begging to be reaped—no longer just the corrupt ones. It was like an itch in his brain, begging for a good scratch. The lure was strongest when he slept, and too often he awoke in strange places, unsure of how he'd ended up there. When his willpower was strong enough, he avoided sleep altogether. Somewhere after the third straight day of no rest, time and space seemed to run together.

A few days ago, Jarrod had begun hearing strange noises in his head. It was like the high-pitched feedback from a microphone. He didn't know the meaning of the sound, yet it didn't feel foreign. Sometimes it merely irritated him, while other times it would turn his brain upside down. Sometimes it lulled him to sleep. Or could that have been his self-imposed sleep deprivation? It didn't matter. What did matter was that he found himself on autopilot more and more often.

Yesterday, the ringing had become more frequent, more distinct, like the tolling bell of a sinking ship. A few hours later, the sound of the horn had started. Blaring louder than the rest of the chaotic tune in his head, the horn intimidated him—it seemed to demand to be heard.

"I'm gonna piss me-self, mate," the voice on the other side of the door pleaded. "Hurry up, you wanker."

Jarrod didn't know why he felt so agitated, but the intense anger within him bubbled to the surface.

"I'll rip your damn head off, you pathetic piece of shit. SHUT UP," Jarrod snapped, making a fist so hard that his fingernails dug into his palms. He was shaking, both from anger and the shock of his outburst. He stepped back from the door, rubbing his head.

What the hell is wrong with me?

He turned the rusty knob on the sink and the pipes rumbled as a slow trickle emerged from the spout. A small pool collected in his cupped hands and he tried to drink. Although he wasn't thirsty, he forced it down. He slicked his hair back with wet fingers, pushing the long, dark strands out of his eyes.

His hands were glowing blue; the aura from his fingertips flashing like a neon sign at a jazz lounge. Wary that the light might be seen through the crack under the door, he reached into his back pocket for his gloves to cover his hands.

He slid into his brown flannel jacket and pulled his black skullcap over his head, his hair jutting out the back of the beanie like metal spikes. As he left the restroom, Jarrod shoved the waiting man into the wall before making his way to the cargo hold of the large ship. He nodded at one of his supervisors and picked up a tool belt.

"'Ey Cooper, wot nickel and dime is it?" his boss asked sarcastically. Jarrod nodded, acknowledging that he was late for work, and proceeded up a flight of metal steps. His supervisor spoke again. "'Old on, mate. I neet-a man down in B-19. We're making our final preps fer Car'iff."

Jarrod nodded again, trying not to make eye contact, and turned to head back downstairs. His efforts to shield his eyes proved useless as his supervisor blocked his path, placing a hand on Jarrod's chest.

"Give me a look," he said, trying to gaze into Jarrod's eyes. "C'mon, now."

Jarrod obliged.

"You been drinkin'?" his supervisor sniffed, leaning in close. While the smell of alcohol was absent, the look in the man's eyes indicated that his mind was turning to more devious things. He pulled Jarrod's sleeves up, examining his arms, and turned out his coat pockets. "What are you on?"

"Nothing, I'm just a bit under the weather," Jarrod said, smacking his lips, trying to give his mouth a bit of moisture. His supervisor went to remove the gloves, but Jarrod snatched his arm back. "I wouldn't do that, sir."

"C'mon, wot ya hidin'?"

Despite Jarrod's protests, he pulled one of the gloves off.

Everything was normal.

"Well, perhaps when you're done assistin' Hank, gettin' those last containers prepped, you can catch some fresh air."

"Will do, sir." Jarrod gave the man a nervous smile.

"Relax kid, the first leg of the journey is over. There's lots lef' ahead yet, though."

"Yes, sir. You couldn't be more right." Jarrod smiled tightly before hurrying off.

"Hey, kid," the supervisor called out again. "Knock i' off with the sir rubbish. I'm no' THAT ol'."

"Sure thing," Jarrod agreed with a nod.

Suddenly, his mind went blank. The itch crawled up from the base of his skull and his hands were no longer his own. The pitter patter of his feet echoing down a hallway, slow and dull like a grandfather clock, was the only noise able to make it through the thick, gelatin wall in his mind. He smacked his face and closed his eyes, taking in a deep breath. Upon exhaling, he opened his eyes and found that he was in a new place. Again.

What?

"I'm sorry, please don't hurt me," a man pleaded. Jarrod turned around to see a fellow ship-hand shaking in fear while another lay inert on the floor beside him. "I think you killed him."

"No, impossible," said Jarrod, shaking his head, although he knew it wasn't. "I can fix this. I've returned them before... Their souls."

"I'm stuck on this ship with a loon," the man wailed, covering his face.

Jarrod knelt beside the unconscious man. When he found that the man was still breathing, a gush of relief washed over him. He removed his gloves and rolled up his sleeves, watching the blue hue snake through his veins. His fingertips moved to the man's forehead.

"Believe, Jarrod, you've got this," he said to himself, exhaling. His arms lit up and a blinding light overpowered anything else they could see.

The formerly unconscious man sat straight up as the energy surged from Jarrod's arms into his body. The gash on his stomach stitched itself back together.

Upon seeing this, the frightened ship-hand bolted from the room like an Olympic sprinter.

"Just... rest for a second." Jarrod patted the now healed man on the back and stood. He was hit by a woozy feeling, but managed to regain his balance and walk out into the hall. This area was familiar.

I'm back here?

He stepped lively, walking with intent towards a restroom. Once inside, fragments of glass cracked under his boots. Brushing the wall with his hand, he searched for the light switch, but there was no response when he flicked it. He unhooked a large steel flashlight from the back of his utility belt, turned it on, and scanned the small restroom. The light glinted off something in the dark and Jarrod stopped dead.

The shattered mirror.

"It actually happened?" he whispered, stepping into the darkness.

Outside, he heard chatter as people approached the bathroom. Their voices were unmistakable—they were his friends, Claire and Austin, and they were looking for him. Turning off the flashlight, he closed the door, leaving only an inch-wide gap. They passed by the doorway without seeing him.

Once the coast was clear, he turned around and flicked the flashlight back on. The area behind the mirror was smashed inward. He compared his fist to the hole. The size matched.

But I didn't hit it. He scratched his head. *Did I?*

He spun around, illuminating the area where his head had been bashed into the wall. His heartbeat raced when he noticed an indentation. His head was fuzzy, unable to shake this lethargic feeling.

I punched out the mirror and bashed my own head into the wall?

His fingers caressed the indentation on the wall as he knelt to inspect it more closely. The evidence didn't jive with his recollection of events.

"You're losing it," a voice whispered in a mocking tone.

Jarrod spun around, but there was no one there. He searched the darkness erratically with the flashlight but couldn't see anything. Closing his eyes, he shook his head.

"I need some air," he laughed, slowly growing more unhinged. "Seriously, I need to get off this damn ship."

"You and me both," the whispering voice replied.

Jarrod opened his eyes, still smiling, but in a deranged sort of way. His right eyebrow rose as he turned his head slightly to look over his shoulder.

"Keep your eyes forward," the voice said.

"Why?"

"You can't take it."

"Do I at least get a name?" Jarrod asked.

"Introductions in due time."

"You're all in my head." Jarrod smirked, feverishly rubbing his face. "Charon put you up to this? You're not real."

"I can assure you, I'm very real."

"Then prove it," Jarrod growled, turning around and smacking another hole into the steel. There was nothing there. "That's what I thought. You're afraid."

Jarrod pulled his hand out of the wall and noticed that somehow his armor had manifested over his hand and forearm. It had never done that on its own before. He shook his hand, trying to command the stray portion of his suit to vanish, but it wouldn't listen to him.

"If I'm afraid, you are," the voice replied. The aurascales crawled further up Jarrod's body, but this time he couldn't stop them. It felt like he was drowning. Worse, he was sure that he could hear Claire making her way back towards him. The voice laughed. "How many of them can you save?"

CHAPTER TWO

Austin I

A door creaked behind them. Claire didn't notice it, and it wouldn't have been fair to expect her to—her hearing wasn't as refined as Austin's, which was heightened thanks to his new animalistic senses. Since first shifting into a wolfish creature, caused by the infection spread to him through gashes made on his back while in Maya's custody, Austin had gradually honed his skills. What he called his new 'super hearing' was the hardest. New frequencies not audible to the human ear—and some he lost when a concussion grenade went off near him during a raid—were gifted to him. At first they couldn't be picked apart. As his skill grew, he was able to distinguish various notes and sounds in a flood of otherwise inaudible or jumbled information.

"I think we passed something," he whispered to her. Claire stopped in her tracks and spun around on a dime. She closed her eyes and leaned in the direction of the perceived noise, but shook her head and shrugged. Austin glared at a spot on the floor, though he didn't see it in the normal sense. His mind's eye was sifting through the sounds. Was it a man or a rat? Could the ship just be making noises? "There's definitely something there."

"You would know," Claire replied, nodding. She led the way back. "To be the only one without powers actually makes me feel like I'm the weird one."

He raised an eyebrow. "Sorry you think we're weird." The way her blood thumped through her veins told him she was embarrassed. He smirked. "I'm kidding. I know what ya mean."

"Which way?" she asked, standing at a T-section in the hall. "I'd like to be good for something more than an ear to gab at or a pair of hands to bring coffee."

He tapped her shoulder and pointed with his thumb to the right. "Not everyone is capable of withstanding that type of monotony. Perhaps your gift is the most important."

"Knowing whether you like cream or sugar in your coffee?" she asked with a half-chuckle. "Is that really a compliment?"

"Keeping up the perception of normalcy in a sea of paranormal and weird? Yeah, it's a compliment." The hairs on his arms stood up. He froze in place and held his hand up for her to stop . "There are eyes on us."

"When are there not?" She stepped back and leaned against the wall.

"I'd like to think while I shower." He knelt and rubbed his fingers along the ground. Black grime stuck to his fingertips. He smelled it and a vision formed. A path walked by a third set of feet flashed into his head.

"What is it?"

"A pair of boots that have been in the lower levels came through here. Could be Jarrod." He stood and his brow furrowed. He motioned with two fingers for her to follow.

"You got all that by smelling shit?" She covered her smile with a hand.

"Not shit. Engine grease." They followed a track mapped out by his nose.

She sighed. "I was joking."

"That's not one of your powers." He bit his lip in order to subdue the laugh swelling inside. It didn't work. She slapped the back of his head. "Hey, now."

A sound reminiscent of a mallet against sheet metal echoed down the corridor from behind them. Austin ducked and Claire dropped to her knees. The muffled tone of a male voice vibrated through the walls, tickling the back of Austin's ears. He turned around and noticed Claire was walking towards a door. A blue light which had been shining through a crack underneath the door vanished. Her hand lifted to the knob. Austin pulled her back and wrapped his arms around her shoulders.

"What was that for?" She pushed away from Austin.

"Go back to the cabin." Austin narrowed his eyes. With trembling lips, he snarled and stared holes through the door. He looked over his shoulder at her. "That wasn't a request."

"Is it him?"

"Go." He said forcefully. She sprinted out of sight.

Austin moved forward, kicked through the door and broke the knob off. He held his flashlight like a club. The restroom was empty. The mirror over the sink was shattered, and in its place was a hole the size of a fist smashed into the wall. The acrid smell of vomit hung in the air. One of the ceiling boards was askew, making a hole just big enough to crawl through.

"Jarrod," Austin sighed, running his hand through his dirty blonde hair to shake the stress out, "What are you doing? We're here to help."

He stepped out of the room and hooked the flashlight to the back of his belt. He thought of all the places he would go to get away. It would've been easy to ask Lian to find Jarrod, but she couldn't hear Jarrod's thoughts even if she wanted, and besides she was sick. No, this had to be done the old-fashioned way. For a second, he knew what Claire was experiencing. All of his abilities were good for nothing. They couldn't make Lian better, let Jarrod know everything was going to be alright, or even help to find his friend.

19

Two ship workers passed by down the hall, one dragging the other. When Austin caught up with them the conscious one turned to acknowledge him.

"Do you need help?" Austin draped the unconscious man's left arm over his shoulder. "What happened to him?"

"You wouldn't believe me if I said." The sailor was shaking. Austin could smell fear oozing from the man's pores. "The world's comin' to an end, I say."

"I can keep an open mind." Austin turned his attention forward so he wouldn't make the other guy feel uncomfortable. "I've heard strange things at night. Weird glowing things too. Probably just my imagination."

"Were they—"

"—Blue? Yes. How did you know?" Austin gawked, faking surprise.

"I seen them too. There's a man possessed among us." The ship worker halted, looking all around as if prying ears were close by. He leaned close to Austin and whispered, "What do you think did this to him?"

"Rum?"

"No. I saw a feller with glowin' blood in his skin suck the very life force out of this poor man. He argued with himself while doing it, as if talkin' to a stranger." His hand latched onto Austin's wrist and squeezed. "Whatever's overtaken him, he's at odds with himself. I swear he looked at me and each side of his face was a different person. I don't know why he let my friend live, but he brought 'em back."

"Back from where?" Austin knew the answer, but was shocked Jarrod could do it. He'd been thinking for a while something was strange with his best friend, but had no idea the extent.

"The dead," the ship worker gasped, ask if his own words caused him to shake. "I say too much. Don't concern yourself with this any longer. Hide in your cabin and lock the doors."

"You think locked doors will work?" Austin tilted his head and cemented his gaze in the man's eyes. He could hear the guy's heartbeat race. "You're probably right. This man who was so conflicted, where did he go? Did he say?"

"When he was draining my friend's life he was mumblin' about fresh air. I plan on staying below." The ship worker pulled his friend away from Austin and scurried down the hall. "Don't go searchin'. I'm pleadin' with ya."

It was cold up on the deck. Not many sailors would dare brave the elements unless instructed. Austin knew if Jarrod was mumbling about fresh air, then he'd be at the ship's front. Austin wasn't a fan of the cold, but knew his friend would do anything to be avoided. He just hoped it wouldn't come to jumping ship—and if it did, he hoped he would be strong enough to stop him.

22

CHAPTER THREE

Lian I

A foghorn blared in the distance, the sound burrowing its way through the dense metal walls. Flickering light pushed through a crack in the cabin's only door. The subtle swaying back-and-forth of the large freight tanker on the waves could be felt just a little when Lian laid flat in her cot.

Her fingers snatched up a fistful of stiff bed sheets. She pulled the covers up to her chin and curled herself into the fetal position. Her forehead was on fire, her nose was red and runny, and a shiver took hold of her spine. The room was drafty. For three weeks straight, frigid, salty air had been circulating through the cabin.

I hope Austin finds him. Lian could hear Claire's thoughts.

"Why are you sitting in the dark?" she asked. Claire flicked a small desk light on.

"I didn't want to wake you." Claire knelt by Lian's side and rubbed a damp cloth over her friend's face. She moved a few strands of black hair out of Lian's eyes and then made her way over to the sink, placing the cloth under the flowing water and wringing it out. "You're slightly warmer than earlier, but I think that's a good sign. Maybe your fever will break soon."

"Land's close?" Lian replied. She spoke more out of hope than confidence.

"Sounds like it." Claire nodded, walking back to Lian's side. "Jarrod wandered off again. He's been ignoring us."

"More dreams?"

"If that's what you want to call them," Claire sighed, gently dabbing Lian's lips, cheeks and head. "It's more like he's following a beacon. The past few months have been crazy for all of us, I suppose."

"You need to stay away from him." Lian shifted her stare downward and made eye contact with Claire. In the middle of the room, Lian could see the outline of Sanderson, like a hazy mirage. Echoes of his voice stirred in her head, constantly explaining things to her and apologizing for past sins.

Means… it matters, the illusion said, phasing in and out of focus.

Lian squinted, trying to give the outline more energy. It didn't work. Lian knew it was a piece of Sanderson stuck in her conscious. For reasons she couldn't explain, she wouldn't let go. Somehow, as the surge of energy from Maya's collapsing starstone tore through Sanderson, the thoughts she'd latched onto in his head copied across, saving a piece of his soul. The yellowish static energy, which only she could see, dissipated.

"Means what matters?" Lian asked herself. She couldn't see how it correlated, nor did she feel like trying to piece it together. Her focus was once again reserved for Claire.

"He's not near me even when his body is present." Claire shrugged, sitting on the cot at Lian's feet. She leaned against the wall and rested her chin on her knees. "He's never really present for any of us, if you think about it."

"I try not to," Lian said, grabbing Claire's hand. They locked fingers. "Have I ever said thank you?"

"Trying to cheer me up?" Claire rolled her eyes and leaned toward Lian. "Were you listening in on mine and Austin's chat about sugar or cream?"

"No. I just wanted to say thank you." Lian shook her head. *Means it matters?*

"You don't have to thank me."

"You don't have to care for me while I'm sick." Lian coughed, pulling the sheet over her face.

"I'm just trying to pull my weight. Try to feel like I actually hold some importance."

"Are you scared?" Lian cleared her throat and lowered the sheet. She puffed the pillow under her head and sat up.

"At first I was. But I've been living with this sickening sense in my gut for a while now. Would it be right to call it fear, or should I just assume this is the new normal?" Claire shrugged, unsure of anything she should feel. She looked at Lian. "Should I be scared?"

"No," Lian giggled, shaking her head, "I meant are you scared you don't matter? But, given that you raised the question, I don't know what to expect."

Claire nodded. "Do you think this woman can help? The one who has your brother, that is? I can't wait to get off this damn boat."

"Sanderson and my father trusted her, once upon a time. If she can't help us, then we're truly on our own."

"So we're just going to disembark and she'll show up? I suppose crazier things have happened."

The definition of crazy had been rewritten long ago in Lian's book. Shortly after working under Sanderson, the word had lost all meaning. The woman they sought may not show when the boat journey was over, but Lian knew whatever part of Sanderson was left inside her would show them the way. Maybe they weren't truly alone after all.

26

CHAPTER FOUR

Austin II

The sound of waves breaking along the side of the massive freight ship echoed through the frost-bitten fog. Austin could see Jarrod leaning over the rails close to the bow of the ship while resting his forehead in his hands. The smell of salt water was sharp. The ship plunged into large waves head-on in an attempt to make up time.

Austin's hands glided over the frigid railing as he staggered towards the front of the ship. He walked up a few narrow steps and stood atop a landing. The foghorn sounded out into the void, bouncing off the windows of the observation deck behind him.

"I'm no sailor, but I'm pretty sure that foghorn means land ahead," Austin said, glancing around for any crew members. "You couldn't wait to get some fresh air? We shouldn't be up here right now."

"There's no such thing as fresh air anymore," Jarrod said through his hands, pressing his palms firmly against his face as he rubbed. He pulled his hands away, gazing at them as they shook. The hairs on the back of his neck stood up and he went rigid. "You're right. We should return before we're seen."

The scent of harsh cologne drowned out the sea air. Austin's gut told him Jarrod also knew someone else was nearby.

"Shouldn't you gentleman be hard at work?" A sailor approached Jarrod from the right. "I don't think you two are cleared to be up here. Let me see your badges."

"Austin, get rid of him." Jarrod winced, turning his face and closing his eyes. A blue light glowed through his eyelids. His knees buckled. A glow, similar to the one described to Austin earlier, crept through Jarrod's skin.

"Yes, sorry sir." Austin stood between Jarrod and the sailor. "My buddy here is a little under the weather, as you can see, and the doc said it'd be good for him to get some fresh air."

"Regardless, your badge, please," the sailor demanded, standing on his tip-toes to get to eye level with Austin.

"Yeah, we're new. Signed up just recently on your last docking in Baltimore."

"Don't make me ask for it again," the man said in a deep, breathy voice as he got in Austin's face.

"I'm sorry," Austin half-heartedly laughed, patting his chest and pants down. He turned and grabbed Jarrod. "It seems we've left them back in our cabin. We'll be on our way."

"Not so fast," the sailor persisted, reaching for Jarrod. Austin latched his palm around the man's fat wrist. The sailor was awestruck by Austin's hand as it grew in size. Austin's eyes took a slight beastly shape. "What are you? Are you one of them?"

"I'm just a guy trying to do his job and look after his friend." Austin nodded with a blank expression. He twisted the ship worker's arm just a little bit. "I can understand how insubordination will hurt a crew, so we'll be off when we dock, first thing. You won't have to deal with or hear from us again. Sound good?"

"Sure, that sounds just fine."

"Alright, then." Austin let go of the ship worker's arm, slapping it to the side. Jarrod stepped away from Austin, holding his left hand up as he walked down the steps with his eyes closed. "Are you sure you're OK?"

28

Jarrod nodded. "I am."

"Let me help you before you hurt yourself." Austin reached for Jarrod, but his friend just side-stepped out of the way. "Come on..."

"I have to learn to deal on my own," Jarrod insisted.

Austin looked back at the ship worker and smiled nervously, shrugging his shoulders. The sailor stood in place, seemingly unable to move. Austin walked back up the steps and waved his hand in front of the sailor's eyes. He didn't blink.

"Lian, you in there?" Austin asked, staring into the man's dark green eyes.

Just hurry up and come back, her voice replied in Austin's head. *He had no intention of letting you just leave. They're all spooked. We can't show them what we've become.*

"I assume you've taken care of his memory." Austin leaned back, smirking, folding his arms and tapping his foot.

"What the hell are you doing?" Jarrod yelled back at Austin. "You know you can talk to her while you walk, right?"

"Yeah, of course." Austin held his breath.

You forgot.

"Oh shut up," Austin whispered to himself.

You know I can hear that loud and clear in your thoughts?

He rolled his eyes and followed Jarrod.

That too.

"You can get out of my head now," Austin grumbled.

Jarrod was already a good distance ahead. A blinking sea buoy in the distance snared Austin's attention as the sun crept over the horizon. He stopped for a second, wondering why the ship continued at its fast pace. A large wave jostled him side to side. Austin turned to make a comment to Jarrod, but his friend was already gone.

Panic struck him. Austin sprinted down the side of the ship and found a door to his left slowly closing on its own. He rushed up the steps and stuck his hand between the door and the frame, noticing the handle had been ripped away.

"What the hell?" Austin panted. He shook his head, wondering what could have done such a thing but already knowing the answer. He walked into the inner corridor, finding the lights off. He removed the flashlight from his belt, turned it on, and scanned the area for his friend. "Jarrod, where are you?"

A light escaped underneath a door at the far end of the hall. He investigated the room. Everyone inside was dead, slouched back or hunched over with their eyes burned out. When his breathing stuttered, Lian poked inside his head.

You're worried, she said. *Why?*

"Don't ask stupid questions," Austin grunted, turning and frantically looking around the ship. He opened another door. Inside were more dead bodies. "Who else can you poke inside to help find him?"

Give me a second.

"I'm headed to the bridge," Austin shouted, sprinting back the way he'd come.

The ship snapped up suddenly and he fell to the floor, hitting his chin. He crawled his way back to his feet. Once out on the deck of the ship he spotted the bridge light, still blazing. A ringing buoy caught his attention. The sun burned through the fog and the hazy outline of a city was now in full view. The freight ship powered in through the Bristol Channel. He stared at a small island between the ship and the city, and noticed that another small land mass was visible portside. Both islands were a little over a mile away from either side of the ship, but more miniature rocky landings were sprouting up in the water all around them. It was only a matter of time before they clipped one.

Just a few people who are in their cabins, asleep. Where is everyone? Austin, what's going on?

"We're not stopping." He took two steps back and then lunged forward. His body density increased. Muscles bulged and his skin stretched until it was gray. Hairs sprouted over his body. The jaw of a wolf formed. His face transitioned, completing his transformation into a beast.

He pounced up the stacked containers, digging his claws into the metal as he leapt forward. Climbing up the makeshift tower, he peeked over both shoulders and saw several helicopters and speedboats heading in his direction. His focus turned forward, crashing through the window of the ship's bridge. He stood on his hind legs and his body returned to its human form.

My god, what'd he do? Lian asked, seeing the dead bodies sprawled about through Austin's eyes.

"How do I slow it?" Austin asked. The rigid coastline of dark greens and brown ambers was fast approaching. "Lian, of the crewmen still alive, which of them knows how to stop this thing?"

Already ahead of you, she responded. His eyes rolled back as she placed the instructions in his head.

Austin fell to his knees, rubbing his forehead raw. He stumbled towards the control panel. The correct stopping sequence wrestled through his mind all at once. The instructions were indecipherable. Another wave slammed over the side of the ship and dislodged a few containers, dragging them down into the water. Suddenly, the sequence was clear.

He reached for the lever to halt the engines. A hand covered in black armor and pale blue Aurascales grabbed his wrist. The beaming blue eyes hidden behind a black skull face stared at him.

"Jarrod." Austin nervously grinned as sweat poured over his brow. He tried pulling his arm back, but Jarrod's grip grew tighter. He casually moved his other hand towards the lever. "I know you're in there, buddy. Let me stop this thing so we can save us all from another disaster."

Jarrod twisted Austin's arm and then slung him around, bashing him into a control panel. Austin rolled onto his chest and shape-shifted back into his lumbering beast form. He tackled Jarrod, slamming him through the glass wall and over the side railing. He watched as his friend fell to the bottom deck, crashing through several containers.

The crew is alerted. Some are heading your way, some towards Jarrod. If we don't snap him out of the funk, he'll kill them.

"I have to stop the ship or we'll all die." Austin stood up, still in his werewolf form, and pulled back on the lever. The ship's propellers started pushing in reverse. The ship creaked, throwing him off balance. "Control the ones headed towards Jarrod. Stop them."

Austin, they're close to you. They have weapons.

Two crewmen rushed through the door, guns drawn. They took one look at Austin and opened fire, landing three shots. Austin stumbled backwards and fell over the side of the snapped railing. He bounced off the edge of a broken container and landed on the deck.

The freighter, unable to slow down enough, hit the shallow seabed and shook uncontrollably. The bow rode up the shoreline, throwing several containers over the side and into the raging waters. One rolled over and crashed towards Austin. Unable to move with his ribs broken, he held his arms up and waited for the impact, closing his eyes. But it never came.

He lowered his arms to find Jarrod standing in his full armor over the top of him. Austin swallowed and smiled with hope. Jarrod tossed the container into the shallow water and offered his hand to Austin as the facial armor retracted.

"Are you... you?" Austin asked, hesitant to give his hand.

"Where are we?" Jarrod shook his head, his eyes blood red, and grabbed Austin underneath the arms. He slung his friend's arm over his shoulder. Jarrod turned to walk back towards their cabin.

The ship ran ashore a stone's throw from the dry beach. People from the seaside village walked out of their shops and homes, even pulling their cars over to the side of the road to look at the large freight ship stuck on their beach. Two helicopters circled overhead.

"Lian," Austin hacked. The stabbing burn in his ribs caused him to pause. Jarrod rested him against the wall. "Lian, can you get rid of the helicopters?" Jarrod and Austin waited for a minute. When no reply came, Austin began to worry. "Lian?"

"You can't hear her?" Jarrod asked. Lian had never been able to communicate with Jarrod telepathically.

"Something has to be wrong." Austin tapped his head. "She's always poking around up here. What if…"

"Don't say it." Jarrod shook his head and picked Austin back up. "They're gonna be fine. I'll get us out of this."

34

CHAPTER FIVE

Set I

The orchestra moved as one, setting an eerie mood as the lights of the opera house dimmed and shifted from a light green to a dark tangerine. Perched in an alcove, high above the rafters in an old, seldom used attic space, Set admired the first movement of Brahms' third symphony. His right hand danced as if he were the conductor. He rocked back and forth, closing his eyes and swaying his head to the stream of violins. The music flowed through his body and carried him to a place far beyond the rats' nests and spider webs which littered his immediate surroundings. The strings and woodwinds were the river and he was a leaf in the current. Briefly, the jarring cold of the drafty storage space was a distant memory. The moment's serenity was a bitter reminder of what wasn't allowed to his kind.

This space, though dingy and repulsive, was all his. No one else knew about it. Life was more tolerable that way. Since happening upon it sometime in the mid-19th century while hunting down and executing a pair of angels who'd refused to fight in the Last Great War, he always found time to stow himself away for a show while on a mission. Since his newest target wasn't too far from here—just a few countries away—he thought a couple of minutes could be spared to rejuvenate and prepare for the incessant whining of Hermes and the dull, slow comments of Sif, his fellow Assassins.

The beacon on his left wrist pad vibrated. Hermes wanted his location. Set double tapped the light and the beacon went away. Ten minutes wouldn't even factor in as a nanosecond on the celestial scale. They could wait. The beacon vibrated again and this time two lights popped up. Both were pinging him.

"Dammit." Set rubbed the bridge of his nose and slowly exhaled. The wood floor creaked as he stood. He took one last admiring glance at the performance and turned off his recording device. The aurascales slid over his face, forming the silver faceguard that resembled a beast long since extinct. Modern humans didn't even have a name for it.

The music he'd just recorded played in his helmet. A crystal with a pink mist inside manifested in his grasp. He let the crystal go and it hovered in place. A quick burst of light spouted out of the crystal, wrapping around him, and sucked him in. Time and space warped, setting him alongside the others just outside a closed coffee shop. Hermes was noticeably irritated, which was normal.

"What were you doing?" Hermes asked, squinting.

"You forget who answers to whom." Set grinned. The music cut off and his facial armor retracted. The three stood in the shadows of urban night life. A gentleman's club was in full swing across the way, and street walkers were busy enticing clientele down the avenue on the corner. "It's always the pigs we're called to slaughter."

"They're all that is left." Hermes leaned against the cracked brick wall. His purple aurascales beamed underneath his black leather trench coat as a metallic orb with angelic inscriptions spun in the palm of his hand. "They find nourishment where others starve."

"How many are there?" Set asked, referring to the infestation of demons in the club.

"I counted about thirty-eight myself. Hermes said another fifteen or so," Sif replied. She stood behind her commander. "I'm ready when you are."

Set looked at Hermes with a raised brow.

"The command is yours, sire," Hermes said in a mocking tone, bowing for emphasis.

"With all the recent action on Earth, we're supposed to keep this low-key. But there's not much fun in that." The exoskeletal armor formed over his face and his eyes beamed a dark green. His voice sounded robotic from the outside. "I rather enjoy the taste of bacon, don't you?"

Before they could soar across the street with blades drawn and spill some blood, a limo pulled up. Out stepped a curious figure. Set recognized the face behind the human flesh from a time long ago. It was Beelzebub, one of the first demons spawned by Lucifer in his attempt to duplicate the power of a soul. He pushed the other Assassins around a corner and out of view. He crouched to watch Beelzebub and a female he couldn't make out enter the club.

"What's the delay?" Hermes asked, trying to push by Set. His leader shoved him back into the wall. "Get your hands off me."

Set's grip grew tighter as he towered over the swift-footed angel. Hermes' hand clamped around Set's wrist and he tried to pull himself free.

"You counted only fifteen or so. Why didn't you get an exact number?" Set barked. His latch on Hermes remained stiff despite the latter's struggle. "What are you trying to prove?"

"Nothing. I just wasn't sure if Sif and I were double-counting them," Hermes grunted. "That's all."

"We don't deal with guesses." Set let his subordinate go. "I prefer cold hard numbers."

"What do you suppose we do?" Sif asked. "Demons of that number are bound to cause a ruckus. We can't complete the mission without breaking protocol. Should we ask the Archangels?"

"No." Set shook his head and popped his knuckles. "Demons are survivors and concerned primarily with self-preservation."

He marched across the street and the demon-possessed security guards at the front entrance noticed him immediately. Their smoky-black auras slithered behind their human faces, snarling at him. Several more lined the four story roof and exited the building, as if each demon was psychically linked to the troubles of others.

"You know what I am and what that means for you if you get in the way." Set folded his arms, waiting for them to reply. They just blankly stared at each other, apprehensive. He could smell their sweat. "Consider tonight your one-time free pass. Judgment doesn't seek you." To his surprise, twelve more demons stepped out of the nightclub. Set's triplet wrist blades protruded out from his right arm, curving over his hand. "Really?"

The demons spread apart, giving way to his demands. His blades retreated and he stepped through the crowd. Sif and Hermes followed. The neon signs and strobe lights of the club dance floor and VIP lounge created a blanket of white, blues and reds inside the fog and misters. Haze from dry ice lingered around their ankles. Half naked dancers twisted their bodies on thin table tops for those stuffing their noses with white powder. A hostess with striped pink and silver hair approached. Her eyes turned to solid black.

"It's not every day we see the likes of angels still in service as guests." She smiled, folding her hands behind her back. Set paid her little attention, scanning the room for their mark. "I take it this is business only. No time for pleasure?"

"This is repulsive," Hermes said, scrunching his nose. "Count yourself fortunate you still draw breath inside your host."

"My kind has to make a living somehow," the hostess replied. "If your precious human pets weren't so weak-minded and frail of will, we wouldn't have much to tether us to this planet. Admit it, though, you need us just as much as they do."

"I don't care to squabble and debate." Set snapped his fingers and the others went quiet. The bass speakers still rumbled through the floor. The gyrating, frantic screeches and bloated squawks from what the newest generation regarded as music gave him a headache. "What ever happened to learning to play instruments with strings or your lungs instead of at the push of a button? Where's the skill in programming a computer to artificially produce the sounds?"

"It's what's hot." The hostess stroked his arm.

Set smirked at her. "So is hell." She withdrew her hand. He brushed past her and motioned to Hermes and Sif. "You know what to do."

The Assassins split, going in three different directions. Set rounded a corner, away from the main area and dance floor, to a part where only the walls could hold the throttle of the music. The hostess tagged along. Two beefed-up guards stood in his way. She nodded at them. Their hands relaxed and they hesitantly parted.

"Third floor, second door on the left," she said, stopping at a flight of stairs. She motioned with her head. "Boss would like to say hello."

"Right." Set was skeptical but not worried. There had to be a reason Beelzebub was showing his face in this neck of woods. Even though other obligations should've held influence over his time, Set needed to feed his curiosity. His hand rose to knock on the door, but it opened on its own. Across the room, standing with his head over a sink, Beelzebub washed his face. Set entered. "No longer inhabiting scientists?"

"Not by choice," Beelzebub laughed, turning around. He patted dry his dark hair and square chin. His body bore battle scars in the form of abrasions from exploding metal, stab wounds and gunshots. "My last meat suit was obliterated into cosmic dust by a starstone."

Set moved further into the room and quickly inspected the surroundings. "Too bad. Elliot Foster was growing on me." He spoke of Beelzebub's previous human host. "I can only hope your new shell holds the same amount of influence."

"Shawn Hershiser has proven to be a valuable commodity, given recent events." Beelzebub tossed the towel to the side and sat down. He gestured for Set to do the same. The Assassin shook his head and remained standing. "I can't believe my time is up."

"Our paths' crossing at this juncture was not my intent. But I must say I'm awfully confounded as to why you're here looking like that." Set walked behind the plush white sofa, his fingertips caressing the arch of its back. "Comfortable."

"Quite. Take a load off and stay a while."

"Still making copies of Zeus?" Set asked, referring to Beelzebub's pet project with the US Government. The way the demon scratched the back of his head in response to the question told Set all he needed to know. "When did they shut you down?"

"They didn't. The scientists in charge of the Double-Helix were both killed." Beelzebub sighed and sat forward, hanging his head between his knees. "And the catalyst used to reshape subjects' DNA was set free and is now MIA. But we both know he can't get far in his condition."

"You let Zeus get out?" Set went rigid. He drove his knee into the back of the sofa and sent it flying across the room. "Please tell me that it wasn't him who sent that horde into Moscow."

"No, that was all Maya and her spoiled little self." Beelzebub looked at his overturned sofa and the antique oak liquor cabinet it landed on and crushed. "That was one of a kind."

"So is the Forge," Set replied through his clenched jaw.

"Ah, and the penny drops. It's not my life's work you're worried about, but a shiny sliver of a fractured amulet."

"You know what it can do." Set's wrist pad vibrated. Sif was trying to get his attention.

"Don't I know it." Beelzebub smiled. "Luckily I'm still in control of the piece I found, and its owner. Soon Hershiser here will stumble upon the notes of Drs. Foster and Sanderson, and he'll get the Double-Helix back off the ground with the second catalyst."

"About that other catalyst..."

"He's still in his angelic cocoon." Beelzebub nodded and raised a hand. "Nothing to fear there."

"So that wasn't him stomping all over Argus in downtown Moscow?" The wrist pad buzzed again. He quickly double-tapped the light to shut it up. "You were successful? The horseman…"

"Rides? He does indeed." Beelzebub stepped closer to Set and spoke softly. "He hasn't quite put it all together yet." The wrist pad vibrated again. Beelzebub took Set's hand. "Who is it you need?"

"One of your lower level thugs has been gutting too many humans and making a scene. We've been sent to burn him."

"Thazmurzia?" Beelzebub asked. Set nodded. Beelzebub shook his head and closed his eyes, temples throbbing. He opened his solid black eyes again. "He'll be waiting out back for you. My more subtle men will have him wrapped up in a doggy bag. Do please come again when you can enjoy the scenery a bit more."

"Why are you here?" Set grabbed Beelzebub by the wrist and twisted, bringing him to his knees. "If this meat suit is so useful then shouldn't you be worried about it losing appendages?"

"I've got many fingers in many pies," Beelzebub grunted and Set let him go. "I dabble in a little of this and that. Some days it's arming Syrian rebels. Others it's coke to the Greek Mafia. Today it's individuals with a fetish for kids."

"I thought you were above all that?" Set asked, shaking his head. He walked to the back of the room and looked out the window. Hermes and Sif waited in the alleyway with a few demons and their target, all tied up. "Is it sexual?"

"I don't ever care to ask. I just know these clients were very particular. They wanted livestock that only my agency could provide." Beelzebub stood and rubbed his arm. "I think you know one of them. He's a former Alpha Guardian from the now defunct Southern Corner. Didn't you kill all of them?"

"Amun?" Set looked over his shoulder, raising an eyebrow. *What would a person like him want with gifted kids?* "You know many of them eluded me. As long as my bosses don't know any different then it won't matter. You said 'they'. Who are the other clients?"

41

"Anonymity is something they've paid very highly for. Just know you would recognize his flaky skin condition if you saw it." Beelzebub lifted the sofa and put it back in its resting place. "Look at that, you've stained it. You've got what you needed—it's time you be gone."

Set jumped from the window, his landing causing the concrete beneath him to crack and cave. He removed the hood from over his target's head and confirmed his identity. He nodded at the other demons and they retreated back into the club.

"Filthy scum. I feel soiled just having to deal with them." Hermes spit on the door as the demons closed it.

"It's all about the end, Hermes, not the means." Set cupped his fingers around Thazmurzia's jaw and opened his mouth.

Hermes removed the silver orb from his satchel and pinched in on the sides. A slit through the equator of the orb opened up, bleeding white light, and two beams of energy sprang from its poles. The orb spun quickly, emitting a whistling noise. Thazmurzia kicked and screamed. A black vapor trail was ripped from the mouth of his host body and sucked into the orb. Hermes grabbed it from the air and placed it back in his bag.

The wrist pads of all three angels vibrated. They examined their message. Set groaned, longing to retreat back to the orchestra. He dropped the limp body to the ground, his shoulders and back aching from centuries of stress. He couldn't let the other Assassins see it.

"They're sending us to Moscow," Sif said with a hint of anxiety in her voice. "They say an angel has reached out. Could it be Azrael? The rumors, do you think them true?"

"Hard to say." Set shrugged, holding his knowledge close to the vest. He swiped his fingers across his wrist pad and a cloudy pink crystal materialized in his grasp.

"Why would it be Azrael?" Hermes asked, coughing in the process. Set whipped his head around and stared holes through his fellow Assassin. "What?"

Set knew the sound Hermes' voice made. He'd heard it several times through the many wars his kind had been through, and again buried in the wails of those he tortured for information and hunted for penance. There was a secret, and secrets were the most valuable commodity in existence; more so than souls, starstones and pieces of the Forge. Secrets unlock mysteries, and there was a mystery Set had longed suspected Hermes of keeping to himself.

No matter. That would have to wait. Set hadn't spent countless ages coordinating his plans to get over-eager and pop his top. He managed the mundane nature of life by taking it one hunt at a time. He could stomach a little more patience.

"Nothing, Hermes." Set handed Hermes the crystal. "After you."

44

CHAPTER SIX

Horus I

A large, light-beige hood draped over Horus' curly umber locks. His cloak was unbuttoned just below the neckline, but securely fastened all the way to his waist with bamboo toggles. His sky-blue woolen pants crackled in the wind, keeping him warm amongst the snow flurries.

He proceeded through the large, crowded market, walking between lines of fire-spouting trashcans. Bakers selling piping hot bread and fishermen touting the morning's fresh catch had replaced the fields of corner stores and liquor shops that used to litter the inner city of Moscow, before what the locals called "the invasion."

"Did we land in the right timeline?" Horus wondered aloud, looking at the clothes of the people around him. To him, they wore modern uniforms. However, he couldn't help but notice things were different with the way they acted. They didn't drive cars, but instead slept in them. Three triangular-shaped drones with cameras mounted underneath zoomed overhead, racing through the buildings. "We must stay close together."

Anubis, who lingered behind Horus, was nearly a foot taller than everyone else. He watched as a butcher carved a pot roast for a woman and her three kids. She dumped a bag's worth of money onto the table, but the butcher yelled at her and pointed with his knife. She undid her blouse, nodding at the fat, bald man. He licked his lips, putting a sign in front of the stand as he led the woman away. The youngest child—a girl—happened to look at Anubis. Her eyes grew wide as his cloak and hood didn't shield his gray complexion very well. Horus grabbed his cousin's wrist.

"We must be quick. According to the information from our point of contact, our rendezvous is close," Horus said, dragging Anubis. They slid between two stands and into an alleyway. The red brick walls were painted with generations of graffiti. Horus' fingers caressed the newest designs; a black skull with blue eyes. "The face of Death," he said, eyeing the fresh painting. "They worship him as they did our ancestors in Memphis, Thebes, Aswan and others."

"They are hungry, yet have plenty to ration evenly." Anubis kept his gaze on the three children who were left waiting in front of the butcher's stand. "She offered money and he didn't take it."

"Would you prefer she offer her children?" Horus looked casually towards the kids and then stepped in front of Anubis. "They did far worse in our fathers' time. Their struggles and penance are their own. We cannot help them anymore."

"What is the difference between those children and the girl Aunt Isis has asked us to retrieve?" Anubis' blank stare moved back to Horus. His cousin pressed on, leading them further into the secluded alley.

They made it to the back of the building. Anubis stopped in place, watching as the butcher bent the woman over a trashcan. He turned his back to follow Horus, but heard the woman cry out. At the sound, Anubis spun and walked towards the pair, but Horus yanked him back. The butcher tangled his hands in the woman's hair and shoved her face into the garbage as she sobbed. A blade slid down Anubis' right arm and into his palm. He tried to pull away from his cousin.

"There's a bigger picture to all of this, cousin," Horus said. Anubis tried half-heatedly to break free but Horus wouldn't relinquish his grip. "We have deadlines. We don't wish to draw undue attention to ourselves."

Anubis looked down, and it was clear from the look in his eyes that he did not understand. Horus knew that his cousin was incapable of comprehending the gravity of the situation before him. When Anubis stopped struggling, Horus breathed a sigh of relief and stepped out of the way.

"I only mean to scare him." Anubis quickly stepped forward before Horus could stop him and dashed toward the butcher, shoving the fat man to the ground. The woman crouched next to the dumpster as Anubis held the blade against the butcher's stomach, standing over him. "Do not get up."

"Very well, then. Let's go." Horus sighed, snapping his fingers. "Anubis. There's time to keep."

Horus knew there was a deeper emotional and psychological problem at work inside his cousin's mind. His mother said Anubis was traumatized as a child by watching his own mother die. She told Horus that Anubis laughed as their Corner fell because his naive mind hadn't yet developed the ability to understand death. Horus knew different; a portion of Anubis' mind had never matured—and never would. That much was evident from the events of the day that caused Anubis to now bear the mark of the jackal.

Anubis had been an outcast among his own kind growing up. The others were afraid of him and his otherworldly appearance. They avoided speaking to him, mostly directing their questions and comments towards the Prince of the Southern Corner, Horus. He was, after all, the only one who ever took the time to talk with Anubis and discover the child-like kindness hidden behind the gray giant's coarse exterior. Horus believed his cousin was oblivious to it all, either willfully or because he was unable to comprehend it—those lines were blurred sometimes.

"I told you it would be fine." Anubis looked at Horus and smiled. The butcher jumped up and lunged for Anubis' blade. Anubis turned and sunk the blade into the butcher's gut with ease. He pulled back and the butcher collapsed face-down onto the Anubis' left foot. "No."

"Anubis," Horus said, standing rigidly. His breathing was erratic. He hated to think of his cousin like a dog, but Horus knew he should have kept a tighter leash. "Anubis, can you hear me? Step away from the man."

"Don't hurt me," the woman pleaded in Russian, crawling back against the dumpster, shaking.

"The animal can no longer torment you," Anubis replied in her language, inching nearer to her. She pulled herself back, pressing tighter against the trash. He placed his hand to her wrist gently and she screamed. "No, do not do that. I will not hurt you." Anubis grabbed the woman, his large hand clasping over her mouth and nose. She struggled to break free, but he continued to hold her tightly, constricting further every time she wiggled. He looked towards Horus, with panic on his face. His lips quivered. "Please... Settle down. I do not mean to frighten." Anubis sniffled, shaking his head.

"Let her go." Horus pulled on his cousin's arms, but the woman remained tightly in his grasp. "You are hurting her."

"I do not mean to. If she would only understand that I am trying to help," he cried, standing up and yanking the woman away from Horus. The force of the motion snapped her neck and her body went limp. Anubis froze, as if unable to breathe from shock.

"Look over here." Horus raised his hands, slowly walking toward his cousin. He touched Anubis's right triceps, slowly taking the woman from his clutches. He laid the dead woman down and stepped away. Horus spoke slow and smooth to help ease Anubis' nerves. "Are you with me? I need your mind present."

Anubis' eyes remained focused elsewhere. Horus turned around to see what he was staring at and found the woman's youngest child standing in the alleyway behind them. Her eyes were locked on Anubis. Horus stood between them. The girl shifted her gaze to her mother. Fear overtook her face.

"Listen, child, you must not cry." Horus knelt and reached to embrace the girl. Her face turned red with fright. "Please, for both our sakes..."

Just as she let out a scream, a short blade pierced into her back and through her chest, puncturing her lungs. The girl's eyes widened. A slow trickle of blood ran out of the left corner of her mouth. The blade was quickly pulled back and the girl tilted forward. Horus, stunned and shaking as adrenaline surged through him, caught the child. He looked up and saw the individual he'd been on the way to meet standing tall.

"I see why your Corner fell so easily," Svarog said, wiping his blade. His head was clean-shaven, giving the illusion that his forehead wasn't as prominent as it really was. The ridge of his nose was wide, but pointed in a sharp angle at the tip. His eyes were large, almond shaped and wide-set. A bushy, yellowish goatee framed his mouth. The dagger dispersed into his armor. He motioned with a finger for Horus to follow. "Are we going to linger, or are we going to move?"

"You murdered her." Horus' hand was shaking as he laid the girl down over her mother. He glared at Svarog as the snowfall picked up pace.

"Your imbecile cousin just killed two of his own, leading to this child's death. I see not the difference you attempt to make." Svarog flapped his long, leather trench coat shut. He slowly buttoned it, still walking. "I guess somehow us middle-guard angels don't have the same privileges as those of you who live in the higher-priced locales."

"She was a child."

"Who would have one day been old enough to carry a weapon against us." Svarog turned around, marching back to Horus. "Again, you make excuses when your anger should be turned elsewhere. I simply eliminated a threat before it drew unwanted attention. That's the problem with you elitist types and the humans you've become so close with—compassion for those perceived to be innocent keeps you from eliminating all threats. The problem is, we live in a fallen world— none of us are innocent. We're all judged equally, and when left unchecked we can be even more dangerous than those who preceded us."

"Fallen or not, the adults knew what they were doing. The child didn't ask to be fallen."

"Neither did I, but here I am. I was dragged down with the rest of you," Svarog replied, continuing on his way. His feet crunched through the freshly fallen snow in the un-walked areas of Moscow's backstreets.

"The man had it coming. The woman was an accident. Anubis didn't know," Horus said, keeping pace.

"Oh, well then, I guess he's exonerated," Svarog mocked, rolling his eyes. "I knew not that ignorance of the law was a justifiable defense."

"Horus," Anubis whispered, leaning into his cousin. "Why is he mad?"

"The mind of a child and the body of a giant. God certainly does have a sense of humor." Svarog smirked, chuckling and shaking his head. He gestured for them to move faster. "This way, abominations."

"We're not abominations," Horus replied, grinding his teeth. He and Anubis followed Svarog through a maze of alleyways. They stopped in their tracks when the antique buildings gave way to the large metal giants of new, towering overhead. Horus looked on in awe as the Russians slowly rebuilt after the battle of Moscow, mostly amazed by the destruction caused when the one they called Death had thwarted Maya's invasion. He glanced over at Anubis, whose head was down in shame. "Don't listen to him. We exist for a reason."

"You exist because of treason," Svarog said sharply. "I was a Muse, not a fighter. I was created to inspire man to make great weapons, not to use them myself. When word of angels producing children with one another came about, some were inspired. Others, like me, were aghast. When angels began fornicating with humans— procreating—I knew then we were truly at the end. I never engaged in any wrongful behavior, but because all those around me acted upon

50

their impulses, I was just as guilty for not reprimanding them. I, an artist, was supposed to tell Guardians—fighters and trained killers—how to live by the law? That was a conversation I am sure would have gone over well."

"If you despise us, then why do you offer your help?" Horus watched Svarog out the corner of his eye, his gaze still directed at the shredded sky-scraper. Cranes positioned several stories high pulled up fresh metal support beams. "Can we get closer?"

"I was in one of those buildings when the fight began. I saw him as clear as you are to me now." Svarog led the cousins along a perimeter created by tall barbed wire fences. He removed his dagger and sliced the chain link, ducking through. The cousins followed. "It was not the one called Azrael, as he was young like you. I could tell, though, that he hadn't been born in another realm, as time here on Earth did not warp him like it does us. His essence wasn't human, nor was it angelic or Angel-born. There were many entities within him, intertwined."

"So he's neither human nor angel?" Horus scratched the back of his head.

"Maybe both. Some sort of new concoction." Svarog stopped and whispered to Horus. "All I know is that he wore Azrael's colors, but was not Azrael. I've seen the humans run experiments before to create what they call 'super soldiers'. Remakes, they were known as, by those from the Western Corner I captured that day and interrogated."

"I heard those stories. Why are you so sure this man isn't a remake himself?" Horus asked.

"My eyes don't fool me." Svarog led the way into a large shopping center. Windows all around were boarded up and temporary lights hung from the ceiling. Workers laid fresh concrete and erected new walls to replace the ones destroyed in battle. Signs all around saying 'never forget' united the workers' focus. "It was here, while I watched on from above, as Death himself took the soul of Maya's field general and reduced him into a plume of ash."

"Death?" Anubis asked, giving a sideways look.

51

"Yes." Svarog nodded, lowering his eyebrows, as if confused by Anubis' question. "I must confess, you're not the only ones to have come here. I have spoken with others."

"Who?" Horus asked, jumping to an alert stance.

"Vishnu sent his own delegates. So did heaven. The infamous Assassins paid me a visit. They hunt this Death. Even some descendants, with a female Angel-born, came poking around and asking questions about what happened." Svarog smiled, smug. "But I didn't show them what I have to show you. You see, I still have prisoners from that battle. Both human and half-breeds from Maya's legion. I believe the prophesized week of years is upon us, and when it starts this planet will see devastation even more powerful than when Zeus and Michael tore continents apart."

"Again, you've not told me why you want to help us if you despise us so," Horus prodded, calmly breathing as his mind tried to make sense of everything. If Azrael wasn't responsible for this devastation, then who was Death and who'd sent him? Vishnu, the Assassins, and others were now ahead of the game. Horus knew his people had to quickly catch up.

"Because unlike you, I don't have a planet of my own to run to. My star is far too weak to go gallivanting around time and space, and sooner or later its power will fade and I will be no more than human. Despite my personal feelings for Angel-born such as yourselves, we share a vision: we both want to be free and stop the upcoming apocalypse. Vishnu aspires to be god, and heaven already has one of their own. But you... You just want to be free. That is the only option I have left."

"Instead of being an ass, it would have been best to lead with that," Horus said. He smirked, nodding at Anubis and then looking back at Svarog. He tilted his head, thinking. "Why do you call him Death?"

"It was a name given to him by the prisoners of Maya's army. They would have nightmares about him and spoke in their sleep."

Svarog walked toward a fresh window pane, looking up at the shattered tower. "Because when he figures out the power of the beast inside him, no entity in existence will be safe. Destruction follows him, they say."

"I want to hear the words from their own lips." Horus paced in circles, deep in thought. Svarog shook his head. Horus thought of many ways to compel Svarog to change his mind, but chose the option he liked least because he knew it would get the best response. "We will bring you back. Safe harbor is yours, but I cannot go back to my people without clear answers. They deserve them."

"But Horus…" Anubis grabbed his cousin's shoulder, but Horus shook him off.

"Silence now, I am conducting business." Horus squeezed Anubis' wrist. He looked over his shoulder to Svarog. "What is your reply?"

Svarog nodded. The air grew cold, frosting their breath, and Horus knew what that meant. They were about to slip through a rift. Pink light sliced through the room and closed just as quickly as it had opened. The first thing Horus noticed was a blood-soaked hole in the wall hanging above a dead prisoner who had keeled over onto a female inmate.

"Another one." Svarog grabbed the body and sat it up. The woman stiffened, breathing erratically. He took out her gag and smacked her on the cheek. "Did you kill him?"

"No, sir," she replied in Russian, trembling.

Various bungee cords and polyester rope connected several blindfolded prisoners, keeping them pinned on the floor next to the wall. Veneered particleboard covered all of the windows and the air vents were stuffed with towels and taped shut.

"What is this place?" Horus held his nose shut, finding the conditions deplorable.

"Ever heard the expression about breaking eggs for an omelet?" Svarog asked. Horus shook his head. "Of course you've not."

"You need to release these people," Horus demanded. He thought this treatment was unnecessary. "There are many other ways of extracting useful information from prisoners."

"Interrogated many people in your lifetime?" Svarog hissed, not bothering to look at Horus. The young prince remained silent, believing it better for Svarog to make his own assumptions. Svarog chuckled. "I didn't think so. As a scavenger on a planet not made for me, I've learned the best ways to stay alive. I've seen the mistakes others have made by trusting or making assumptions about this pathetic, cowardly race. Humans and half-breeds are at their best and most trustworthy when you keep a heavy boot on their throats."

"P-please let me go," the woman begged. She continued to plead, but Svarog shoved the gag back in her mouth.

He stood and exchanged jabbing glares with Horus, clipping Horus' shoulder as he passed. Anubis stepped forward to grab Svarog but Horus stayed his hand with a confident gaze, as if saying 'relax'.

"You came to seek answers." Svarog pointed at the prisoners. "Seek them."

Horus knelt before the woman. As if sensing his presence, she turned away. He turned her face toward him and removed the gag, gently rubbing her cheek.

"I will not hurt you," he reassured her. Svarog laughed from the kitchen. The woman was visibly unnerved by the sound of him emphatically banging pots. Horus tenderly touched her hands, ignoring his informant. "Why did he bring you here?"

"He says I... I saw... him," she cried, biting her lower lip. Horus' knee felt wet. He looked down at a puddle of her urine. "I worked downtown. It started there. That's why he says I'm here. I saw... him."

"Death?" Horus asked.

"His real face. For a second... he looked normal. The black skull crawled over his face. Those eyes... haunting. I'll never forget their stare."

"Did he hurt any of you?" Horus had to know more. Specifically, what drove this new divisive figure? Could he be an ally? "The army that invaded; they were stopped by him, no? I've seen the musings and shrines to this Death."

"Not a finger..."

The mumbling of the man next to her overpowered her mumbling. She froze. Horus gently stroked the side of her face before moving to the man on her right.

"Speak," Horus commanded, removing the man's gag.

"You seek him out, but you be a fool," the man hacked, laughing, speaking Greek. His snarling smile showed contempt for Horus, but the young prince didn't know why. "Your accent, you're from the Southern Corner."

"What be it to you?" Horus could see an aura about this prisoner. The man was a changeling. "You're a Satyr. A straggler from Maya's legion."

"Perceptive, you coward. Your people left us to perish. My grandfather died in the last great war, a battle your people failed to show for."

"You know nothing about that of which you speak." Horus remained steady despite the man's taunts, recalling the training he'd received under his uncle, Sobek. *A steel reserve will push an enemy off kilter far more than sparring words.* "Say something useful or remain silent."

"I will tell you something useful," the Satyr chuckled. His boisterous laugh quickly avalanched. "This man—Death be him—he will end you all. I heard the rumblings of the Blood Queen and the Ferryman. They feared him, and they were too ignorant to fear anyone. When Death slaughtered Argus on the battlefield, he turned him to ash." Horus looked over to Svarog in the kitchen, who nodded. The prisoner kept talking. "If I knew better, my mind could make sense of it. He took his soul, I say. He will take all of ours."

"My kind have not souls," Horus said.

"You believe that?" the Satyr laughed.

"It was written as such." Horus squinted, finding the prisoner's laugh odd given the circumstances. The man acted as if he were the warden.

"It was also written that your kind have not the ability to reproduce, yet here you are." The Satyr continued to prod. "Do you still believe?"

"You are in no position to debate or lecture me. My thoughts and beliefs are my own, and not for your musings." Horus stood up, walking over to Svarog. "What is your play?"

"As agreed upon, I want immunity, and after that I don't care what happens. You and your giant freak here can run off and find more answers, or sodomize each other, or whatever takes your fancy. I just want to wade through the coming week-of-years from whatever perch you've chosen."

"No," Horus replied. "You are not worthy."

"What?" Svarog snarled. His fist grew tight. "I brought you here, gave you the information you wanted, dealt with your imbecile cousin, cleaned up your mess, and you think you're going to just deny me?"

"Yes. Interrogation tactics. Did they meet your standards?" Horus turned and walked away. Svarog lunged for him but Anubis snatched his arm and twisted it around, bringing Svarog to his knees.

"I relent!" Svarog screamed as Anubis tightened his grip.

"OK. So you relent." Horus cut the woman prisoner free and stood her up. He moved her to the door and whispered. "When I move you forward, walk ten steps before removing the blindfold and then run. Do not look back."

The woman nodded. Horus kicked the door open. He lightly pushed her and she stepped through the doorway.

"Why is he still twisting?" Svarog's face pressed against the floor, tightly scrunched and turning red. "Mercy, please. My arm is on fire."

"The Assassins saw you and I assume refused your proposition. Given your disdain for us, I'm sure we were on the offering plate."

Horus cut the other human prisoners free and pushed them out the door. He briefly stood above the Satyr and moved on, leaving him tied. "Why did they let you live?"

"Are you questioning me now?" Svarog spit at Horus' feet.

"Judging by your earlier tone, I figured we could use the interrogation practice." Horus nodded at Anubis—a command. Anubis snapped Svarog's arm backward and yanked. The pop of Svarog's shoulder was drowned out by his screams. Horus pushed Svarog onto his back and stood on his throat. "This is the optimal position for information retrieval, no?"

"I have no reason to lie," Svarog coughed, gripping his arm.

"You have every reason to lie." Horus put more weight on Svarog's throat. "This is what I think happened. You were too afraid to fight in the war—"

"Says the Southern coward," the Satyr interrupted. Anubis punched him in the face.

"As I was saying," Horus said, rolling his eyes, "you wanted back into Heaven, but the illusive Assassins are far too callous and high-brow to work with a groveling worm such as yourself. So they cut you a deal. Make connections with as many factions as possible, earn your way in with them, and pave a path for their journey into our realms."

"You don't know what you're up against." Svarog connected his gaze with Horus'. "There are so many spinning cogs in this machine—you're the smallest and most insignificant. I can make you important. You know that?"

"You have nothing left to barter."

"But I do." Svarog smirked. "I know something about the Assassin's leader. It would shake both of you to the core."

"Do not care." Horus shifted his weight onto the foot over Svarog's throat. Svarog's body shuddered briefly as blood bubbled from his mouth before going still. "Finish off the last prisoner, Anubis. We must be on our way."

"Are we headed to Cairo to retrieve the child Isis asked us to get?" Anubis asked, stabbing the changeling.

"We are."

CHAPTER SEVEN

Madame Patricia I

The streets were calm. They carried an eerie aroma not commonplace since the time steam engines were popular. By 'aroma', Madame Patricia didn't necessarily mean the stench. Stinging hot vapor emanating from subway lines, and the dull gut punch of exhaust, still littered the air and she tried desperately to inhale as little of it as possible. This unusual scent was something that could only be detected by someone with her level of attention to detail. The hairs on the back of her neck stood tall—apparently they agreed with her discerning nose. There was something here.

London was like a ghost town at night. Ever since Oreios sent a fault line stretching from Rhyl to Brighton, splintering the county apart and giving the British Isles one more member in the Commonwealth, curfew was established for the entire kingdom. That didn't necessarily mean everyone stayed locked inside, but it was good enough for the law-abiding majority and the human scum smart enough to know when they'd been outclassed—people she didn't have a use for. Those brave enough to venture out into the avenues under moonlight and neon signs were left alone by the police, who also knew when they'd been outmatched.

When Oreios killed Athos, taking the gem of Durga for himself and leaving Madame Patricia clinging to life on the shores of the Irish Sea, it was as if an unspoken agreement between the underworld and mankind had finally been reached. The humans would have their time in the sun, and those of the underworld—half-breeds, changelings, demons and more—would have their peace at night. War would be avoided between the two and everyone could live together, willfully ignorant but safe. No one would admit it, because speaking it aloud meant believing in superstitions, and no one wanted to be known as a believer in the paranormal. Blissful denial was a state enjoyed by angels and humans alike. Maybe they weren't so different after all.

Madame Patricia folded the hood of her fur coat over her head and held the sides of it up to her face. Her high-heeled boots clacked against the cobblestones as a pair of demons passed by her. Their smoky and snarling faces made it crystal clear what they were. Seeing her, they scampered quickly away—they must not have recognized her aura. Demons were always the most self-preserving. 'If you don't know what it is, don't mess with it' was their motto.

She couldn't shake the feeling that there was pair of eyes on her. They'd been trained on her back for the past few blocks, and there had been more than enough instances when the owner of the eyes could have pounced and tried to take her out. Whoever it was didn't mean her harm. Not yet, anyway. She turned down an alleyway and walked past a group of whores. A lucrative new market had been established in allowing demons to temporarily possess you, giving new meaning to the term 'penetration.'

Finally, she reached her destination. It wasn't glamorous, or really the sort of place she approved of—the gentlemen's club was overridden with the demon-possessed. The bouncers out front seemed nervous and more standoffish than usual. She opened her mouth to speak, but they moved out of her way and opened the door.

"Don't trouble yourself," the bouncer muttered, or something close to that. Madame Patricia moved up the steps and nodded politely at them.

"Another one?" she heard a voice ask. "Who they be huntin' now?"

The lights and music inside caused a pounding in her skull, and there was so much cigarette smoke that she couldn't even taste her own saliva. Her senses were all drowned out. A hostess with pink and silver striped hair approached from the cloud of strobe lights. Two naked dancers followed behind her and then moved into a private room on the left.

"My name is Tunrida," the hostess said. "I have been expecting you. May I take your coat?"

"Is there a place you could take it to keep the stench of an ashtray from impregnating it?" Madame Patricia asked, not bothering to make eye contact with the hostess.

"I suppose not."

"Then no," Madame Patricia snapped. "Show me to the room so I can be done with this place."

"Right this way," Tunrida said, curling her index finger a few times. Black leather spandex covered her from ankle to wrist, opening into a plunging neckline down her chest. As she walked, the sound of it squeaking jabbed at Madame Patricia's ears, even over the throbbing of the bass-heavy music. "Pardon the mood. We've had a busy night."

"I don't care about the sort you entertain." Madame Patricia turned her nose up and followed Tunrida up a flight of stairs. This sleaze-fest was nothing like her place, the Progeny Lounge.

"Not just busy with patrons, mind you." Tunrida turned back with an infantile smirk. "Never mind, you claim no interest."

"Take that look off your face or I'll do it for you." Madame Patricia didn't bother looking up at the hostess, but she knew the expression was there. It was easy to sense by the tone of her voice. She was above giving a demon the gratification of eye contact, but not above smacking one senseless. "I helped shape this spherical rock you live on. Don't test me."

Tunrida's face fell flat. She opened the door and stepped inside to announce Madame Patricia, but Beelzebub held a hand up and shooed her away. He bowed his head reverently and offered a hand. Madame Patricia didn't bite, choosing to walk right by him.

"Please, be seated," Beelzebub said, sipping from his glass. "I'm honored by your presence."

"I'll stand." Madame Patricia combed her fingers over the back of the couch and then rubbed them off on a stack of cocktail napkins. She didn't try to hide her boredom. "I can feel him. Is he waiting to build the suspense? I lack patience."

"He's currently busy with other matters. He asked if I would be willing to entertain you."

"Burn yourself alive and see if it draws a chuckle." Her eyes moved around the room, purposefully ignoring him. "Wait, on second thought, I wouldn't want to spoil the surprise of what's in store for you in hell."

"Yes. Indeed you wouldn't," Beelzebub laughed and sat on a massive brown leather recliner. "I trust you didn't have too hard a time finding the place."

"I don't like small talk, either." She exhaled loudly in disdain and folded her arms.

The door opened and her eyes came alive as she stole a glimpse of the tall angel. His face was round, his hair inordinately long and his aura unmistakable. He was from the Southern Corner, but his identity escaped her. He quickly moved out of view as Ra entered the room and shut the door behind him.

"Moved on to men, have we?" she asked Ra. He chuckled in response. "I hope your lips didn't burn his cock. Perhaps just a light suntan?"

"You would know best the warmth I give inside," Ra retorted. His iron mask muted his voice slightly, but not the piercing glare of his starlight eyes. He walked in her direction and passed by a fish tank. The thermal discharge of his body boiled the tank water. He stopped and laughed. "Sorry about the puffer. I trust it wasn't too expensive."

"You're paying me enough to buy a new one." Beelzebub lifted his glass in appreciation and took a sip. He looked at Madame Patricia. "Are you sure I can't offer you a glass of champagne or something stronger? You look like you need a stiff drink."

"Perhaps a glass of cabernet squeezed from the grapevine I'm about to make grow out of your ass," she replied. "Ra, I don't have time for this. I thought that much was clear when you visited my realm after that incident with the Ourea."

"Yet here you are." He smiled.

"Indeed." She paused and squinted at him. "I'm not beyond making a scene."

"Never were." Ra seemed intoxicated with her. His voice was sultry. She knew he remembered what she liked and turned those switches off. "My sweet Danu, whatever came between us?"

"All the other women you came in."

"Yes. My stupid mistake." His hand went over his chest. "I ask that you cast aside old grudges and fractured emotions. There are possibilities out there which demand we explore them. I will, with or without you…"

"Like giving terrorists the elemental powers of the Ourea?" She giggled. That plan was utterly preposterous. "What were you thinking? Poor Durga."

"She'd been dead a long time." Ra shrugged dismissively. "I figured if anyone was going to have our sister's gem it might as well be me."

Durga had lost her life getting caught up in the affairs of angels and humans. She'd received her warning just like the rest of the Architects, and Madame Patricia wasn't about to make the same mistakes. Ra's game wasn't passive enough. It would eventually attract God's attention, and when it did he would be sure to send Michael. No one could defeat him—a lesson many had learned the hard way.

"I'm afraid I don't know what you're talking about, nor do I care." She marched for the doorway but Ra stepped in her path. His warmth enveloped her. The closer they stood, the more their skins illuminated with cosmic energy. She stepped away, quivering. "Please move."

"No." He shook his head. "You came here because you have an interest in what I've to say. Do not deny that. When I've said my piece, the decision will be yours and I will not oppose you."

"You have a minute."

"The game with the Islamic radicals was merely a ruse—a bartering token I never intended to deliver on. I knew the Ourea were backstabbing cocksuckers. I counted on it." He stepped towards the window. The glass fogged up in his presence, steaming the chilled rain that had collected on the other side of the windowpane. "No one can traffic children quite like Muslim extremists."

"You make me sick." What kind of twisted fetish was he addicted to now? The thought of him defiling young boys and girls the way Jihadists in Syria did goats made her stomach turn.

"Why? Because the taste of innocence gets me off?" He chuckled and looked over his shoulder. "Please, give me more credit than that."

"You've wasted half your time." She tapped her wrist.

"There was one among your realm. A boy, I believe. I felt him tingle my nerves when I stopped by." He turned around and leaned over the desk. His hands charred the oak desktop.

"That is a tad less replaceable." Beelzebub pointed at the desk and bit his lower lip in anguish. "The Resolute desk," he whispered loudly, not really intending for it to be a secret. He was actually quite giddy. "It was a gift from her majesty for an inordinately long life to keep her son off the throne—and for sending some overzealous paparazzi to Paris, if you catch my drift." He smiled, leaned toward Madame Patricia, and cupped his hand around his mouth. "She hated that blonde bimbo."

Madame Patricia narrowed her eyes at him. "I understood the reference."

"Just wanted to make sure everybody got it." He looked around nervously, but the cold stare from Ra and Madame Patricia caused him to sink back in his chair. "I'll shut up."

"You don't know what you have." Ra's voice sounded as if he were smiling, and the way the iron mask raised off his face supported that theory. "Don't be ignorant, my Gaia. The chosen few described in The Word are more literal than we thought."

However, Madame Patricia *did* know what he was talking about. She only hoped he mistook her flushed face as attraction for him and not nerves giving away her hand. She knew exactly what he was implying—once upon a time there was a pair of siblings that were separated to keep the existence of their kind secret. Ra must be looking for the others like them.

Her eyes washed over Beelzebub. It was widely known he was a part of some government entity from America—the one responsible for creating the individual rumored to be Death. They also dabbled in human trafficking of their own, though it was under the guise of global security. Her contact in that agency, the one who'd brought her the siblings and called attention to what they were, had informed her of all their goings-on in exchange for information about angels and the supernatural.

It was all coming together. The American agency had half the stronghold in the Middle East, and the terrorists had the other. Ra was being supplied by both. Though it was obvious what the radicals thought they were going to get out of the partnership, it escaped her how Beelzebub could possibly benefit. Ra's endgame and Beelzebub's couldn't have been more at odds. Finally, the aroma that had aroused her suspicion on the walk over resurfaced. It was time to leave.

"I'm afraid the minute is up." She nodded at the two and opened the door. "Your hospitality has been much appreciated and found not entirely lacking for a demon."

"She acknowledges me," Beelzebub laughed.

Madame Patricia quickly left the infested melting pot that was the gentlemen's club. She leaned over a car hood to catch her breath. Immediately, the eyes which had followed her through the streets were upon her again. It was time to learn their identity.

She hurried down a small side street. The buildings all began to look the same. The frosty rain stung her cheeks. She managed to corner herself in a dead end, hoping to draw whoever was following her out into the open. Instead, a trio of changelings emerged from the shadows.

"Hello there, ol' lady," said one of the thugs. She looked him over. He was a Centaur; a rare site in this part of the world. The two behind him weren't born changelings, but converted. It was hard to know what exactly they would turn into. Their lack of sight kept them ignorant to who they were dealing with. The Centaur grabbed at her. "I'd like ta dance wif you."

"No thanks. I was just on my way home."

"Perhaps we shoul' leave 'er?" one of the Centaur's mates, who was wearing a blue parka, suggested. He was nervous, which said he was smart. "If she be ou' here all on her Tobler, then maybe she belongs. You know wot I'm sayin'?"

"Naw, she jus' look like she needs a bit o'luck." The Centaur towered over her. Drool soaked his chin.

Behind him, on the rooftop, a silhouette took form. The shadow crept to the edge and jumped from six floors up with a sword in hand. The short blade jabbed through the back of the Centaur's head and out his mouth. The tip of the weapon stopped just a few inches from Madame Patricia's face. Thick crimson doused the blade and dripped slowly from the point.

The Centaur collapsed to the side allowing the purple aurascales of Athena to shine brightly in Madame Patricia's eyes. Athena crouched and pulled the sword from the Centaur's head. Her beaming eyes were intensely fixed on Madame Patricia. The other two changelings scampered away.

"Just one second," Athena huffed, her voice robotic from behind the aurascales. She sprinted after the two men and leapt for them, springing off the wall of a building. Her legs wrapped around the first man's head as she swung off him like a pendulum and tackled him to the ground. The quick crunch of his neck soon echoed down the way. The thug in a blue parka took a swing, but her sword sliced through his hand down to the elbow and split his arm in two. She pulled the blade back and severed his head with a quick stroke. She called out to Madame Patricia, her surrogate mother. "What are you doing here?"

"I should be asking you the same thing." Madame Patricia stepped over the bloody corpse with her hands firm against her hips. "You know better than to come rifting out here all alone. What if Heaven picked up on you?"

"I used the crystal, just like you taught me." The silver exo-armor retreated from Athena's face and the vibrant orchid aurascales upon her head vanished shortly afterward. Her nearly platinum-blonde hair was soon soaked by the rain. Madame Patricia couldn't help but think that she looked like her father, Zeus, although she had her mother Hera's almond-shaped blue eyes. "That's not the point. You could have been hurt."

"Really?" Athena looked around at the changelings she'd just disposed of and smirked. "What about you? Why were you at that demon place?"

"They didn't see you, did they?" Madame Patricia asked, pulling Athena in close for a hug. She breathed in the scent of Athena's hair and relaxed. It wasn't really fair to be angry with her. Since closing the Progeny Lounge to outsiders, Athena had only had Jaden, Harold and Rob to keep her company. "Who's looking after Jaden?" she asked. "Harold is on a mission."

"Rob was more than happy to oblige." Athena giggled when mentioning the tender hearted Cyclops. "Jaden loves him."

"Jaden can run circles around him." Madame Patricia put a hand on Athena's shoulder. The young girl Hermes had once brought to her for safekeeping had quickly grown into a beautiful and strong woman—it had only taken her a few thousand Earth years to do so. "It's very important you listen to me, more so now than ever." Athena opened her mouth in protest but Madame Patricia quickly put a finger to her lips. "Just trust me. Things have changed. It's not just the Ourea we've recently encountered, nor the events in Moscow—Jaden and his kind are being hunted. He especially needs our protection. Not to mention those who may be looking for you."

"And what about those looking to harm you?" she asked.

Though the notion of someone harming Madame Patricia seemed a silly thought, it wasn't to Athena. Madame Patricia worked hard to never use her powers to harm anyone. It wasn't in her nature. For all Athena knew, the woman who'd raised her was a delicate flower just as in need of protection as Jaden.

"I'm a grown girl. I can handle myself." She kissed Athena's forehead. "And so are you, I suppose. It's time to stretch your wings." Athena swelled with excitement. "Temper your expectations. We must keep a watchful eye and ear. If my hunch is correct, someone with a stronger claim to Jaden will come looking for him. Keeping them apart will be impossible."

"No one can take him from us." Athena squeezed Madame Patricia's hands emphatically. "They'll have to go through me."

"I wouldn't make such statements." Madame Patricia's eyes grew large. "There may be one with Jaden's sister who can do just that. Sooner or later they'll pop up on the radar, and when they do, I'll send you and Harold to retrieve them. But stay vigilant."

CHAPTER EIGHT

Lian II

Lian awoke behind the bar of a tavern, lying on a pile of blankets. Her head throbbed. The lights were off but there was enough moonlight pouring in from the windows that she could see. She couldn't recall how she got off the ship. Flashes of the freighter tossing about and throwing containers into the sea as it ran ashore were superimposed on the back of her mind. They were visions from the ship workers she had mind-melded with while helping Austin track Jarrod. Suddenly she couldn't breathe, drowning in her own visions. Her heart pounded and she was not able to shake the anxious feeling. Lian clawed at the ground and cabinets, trying to swim. All she could see around her were green waves pulling her under, and then a black void.

She gasped, sitting straight up.

"Shit," Lian groaned, grabbing her back. She felt like an eighteen wheeler had plowed into her.

"Don't move," Claire said, walking up behind Lian. The left side of her face was purple and blue, and a large gash was crusty on her knee. Claire tucked a few brown strands of hair behind her ear and more bruising became visible.

"Where are we?" Lian asked, reaching for Claire. She lightly touched her friend on the chin and examined the marks. "Is it serious?"

"We didn't know when you'd wake up and we wanted to let you rest," Claire replied, lowering a glass of water with a straw in it for Lian to drink. "It's a good thing you did wake. This place is crawling with helicopters and soldiers. We don't know how many of them saw us."

"Claire," Lian said, putting her fingers to her friend's hand. They connected eyes and Lian took a deep breath. "Where are the boys? The last I saw..."

"They're fine."

"Really?" Lian frowned in disbelief. What exactly counted as fine? "No more crazy?"

"I didn't say that." Claire peered over the bar and whispered, "But they're fine."

"What about you?" Lian asked. Claire went silent, offering only a quick nonchalant glance. The more she shook the haziness from her eyes, the worse Claire's face looked. She needed to know what they were dealing with. "Did... Jarrod do this to you?"

"No, you kidding?" Claire shook her head emphatically. Lian's mind stole a few of Claire's thoughts. It was the truth. Jarrod hadn't laid a finger on her. That didn't stop Claire from nearly crying over how she now feared him. Lian hopped out of Claire's head to give her privacy.

Lian let out a relieved breath. The monster inside Jarrod was still hibernating.

"I didn't mean to upset you." Lian pulled herself up and leaned over the bar.

"What's going on?" A tear hung in the corner of Claire's unswollen eye. "The three of you are so alike. You act like shutting up keeps me safe and strong, but really it just heaps more weight on my shoulders. I don't have super strength."

"What's that supposed to mean?" Lian huffed.

"You're all still keeping secrets." Claire stood and moved around the bar to stand opposite Lian. "Some of us don't have powers to protect us."

"We'll try harder." Lian coughed and dug her hand into her right side to mute the sharp burn. "I'll try harder. I'm an open book."

"Starting when? Now?" Claire scoffed. Lian couldn't help but hear Claire scream *'yeah right'* in her thoughts. "All I want is to be that person who keeps faith during the storm, but you've got me questioning what I've got faith in. It doesn't help that the scariest of you all can't stand the sight of me."

"That's not what it is…"

"Sure seems like it," Claire snapped back. "Heaven forbid I whisper 'how are you' his direction or he's off to the races."

"Is this one of those emotional girl moments?" Lian asked, serious and giddy. It may have seemed odd to some, but this was a dream situation for her. All her life she grew up surrounded by adult men who did nothing but bark orders. Something as simple as having girl talk excited her. The only way she could ever experience it before was through a book or watching a movie online.

"You don't have to be a bitch." Claire rolled her eyes, folding a towel in her hands and then throwing it to the ground.

"No, I'm not." Lian tugged on Claire's shirt and pulled her back. "I've… I've never done the girl talk and confidante thing before. I didn't mean to sound too excited. This is all very serious."

"Uh huh."

"These are uncharted waters for all of us." Lian propped herself up and walked around the bar to sit on a stool next to Claire. "Something you said a second ago is bothering me. Why are you afraid of us? We would never hurt…" Lian stopped mid-sentence and diverted her eyes away from Claire. Her friend was right. Powerless didn't have to mean helpless, but it could when you didn't know the whole truth—secrets will rot the strongest oak and corrode the thickest metal. It was as if Sanderson were talking in her ear.

Lian wanted to reassure Claire, but there was no way she could. Her friend's thoughts were screaming that loud and clear. Only hearing the comforting sound of Jarrod's voice could really alleviate the fear festering in Claire's heart, because he was the source of most of it. "If you feel like you're losing him, imagine how he feels. He lives every day afraid he's going to destroy the only people he has left in the world. One of you is not going to get what they want. Frankly, I'd rather that be you."

"Really?" Claire flashed a crooked smile.

"Well, it kind of means you'll stick around a bit longer to keep me well." Lian playfully rubbed her hand over Claire's back.

"Is that what you saw?"

"What do you mean?" Lian shook her head, confused.

"Just something you said in your sleep." Claire shrugged, looking out a window to her right. The moonlight illuminated her face with a pale glow. Lian poked inside her head, but Claire's mind traveled to another thought. "It's pretty out."

"It is," Lian whispered, her eyes blankly staring a hole into the wall. What could she have said while asleep?

"You're awake," Austin said cheerfully, rushing to the bar. He leaned next to Claire and spoke to her, pointing at Lian. "Can I take care of her for a bit?"

Claire smirked at Lian, squeezed her knee and walked away. Austin smiled and ran his fingers along the side of Lian's face, pulling her in for a kiss. Lian allowed her muscles to go loose as she crawled into his lap.

"I saw you get knocked over the railing. How did you not break your back?" Lian asked.

"One of the perks of being scratched and infected by a werewolf is advanced healing." He lifted his shirt to reveal no bruises, cuts or any other sign of injury. She quite liked looking at his chiseled abs.

She smiled, rubbing his stomach. "What are the others?"

"An increased metabolism that lets you guzzle as much beer as you'd like and keep your rock hard eight-pack." He tilted a glass under the tap and filled it to the brim. He chugged it and repeated the process. "But that's sort of a double-edged sword, because you don't feel a thing. Which pretty much means you're drinking for taste, ruling out Keystone."

"That's a bad thing?" she giggled.

"It is for your wallet. Good tasting beer is expensive." They sat in silence for a few minutes just looking each other over to be sure they were OK. His fingers sifted through her hair and his thumb rubbed a sensitive spot on the back of her head. She could tell he wanted to say something.

"I thought for sure you were... that Jarrod was going to do something to you, too." Lian struggled to talk, on the verge of breaking down. Her hands pulled tightly on Austin's shirt. Her arms shook. "I'm not sure if I'm qualified to handle all this. If Sanderson were here, he'd know what to do."

"You've done a bang up job baby-sitting us so far." Austin pulled her into his arms. She rested her head on his chest as he took in a deep, controlled breath. "You're the glue. Don't un-stick now."

"Bang up job?" She laughed. *Banged up* was more like it.

"Poor choice of words," he said. It was like he could read minds too.

"Me, the leader?" she chuckled, snorting. She covered her face, hoping he didn't hear it. "All I did was spin the wheel and see where it pointed. You've done all the grunt work."

"I have." Austin nodded.

"Asshole." Lian reached up into his shirt and pulled on a few chest hairs.

"What's next?" he asked, kissing the top of her head.

"I don't know. I'm making this up as I go along."

"We all are." He breathed against her neck as he held her tightly.

She didn't quite agree with that last statement. Not all of them were improvising during this journey. Lian stood and smiled at him, reassuring him that she was stable enough to walk unassisted. He let go and for the first time in a week, since getting sick while on the ship, she stood on her own power.

She was happy to see something other than the dark cabin they'd all shared on the boat. The pictures on the walls of the tavern were interesting. They chronicled decades of time for the tavern, all the way back before the start of World War One. Her gaze fell on a picture taken nearly ten years prior. A memory flashed in her mind. She stumbled, shaking her head, falling over a table. Austin caught her, but she put her hand up and motioned for him to step away.

Something about the picture screamed that it was important. She took the picture off the wall and stared at it while sitting on a chair. Her vision became static. The picture moved.

"Did you see that?" Lian looked over her shoulder at Austin. He shrugged.

The flash of a camera sent her mind back in time. She sat watching a rugby group gather for a photo as a stranger in the pub took their picture. After the collective smiles had been etched onto film for eternity, the man gave the camera back to the group. It was Sanderson.

"Thanks, mate. Can we buy you a pint?" One of the tall, brutish looking rugby players drunkenly slung his arm around Sanderson's shoulders. "C'mon yank, live a little."

"Let's get on with it, you munter." Another rugby player pulled on his friend's shirt. "We're drinking single malt now."

"I'm fine, thanks." Sanderson nodded, moving away from the drunken group. He adjusted his dark plaid hat. "But thanks for the offer."

"I'm not leavin' til ya have a glass. So, what'll it be?" The man swayed in a circular motion, putting his hands to his hips.

"A Guinness, then," said Sanderson, shrugging.

"Fuck that." The rugby player belched.

"Excuse me?" said Sanderson. He shook his head and Lian could tell he didn't know if the man was swearing at something else or if he should be offended.

"Oh, nothing." The man burped again. "I thought me fish 'n' chips was working their way back to the party."

The group waddled over to the bar, leaving Sanderson to his own devices. He pulled the sleeve up on his sweater and checked his watch.

She's late, Lian could hear him think. Lian walked around him, looking intently at the lines of his face, in awe at the detail of her vision. He was so young.

He looked right at Lian but didn't see her. She turned around to find a skinny blonde woman with curly hair walking with purpose toward Sanderson. Her long, brown fur coat swayed behind her. Sanderson stood up and reached through Lian to shake the woman's hand. The lady placed her coat over the back of a chair. Lian stepped back to give her vision space to play out.

"How did you know I was the one coming to see you?" she asked. Her voice was smooth and she had an Irish accent.

"You had that look about you." He sat down, seeming a bit more reserved than Lian remembered him to be. "I can tell when someone has seen... things."

"Yes, there's something unmistakable about it," the woman replied, sliding her lace mittens off. She folded them neatly on the table and crossed one leg over the other. Her long dress nearly hit the floor.

Lian tried to force her way into Sanderson's mind to find out who the woman was, but the vision went fuzzy. She stopped trying to snoop, hoping she'd find out soon.

"It is, indeed, Miss..." Sanderson said, waiting for her to finish his sentence.

"Those who know me refer to me as Madame Patricia. But you can just call me Patricia." She held two fingers up, signaling the bar keeper. She prodded Sanderson with her eyes. "So, you have two kids?"

"W-with me, yes," Sanderson stammered, looking at the table as he focused. "Well, not with me here. They're at the hotel, sleeping. And they're not mine. They're a colleague's. I heard you take in their kind."

"Descendants, yes. Why do you have a friend's children?"

"He's dead and the people who killed him are after them." Sanderson paused for a second to regain his composure. "He knew only I could protect them."

"He's talking about me and my brother," Lian whispered.

"Yet here you are, seeking me," Madame Patricia said. "How did you learn of me?"

"I recreate, let's just say, *remarkable things*. I know there's more out there. Urban legends and all that—they're true."

"Mostly, anyway." Madame Patricia turned to the side and leaned back into the chair, uncrossing her legs. Her eyes scanned Sanderson. "Those and the ones who follow me try to clean that up. It's a delicate balance to keep—well, let's just say 'the authorities'—out of everyone's hair. Nothing would be worse than having our kind all over the evening news."

"Your name came through the grapevine. I got a few gifted ones to talk."

"Really? How?" she asked, leaning forward.

"I'm talented like that." He looked at her with the confident, unrelenting gaze Lian remembered. "I've been told that if I need somewhere to hide, I should come to you."

"That's half true." She took the tea from the waitress and sipped it.

"Just half?"

"I don't take in your kind," she said, setting the cup on the saucer. "You'll have to leave the children."

"Oh, no." Sanderson shook his head. "I don't mean for you take us all in. Just one of them."

"You want to separate the siblings?" She squinted, crossing her arms. "I work on my terms only. You won't dictate to me."

"When you meet them, you'll understand why. They can't be kept together," Sanderson whispered, scooting closer to Madame Patricia. "Their father hid something inside each of them that grows stronger and more unstable the longer they're together. Until they're old enough to control it, they'll have to be apart. You'll see."

"Which shall I take?" Madame Patricia turned her head and gave Sanderson a sideways look. "I assume you have one in mind."

"I'd like to keep the girl. I think I can hide her."

"What is the power?" Lian asked, trying to force herself into Sanderson's head. The vision flickered. She couldn't force it to work at her pace.

Austin put his hands to Lian's face. The vision waned and quickly disappeared. His forehead pressed against hers.

"You were mumbling gibberish," he said. His hands slowly wrapped over hers.

"Was I?" Lian looked down at the photograph, finding the frame had snapped. Pieces of the glass cut into her palms. "I, uh, don't recall."

"Your eyes rolled into the back of your head. You were going full-on undertaker." He pulled shards of glass from her palms and wrapped a towel around her hands. "We'll have Claire take a look at this. You need to be more careful, if you can. You were yelling for Sanderson and Madame Patricia. Who is she?"

"The lady who has my brother." Lian bit her lip to keep from crying. "And she knows why Sanderson separated us."

78

CHAPTER NINE

Jarrod II

Jarrod sat on top of a round table with his feet propped up on a bar stool. He was hunched over, hands in lap, gazing out the window. His eyes glimmered with blue light. They reflected off the window, growing brighter and dimmer in sync with the waves on the shore. The door into the dining area squeaked on its hinges as it swung open. Claire entered. Jarrod blinked and the blue glare vanished from his eyes. Claire stood to his right and lifted her hand but pulled it back apprehensively. He grabbed her palm and brushed it along his face.

"It's good to see you happy," Jarrod said. "You are happy, right?"

"I'm getting there." She nudged him over and sat with him on the table. She squinted out the window. "Not much of a view."

Jarrod looked back outside. His eyes could decipher the chaotic scene hidden beyond the darkness. The tanker sat parked in the sea with a large hole gashed in the side. Several of the cargo containers barely stuck out of the tide. His eyes refocused and connected with hers in the reflection.

"It's an incredible view," he whispered, putting his arm around her back.

"Flattery," she smiled, laying her head in his lap. She yawned and closed her eyes. "It works."

The stray beams from a helicopter in the distance briefly flooded into the windows. The light cast the outline of three dark figures into his field of view. One of them was a giant. He blinked and the blue beam in his eyes came back. The figures were gone. The glow vanished from his eyes. Claire slid her hand behind his head, pulling him down for a kiss. It did little to calm his nerves.

"Relax," she said with a breathy voice.

"This will have the opposite effect." He winked at her, grinning. The battered contours of her face caused a hole to burn in the pit of his stomach. His hand balled up into a fist to keep from shaking. He kept hammering himself about causing the ship to crash and hurting those closest to him. His left hand caressed her forehead. "I'm dangerous. This is all my fault. I'm losing control and next time I might not be able to stop. I almost killed Austin. I could see what I was doing, hear what I was saying, and knew what was coming next, but I couldn't prevent it."

He stopped short of telling her that it felt good.

"But you did stop. Austin says you got control." Claire rubbed the back of his arms. "Lian says this woman we're looking for can help you."

"What if she's wrong?" Jarrod looked back out the window. His reflection snarled at him. "What if the woman from Sanderson's memories is dead? I remember how afraid of me he was when I was a child. I remember the voices..."

"You were a kid then." She put her hand to his chin and refocused his attention. "You're more capable of dealing with it now, right? Kids are scared and lack the refined skills of adults."

He wished that were true. He'd grown up, but he was still scared and unable to control his powers—now it seemed more like his powers were controlling him. It was all muddled.

"You'll get whatever this is under control. We're all here to help." She sat up and kissed him. For a moment, they allowed themselves to forget where they were.

An hour passed. Jarrod stood with his right arm arched against the window and his forehead pressed into his bicep. The breath from his nose fogged up the glass. His eyes briefly glanced down at Claire while she slept soundly. He knew he should rest too, but his body couldn't. Instead, he continued to look aimlessly out the window.

He swore he'd seen something earlier—the three dark figures. Who were they and what did they want? Where did they go? He wouldn't let himself believe it was another lie conjured by his own consciousness.

"It's not," a voice said. It was his, but his lips hadn't moved. He didn't bother looking around, knowing there was no one else besides him and Claire in the room. He hesitated before responding to the voice, not wanting to encourage it.

Why should I believe you? The itch in the base of his skull grew. He didn't want to scratch. The voice couldn't be trusted, yet he couldn't resist. *You hurt those closest to me.*

"Closest to *us*. I haven't killed them. I need you," the voice replied. "You will need me too. Those figures are after you. I have no reason to lie—I'd never lie to you."

Really?

"Really. If they get you, they get me..."

The blue vision poured out of Jarrod's eyes. Across the street stood a towering Cyclops. Jarrod's heart raced. His control of the aurascales slipped. He grabbed his chest, fighting back against the armor. The blue and black aurascales slithered through his veins and skin, tearing at his will like shards of glass. He looked up, noticing the Cyclops marching toward him.

"She's alive," Jarrod panted, sweating profusely as he tried to fight the armor. "Maya found us." He looked down at Claire. Protecting her and the others was most important. "I have to get away from here." He snarled at the Cyclops through the window. "But I have to stop him first."

The aurascales won the struggle and he jumped through the window. He rolled to his feet, dressed in full armor and ready to fight. He drove a shoulder into the lumbering giant's torso with all his might. The Cyclops flew backwards fifty yards, crashing on the beach. Jarrod leapt and landed on top of the frightened giant. He squeezed tightly onto the Cyclops' throat.

"Kill him!" the voice yelled at Jarrod.

A shockwave of sonic energy surged though Jarrod, attacking from the left. It blew him off the Cyclops and caused the aurascales to ripple. The exoskeleton armor adjusted, growing thicker along the front of his body to defuse the vibrations. A pudgy, bearded man raced to the Cyclops' side.

A shield sprouted from the aurascales and deflected the frequency flowing from the pudgy man's hands. Gusts of wind jetted away from Jarrod in ninety-degree angles, causing all the shop windows along the main street to shatter.

A pair of hands snatched Jarrod from behind and slung him to the ground. He tore the hands away from his eyes and saw that it was a blonde woman he thought to be about his age. She shoved his face into the dirt. Her bulky silver-plated armor shifted around her left arm, locking onto the back of his head.

"Athena, do you have him?" the stocky man asked the blonde, coughing as he tended to the Cyclops.

"I do," she replied. "Piece of..."

Jarrod wrapped his ankles around her neck, twisted her arm around, and tossed her over his head. He kicked off his back and to his feet. Turning around, he analyzed this Athena. Billions of purple dots formed together over her skin. The aurascales covered every portion of her body except her face. Jarrod thought she looked like a female version of Jackson, or at the very least there was a strong family resemblance.

"They're recruiting women for the Double-Helix?" he wondered aloud, locking eyes with her. The sharp wind slapped across his face. They lunged for one another.

Athena swung first but Jarrod rolled under her blow. He jabbed at a gap in her exo-armor, striking her ribs, and then kicked her feet out from under her. The Cyclops pulled Jarrod away from Athena and tossed him across the ground. Light beamed from the pudgy man's hands. Jarrod sprinted toward the trio, rearing back for another jab. A cinder block of ice manifested around his right hand and pulled him to the ground

"Do you have him, Harold?" Athena asked the pudgy, red-bearded man. He nodded in reply.

Athena cracked a roundhouse across Jarrod's face, sending him to his back. He followed the momentum of the kick and used it to his advantage by sending it through his hand with the ice-block. He lifted his right hand off the ground and bashed the ice-block into Athena's back. The ice splintered apart.

"You're a nifty ol' buggar, aren't ya?" Harold grunted, waving his glowing hand through the air as if he were trying to write his name with sparklers. A super bright flare erupted, momentarily washing out everything Jarrod could see. When his vision came back, Athena was inches away. Her right hook sent him barreling like tumbleweed.

Jarrod shoved his left hand into the sand and slowly came to a stop. As he looked up, Athena was already high in the air soaring towards him. She landed on him, driving her knees into his shoulders. Putting her left hand to his throat, she pressed it into the ground. Her right fist raised and a dagger appeared in her hand. He latched onto both of her wrists and pushed against her.

He was woozy and still recovering from the flare. The blurry outline of Lian and Austin raced his way. Lian's eyes went white and her hand lifted toward Harold. In turn, his eyes blanked and his hands grew transparent with light. A sound-blast erupted from his palms, nearly ripping all the aurascales from Athena's body. She soared away from Jarrod and landed several yards away with a thud.

"Kill them," the voice in Jarrod's head urged, speaking frantically. "Kill them all now while you've got the drop." Jarrod stood and staggered around, pulling at his hair. A pale blue glow crept through his skin. "Can you feel them? Their souls beckon."

"Stop him." Austin nudged Lian and pointed at Jarrod. "I really think you should stop him now."

"I can't reach in his mind," Lian replied. Her eyes locked onto Harold. "Perhaps it'll work again."

The light from Harold's hands surged over his entire body this time. He lifted off the ground and clapped his hands. A tidal wave of sound rippled across the beach. The force of the sonic boom smacked Jarrod in the gut. The aurascales retreated back inside his body as he rolled across the ground and threw up simultaneously.

Lian lowered her hand and Harold collapsed. The Cyclops stood motionless, scratching the back of his head. Lian walked by him and patted him on the shoulder.

"It's OK, Rob. I'm not gonna hurt you." She winked, walking over to Jarrod with Austin by her side. She stood at Jarrod's head and held her fingertips up to Austin's lips before he could speak. "I read their minds. That's how I know their names."

"Fair enough." Austin nodded. "Who are they?"

"It seems you are the posse we've been sent to retrieve," Harold said as Rob helped him up. "Miss Lian here was able to divulge as much to me while crawling around in my head. Sorry for the misunderstanding, but we were caught off guard when one of your own attacked us. Strange, though. I've never come across the color of those aurascales before."

"Yeah, yeah. I've heard that story before." Jarrod grimaced, gripping his ribs as Austin assisted him to his feet. He eyed Lian. "Did you have to do it so freaking hard?"

"Look at what you did to the ship." She put her fists to her hips and lowered her head. "I'm not going there again."

"Don't blame her," Austin said. "I told her to put you down."

"Right." Jarrod nodded, trying to catch his breath. He walked over to Athena, who was still kneeling with her hands covering her face, and offered her a hand. She slapped it away before standing and marching over to Harold's side. "It was a valiant effort."

"Valiant?" She looked over her shoulder and scoffed. "I had you until your friends intervened."

"Because it took three of you to distract and sneak attack me." He stopped mid-statement and bit his lip. His head hurt too much to argue. "Whatever."

"You have no retort." She grinned. "Victory is mine again"

Jarrod rolled his eyes. Was this chick being serious or playful? Who was playful after a fight like that? And all this time he'd thought he was the one going crazy.

"Is everything OK?" Claire called out, sprinting towards the group, on edge because of all the commotion. "What in San Jacinto is going on?"

"Are you ancient, too?" Athena asked. Harold put a hand on her shoulder and shook his head.

"I am Harold and these are my companions, Rob and Athena," Harold said, putting his right hand to his chest as he bowed and walked toward Lian. "And you're the one."

"I suppose," she replied, gazing awkwardly at him. She stepped behind Austin, whose eyes shifted with animalistic ferocity. Harold stepped back.

"The one what?" Claire asked, breathing onto her hands to warm them up. The wind blew against her light coat, making it crackle.

"The child we couldn't keep." Harold waved Athena over, whispering to her.

"No secrets!" Jarrod yelled, storming over to Harold and grabbing him by the arm. He yanked and turned Harold around.

"There are none," Lian interrupted him. She tapped her head. "He couldn't, even if he tried. I got him in here."

"Very true, mate." Harold held his hands up and sighed heavily when Jarrod let him go.

Athena walked toward Lian. She nodded at Claire—who didn't seem to share the same enthusiasm—while passing by her. Athena reached for Lian's hand, but Austin's wolf-paw snatched her wrist.

"A changeling," Athena gasped.

"Excuse me if I'm not so trusting," Austin said through his teeth, glaring at Harold. Athena pulled away and stood back next to Rob.

"Sorry about the shoulder-tackle." Jarrod leaned toward Rob, who was standing to his left, and slapped the Cyclops on the back. "Nothing personal."

Rob whimpered and rubbed his chest.

"Sorry about my cross." Athena playfully mimed a punch while biting her lower lip, surveying Jarrod. She pushed her hair behind her ear and tapped him on the right shoulder. Touching Jarrod's chin, she shifted his face down to look at his eye. "I think that will leave a mark."

"Excuse me, but I'm with Austin on this one. I don't trust you guys one bit," Claire said, stepping between Jarrod and Athena. Her hands caressed his face. "Are you hurt?"

"No, I'm alright." Jarrod shook his head, looking cross-eyed at Claire. She pressed her face into his chest, practically leaping into his arms. "Um, OK."

"We must be on our way," Harold said, whistling at Athena. "We've already attracted too much attention from the locals."

Athena nodded in reply, grabbing Jarrod and Claire by the wrists. A crystal with pink mist sprouted from her armor and hovered in place. Harold touched Austin and Lian. A pink cloud swirled around the group, slowly taking hold of them. Jarrod pulled Claire in tight.

"This is going to be uncomfortable," he whispered to her.

Reality became flimsy, like cold gelatin. A pink light pierced through them, splitting apart the molecules that held them together. The cold sting subsided as they were pieced back together on a hillside overlooking a steep drop off into the Irish Sea. Claire inhaled, pressing a hand against her chest. Jarrod scooped her up and followed Athena towards a small hut at the top of a slope.

"I think I remember this place," Lian said, pushing into Austin's embrace.

"You should," Harold replied. "You've been here before."

"Where is here?" Austin asked.

"The Progeny Lounge," Harold replied, turning to face the group as he twisted the door knob and pushed into the hut.

CHAPTER TEN

Isis I

Isis watched her eight year old son Horus train with his uncle, her brother Sobek. One day Horus would be expected to be a leader. Part of being a capable commander was holding one's own in battle, and killing if one must. She stood on her balcony, viewing him through a window which allowed her to be unseen by those on the other side. Her reflection looked haggard.

Her brother Sobek—that thought was humorous to her. She'd always been told he was Nephthys' twin, and a few years her junior. She didn't remember ever being a child like her son, though. The thought of being little once upon a time was both silly and somehow strange. The angels were supposed to have always been, created from the light of stars.

Really, she was related to all the angels. Wasn't she? How could they all simultaneously be her siblings, lovers, friends and allies, but also be singled out specifically? Osiris and Set were brothers. Michael and Gabriel brothers, and related still to Osiris in that they referred to him as brother, but not Set and Sobek, or her as a sister. Why the distinction?

It was a fool's errand to try to understand. That was why the humans remained so frail—they were always caught up with where they came from instead of where they were going. What's done is done, she always said. The important thing was what lay ahead. Horus and her nephew—and surrogate son—Anubis deserved a tomorrow.

89

Of course, she convinced herself of all that as a way to cope. There was truth hidden in the light of their eyes. Something devious that put a crack in Father's foundation. Even though she always thought Zeus a bit of a radical, there was truth in the grand speeches he would give the other Archangels just before the Last Great War. A truth she would overhear when Osiris and Zeus would seek council with one another and draw plans of merging their Corners. It was a truth Osiris died for. It was now embodied in her son, and she would do anything to protect it, whatever it was.

"Get up." Sobek's voice was stern. His blade ran parallel to his right leg, the tip pointed at the ground. He walked in a circle around Horus, stepping sideways. The young boy slowly pushed himself up. Anubis sat on a step in the far corner of the room with his eyes more curious of the sparring than the lessons he was instructed to read. Sobek commanded once more. "Your fight is not over."

"It's no use. You're too fast and strong," Horus replied, on the verge of tears. He slammed his fist into the gray floor, grinding his teeth together as he stared down his trainer.

"Surrender is a state of mind settled on before battle. If you're truly done, then you never had a chance." Sobek lunged forward and swiped down toward Horus. The boy jumped, rolling to the left, barely avoiding the edge of the sword as it hit and splintered the floor.

Horus snatched his weapon off the ground, spinning and jumping to his feet. He slung the sword over and around his head, slashing across his body at Sobek. A shield materialized out of thin air, deflecting Horus' blow. Sobek followed the block with a swipe of his blade-turned-staff to take out his nephew's legs. Horus landed with a thud, drawing a concerned look from Anubis who quickly rose to his feet.

"No fair—you used your aurascales!" Horus shouted, rubbing the back of his head. "If I had a starstone of my own, I'd cut you to pieces."

"But you don't." Sobek pressed the ball of his foot onto Horus' sternum and placed the tip of the staff to his young student's neck. It shifted back into a sword. "There is nothing fair about your existence. You can't let it get you angry. You have to rise above the rage, stay collected, and never give up."

"That's easy for you to say."

"Is it?" Sobek squinted, his jaw tight. "Despite all this power I have over you, I am still but a speck of dust among the stars. There is always someone more powerful lurking in the shadows. Don't make it easy for them by defeating yourself—your father taught me that."

"A lot of good it did him." Horus slapped the sword away from his face and crawled backwards. He turned onto his stomach and pushed off the floor. Wiping himself off, he straightened his clothes. "He couldn't even save his Corner. He was useless. He—"

"He was outnumbered and alone!" Sobek roared, cutting Horus off. He opened his hands and his weapons vanished into his armor. "There was a time when your father single-handedly defeated a whole brigade of Lucifer's legion. There were few as capable of wielding the HALOGUARD as he. It was a sight to behold." Sobek paused and his tone shifted from stern to sincere. "It is because of your father that we have this place and have a chance. One day, when those who followed him are gone, the ones we birthed will look to you for guidance and wisdom. If you could end up being a quarter of what your father was, then I would consider my time with you a success."

"I will lead our people home and off this blasted rock," Horus snarled, turning his back and crossing his arms. "I won't get myself killed like my father. I'll be powerful enough to destroy anyone that gets in my way. I could now, if I had a starstone."

"There will come a time when none of us have the power of the stars to protect us." Sobek sighed, shaking his head, visibly frustrated with Horus's immaturity. "What will you do then? How fair will it be when the power that protects this place—your people—runs out? The energy of our starstones doesn't last forever, and when they fade so do we. How will you save your people then, Horus? When your mother, the elders and I are no longer here, and you and the other Angel-born, not tethered to the stars, are all that's left?"

"I'll keep fighting!" Horus yelled, spinning around, kicking his foot underneath his sword, lifting it into the air. He grabbed it, smashed the edge into Sobek's sternum plate, and then swiped his legs under his teacher, bringing Sobek to the floor. The blade stood at attention next to Sobek's neck. "I'll get our enemies right where I want them and then take off their heads, because our enemies are weakest when they think we've given up."

"He's a stubborn child. Hopefully it serves him well," Amun said as his reflection appeared in Isis' window. He stood a good foot taller than her, but appeared much larger when dressed in his lavender ceremonial robes and long white hat. A thick, burgundy goatee stood strong on an otherwise cleanly-shaven round face. "It reminds me of someone."

"Osiris was firm, relentless and strong-willed, but was also kind," Isis replied, keeping her focus on Horus. Her arms were folded over the top of each other as she leaned against the wall. "Stubborn, he was not."

"I was talking about his mother." Amun smiled at his own wit. Isis briefly looked at Amun through the reflection, allowing her silence and stone-cold glare do the talking. She returned her attention to her son. "We've spent eight years in the warped shadow of this collapsed star. It's time we began speaking," Amun said, touching her shoulder. "Do you remember when you first joined us here?"

"My skin crawls at the thought." She shook him off.

"I thought it made you perspire?" he said, almost breathing down her neck. "The things we do for our loved ones. Why not experience it again?"

"Can't imagine why I avoided it all this time," Isis snickered. She rolled her eyes and turned to walk away. Amun followed. She spoke again. "You're relentless, I'll give you that. But I won't give you what you want. You're in my chamber now. I insist you leave."

"Then come with me to mine." He smiled, but she groaned. "Isis, you're being unreasonable. An arrangement between us is the only natural course."

"I've a husband," she rebuffed. He grabbed her right arm and twirled her around, pressing her into the glass wall that overlooked her son training below. He towered over her, looking down the top of her blouse, before gently letting go and smiling nervously. The dagger tapping his inner right thigh was firmly in her grip. "Touch me again and I'll show you where Horus gets his temper."

"And his quick draw," Amun chuckled, stepping back.

"That, he inherited from his father—"

"—Who is dead and not returning." Amun took another giant step out of her reach when her nostrils flared. "This is my fortress, remember? After the fall of our Corner, we found you content to flee and live in solitude with your child and nephew. Would you have come looking for the rest of us had we not found you first?"

"You're married." She pointed the blade directly at him.

"She pales in comparison to you."

"You have a daughter," Isis said through her teeth. Her gaze and the steadiness of her weapon were unaffected by her emotion. "She plays with Horus."

"If unity between us is something that won't happen, then perhaps Hathor can grow into a suitable bride for Horus. It seems only fitting that our lines should be joined somewhere, seeing as your starstone was the one selected to protect this fortress. Unless he's still betrothed to Athena... Likely dead as she may be."

Isis narrowed her eyes. "It is unwise to push me."

"You're not an Archangel, Isis. They were a powerful, but rare, breed. I am the next highest-ranking official in our Corner, so let's not lose sight of the fact that your throne sits atop a pedestal carved out of guilt for the loss of Osiris. The people know your power won't last forever—you're a mere muse. I'm an Alpha Guardian..."

"*Were* a guardian. Those titles no longer fit us."

"So what be us now?" Amun spread his arms as if speaking to a crowd and then plopped them next to his sides. "Are we gods to those who know not any better?"

"We're free."

"A label the naive give themselves," Amun replied, stepping closer to her. She raised the dagger. He continued forward and she swung at him. He stepped inside her strike, grabbing both wrists, and pinned her to the wall. He pressed against her and licked her cheek. Her muscles strained as she tried unsuccessfully to pull away. "What happens when your aura starts to fade? Feeling sorry for you won't be enough to keep you in charge."

"If my power ever wanes, then the crown can be yours." She turned her face towards him, their noses touching. She relaxed a bit, breathing heavily as she looked at his lips. She breathed down his neck, feeling him excite.

She looked over her shoulder at Horus. She had the support of many angels, but how long would it last when tested? The only thing keeping her boy safe was making sure potential threats remained docile until he was old enough to fend for himself. She looked back at Amun and her bright eyes scrutinized his physique. She licked his lips and bit his ear playfully.

Amun pressed his lips to hers and shoved his tongue into her mouth. At first she wanted to clam up and curl into a ball. Coming to terms with the fact that this was the only way, she began to tell herself that it was enjoyable. Slowly, it became so. Her fingernails raked across his abs as she returned his kisses, massaging his tongue with hers. She spread her legs and he tore her skirt apart. Sliding his pants down, he turned her toward the window and pressed her against the glass. The sway of his thrust pushed her into the window and then pulled her back again. Between each forced moan to stroke his ego, she shielded her gaze, not looking at her young boy. She noticed Anubis turn his head up to the window, though he couldn't possibly see her.

Amun grabbed her hair while thrusting harder, trying to cause her breathing to grow shallow. She wouldn't let him dictate the depths to which he enjoyed her. She spun, curling her legs around his hips, and twisted him to the ground. Her back arched and her hands sifted through her hair as she pulled her own head back. She leaned forward and forced her hands around his throat. She crouched on her feet and closed her eyes, thinking of Osiris as she took command.

Amun moaned. His arms and body rattled between her legs. His breathing softened as sweat ran down his face. Isis finally collapsed over him with her mouth locked in the open position as she pressed her forehead into his shoulder and breathed heavily. She fought back the tears, hoping Osiris wasn't judging from above.

"If Horus inherits the strength and skill that Osiris had as a fighter, and the tact and manipulative ability of his mother, he'll be an unstoppable leader," Amun panted with his arms sprawled open on the floor. He took a deep breath, his lungs stuttering.

"I'll be sure he's ready to lead. He's destined for great things," she said, slightly grinning. Her breasts were soaked in sweat and visible through her white top. She stepped off him and wrapped a shawl around her waist. "I'm satisfied. You may leave."

"Indeed you are." Amun nodded, examining what she left behind on him. He stood and brushed the wrinkles from his robe. "Osiris may have been powerful and just, but you're a far more ruthless and suitable leader. You play the game well."

"You play well, too." She smiled, trying to be provocative and enticing. Really there was nothing that made her sicker. The day she could put a dagger through the back of his neck couldn't arrive soon enough.

Amun turned and walked away. Isis stared him down, grinding her teeth together. The game terms were now set. They both would have to play by them until better options became available. Isis searched for hers every day. She was not naive enough to think Amun wasn't doing the same. She turned back to watch her son and noticed

Anubis was gone. Just Horus and Sobek remained, continuing to spar. Both boys would remain safe under her watch long enough to one day take possession of what Osiris had charged her with harboring: his piece of the Forge.

CHAPTER ELEVEN

Isis II

Isis' brother Sobek sat across from her with his loyal lieutenants at attention outside the door and out of earshot of their conversation. He was literally suggesting abdication to his sister. It wasn't quite clear to Isis how her situation had come to this. Perhaps it had something to do with her limited desire for real politics. She'd done everything in her power to hold influence. She'd even preyed on the goodwill of those who still pitied her for the tragedies that she'd endured during their Corner's expiration. The majority of their people were spared death because of Osiris' quick thinking and sacrifice. To honor him, his heir—and by extension she—should be lifted up. Their Corner owed it to their onetime Archangel.

It seemed now all they remembered was Amun swooping down like a god from the sky, casting his wing over them and carrying them away. However, he did so by order of Osiris. How quickly the ignorant masses forget those truly responsible for salvation or devastation. Amun hadn't uttered a word of ascension to Isis or in public. Of course, there was no telling what went on behind closed doors. Isis knew that all too well.

Though Horus was now grown, and more than capable of taking care of himself and her, the notion that she would step aside for an angel like Amun was preposterous. She tolerated him being inside her because she could tell the type of dark individual he really was; a trait she sometimes saw in herself.

Her brother's words angered her so much she nearly had Sobek thrown into the subterranean mines for speaking them. But then where would that leave her? Down an ally and a reputation shot to pieces.

"This wasn't the way it was supposed to be," she said, leaning back in her chair as if completely unfazed. It was important to always project an aura of confidence. "The Angel-born were meant to rule. My son is to be king one day with Hathor as his wife."

"I see not how that changes." Sobek couldn't see the truth through the clouds. He must've been desperate like the rest of them.

The energy of their stars was nearing an end, and the shields and life support systems they powered would soon fail. The energetic radiation that loomed beyond their walls would tear through everything with unrelenting force. The time dilation they enjoyed, helping to keep them young all this time, would slip and reverse stream instantly, and they'd be torn through a sort of temporal flux. In short, it wouldn't be pretty.

He reached over and held her hand, attempting to console her. "They would still be betrothed," he said, as if matters of betrothal and marriage were taken to heart by a beast like Amun. "He would assume kinghood through his wife. What difference would it make?"

"All the difference." She squinted. "You're a bigger fool than I took you for if you think Amun would take command and then just hand it over."

"And why is that? He's shown no ill will toward you or Horus in the past. He's always been your biggest champion." Sobek stood, obviously insulted by what Isis had said.

Of course he was her biggest champion. She rode him well.

"Maybe he should lead." Sobek nearly pulled out his remaining hairs. "A calmer head sits upon his shoulders, clearly. His star has not faded a day since we've come here. It is limitless. I could see us ushering in a new era like never before. Perhaps it would be right for him to remain king for a while. My nephew could learn a thing or two."

"Do not bring him into this lest you speak his name with caution." Isis sat forward and glared at her brother. "I won't entertain this further. If there be something else you wish to discuss then I'll hear it. Otherwise, leave me be."

"Where did you send the prince and his cousin?" Sobek softened his tone. His long face told her the bickering was wearing on him. "I think I have a right to know that."

"Earth," she said. He was aghast and turned pale. "That look, there." She pointed at him. "That's why I kept it close to the vest."

"You are mad," he said, nearly hyperventilating. He propped himself against the back of the chair for support. "You know what's happened there. They're exposed."

"We don't know what's happening there. Have we seen it for ourselves?"

"The scouts sent earlier…"

"By Amun. I trust them not." She stood and pulled him close, speaking at a whisper. "Steady yourself."

"I can't for the life of me understand why you view him as a threat." Sobek caressed his fingers along his sister's soft face. "There is plenty you've not shared. Just unburden yourself."

Isis wanted to tell him how Amun would frequently slither his way inside her quarters and her body, a fact she'd long regretted but couldn't seem to change. She both hated and enjoyed it. Mostly she pretended it was her husband.

Her sorrowful eyes turned up to him and held tears at bay. He waited patiently for a revelation, but it wouldn't come. One of his men entered the room.

"Sir," the young Angel-born lieutenant, Khepri, said as he marched into the room with his eyes cast to the floor. His superiors graciously gestured for him to speak. "There is a visitor from the East. Lady Khali has come to speak with our people."

Isis looked at Sobek with a sense of mistrust.

He shrugged. "I know nothing of this. I swear." She knew when her baby brother was lying, and this wasn't one of those times. He spoke to Khepri. "Is she alone?"

"She is." Khepri nodded. "And claims it is urgent."

"Bring her here immediately. Do not let her speak to anyone else." Isis stood and marched in circles. If Vishnu was sending delegates then something was afoot. He only ever let those under his wing loose when he had demands. Or could it be something closer to her heart? Maybe his scouts to Earth had grave news regarding Horus.

"The small council needs to convene," Sobek urged her, but she ignored him. "Look at me, sister—you know as well as I do what someone on the level of Khali visiting our inner halls means. We have to play this right."

"I'm aware." She briefly glanced at him while pacing. "You need to go."

"Vishnu was there at the Last Great War." Sobek stood in her way and grabbed onto her. His hands went clear around her arms with nearly a finger's length to spare. "Michael destroyed the Western Corner. They were dismembered so badly that a spoiled half-breed cunt was able to ascend as queen."

"I know this." Isis shrugged, wishing Sobek would just get on with his point before Khali arrived.

"Vishnu, from what I know during my brief encounters and the words your husband and his brother would share about him, is a very greedy, untrustworthy and nefarious individual. His selection to the ranks of Archangel was far from unanimous, sneaking in through a three-way split vote because of the incredible influence he held over a large population of our kind."

Khepri leaned in through a small opening in the door at the far end of the chamber. The siblings looked at him, each holding up a hand for another second of privacy. Isis rubbed Sobek's chin and pulled his head down to kiss his forehead. He sighed and closed his eyes.

"When you share a bed with someone, you are uniquely in a position to know all sorts of truths. Osiris would confide in me things that would make your bones crumble," she whispered, pulling her brother's head down and into her shoulder. "I know what kind of man Vishnu is, and I also know the man you would have me bow to."

"When the choice isn't one you'd like to make, but you are forced, I always choose the lesser of two evils." Sobek pushed away and knelt, bowing his head. "Vishnu experienced no losses in the Last Great War because he offered Zeus on a silver platter to Michael. I cannot prove it, but there could be no other explanation." Sobek looked up and stood. "And if you believe that not to be the case, then you're the biggest fool I know."

Sobek left Isis' private chambers as Khali was escorted in. He stopped for a moment, looking back pensively. Khali's armor was manifested. The mandarin glow of her aurascales and the charred silver exo-armor that grew from them must have triggered Sobek's alarms. A sword materialized in his right hand, but Isis squinted and shook him off. He left reluctantly without Khali noticing he'd drawn a weapon.

"Queen Isis." Her tone said she was all business. Khali knelt and remained on a knee until Isis tapped her shoulder. Vishnu had his followers trained well. "Lord-god Vishnu extends his warmest thanks for accepting my visit with no advanced notice, along with his deepest heartfelt sorrows for the loss of his beloved Archangel brother Osiris."

"A tad late on that last one, no?" Isis asked, offering her hand for Khali to kiss; which she did without hesitation. "Please, tell him both his thanks and condolences were well received and accepted."

"Please pardon the abrupt nature of the change in subject, but I would like to discuss why I am here."

"Me too." Isis sat and motioned for Khali to sit alongside her. The offer was refused with a casual shake of the head.

"My emperor wishes for those under the green banner of the Southern Corner to pledge their allegiance should an attack fall upon the borders of the Eastern walls." Khali was able to speak with a straight face, though her eyes relayed to Isis that she didn't have complete faith in the message.

"Why would battle come at this time?" Isis asked. She waited in silence for an answer. Khali didn't give one. "Are you trying to imply this is simply a good faith agreement? Like the one Zeus reached with Osiris before aligning with Vishnu in the Last Great War?" Khali remained stoic. Isis didn't care if her words were going to illicit a response from the Guardian; she wanted the cathartic release of saying them. "If Vishnu honors our alliance and fights as hard as he did for Zeus, I have no doubt in the fate of my people."

"Yes, you will be well protected." Khali nodded.

"Oh no, I didn't say that." Isis smiled, standing from her chair and moving over to the door. "I just said I had no doubt in the fate of my people." Khali's lips pursed and her fists curled up tight. Isis opened the door and spoke to Khepri, who was stationed outside, though she'd expected to find Sobek waiting. "Khepri, have Sobek assemble the small council."

"Yes, my queen." He bowed and scampered off.

"Your insinuation is wrong."

"I am more than capable of deciding the validity of my own insinuations, thank you." Isis snapped her fingers twice at Khali, hoping to illicit an emotional response. There was none. That was far more unsettling. "I don't suppose it would be too much to assume your conscience would get the better of you and you'd divulge the truth to me, woman-to-woman." Isis walked circles around Khali and analyzed her body language. "At least I know you have a conscience. I can see it in the way you steady your breath, though what you fear far outweighs any guilt you have in delivering your message or its repercussions should you act upon it."

Khali remained stoic. This was an exercise in futility. However, with a quick flicker of her eyes, Khali betrayed her intentions unknowingly. Her gaze swiped across the fractured artifact hanging around Isis' neck. Maybe it wasn't unintentional. Maybe it was Khali's inner sense of right and wrong calling out. Either way, Isis had more than enough information to make a decision.

"Tell your Lord-god, emperor, and majestic-supreme king that I politely refuse his offer. Seeing as Michael, in all these millennia, hasn't attempted to track us down, and pretty much lets us do as we wish even though he must know we're here, I think we are safe."

"But the failed invasion…"

"Was just that. Failed. That was another Corner and another problem. A Corner we would've been a part of had Vishnu not tugged away Zeus' affections." Isis smiled. Sobek entered the room with a few guards behind him. "I suppose, given the alliance the East had with the West, that would put you guys in the line of fire, right? Maya was brash, but she wasn't well-supplied enough to carry out an attack of that magnitude. And since the North is dead, and we didn't do it, that leaves one supplier—the Corner who fled with their tails tucked between their legs during the Last Great War. Good luck with that."

"As you wish." Khali knelt again and bowed her head. She waited for Isis to release her with a touch once more, but none came.

"Brother, get her out of my sight." Isis turned and clapped her hands.

"With pleasure." Sobek marched forward and grabbed Khali by the arm. He tugged her up but she kicked her legs behind his feet and drove her forearm over his chest, throwing him to his back. Sobek's soldiers drew their weapons.

"Do not touch me," Khali sneered.

"So she has emotion after all." Isis smirked. "Be gone."

"I came here in kindness," Khali said with an eerie calm as she stood up. "The disrespect was uncalled for."

"Disrespect was waiting an eternity to send flowers to a funeral for a supposed brother." Isis motioned toward the door with her head. "Thank you, though."

CHAPTER TWELVE

Anubis I

Anubis and his cousin returned from their journey to Moscow and Cairo. On their travels they rescued a little girl. By the looks of her, she was about seven years old. Anubis felt sorry for her. She'd just lost her entire family. He didn't know why Horus insisted they stay back and let them be slaughtered, but he had to trust his cousin because he knew better. Had his advice been heeded before meeting with Svarog, perhaps the young Russian girl and her mother wouldn't have died in that frozen alleyway. At least he felt as if he'd made amends by saving this child. Now they just needed to know why his Aunt Isis insisted they bring her back. Again—he slapped himself in the forehead—that's not something he should be concerned with.

The young child's head dangled over Horus' arm as he carried her through their fortress. They tried to remain undetected by the others. A thin white blanket had been placed over her body and face, allowing her to rest without too much intrusion from the light. He noticed her eyes blink through the loosely sewn fabric.

His facial armor retracted, leaving his grayish complexion and shaved head exposed. His eyes were almost as dark as his armor. He smiled at her and she quickly closed her eyes. It must've been a game. Anubis liked to play it as a child; to pretend to be asleep and fool the grownups. He wanted to play with her.

However, a ringing noise entered his mind not long after they rescued the girl. Horus heard it too. It was poking at the back of Anubis' head. He yearned to cut it out.

"Can you hear it?" he howled at his cousin. "Make it stop."

"Calm yourself, Anubis," Horus ordered as he gently placed the girl down on a soft bed. "You'll wake her."

The child's half closed eyes turned up to Horus. She didn't shy away from him like she did Anubis. His beautifully feathered mask probably appealed to her. It slowly shifted back and revealed his chiseled cheekbones and squared jaw with a cleft in the chin. His hair was thick and wavy, and his skin a honey-amber. The girls always swooned over Horus. Anubis was used to it.

She sniffled and then went rigid. Horus was aware she'd woken up. He knelt beside the bed and slowly pulled the blanket away from her face. He gently ran his fingers over her head, whistling a tune to ease her nerves. It was soothing to Anubis too.

"You've returned," Hathor, Amun's daughter, said, entering the room. Her father was the highest-ranking Guardian left in their Corner: an Alpha. She was a bit fairer in complexion than Horus. Anubis found her utterly beautiful, though others around their fortress regarded her as plain. His gangly looks kept him from ever getting the courage to really speak with her. That and other things he once did as a child stifled any interaction before it ever started. She was dressed in silk linens the color of turquoise and lavender. She looked down at the girl and her brown eyes widened. "Oh, you brought one..."

"How's my mother?" Horus cut her off, looking at her out of the corner of his eyes. He felt the little one tense up as he began to move away, so he returned his knee to the floor and stayed close to her. "How's she handling the call of Gabriel?" That was the ringing noise in their heads.

"She's fine, but the others are getting anxious. What's going on?" Lines formed around Hathor's eyes. She moved behind Horus, peeking over his shoulder at the young girl. Most of the other Angel-born had never seen a human up close before. Travel to Earth was forbidden to those not authorized. "Your Uncle Sobek is on edge. He believes Gabriel's beacon is a sign of forgiveness, in light of the recent assault by the Corner of Olympus."

"Sobek is always on edge," Anubis said, trying to stand where Hathor would notice him.

"What do you think Horus? You were out there." Hathor rubbed the prince's shoulder, visibly disregarding Anubis' opinion as she rolled her eyes.

"I was there too," Anubis said bashfully, still trying to lean forward into Hathor's sight. She continued to ignore him, so he slunk back and away.

"Khali was here." Hathor focused her attention on Horus as she massaged him. Anubis stared longingly at her fingers as they dug into his cousin's muscular back. Horus stood, shrugging her off. She looked towards the ground, quickly pulling her hands behind her back. Anubis smiled on the inside.

Horus snapped his head around. "What did she want?" His steely gaze was unnerving. It was unusual for other Corners to send such high delegates to relay information. Khali was a warrior and often where she traveled so, too, did her husband Shiva, a man with a formidable reputation of his own.

"She spoke with your mom in private. Sobek believes Vishnu's Corner intends to move against Michael. Some of us are fearful your mother may align with them, you know, because..."

"Because why?" Horus stood closer to her.

"Because of what Raphael did to your father and uncle." Hathor turned her head up, closing her eyes as she leaned towards Horus, slightly biting her lower lip. Anubis wanted to pull her away, but she was betrothed to Horus—if he'd ever have her. "They think you'll bring us to war and doom us."

"What do you think?" he asked, semi-oblivious to her body language.

"I... trust you," she replied.

"We must address them, now." Anubis stood between the two. The girl threw the covers over her head when he got close. He looked down at her and his face fell. The child's reaction was one he was all too familiar with. It was the way he viewed himself. "We should probably help mother."

"You mean my mother?" Horus looked at Anubis strangely.

"Yes, that's what I said."

"Can you watch her?" Horus asked Hathor as he touched the back of her arm. A smile grew on her face as her shoulders rose back up. She nodded. He whispered. "We can't let anyone else know she's here."

"Why did you bring her?" Hathor asked.

"Mother asked me to." He looked back at the girl and smiled at her, nodding, then briefly glanced at Hathor and turned to walk out of the room. "Anubis, come."

"Of course," Anubis replied. He stepped out of the room and stood around the corner, out of sight. He snuck a glance at the two girls in the room.

"Hello, child. What is your name?" Hathor leaned forward slightly, placing her hand on the girl's knee. She smiled and spoke again while leaning forward. "It's OK. I promise I won't bite."

"I'm Rashini," she replied, her eyes red. A large frown hung on her face and her hands shook.

"You're safe now. No one can hurt you here." Hathor wiped a tear from the young girl's cheek.

"That's what papa said," Rashini pulled her knees up to her chest and wrapped her arms around her legs. "But they came and got us. We tried to hide, but the bad people... They brought us to the burned man."

"The burned man?" Hathor asked.

Anubis had heard stories as a child—an angel who predated time itself with stars for eyes and lava-chiseled skin. The very ground he walked on sizzled and smoked beneath his feet. But he was a myth; just a tall tale to scare young Angel-born into listening to their elders, and to tarnish the lure of traveling beyond the borders of their fortress. Rashini couldn't possibly be speaking of the same person.

Hathor cradled the child. She rubbed Rashini's head and rocked back and forth.

Anubis turned and pressed his back against the wall. He listened to Hathor hum the child a song, but noticed Horus was well out of sight. He stole one last look at Hathor before hurrying to join Horus and the others in the grand hall, where he knew Isis and the elders would be waiting for answers. He only hoped they wouldn't be too angry with him for being late. The thought made him sick to the stomach.

CHAPTER THIRTEEN

Horus II

Horus walked into the Great Hall followed by Anubis. Before them stood the higher ranking officials of their Corner, all of them Angels just like his mother. He regarded them as much wiser beings than himself. The group split in half as he walked between them towards his mother at the far end of the room.

Their Great Hall was boxy, made of the same angelic metal as their starstones. Small holographic lights hovered in place, illuminating the cold looking room, powered partially by the star of Isis. His father, Osiris, and uncle, Set, had constructed the fortress and navigation systems before they were murdered. They had intended to rendezvous with Zeus on a planet cultivated by the Archangel on the far side of the galaxy. However, Horus was told, the events on the day of his birth had changed all that.

Instead of heading to that virtual oasis, Isis had transported Horus and his cousin to this desolate planet using the limited power remaining in Osiris' star. Later, the remnants of Osiris' legion, under the command of the Alpha Guardian Amun, arrived to make this planet a home for all their kind. At least, that was the story as Horus had been told by his mother, and he never questioned it.

Built into the walls were large floor-to-ceiling windows, originally intended for their Corner to gaze upon the wonders of Zeus' new haven. Instead, the Great Hall overlooked the desolate cold of space, with large chunks of rock half the size of the human moon floating in the sky. Their planet had no atmosphere, and no way for them to build new life of their own. Those who'd fled the day of Horus' birth were the same individuals who acted as the elders of their Corner today. They faced extinction at every turn, and Horus silently vowed to himself that he would change that. He would deliver on the promise his father made.

"My son." Isis beamed from ear to ear as she stood and raised a hand. Horus walked up the steps and knelt before her, taking her hand and kissing it. "I trust you were successful in scouting."

"I was," Horus replied, turning to look at the group.

"So you've seen the destruction brought forth by the spoiled brat Maya?" Khnum called out, stepping to the front. His full beard was turning gray, an unusual sight. "You've naturally heard the call of Gabriel, and know of the impending judgment they're waiting to bring upon the remnants of the four Corners?"

"It's not judgment, you fool!" Sobek shouted, charging towards Khnum. "We hear the messenger's call because Father intends to welcome us back. Michael has had ages to snuff us out. This is clearly a sign of forgiveness if we repent and fight against the wicked ones. Why else would Father allow Azrael to return to vanquish Maya and send her heretical forces back to wherever they came from?" He looked up at his sister and nephews with a pleading glance. His long, weary face was riddled with age. "Think of it, sister. Why else would we still be alive unless Father had instructed Michael to leave us be?"

Horus began feeling a bit light headed. Their arguing faded in and out of his mind, and his concentration slowly began to wane. Anubis shook his arm.

"Are you OK?" Anubis asked. Horus' head shot back up and he shook the funk from his eyes. A faint light grew in the far end of the room. He looked at Anubis and nodded, turning his focus back towards the argument.

"You know not if it is Azrael," Khnum said through his tight jaw. He leaned close to Sobek's face, growling. "Vishnu and his Corner have offered their hand. He's the only remaining Archangel in any of the four Corners. Zeus, Thor, and our commander have all perished. I would think Vishnu knows best."

"For all we know, Vishnu is the reason Zeus never came to our aid." Sobek grabbed Khnum by the robe. "Don't act like you never heard the rumblings."

Anubis looked towards Horus, who nodded. He walked down the steps of the throne and wrapped his large hands around the arguing angels' arms. After pulling the squabbling Beta Guardians apart he stood between them. He crossed his arms and stood with his feet shoulder-width apart.

"Don't stand there silently." Khnum looked up at Horus. "If we're not allowed to hash out our differences, then speak up. Tell us what you saw."

"Amun would never treat us as such," Sobek grumbled. Isis swiveled her glare toward her brother. Sobek smoothed out the wrinkles in his clothes, glaring into Anubis' face. "I expected more from you, nephew."

Anubis raised his hand, ready to strike Sobek, but Horus grabbed his cousin's arm and steadied him.

"It's true that the remaining Corner of Olympus invaded the realm of man," Horus said. A slowly-building, eerie tone filled his gut: an orchestra playing a jumbled melody. The light that only he could see flared. He tried to ignore it. "They were thwarted by one appearing to be Azrael. However, Anubis and I were unable to confirm if indeed the Angel of Death has returned from his banishment."

"Impossible—how could you not know?" Sobek slammed his closed fists together and paced in a circle. "It was him. I know it. I saw him once..."

"That was ages ago." Khnum rolled his eyes, filled with contempt.

"My memory is still fresh!" Sobek shouted, his pale green Aurascales shifting over his face, projecting a long snout until it looked like a crocodile. "Need I remind you how well I led my part of the legion against Lucifer?"

"If it is Azrael, then he's not at full power. He has no wings." Horus walked between the two squabbling guardians, looking at the many angels his father once commanded. They turned to him, silent, yet he was still a bit unsure of himself. Isis nodded at him, almost as if she were aware of the sights and sounds growing in his mind. "This alone doesn't tell us anything. Maybe he has to earn complete reinstatement in Heaven before granted full form with use of his starstone and aurascales. Nevertheless, there has been destruction in other places following that incident. Whatever happened wasn't a one-time thing..."

"So what you're saying is you don't know anything," Khnum laughed.

"Watch your tone when speaking to him." Anubis wrapped his hand clear around Khnum's neck and lifted him off the ground. Anubis was an odd sight in the room, almost two feet taller than the next largest angel, with skin the color of wet clay on the banks of a slow-moving river. Not a single bead of sweat broke from his skin, nor did his arm tense as he lifted Khnum to his eye level.

"We can't say it was Azrael because we didn't see him in person. Some of the descendants of Olympus that were captured also spoke of a fake Zeus. Remakes, they call them. They claim the humans have figured out how to duplicate our kind." Horus put his hand to the back of Anubis' shoulder. His cousin dropped Khnum to the floor. Horus' back and neck started to perspire as the light he saw began to give off heat.

"So the favored ones have themselves turned away from Father," Khnum cackled while glaring at Anubis and rubbing his own neck. "The end is near and we have no faction head. Instead, we're split between two leaders."

"My mother leads this Corner!" Horus yelled.

"She's not an Archangel, and it's obvious to all those not blinded by loyalty that her power fades," Sobek said, though it obviously pained him to do so. His words were the most deafening of all. "Amun has every bit as much of a claim to head this legion as she. They both have seniority. After all, he was the one who saved us."

"It's time to join Vishnu's Corner and try to salvage a future before tribulation is upon us," Khnum interjected, ignoring Horus and talking to those around him who he still held influence over. "The last war is ahead. The signs of the end times have shone brighter than the first morning star. Soon the seven years will be here, and by then it'll be too late to choose a direction."

"I don't think you understand what you're suggesting," said Sobek. "What do you honestly expect to accomplish?"

"To save our kind, just like Khali suggested." Khnum glared at Horus for a second, and then turned back to the others. "It can be done, if enough of us stand together. There is power among our stars still."

"That was tried by another in the beginning, Khnum, and he failed miserably. Zeus' and Thor's legions were wiped out in similar battles," Isis said, leaning forward on her throne. "We're neither strong nor prepared enough for any such action. We can only hope for forgiveness."

"So you're in agreement with Amun?" Sobek asked, looking towards Isis. "Please, sister, I would not lead us astray. You know this."

"Not intentionally," Isis replied.

"Father offers no such thing to us." Khnum turned around, walking up the steps towards Isis before Anubis and Horus stood in his way. He looked at the two cousins, raised his hands in surrender, and stepped backwards. "Take it from someone who has visited man's realm from time to time. There are more of us hiding in the shadows— factionless—than we're allowed to believe. We lack a true leader.

Vishnu is the last who is powerful enough to take command. Together we can outnumber the assault Lucifer helmed."

"Vishnu isn't half the angel Lucifer was," Sobek sighed. "The energy from his star would be enough to wipe whole legions out. I think many forget just how magnificent he was. If he couldn't win..."

"So you just accept defeat?" Khnum's voice boomed.

"I don't believe this is defeat," Sobek replied, shaking his head.

"I won't entertain this debate any further." Isis stood, slamming the end of her staff onto the floor. The tap resonated for a few seconds before dying a slow death amongst the blank stares of the other angels. "To ignore the warning signs of tribulation would be foolish."

Khnum smiled, folding his arms and winking at Sobek.

"To challenge Michael and his legion is just plain stupidity," she continued.

Sobek chuckled, turning his nose up towards Khnum and silently clapping. Khnum lowered his arms, clenching his fists as he squinted at Isis. She looked him square in the eyes, her resolve not wavering, and stood between Horus and Anubis.

"Khnum, I acknowledge your fears and appreciate your concern, but we will not align ourselves under Vishnu's star." Isis folded her arms around her son and nephew, turning her gaze up towards Horus. "Come, son, there is more to discuss."

She nodded at her brain trust and then walked into the darkness with Horus alongside. Khnum continued to shout at her, but his words fell on deaf ears. A large wall slid up from the floor, separating the throne room from Isis' private chamber, muting the grumblings of her faction. When she and Horus were out of sight, she collapsed onto her bed. Horus rushed to her side, wrapping his arms around her.

"Are you ill?" he asked, gripping her shoulders firmly. He lifted her and laid her flat on the bed, propping her head up. Kneeling down, he took her hand. "How long has it been fading?"

"I was about to ask you the same thing." She smiled at him, caressing his soft face with her fingers. "Every time I gaze upon the sparkle in your eyes, I see your father looking back at me."

"Let me return the power I borrowed." He held his hand up and a pieced-together starstone constructed itself in the palm of his hand. The energy between the two mismatched halves surged over the outside of the stone, fluctuating in color between pink and green. He split the stone apart, a jagged line forming along the edges of both halves, and revealed two different glowing centers. "Take it. Keep your strength so those growing in allegiance to Amun no longer question you."

"It would save me, but not for long. It is true that his power remains steadfast. I know not how he is able to maintain it." She closed his hand around the stone and pushed it back against his chest. "But your light can grow beyond anything creation has seen—if only you'd believe it."

"I don't understand." His head hung over the starstone in his lap.

"Go and be the link to bridge the lost." She yawned and closed her eyes. "The answers to everything lie somewhere between Khnum and Sobek. They're not completely wrong."

A gut-wrenching symphony blast shook through Horus' body, and the light that hovered in his sight surged. He crumbled to the ground as his mother's words were drowned out by the deep, pulsating rumbling of brass instruments.

His eyes glazed over. Everything in his field of view disintegrated. Formed together by stray bands of light, a palace took shape behind large golden gates. He looked around as others marched towards a man blowing a horn. They were illusions, and soon everything returned to normal.

"What was that?" he asked, dry heaving. His mouth trembled and his clammy grip slipped from his mother's arms. "That wasn't a normal call."

"It was the call for the Archangels," she whispered. "Your father was an Archangel. You've inherited his hearing and sight. When

Gabriel calls the other Archangels, they hear the same thing. Your father used to react this very way."

"Can they... see me in turn?"

"We are shielded from their eyes here," she replied, turning him around and rubbing the side of his face. "I would suspect the sounds you hear are in response to the troubles recently. Heaven is surely on edge, if indeed this isn't Azrael."

"The contact, Svarog, was adamant it wasn't." He paused. "Maybe Khnum is right."

"Maybe Sobek, too." She straightened his face out and gazed lovingly into his eyes.

"How so? If Azrael is not back, then why would Heaven have supported this Death?"

"He is a horseman, though nobody knows if that is literal or figurative." She delicately slid her fingers through his hair, rubbing him the same way she did when he was a child. "Go back and find the one who wears Azrael's armor. See if he can be made our friend, or if he brings the end of time."

She pushed her starstone towards Horus, fusing it once and for all with Osiris' stone. The energy pulsated together and became too much for her to grasp, so Horus took hold of the beaming artifact. The angelic armors of his parents surged over him. Only the blood in his veins could command the energy.

"Take this as a token of where we came from, so that you can shape where we're headed." She placed a triangular medallion that looked as if it was one part of a larger set around his neck. "Safeguard it as you would your own heart."

Their entire palace went dark, and the moans of the walls pushing back against the vacuum of space filled the air with apprehension. His facial armor formed, returning balance to the darkness and bringing his mother into focus. She couldn't see him, but knew her son continued to watch over her.

118

"You don't have much time," she said, leaning back and resting her eyes.

"The others will turn against you when they realize what you've done," he said.

"Then I guess you have less time than you thought." She smiled, pulling the sheets up to her chin. "It was only a matter of time before Amun made his move to usurp command. He's been making the play for a while now."

"I'll leave Anubis—"

"You'll take him," she said. He turned to look back at her, but she didn't move. "Have Hathor bring the child to me. The future is with you now: the Angel-Born."

"Why did you have me rescue her?" Horus asked, remembering child he'd brought back from the human realm. "What was the point?"

"It was something your father once said," she yawned, squeezing his hand several times. "Something he said could give us hope, or make us cower and hide. I need to talk to this girl and find out for sure."

"Tell me..."

"You carry too much burden, my son. I have faith in you." She opened her eyes and smiled. "Now go."

Horus pushed away from the bed and hurried along. Energy flowed from his fingertips and through the door. It opened and closed when he passed through. Anubis was waiting for him.

"What is happening?" Anubis asked worriedly.

"My mother must be delirious to ask that I leave her here alone and unguarded." Horus shook, breezing past his cousin. There was no way he would let her be vulnerable. He looked at Anubis. "You must watch over her. If anything were to happen... Guard her with your life."

"Of course." Anubis nodded.

"Command Hathor to bring the child to my mother. The matter is urgent." Horus pushed into his quarters and knelt at the foot of his

119

bed. His fingers clamped over the medallion around his neck. He stuffed it under his shirt and looked up at Anubis. "You're still here."

"You're leaving?" Anubis asked in shock, feverishly rubbing the back of his head. "When will you be back? Have I done something wrong?"

"No, you've not." Horus took Anubis' hands and squeezed. "This is me trusting you. If I didn't think you capable, I would have you by my side." Horus stepped over to a control panel and swiped. A thin laser stream erupted from a mechanical pen and fabricated a crystal out of thin air. Three more beams shot into the center of the flickering glow, constructing the edges of the crystal. A pink light emerged in the center. "I travel back to Earth to find the one from Moscow. He will either become our friend or die by my sword."

CHAPTER FOURTEEN

The Observer

The walls of the Southern Corner's fortress groaned as the vacuum of space sunk its fingers into the metal hull. The entire ship had lost power and emergency systems rerouted all reserve energy to stabilize the atmosphere and pressure systems, leaving everyone in the dark.

The young girl, Rashini, clung tightly to the back of Hathor's skirt, sticking her nose into her new friend's back. Hathor reached behind, covered the girl's head with her arm, and pressed her against the wall. Two men approached. Their aurascales beamed a path for them to follow. Hathor crouched and pulled Rashini down into her lap. The men passed. They were Sobek's men.

"We're almost there," Hathor whispered into Rashini's ear. They resumed their journey. *I must've taken this route a thousand times growing up. Three steps here into a left turn, and then straight on into the Great Hall.*

"Where are we going?" the girl asked, her eyes helplessly searching for light to absorb. There was none until they got to the Great Hall. She stopped breathing when she saw the shattered moon of the desolate planet floating in the sky just as casually as low hanging clouds would back home.

Where am I? Rashini trembled. The dusty white of the fractured moon's surface reflected off her pasted-open eyes. Her hand slipped from Hathor's shirt.

Hathor stood by Rashini with her arms over the girl's shoulders and looked out at the scene. *What has her in such a trance?* Hathor asked herself. *Is the sky not like this on Earth? Of course, their atmosphere turns it blue. A blue sky... The magnificence.*

"Come on, little one," Hathor said, pulling Rashini along. "All will make sense soon enough. I promise."

"Am I going home?" Rashini asked.

"I don't know." Hathor shrugged. Her response seemed callous and cold. She was oblivious to how her tone made tears scurry down the child's cheeks.

Hathor pressed her hand to the door and a light erupted underneath her palm, scanned her hand, and illuminated the entryway like a teal searchlight. The door split open. She scooped Rashini up and hurried through the entryway. The door quickly snapped shut and sealed behind them.

Isis sat up, gliding her hand over a control panel next to her bed. Four gently glowing orbs shot up from the floor and escorted Hathor and Rashini over to the bedside. Isis smiled at the young child, extending her left hand. Rashini silently sought permission from Hathor who nodded.

"There now, child, all will be fine. I promise," Isis said, firmly hugging Rashini. She moved over and pulled the girl up onto the bed. When the girl was closer to Isis, she noticed the lines of age along the queen's tanned cheek.

"Are you my papa's age?" she asked.

"No, child. I am much older." Isis smiled. "I will try to make things better, but you have to answer some questions. Is that OK? You're going to have to think about some bad things and they might upset you."

"She's been through a lot," Hathor interjected, sitting at the foot of the bed, folding her small, delicate hands into her lap.

"She's a strong girl. Aren't you sweetie?" Isis gave Hathor a firm gaze, keeping her head directed at Rashini. "I need you to think back. Do you remember what happened before you got here?"

Rashini broke down, covering her eyes. Her black hair fell over her face and her body shook with a forceful wail. Isis gently massaged Rashini's back, shushing her with a soothing tone.

"Someone will hear." Hathor stood and looked around worriedly.

"I can't!" Rashini bellowed, shaking her head. Her hands clamped over her ears. "Papa," she cried, cringing. "The guns were loud." She shoved her face into Isis' chest and wailed. "They killed my sisters."

"I know." Isis moved her hand gently through Rashini's hair and along her left cheek. She pulled the girl in closer and connected their foreheads. "But that's not what I'm talking about. What did you see? Before that. Before the men dragged you away. The burning man, you called him."

Rashini froze. Air couldn't even weasel its way into her lungs.

"Yes." Isis grinned. "You know him."

"I..." Rashini stopped speaking and tried to pull away. Isis' soft, reassuring hug turned into shackles. Rashini pulled back with all her might, but Isis yanked her into her clutches, wrapping her arms all the way around the girl.

"You're scaring her." Hathor jumped up, breathing heavily, initially lunging for Isis before hesitating. She turned her head to the floor, unable to watch Rashini struggle.

"The burning man, little girl. Tell me more," Isis commanded. "Who else knows?"

Screams erupted from the other side of the chamber door. Hathor's nervous gaze shifted towards the barrier. The center where the two sliding doors met glowed with radiant orange heat. The metal sizzled as steam rose off the door.

"Tell me now before they come." Isis squeezed tighter around Rashini's wrists. "I cannot help you if you don't tell me everything. The burned man, child. Tell me."

"Ma'am, what's going on?" Hathor asked, hyperventilating. Hathor grabbed Isis by the arms, yanked them apart, and pulled the young girl away to cradle her. She moved backwards, stopping in the dark corner of the room.

"It's too late." Isis shook her head and pounded a pillow.

The barrier to her room melted apart. Amun walked through and placed a palm to Isis' shoulder. She slapped his hand away and he threw her to the floor.

"You've been poking around where you shouldn't have been." Amun towered over Isis, appearing as if he were about to stomp on her. "Where's your starstone?"

"Gone." Isis covered her face to safeguard from any strike. "How long have you been conspiring outside our borders? How long have you bartered with the Architect to repower your star?"

"Father, what is going on?" Hathor cried.

Rashini came to, gasping at the sight of the Amun.

"No, not you!" she screamed. "You won't take me back to the burning man."

"His name is Ra," Amun replied, grabbing Isis by the shirt and banging her head against the floor. He stepped toward his daughter. Solar flares of pure white erupted over his body and brought forth his aurascales. "Hand her over."

Hathor shook her head and slouched back. Amun dug into her arm and jerked it end-over-end. His gloves seared her flesh. Her screams echoed through the corridors. Amun let her go and lumbered after Rashini as she attempted to crawl away.

"My head," Isis said, rubbing her forehead as she stood and swayed in a circle. Her knees buckled and she caught herself on the bed. "Where are you taking her?"

Hathor lay injured on the floor. Amun glanced at Isis and snatched Rashini up. He covered the girl's mouth and walked toward the exit. Isis stood in his way. He lifted her with one hand around the neck and choked her until she passed out.

124

"Leave her alone!" Hathor yelled, trying to stand. Her arm felt like it was going to slide apart at the burn.

"We're at the precipice, daughter." He grinned. "The days shall revolt. You can join me or be left behind to die. The choice is yours."

Amun marched out of the room and around a corner. Rashini reached for Hathor, screaming for help, but disappeared with her abductor into the black hallways. Hathor, seething with anger, glared at Isis.

"What was that?" Hathor roared, standing up. She jumped onto Isis. They slid along the ground and stopped against the wall. Hathor grabbed Isis by the shirt, lifted her, and struck a blow with her right fist. "Where did he take her?"

"Stop. Please," Isis gasped, raising her right arm in a lethargic fashion. "I don't know."

"Liar!" Saliva formed spider webs in Hathor's teeth as she screamed.

Sobek and Anubis entered Isis' private chamber. They grabbed Hathor and threw her onto the bed. Anubis leapt and landed over Hathor. He twisted her arm behind her back, lifted her up, and pinned her against the wall. Sobek offered a hand to Isis, pulling her up and wiping a trickle of blood off her mouth.

"What happened?" Sobek asked, moving Isis over to the bed. The lights of their fortress came back on, but the walls still wept under the unforgiving forces of space. Sobek pointed at Hathor, commanding Anubis. "Remove her."

"She's the traitor!" Hathor tried to pull away from Anubis while grabbing at Isis. His massive hands went clear around her arms as he forced her out of the room. She dragged her feet and kicked on the walls, trying to pull free from his grasp. "She's responsible for all of this."

"Remove her now, Anubis," Sobek said, raising his booming voice.

Anubis put Hathor into a choke hold, forcing her to sleep. He slung her over his massive shoulder and carried her away. Sobek turned to his older sister.

"What child does she speak of?" he asked.

"Amun... The one he took," Isis replied, still rubbing her temples. She looked at Sobek, but he was clearly lost. "He is a traitor. An Architect has been reigniting his starstone. The extent of their alliance, I know not."

Sobek analyzed the door. It was melted down the middle. He peered over his shoulder at Isis, biting his lower lip as his eyebrows furrowed with suspicion.

"I speak the truth," she insisted.

"You should come with me. It's not safe in here," he said, massaging his hand through her hair. "Our shields are down. Most of the station is without power. If we don't reinforce the power supply, the time flux will affect us exponentially. We need the power of your star."

"I sent it away." She shook her head and held his hands tightly. "My son guards it now. Along with his father's."

"Then we've not a moment to waste. We must make our way to a chariot." Sobek wrapped his fingers around Isis' wrist and pulled her from the room hastily.

They marched through the Great Hall and the swirling lines of the event horizon came into view. Their side of the planet slowly turned to face it. The edge of the fourth dimension could be seen in their physical realm, mixing with the tangible like a cocktail. The light spectrum flared until it was sucked into the center of the abyss, no longer carrying any meaning.

"This has gone on long enough," Khnum said. His chartreuse aurascales and silver armor were fully manifested; his helmet the shape of a ram. A large mallet materialized in his grasp. His lieutenants, Serket and Khonshu, stood behind him in their warrior regalia. He snapped his fingers and they moved into offensive positions. "Hand over the traitor queen."

The large pieces of the shattered moon swayed as they were sucked towards one another. The two largest pieces collided, splintered off into millions of projectiles, and released countless meteors towards the planet.

"We don't have time for this. We must take cover underground where the reserve shields can safeguard us until we can rift to a new home," Sobek replied, shaking his head to Khnum's demand and stepping in front of Isis. A beam of light radiated over Sobek. Billions of sentient dots raced over him, giving off a green glow. A scimitar and shield sprouted in his grasp.

A scorpion tail grew from Serket's aurascales. Sobek spun across the floor, evading her sting. Two skinny blades curved over her wrists and hands like pincers. She jabbed and flung a cross hook, missing. His scimitar cut upward in a diagonal motion. Serket's tail bounced off the floor. His shield jabbed into her shin and brought her to all fours. He kicked her face and knocked her out cold.

Outside the large windows, the fractured moon pieces pelted their planet. The rumbling from the meteor strikes ran through the floor, shaking the brawlers.

"Vishnu is using the power of his star to protect us now." Khnum directed his words toward Sobek, but his gaze was fixed on Isis as he gave chase. He grappled her tiny waist and threw her into the wall.

Isis bounced off and rolled backwards onto her feet. She grabbed a stone statue off the floor, crouching. The majesty of the meteor shower reflected off Khnum's breast plate. She swung the statue. His fist pulverized it into dust.

"You're an imbecile," Sobek shouted, jostling with Khnum's other lieutenant, Konshu.

Konshu moved behind Sobek and put him in a full-nelson. Sobek broke free, jamming himself inside his foe's reach. He pinned Konshu's arms in the air and used the back of his crocodile helmet as a battering ram, snapping Khonshu's left arm at the shoulder and throwing his enemy to the floor.

"And you've no way off this rock," Khnum replied, his lungs heaving.

Isis ran to Sobek, but Khnum grabbed her hair and pulled her backward. Her head bounced off the floor like a tennis ball, rendering her unconscious. Sobek tackled Khnum. The two skidded along the floor, exchanging short jabs.

Khnum stuck a katar into Sobek's ribcage, twisting. Both of his feet pressed against Sobek's chest and pushed him off. He jumped to his feet, conjuring the mallet once again, and swung with an uppercut motion. The hammer caught Sobek under the helmet. Half of the crocodile faceguard splintered into pieces. Sobek fell to his knees. The mallet bashed into Sobek's right shoulder blade. The bones in his shoulder, arm and collarbone cracked, making a sound like an insect being squashed.

A meteor collided with the Great Hall, extinguishing the outer shields and rupturing the hull of their fortress. The windows on the far end of the hall shattered and the air in the room raced to escape. The vacuum of space wrapped a noose around Khonshu and dragged him into the cold depths of oblivion. Time and space ripped into him as the edge of the event horizon drained his starstone. Radiation melted him in a matter of seconds. The exploding starstone sent a shockwave through their planet, fracturing it. The core of the planet shifted from the surge of energy, tilting the planet onto a new axis.

Sobek slid towards the opening. With his one good arm he latched onto a door and wrapped his legs around Isis to keep her from flying away. To his right, Serket's legs were flailing from the suction while her two wrist blades were dug into the ground as an anchor. Sobek made eye contact with Khnum. The emergency doors rose up, sealing the inside, removing any fear of being sucked into space. The planet, however, continued to crumble.

Khnum stumbled over to Sobek, twirling the mallet in his hands. His facial armor retracted, revealing a snarling, contempt-filled glare. Anubis ran onto the scene.

"Vishnu has sent Shiva," Anubis said. "Where is Khonshu?"

"You betray your own uncle and aunt?" Sobek yelled.

"They never treated me as such. I do what is needed for the survival of our people." Anubis stuck a sword to Sobek's neck. "I would take your life, uncle."

"They always treated you harshly," Khnum responded, collecting his breath. His eyes were unsure. "Sucked out into the darkness, Khonshu was."

"Regrettable." Anubis stood over Sobek, turned him onto his stomach, and locked shackles around his wrists. "We're to coordinate forces and track down those who remain loyal to Amun."

"There's no point in taking prisoners." Khnum raised his mallet, but Anubis stood in his way.

"I was told by Shiva that I could deal with my kin as I see fit."

Khnum groaned, his jaw tight, and then nodded reluctantly. He lowered his weapon, gesturing with his head for Serket to follow. The two left and Anubis pulled Sobek to his feet. He slung Isis over his shoulder and pushed Sobek through the corridors. Sobek looked at his nephew with a curious expression.

"Vishnu's delegates arrived shortly before the meteor storm," Anubis said, answering Sobek's silent question. "I put Hathor in one of the chariots and locked it off."

"I take it Amun and the others didn't survive?" Sobek asked.

"When the moon fragments entered the hazard zone in the event horizon, they shuttled down to the planet's core. The gravity warp ruptured the shuttle line, and all readings say the core has begun bleeding out. There's no telling if they're still alive."

"How much longer is the planet feasibly safe?" Sobek grimaced as the weight of his cuffs pulled on his broken body.

"Are you sure you're up to this?" Anubis undid the cuffs, referring to Sobek's broken body.

"How much longer?" Sobek grunted, grimacing.

"An hour, maybe less." Anubis sat his aunt on the floor. His armor slid up his arms then ran down to his feet until his whole body was covered, except for his head. "Shiva brought Khali and their Angel-born son, Skanda. There are several lower-ranked among them, not counting those of ours who've joined their side."

"That's exactly what you do when you're looking to join forces as equals," Sobek said with a frustrated laugh. "You send your strongest and best fighters to extend the olive branch. Khnum is a fool."

"You don't think they really mean to adopt us?"

"No." Sobek shook his head and then looked worriedly at Isis. "They're here for something specific. You don't send Shiva when you expect things to go well."

***

"Welcome to our realm," Khnum said as his ram's face armor slithered back into his collarbone. His bushy apricot eyebrows ran together over his steel-blue eyes. It was a jarring contrast to his freshly shaven head. He nodded, acknowledging Shiva, who returned the favor. "Vishnu honors us with the presence of his most trusted. Your reputation as a skilled warrior precedes you. I know we can quickly quell any rebellion in good faith of a merger."

"This place is pathetic," Shiva replied, his upper lip curling. His nose wrinkled and his mouth held back a gag. "How repugnant. You have my pity."

Khnum opened his mouth, but shock held the words in. He exchanged confused glances with Serket. Her eyes locked on her toes to avoid any discussion. His gaze reconnected with Shiva's pitch black eyes.

"Where are your others?" Shiva asked, walking past Khnum and peering into the corridors. His hair was extremely short, black, and curly and his taupe skin had a sheen to it. He stepped back, slowly shutting the door to the engineering room.

"Those loyal to Amun, the very few they may be, followed the crisis protocol. If they're still alive, they won't be a problem..." Khnum's back stiffened when the sound of Shiva locking the chamber door interrupted him. Khnum turned around, anxious. "The civilian population, have they been evacuated already?"

"I'm sure you've surmised by now that god Vishnu has only sent enough power to keep life support systems in place for a select few," Shiva said, walking with his hands behind his back. He nodded at Khali, giving her a silent signal. "We've secured all those of any use or value."

A pair of Urumi materialized in Khali's grasp. With a quick flick of the wrist, the whip-like metal blades wrapped around Serket's neck, slicing her throat. Serket fell to the ground, bleeding out instantly. Khnum moved to engage Khali, but Shiva stood in the way, raising the point of his sword to Khnum's neck.

"We've already moved those we require to our realm. We don't need any more leeches." Shiva squinted at Khnum, gently prodding the blade against his prisoner's flesh. He winked at Khali, sending her on her way. His voice became stern and imposing. "We can make space for a few more. I would prefer Isis be among them unless you can make our need for her obsolete."

"She's not here already?" Khnum asked, scratching the back of his head. His eyes widened. He spoke under his breath. "Anubis... I should have known he'd remain loyal to his aunt and not his people."

"Speak up."

"She's useless. That is, if you're looking for her starstone..."

"The Forge," Shiva quickly replied, squinting at Khnum.

"Yes, of course." Khnum begrudgingly smiled with the realization that he'd been played. "Her son. He has what remains. She thinks I don't know, but I have my spies just as she has hers. Isis merged the power of her starstone with that of her late husband's. Horus uses it to travel to the human realm. He and his retarded cousin are looking for Azrael. They're hoping salvation and forgiveness lies with his return."

"They will be bitterly disappointed with what they find." Shiva smirked, shaking his head, trying to suppress a chuckle.

"Impossible."

"No, I have my sources too." Shiva lowered the blade, but Khnum remained petrified. "While your Corner has been hiding here on the edge of this collapsed star for ages, some of us have been hard at work."

"Do tell."

"Insider information only—but we are open to expanding the club." Shiva shoved Khnum into the wall, causing the hull to bend. He threw the frightened member of the Southern Corner to the floor and stood on his chest. Shiva's sword hovered inches from the bridge of Khnum's nose. "Just because Isis doesn't have the artifact I seek doesn't make her useless. It makes her collateral. You've failed by every measure to prove your worth."

"Please, I can still be of use," Khnum stuttered.

"I would get to saying how instead of pissing myself."

"I know the ins and outs of this fortress. I know where they would hide her. And I know the pressure points to get her to speak." Khnum closed his eyes and breathed deeply. "At the very least I hold possibility. If I fail to deliver a second time, have my head then."

"Your starstone." Shiva stepped off Khnum, keeping his sword trained on him. He lowered his empty hand. "Give it to me so I know you're defenseless."

Khnum nodded and rolled onto his knees. His body shook with trepidation. A green light sparked between his hands. Billions of slate-gray metal cubes melded together into an egg shape a little smaller than a basketball. He handed it to Shiva.

"Very well." Shiva nodded.

***

Anubis laid Isis down and scooted over to Sobek. His uncle's armor retracted completely to reveal a large gash over the right side of his collarbone. A bone protruded from the skin and blood bubbled out slowly. Anubis tried to stabilize the wound, but Sobek put his hand to his nephew's and shook his head.

"It's no use," Sobek sighed. The color in his face faded by the second. "You've got to get her out. There's nowhere safe for her here."

"She wouldn't want to leave you behind," Anubis said, hesitantly lowering his hands into his lap. He stepped away from his uncle, nearly in tears.

"Apparently you don't know my sister very well," he chuckled. "You and Horus have always been what are important to her. The urge for a son never came upon me, because I had you both. I only regret that I didn't see you more for who you really are, instead of listening to the rumors of what many held you to be." Sobek closed his eyes and took a deep breath. He coughed and little spurts of blood covered his lips. "Can you get her to the chariot? You can save her and Hathor. Get off this ship and find Horus."

"It depends on how much attention Shiva is paying to the launch bay. I would assume plenty."

"I'll draw them out," Sobek grunted, pushing himself up. Anubis offered a helping hand but Sobek shrugged him off. The Beta Guardian stood on his own power. A green light sizzled out from his skin as the aurascales penetrated his wound and sealed it. "I hear them. Go."

Anubis carried Isis out of the mess hall. Sobek stumbled through the hall, tossing about stainless steel chairs and tables. Khali kicked through the entrance and the twin doors flew off the hinges, tumbling end over end. She grinned, elated at Sobek's current condition. Two additional blue arms grew from her aurascales, curving around from under her shoulder blades.

She kicked a chair, launching it at Sobek. His sword appeared in his right hand and sliced through the flying object. The two sides soared past him. A spear took shape in his hands and he thrust it toward Khali. She kicked one leg over the other, flipping herself sideways into the air, rotating. The spear went under her. She unwrapped her arms. The Urumi blades crackled out and snapped across Sobek's chest.

He tripped backward. Khali pursued. Her weapon wrapped around his ankle. She tugged and his feet gave way. He landed on his back and stomped on her metal whip. The tug bent her forward. His elbow swiped off her chin as he kicked to his feet. Jab. Hook. Roundhouse. Sobek pushed her back despite his shoulder bones grinding into dust.

Khali's two Urumi stiffened, forming long serrated blades. She spun. The swords whistled in the air. Sobek's spear morphed into a shield and the two opposing forces sparked. Deafening bursts filled the room. Sobek shoved forward, his shield up, covering his shoulder. He pivoted with his back foot as his scimitar deflected one of her strikes. The rim of his shield shoved into her throat. Her trachea ruptured. She slid across the floor with arms outstretched. Her facial armor crawled back into her breast plate. She hacked, unable to breathe cleanly.

Sobek lowered his shield, panting. He labored to move closer to her, standing tall at her feet. Small trickles of blood slid out of her nostrils. His shield vanished and he folded his hands. A broad sword took form. He painstakingly raised it over his head, ready to drive it through her. Her glance twitched, looking behind Sobek in an unintended giveaway. He spun around, swiping his sword down in a diagonal motion.

Skanda, Khali's son, rolled to his left and evaded the hulking blow. He was a blur, seemingly in one spot and then another on the opposite side of the room. His speed was such that he looked to have eight or nine doubles. Before Sobek could raise his shield, a dozen cuts slashed across his body. He fell to his knees, writhing in pain.

The shaking haze that was Skanda slowly fused, almost oozing together at a snail's pace. His body vibrated so fast it looked like there were several heads and arms connected to his torso. Finally, he turned into a solid state. He knelt next to his mother and she grabbed his right wrist, squeezing tightly.

"She'll live," Sobek coughed, his face down but his focus turned up and locked on Skanda. As he ground his teeth together underneath his helmet, his eyes grew dimmer on the outside of his mask.

"But you won't," Skanda whispered, rubbing his mother's face with the back of his hand. He squeezed her arm and lowered it to her chest. He slightly turned his face toward Sobek.

Sobek roared, using all his strength to lift his sword with his one good arm. He jabbed it at Skanda, but his enemy just chuckled in reply. Before Sobek could even finish his lunge, a hundred stings burned his nerves. He collapsed, bleeding from puncture wounds all over. Skanda kicked Sobek onto his back. Two small knives in Skanda's hands dripped with crimson. Sobek's crocodile helmet vanished.

"Old and slow." Skanda cocked his head with a taunting smile. His teeth were slightly crooked but still perfectly white. He resembled a young Shiva, but had Khali's radiant eyes and long, straight locks. Kneeling beside Sobek, he ran his fingers through his prey's thinning hair. He spun the knife in his right hand between his fingers. The whizzing blade sounded like a lumber saw. "Make way for the new."

Sobek stuck a short knife into Skanda's armpit and rolled out of the way. He crawled for the exit. Skanda pulled the blade from his flesh and stood. A whip took form in his hands. He cracked it, wrapping it around Sobek's ankle and pulling him back. He kicked Sobek in the chin and knocked him out. Bringing his duel daggers back, he kneeled behind Sobek, ready to slice his throat.

"To all of Vishnu's scum who've infected this ship, and those under the Southern banner who've turned against us, know there is still one that remains who opposes you." Horus' voice echoed out through the intercom systems. "I know what you're here for, and I'm in possession of it. Both sides of this battle are running low on time. This planet crumbles beneath our feet and soon we'll be sucked through the event horizon. There are hundreds of innocent lives that hang in the balance, and a few old warriors I'd like to save. Deliver them to me and you'll get what you came for."

Skanda looked over to his mom, ready to take Sobek's head. Khali waved him off. He dropped Sobek reluctantly.

CHAPTER FIFTEEN

Horus III

Two angels in orange aurascales—the banner of Vishnu—surrounded Horus. They stared him down like poachers with an arrogant gleam in their eyes. The reward for the prince had been announced for all to hear. Bring him to Shiva, dead or alive, and receive higher rank and the spoils which accompany it. This pair salivated just as the rest had. Over-confidence would be the end of them as well.

They lunged but Horus was too well trained. He countered the first assailant's blade-swipe by stepping to the left, pushing their sword up, and sliding his weapon down theirs to slice across their belly. The angel hunched over and pressed his hands against his stomach to keep what rushed from the wound inside.

The second swung a bo staff. Energy sizzled from the ends of the metal rod. Horus rolled forward and the strike intended for him punctured the wall instead. He slid to his knees and cut the enemy's Achilles tendon. The angel toppled backward. Horus spun and shoved his weapon into the collapsed angel's neck.

There was someone else behind him. From his knees, he turned back and stuck his sword on the precipice of Anubis' neck, only stopping when realizing it was his cousin. Horus stood and his weapons dematerialized into his aurascales. The feathered head guard retracted into the shoulder plates.

"You've not gone?" Anubis asked. He held Isis like a young child in his arms.

"Mother—is she..." Horus ran his hand over the goose egg on her forehead. He grabbed Anubis' shoulder tightly. Words couldn't express the burden lifted off his chest, or the gratitude he felt towards his cousin, knowing his mother was safe. "My heart said to return. My instincts were correct."

"It is a good thing you had me stay." Anubis offered his aunt to Horus who gladly accepted her. The snapping gears of readjusting walls around the corner, at the end of the corridor, snared his attention. "I have a chariot ready to make leave."

"See my mother makes it safely." Horus attempted to give his mother back to Anubis, but his cousin stepped away, refusing. "Take her."

"You'll stay behind." Anubis folded his arms.

"Are you disobeying me?" Horus squinted, though he couldn't really be angry with Anubis. He'd do the same thing. "I suppose you feel like fighting by my side?"

"Sobek said to leave." Anubis shook his head. "We should."

"I can't do that." Horus motioned for them to duck into one of the private quarters just off the hallway. Inside, blotchy patches of rust lined the walls and floor. A small, puffy, white sheep doll at his feet was stained cabernet. Just inside the entryway, three bodies lay piled in the dark. The child, a girl of maybe three years, was draped backwards over her parents with her arms sprawled out, her mouth gaping, and her eyes wide and staring blankly. Anubis averted his eyes, but Horus stared down at them. A fire roared inside his chest.

The apartment was four small rooms. Two fit for beds, one a living area, and the last a small closet with a toilet. Showers were granted on a scheduled basis for all common-level residents at a community post on level five, and their meals were had at the mess hall.

This style of unit was common for the families of their Corner, but it was dwarfed in size by Isis' private sleeping chamber. This apartment used to be a barracks for those in Amun's legion. Since their Corner downsized to a single Armada cruiser after the Last Great War, the military housing was restyled for a more domestic feel, though it never seemed it. The standard one-child policy was implemented for the lower guard angels when Horus was in his teens—rules the likes of Khnum and Amun never had to obey.

The disparity in treatment had always infuriated Horus. Though he understood that those governing and doing their duty to protect the population needed to be safeguarded and separate, it angered him the elders never tried harder to remedy the conditions of their Corner. It was as if they were content to live on this outpost because they didn't have to pack in like rats, and didn't have to follow their own rules. Mostly, none of them ever felt the need to deliver on his father's promise.

"Our people deserve better, Anubis." Horus moved into the parents' room and laid his mother down. Even though he loved her more than the others, he couldn't help but resent her for their current situation. He tried to think about what his father would do in moments like this, and then it hit him like Sobek swinging a mallet during a training session.

The great Osiris had already overcome the same type of odds and obstacles the day his son was born. Victory cost him his life. In that moment, Horus completely understood everything that Sobek had tried to teach him. The survival of the Southern Corner would require a similar sacrifice. Horus was ready.

"What would you have me do?" Anubis stood behind Horus, leaning in the doorway.

"I'd have you take her to the chariot and leave, but I know that is not a possibility." Horus cupped Isis' hands in his palm. "If you intend to fight by my side, then we must follow the plan. Tell me, how many on our side remain?"

"Perhaps a handful." Anubis shrugged. "Khepri and a few in Sobek's platoon are held up near the bridge. How many is a mystery."

"What of our dear uncle?" Horus could tell by the long expression on Anubis' face that the answer wasn't good. It was best not to dwell on it. Anubis was over emotional and needed distraction. "Amun and his guard?"

"Strange, that one is." Anubis stepped away from the doorway, pacing back and forth. "His daughter awaits us in the chariot. She was stark raving mad. She attacked your mother…"

"Why?" Horus pressed, thrown off at the notion of Hathor fighting Isis. "What of the girl we saved from the human realm?"

"She kept saying he took her, but shut off when asked for clarification."

"It's possible she blames my mother for the situation. Could it be Shiva she was speaking of?" Horus asked.

"Probably so."

"If we can make contact with Amun's people, then perhaps we can mount a force to free Khepri and the others and take back our home."

Horus proceeded to coordinate a plan with Anubis. He kept it simple, but effective. Horus would deliver Isis to the chariot and talk sense into Hathor while Anubis got into position to rescue Sobek's direct reports. With all eyes trained on bringing Horus to Shiva, Anubis would hopefully not be regarded as a real threat.

Three angels standing guard at the chariot hangar dropped like flies with scintillating holes burned into the back of their heads. The plasma crossbows that had sprung from Horus' wrists fell back into his aurascales. He scooped his mother up and proceeded to a shuttlecraft known as a chariot. He found the one Anubis had marked, although it wasn't easy as there were nearly a hundred chariots in the docking bay. The rear entry to the chariot slid open with the ease of a rusty window screen. The motion was mirrored by an uneasy shock up his spine.

"Hathor," Horus whispered into the chariot.

He moved up a few steps, ducking under a ceiling ridge and into the shuttle. The back hatch closed behind him. His mother groaned, so he quickly sat her on one of the seats and reclined it. There was motion to the left. Hathor stuck her head out from under a bunk bed. He looked over his shoulder and rolled his eyes. "What are you doing?" he asked.

"I figured they might look in here, so I didn't want to make it easy for them. Anubis just left me." She crawled out from under the bed, stood, and sneered at Isis. "You do realize what she's done?"

"She is still your queen." Horus slapped her hard, leaving behind a red mark. "If indeed she is guilty of wrongdoing, you of all people should know we're not always judged by our actions. I still remember the leeway granted to you when we were teenagers."

Horus referred to the incident that had left her brother maimed by Anubis. The other kids had never admitted it, but he knew it was her plan to torture Anubis. Though she'd seemed to long outgrow the spoiled brat phase, even showing contrition a time or two, she never really apologized directly for the torment she'd caused Anubis, or even acknowledged him as a real individual. Horus kept that forever in the back of his mind when Hathor would rub him, flirt, or talk of their future betrothal.

"I'm sorry for touching you in that manner." He rubbed her face and lowered his head in shame.

He didn't like that he'd had to strike her. Not because she was a woman—their Corner had long since abandoned the idea of gender inequality and a weaker sex, unlike humans who still thought it socially unacceptable to strike a woman under any circumstance. No, he loathed laying a hand upon her because she was not a warrior. There were plenty of female fighters between their Corner and the others. Khali, Shiva's bride, was well regarded as a fighter. Thor's mistress Sif was another great warrior, thought to have perished by his side.

However, Hathor represented those who needed protection, and Horus tried to always stand up for them and never be domineering.

Still, Hathor needed to be shaken up and understand that disrespect for the chain of command would not be tolerated.

"You know not the things she did to that poor child." Hathor stepped away from Horus and continued to apply pressure to her cheek.

"Anubis said you were incoherent. What happened?" Horus squinted, shaking his head at her in confusion. "We don't have time for this. Whatever happened with the child, we will uncover it. The important thing is to dislodge ourselves from the docking bay and save the others."

"This shuttle won't launch," she replied.

"We won't know that until we try it."

"Already have." She folded her arms and tapped her right foot. "I wasn't going to let Anubis just lock me in here until he thought of a punishment for me. I was leaving."

"If we weren't on the brink of annihilation..." Horus turned around and squared his shoulders as he towered over her. She sunk back. He thought better of his words. "Anubis isn't the sort to be like that."

"But we are on the brink. So what are you going to do?" Hathor uncrossed her arms and stepped toward his face. Horus calmly looked down his nose at her. She took a small step forward and rested her head on his chest. "The override was set for all the chariots. We can't detach until it's taken care of from the main helm and this cruiser is off the ground. It's part of the emergency protocol."

"How did they get the codes?" Horus scratched the back of his head. His eyes widened, sure of the answer. "Khnum. How could he be so blind?"

"You seriously think he believes them? That they don't intend to kill us?" Hathor grabbed his hand, stroking his arm. He knew the game her touch tried to play and yanked his arm away. He would have none of it. "You can cancel the override, can't you?" she asked.

142

"Khnum's a fanatic, desperate for change. There is no telling." Horus leaned over the chariot's control panel and looked out the front window. A few shadows moved across his line of sight. He crouched and pulled her to the floor.

Horus extended his right arm to his side, down at an angle. A plasma beam erupted from his hand, crackling with green static, quickly turning into solid metal to form a sword. His face guard took the shape of a silver hawk. He snapped his fingers and pointed for her to sit in the co-pilot chair. He stepped out of the shuttle and the door shut behind him.

Horus rolled under the chariot, watching numerous sets of silver armored boots pass by as he stood on the opposite side of the chariot and shadowed whoever it was. He twirled around and deflected a strike. The steel sparkled. The would-be attacker knelt. It was Taweret. Bastet was with her. They had Amun's family: his son, Hapy, and wife, Sekhmet.

"Where is your commander?" Horus asked. His posture relaxed, but not his grip on the weapon.

Bastet stepped forward. Her black exo-armor mask was in the shape of a feline. "We made sure Amun made a hasty escape when the power cut off."

That was an odd thing to do. Horus didn't quite buy it. He stole a glance at Hathor in the chariot, staring at them from a window. Her skin was pale and her eyes nervous. Horus remained vigilant.

"Probably for the best," he said. "We don't want all the high council members at risk. Where did you send him?"

"The navigation in this crystal holds the answer." Bastet held up a crystal with a pink mist inside. "I've instructions to destroy it if captured."

"Right." Horus mumbled. He scanned Hapy and Sekhmet over. Hapy was drooling and rocking back and forth. "There are a few of Sobek's men trapped near the bridge. We are going to draw attention away from there."

Tawaret and Bastet looked at each other apprehensively.

"We have orders to…"

"And now you've new ones," Horus cut them off sternly. "Sekhmet and her son will wait in this chariot. Her daughter is inside."

"My Hathor." Sekhmet's face lit up. Hapy clapped with excitement. "How is she?"

"Unharmed." He assumed her elation to be nothing more than a ruse.

The fortress' gravity systems went offline, as did the lights. His armor illuminated the dark hangar as they began to float in the air. He guided Sekhmet and her son into the chariot. The shuttle remained pinned to the floor with clamps securely fastened to its hull at all four corners. He allowed Tawaret to stay for the group's protection and closed off the back hatch.

He and Bastet made their way to the bridge. His left hand pressed against the wall and it shifted to his touch, rearranging into a secret passage that he was told only Sobek and he knew about. Once again, Bastet was confused.

Horus was relieved that some systems still had power. Khnum must be trying to draw him out and had to know something was coming his way. Horus crept down the new route, both hands gripping his sword. He reached a dead end, perplexed. He remained as focused on any enemy ahead as he was on the potential foe to his back.

"You have us lost," Bastet grumbled. Her words were ignored.

The wall behind them closed off and slowly squeezed in. Gravity returned. He pinned his back to one wall and pressed his feet against the opposite, trying to keep the walls from coming together. Bastet did the same. It was a futile effort. The floor opened up. His wings expanded but hers did not. She impacted like a brick, barely bouncing. He landed softly and in a back stance for defense.

The hole in the ceiling sealed and lights came on. Two sets of footsteps made their way toward them. An arrow of crystallized light struck him in the torso, blowing him off his feet. He propped himself against the wall, trying to stand straight and readjust his hazy vision. Bastet crawled out of view. Khnum's large fist struck Horus in the face and knocked him to his back.

"You and your retarded cousin try and play me?" Khnum yelled, kicking Horus in the ribs. "I fight for our survival, you spoiled brat."

"For our imprisonment." Horus tried to push up but was met with another fist to the face.

"You no longer have authority to speak to me in such a tone," Khnum said.

"That's enough." Shiva snapped his fingers. "Pick him up."

Khnum did as commanded.

"Like a dog." Horus slammed his armored forehead into Khnum's unguarded face. Blood smeared across his helmet. "Do you sit, speak and roll over too?"

Shiva crushed Horus's chest with a Spartan kick. Horus slammed into the wall with a momentum he'd never felt before. Falling to the ground, he wondered how a mere kick could pack more force than he'd ever experienced from the blow of any weapon.

Horus grabbed his sword, about to lunge at Shiva. Khnum raised a hand, his eyes wide, shaking his head as he implored Horus not to follow through with the attack.

"He's an Alpha Level Guardian," Khnum said through his left palm. Blood seeped through his fingers. "Don't be stupid, Horus."

"Yes, Horus, don't be stupid," Shiva taunted, grabbing Horus by the back of his torso plate. He dragged the Angel-born down the corridor. Bastet stepped from the shadows, and instead of pursuing them to help Horus she retreated. Shiva tossed the prince to the ground and moved over to the main helm of the large space fortress. "We have no time to spare, Khnum. We must detach."

Even though the plan hadn't gone as intended, he was now at the bridge. He could disengage the locks on the chariot hangar. He kept a careful eye on the codes Khnum was typing.

Khnum flung the blood off his hands and stood at the helm. Holographic constructs of lavender, yellow and cobalt sprouted up from the control panel. Like a maestro, he placed the spherical and oblong hard-light constructs in exact positions. Horus tried to crawl away, but was really hoping to keep Shiva's attention. It worked. Shiva stood on him. Any moment now Anubis would be powering into the bridge with Sobek's men, since Horus had successfully distracted Shiva and Khnum.

"Please, be our guest." Shiva kicked Horus onto his back. "Let me introduce you to the rest of the party," Shiva laughed.

A door split open. The light in the hallway outside was blinding, but several silhouettes took form. They marched forward and the doors closed shut. Skanda, leading a group of fighters, had corralled all of Sobek's men. Anubis wasn't among them.

"There, I'm finished." Khnum spread his fingers and swiped his arms apart like he was swimming underwater. His right hand hovered over the system lock and a white light scanned it. The display screen relayed the progress for launch.

The ship's gears rotated for the first time since it had landed on the planet. The clamps which clung for life deep in the planet's crust detached and the force of the thrusters rocked them back and forth. Shiva stepped off Horus and held firmly to the control panel.

Anubis, who was hiding in the shadows, caught his cousin's attention. His index finger was upright against his lips. Horus nodded in reply and then looked toward Khepri, Sobek's first lieutenant. He was incoherent, but perhaps once the fight was underway he and the others would join.

Silver and gray aurascales assembled over Anubis until his face looked like the animal he was forced to wear like a scar: a jackal. Horus rolled and jumped to his feet when Anubis attacked. The prince boxed with Khnum. His youth and agility proved too much for the older angel. He spun into a roundhouse, knocking Khnum onto all fours.

"You deserve whatever fate Vishnu has for you," Horus said, kicking Khnum in the gut. He leapt for the control panel and undid the lock on the hangar so he and the others could escape in the chariots. He grabbed Khnum by the breast plate. "But I won't let you take the rest of us down with you."

"You forget that I helped train you." The seasoned vet wasn't done yet, propping a shoulder under Horus and lifting him off the group. "I know all your moves."

Khepri and the others attacked, even though their hands were bound. Skanda moved like a flash, laughing as now he had an excuse to behead those who revolted. Anubis took him by the throat and choke-slammed him onto the floor. Skanda fell unconscious. Anubis broke the shackles off Khepri and the others.

Horus positioned himself behind Khnum and placed a blade to the traitor's neck. Khnum's aurascales shifted and grappled onto Horus' extremities. An electric surge threw Horus backward. He pushed off the ground, but Khnum twisted the prince's ankle, keeping him on the floor. Anubis drove Khnum's head into the wall and then threw him backwards with unforeseen power and fury.

"Go!" he yelled at Horus, but his cousin refused as he staggered to his feet. Anubis looked over at Khepri. "The royal line is all that matters. Sobek would agree."

"Indeed," Khepri replied and was assisted by a few others in wrangling in Horus.

"No," Horus screamed, having flashbacks of the time Sobek dragged him away so he wouldn't share in the wretched lashing Anubis was to receive. He broke free of their grip and attacked Khnum again, savagely beating him.

"You think the numbers are in your favor," Shiva laughed. He put two fingers up to his lips and whistled. More than half of those who were fighting on Khepri's side halted and then turned on their own kind. "The influence of the Eastern Corner is far-reaching."

Anubis attacked Shiva and rained down with ferocious haymakers. The blows were chaotic and relentless. He took the invader by the throat and slammed him through a wall. His strength and force lifted Shiva off the ground with one arm. The enormous Angel-born roared like a wild beast as his free hand battered the Alpha Guardian like a jackhammer.

Shiva conjured a knife from his aurascales. Blades protruded from the toes of his boots. He kicked Anubis under the armpit, sticking with the toes, resulting in his release. The knife penetrated Anubis' ribs and twisted. Shiva dug an elbow into Anubis' throat and followed with a flurry of strikes to the head. The final uppercut fractured the jackal helmet like dried clay. Pieces of aurascales fell to the ground. Anubis' bare face followed. Shiva grabbed Anubis by the arm, lifting the limb, and kicked down on his foe's shoulder, dislodging it.

Anubis screamed in agony. Khepri and those still loyal jumped in to help, but Shiva quickly muted their resistance. Anubis crawled forward with his one good arm. His eyes watered as he tried to yell for his cousin.

"There's no time for this." Shiva kicked Anubis' face and rendered him motionless. He walked through the holes in the wall and back to the main helm.

Soon, all that was left was Horus. He was surrounded, stilling fighting with Khnum and a few others. By this time, Skanda had come to. The group was just about to take Horus down when Shiva halted them.

"Stand your ground," Shiva commanded. He looked at Khnum. "Continue. Prove your worth." Khnum swung but was no match for Horus' stamina. The Angel-born grabbed the jab and twisted Khnum to the ground. "Are you going to finish him, already?" Shiva asked in a bored tone.

"I'm working on it," Khnum replied.

"I wasn't talking to you." Shiva's eyes remained forward.

Horus pulverized Khnum in the diaphragm causing him to expel all air. Horus' battered armor repaired while he turned to face Shiva. He looked around. The situation wasn't good. The two manifested their weapons of choice and stared holes in one another. Horus' grip on his weapons wasn't as tight as it once was.

"Your cousin yet lives. As do your friends and uncle." Shiva smirked, but still spun his weapons around his fingers. "I do not care what happens with you, your mother, or the rest of your slowly dying Corner. The many we have yet to slay will be freed, and you can carry them away to wherever you wish. What we want once dangled around your father's neck. I assume you know what I speak of." Horus remained silent, drawing a chuckle from Shiva. "I admire your steadfast resolve despite the mounting odds. You and your cousin would be a beloved addition to my platoon. Just know that I will not kill you, for your life holds too much value. I will merely cripple you and sew your eyes open as those who are innocent, and the ones you hold most dear, are savagely raped and slowly killed in front of you. Do you understand, child?"

There were three exits, but all of them blocked. Horus continued to glance around, drawing up routes in his head. A puddle of blood grew around Anubis' face. The three angels behind him could easily be dealt with. No, that route wasn't an option. Anubis would be left behind.

"He disrespects you, Father, by not speaking," Skanda yelled, squatting in an obvious preparation to attack.

"So do you, by assuming I need the situation dictated to me." Shiva glared at his son and then at Horus. "What'll be?"

"All of us are free?" Horus asked, lowering his weapons. They vanished.

"Every last one." Shiva nodded.

"It is yours." Horus reached inside his armor and retrieved the necklace Isis had placed there. The chipped triangular medallion dangled from the gold chain. Shiva's eyes grew large. Two of his angels placed their hands on Horus' shoulders and reached for the medallion. Before their fingers could touch it, his weapons sprouted forward and he severed their hands.

Skanda attacked. Horus jumped into a butterfly kick and snapped his heel across Skanda's face. He landed and thrust his blade immediately through another of Shiva's men. Shiva's focus zeroed in. He and Horus lifted for blows, but the cruiser's display monitors to the right showed meteors puncturing the ship's hull. The artificial gravity was warped. Everyone was thrown off balance and floated off the floor. Shiva took hold of the control panel and pulled himself down, working quickly to rectify the problem.

Horus pushed toward Anubis while Shiva was preoccupied, but stopped when six enemies blocked his path. There was no way to rescue his cousin. He knew if the situation were reversed he would tell Anubis to run. He cried out and took the opportunity to leave. The gravity systems restored, and everyone hit the ground.

"Bring him back," Shiva calmly ordered, not bothering to look at Skanda.

The thrusters kicked online underneath the ship, shifting the center of gravity. Horus lifted into the air, slammed into the ceiling and rolled along onto the wall. The axis of gravity realigned, making the right wall the new floor. He grabbed his aching ribs and hobbled down the shaft. Skanda gave chase.

The hull rumbled, warning of another shift in thrusters. Horus leapt as gravity spun again. He kicked off the wall to his left, flipped, and landed on what was once the ceiling. Skanda wasn't as prepared and was thrown about.

Flashing arrows in Horus' vision guard led the way back to the hangar bay. The halls screeched with a deafening roar. Horus covered his ears. The force of the black hole must've been stripping away the ship's outer layers while it struggled to leave the singularity's gravitational grip. Horus felt the Armada cruiser swivel beneath his feet. The only explanation was that Shiva was pointing the bow back towards the center of the planet, but there was no way he'd be crazy enough to try and travel through the planet to get away from the black hole, unless he was hoping to use the planet's dying gravitational pull to sling the ship away from the void.

Horus made it to the hangar and locked the door behind him. He jumped nearly fifty yards to the feet of the escape chariot. Hathor put her face to a side window, waving for his attention. She opened a hatch and tried to crawl out of the shuttle before Tawaret corralled her back in.

"Horus..." she yelled before her voice was muffled.

"Get back in." Horus cleared larger crates out of the chariot's launch path.

"You need my help." Bastet hobbled over to a light panel. After a few quick swipes of her fingers over the glowing buttons, a mechanical arm latched onto the chariot from underneath. The ship was moved onto a rail chute in order to launch it out of the hangar. "I'm entering the coordinates."

"How do you know where we're going?" Horus asked.

"I have the crystal," she replied and shoved the crystal back into her breast plate. She scurried back to the chariot but stopped in place when an emphatic thud echoed through the chamber. To her left a large mallet-shaped dent protruded through the door. "We've got company."

"I have him." Horus' aurascales sizzled. Two crossbows formed over the top of his arms and hands. Another thump erupted at the door, this time breaking a small hole. Skanda's face shone through. Horus lifted each hand in succession, shooting two arrows of crystallized energy. The first arrow blew through the door. The second liquefied Skanda's breast plate, eating away at his skin. A third arrow cut through the air, but Skanda raised a shield to absorb the shot.

Bastet limped up the back hatch of the chariot and Horus followed. He reached a hand for Taweret but she slapped it away and kicked him in the face. Horus rolled across the ground while Hathor screamed for him.

The airlock opened. Everything not bolted down was sucked into space. Horus drove his sword into the floor, holding on for dear life, and watched as the mechanical arm slung the chariot through the chute. The rear thrusters kicked on and soon the shuttle was out of view. The airlock closed.

"Mother," Horus screamed, crouching over.

Everything had come to ruin. The dream of succeeding where his father could not shattered to pieces and stuck in his heart. At least Osiris found victory in death. There would be none for Horus. He lowered his hands, kneeling down, and looked at his father's piece of the Forge in one hand, and the crystal he'd constructed to leave for Earth in the other.

Skanda and his minions soared toward Horus. The seconds seemed to span an eternity. The words of Sobek rang loud in his head. *Surrender is a state of mind settled on before battle. If you're truly done then you never had a chance.*

Just then he remembered the arrogant determination of his younger self and embraced it. Just as he'd kicked his mentor's legs out from under him during that training session, he would do the same to Vishnu's men. It was time for a bold strategy. He only hoped this potential new ally wouldn't be his death.

His fingers curled around the crystal. A pink vapor trail sprouted around him. In an instant, with Skanda merely inches from delivering a killing blow, the walls of his only home vanished and a dense, cold forest somewhere on Earth appeared.

CHAPTER SIXTEEN

Set II

Three pairs of shining armored boots pattered up the marble steps. The chromed feet lifted in unison and lowered again onto the salmon and crème swirled pathway. The sky was a baby blue and the air smooth and devoid of any humidity, like always. Golden buildings towered over the streets and steps, adding to the perpetual feeling of walking in a maze. Despite the grandiose nature of new Zion, in which new homes were built every day in preparation for their future tenants, to Set it seemed more like a prison than an actual dwelling for believers. After all, the many things he'd grown to enjoy while on Earth were nonexistent here.

Though seemingly perfect in every detail, Heaven remained silent. The souls of mankind chosen to spend eternity protected by its gates awaited their new form inside the Light of Souls. Whether that would actually happen or not was still to be determined. That was all contingent on whose belief system was right.

"Found out a bunch of nothing while in Moscow, if you ask me," Hermes grumbled.

"I didn't." Set followed a signal beamed into his aurascales, directing him where to go. After eons of doing their dirty work, the Archangels had finally extended him an invitation to their council room. Perhaps this was it and the deal he'd struck with his silent partner the day he killed Osiris was finally coming to fruition. Of course, it could just as likely be another grunt mission to incinerate some changeling or half-breed, something he regarded as nothing but busy work. "We report what we find and that's the extent of our duty. It is not for us to decide the information's validity."

"Since when do you care when opinions are expressed?" Hermes folded his arms and squinted with contempt at Set.

"Since we started getting invited to the high council, and there is more than one of them willing and able to sever my head." Set couldn't tell if Hermes was really that stubborn or just playing the fool. Mocking the wisdom and intent of the higher angels, serious or not, was typically met with a flaming sword through the neck.

Set had always found something fishy about Hermes' version of how the Western Corner fell and the fate of Athena—especially since they didn't match Set's own recollection of events—but he couldn't ever say as much aloud. As far as everyone else was concerned, he was never there.

Set's prominent brow ridge gave his dark eyes a sunken look as he stared at the ground. Stubble dominated his face and neck, and his hair was buzzed short. His skin was a reddish-tan, almost copper in tone, and it cracked around his knuckles, elbows and other joints due to its dry nature.

"Majestic, isn't it?" Sif commented, her brown hair glancing off her silver shoulder plates. She looked up at the tall buildings. Her tears of joy were accentuated by her large smile.

Set rolled his eyes, but was careful to make sure no one noticed. Disguised behind his nonchalant eye roll, he glanced at her alluring features. Milky-white skin and dark eyes formed a compelling juxtaposition. His gaze moved down to her full lips, over her smooth neck, and stopped at her ample chest. He imagined the warmth of her bosom against his face as she cuddled him to sleep, but the thought vanished quickly when he remembered that her breasts had probably played host to Thor's flesh hammer on many occasions. The possibility that there were remnants of little Thors crawling on her tits turned his stomach.

"Is something the matter?" Sif asked him, grabbing his elbow. "You look sick."

"Only in my head," he said with a smirk.

"Truer words," Hermes interjected, drawing a chuckle from Set. "I'm sorry. I thought my words neither sarcastic nor funny."

"They're not," Set laughed, grabbing his sides. "Just your whole attitude all these years. On one hand, I've nothing to hide. I've more than repented for my rebellion. I brought down my own Corner in service of Father's will. On the other, you're still keeping secrets, which is why you follow my lead. If you'd like that to change at any point during the course of existence, I'd suggest your attitude lead the way."

"I've nothing to hide either." Hermes stomped. His stark red hair stood straight as he became agitated. "I just don't like you. Anyone who would deliver their own flesh to certain death, rather than try and negotiate for them a peaceful end, deserves none of my admiration."

"I don't require your admiration." Set turned around and continued to walk backwards. He snapped his fingers at Hermes and whistled at him like a dog. "Just your unrelenting obedience. Now, hurry along boy, get back in line. We don't want to be late."

They came to a large wall. It was built from clouds and vapor though it carried the outline of a brick and mortar construct. Set held his fist up at a ninety degree angle. The other Assassins stood in place as he pressed his hand to the wall. Moving like a slow gel, the clouds enveloped his hand. A white light sliced through the wall and the form became rigid. His hand was released and the section in front of him split apart, opening a path for the three.

As they stepped through the opening to another side they couldn't see, Set's anxiety nearly got the best of him. His orders usually came via Michael's carrier pigeons. He'd always assumed that the Archangels watched him work while they sat perched on a cloud, never having to dirty their hands. Maybe this would finally be the end of all that. Reality shifted around him and sucked him in through a portal of pink light.

"I know not how one manages to be both foolish and a bull-headed coward, but you accomplish the feat flawlessly. Action is required now." Gabriel slammed his fist onto the table, standing up. His shoulders pointed forward at Michael, as if ready to lunge over the table and attack. "With every moment we hesitate, mull over plans and only discuss, we delay finding the lost souls who are promised a home and our protection."

"You think he knows this not?" Raphael stood, his chair sliding backwards and toppling over. The veins in his biceps surged to the surface of his chocolate skin. "You don't think the ramification of every little action weighs heavily on his heart?"

"I see only a shell of the leader who once commanded our respect." Gabriel looked at Michael, sneering.

"You should hold your tongue." Raphael glowered as his jaw grew tight. He walked towards Gabriel, who appeared more than happy to meet him halfway. Uriel and Chamuel stood between the two. "Who should we listen to, Gabriel? You? You're not as heralded as you once were."

"No one is closer to Father than me!" Gabriel yelled. Uriel struggled to pull him back, but his brother slipped through his grasp. Gabriel's right hand clasped Raphael's throat. "When have you ever heard Father's voice?"

"When was the last time you did?" Raphael replied, squeezing out the words despite the hand at his throat. "He's not spoken to you since John at Patmos. What use do you serve now? You're no different than any of us."

"Shut up," Gabriel barked.

"Enough." Michael's voice halted the bickering. He leaned back in his chair, slouched, covering his face with his left hand. His dark locks were longer than usual, splayed out in all directions, helping to shield his eyes.

"So this is how the better half lives," Set chuckled under his breath.

"There are several problems that need attending, and not all of them can be solved at once. None of them if we continue to tear ourselves apart." Michael sat forward, moving to the edge of his seat, and leaned on the table. With a tired face, he looked at Gabriel, almost pleading. "You and I have not seen eye to eye for some time. I've long given up hope that my onetime closest ally would again open his heart to me, but I still expect us to do as required and protect those who count on us."

"You mean believe in us?" Gabriel narrowed his eyes at Michael.

"Those two aren't always the same," Michael replied, slowly standing. He took a deep breath, closing his eyes as he inhaled. He looked over at Set and then towards Raphael. "Did you send for them?" he asked, meaning the Assassins.

"I did," Gabriel said, pushing free of Uriel's grip. "There are whole countries that are lost and need us, but they've had their chances. Our focus should be on our promised ones."

"They'll continue to have their chances until the seven years. For now we crawl, bleed and respond to their needs," Michael said through his teeth, not bothering to look at Gabriel. "For someone who spent so long at Father's side, you exhibit none of the patience, understanding and grace he had for his children."

"No, I exhibit the harsh truths of his word, a line you once toed along with me." Gabriel walked past Michael and over to Set and his two fellow Angel-Assassins. He swiveled around and looked back at Michael. "You can't handle another war, and we both know the last one is still coming."

"I can't handle any more insolence..."

"I think you still sympathize with the old four Corners," Gabriel interrupted him. "You've not been the same since their destruction."

"Hardly a secret." Michael shrugged.

Set did his best to not smile, biting the inside of his lip. Things were more desperate than he'd been told. Maybe the plan would work after all.

"When we decided that our role in the lives of humanity would be a more distant and quiet involvement, we agreed that it wasn't in their best interest but ours. Having that sort of close relationship with mortals is what made the Corners weak and susceptible to the earthly lifestyle in the first place." Gabriel looked at the other Archangels. Set was envious of Gabriel's charisma and his ability to turn the argument his way. The first messenger stood on a chair. "There would be no more random acts of kindness. No more parting seas or moving mountains. No more raising the dead. Instead, our gifts and abilities were reserved for those who believed and then asked for help. I can't seem to shake the feeling that Michael wants to change that."

"You think this is better?" Michael shook his head, just about done with the whole debate. "You seem ready to pull the sword from existence."

"Someone has disrupted the flow of souls, Michael." Gabriel jumped from the chair and skipped toward his leader, but Raphael stood between them. Gabriel pointed at Set. "Why not send our best to track them down?"

"I was wondering if you had another world leader or rogue angel for me to hunt down," Set laughed. "What about the terms of my service?"

"Shut it, assassin," Raphael spat. "You will yet have a turn to speak."

"Of course." Set nodded with forced humility.

Michael waved the room silent, looking at his five fellow Archangels. Though none of them showed their attitude as brashly as Gabriel, Set could tell they agreed with Father's former top messenger. Uriel and Zedkiel looked at the floor. As former messengers themselves, they'd always follow Gabriel's lead. Chamuel had a weary, long-faced look with his hazel eyes hidden behind his blonde hair. Raphael, once Michael's most trusted Alpha Guardian and now fellow Archangel, nodded as he and their commander had a silent exchange with their eyes.

"I've not grown weak," Michael said softly. "There's no written guideline for these events. We move on faith alone. Without that we're as lost as any of them."

"No one's saying you're weak," Uriel replied. His tan skin seemed pale in the midst of the in-fighting.

"I can't help but feel like there was more to be done before the Last Great War. We'd already suffered so much. To lose four factions the way we did... I'm cautious that we don't lose sight of what He really stands for," Michael said to Gabriel. "You would know best his compassion."

"I also know best his intolerance for repeat offenders. At some point, you are what you are."

"We don't know the plan. The words say that's something He's reserved for Himself." Michael hunched forward, pressing his hands onto the table.

"I know those words," Gabriel said, placing a hand to Michael's shoulder. "I delivered them to the prophet myself. However, until we hear otherwise, we should carry on as we always have. And right now, those souls are missing. We must find and annihilate the one responsible for closing the gateway from Earth to Heaven."

"And what if that was part of the design all along?" Michael looked at Gabriel, standing mere inches from him. "We could very well be starting the war before it's time."

They talked as if war was a foregone conclusion. Resignation to an outcome and doing little to prevent it was not divine craftsmanship; it was nothing more than a self-fulfilling prophecy. Set knew there was more than one way to snuff out the war before it even started. It would take slicing a few throats, but as long as they were the right throats then the desired outcome was more than possible. He found free will a thing of beauty, not burden. Unfortunately the others didn't share this belief, so he kept quiet.

"I believe we're divinely inspired. Not divine in and of ourselves, lest you think me prideful." Gabriel sighed. The debate had seemed to age his spirit several celestial cycles. "If he guides our actions, how can we be wrong?"

"Does he guide all of our actions?" Raphael asked.

"We're all here now, aren't we?" Gabriel asked. "How could we be unless he willed it?"

Set knew that their silence in response to his questions said more about how lost they were than how much faith was left in the tank. If the Light of Souls was indeed thrown out of balance, then surely other falsities had come to light. Whether or not they knew how to look for them was another matter. One thing he was sure of: there were more secrets in the air. He could smell them. He may have never been a child, but that didn't stop him from feeling like one, giddy on the inside. It was only a question of who they would blame when all the facts were laid on the table. Would it even come to that? It was hard to believe there was much left tethering the Archangels together. Getting everyone back on the same page to listen to truth and reason when so much denial and faith was clouding their judgment could prove to be an impossible task.

"What of Moscow?" Uriel asked. "It's whole reason we summoned the Assassins to begin with."

Finally, someone was bringing everything full circle. Set was dying to speak.

"Is it Azrael?" Raphael asked, glaring at Set. "Tell us."

Set shook his head. "The coward Svarog wasn't sure." Hermes shifted in his seat, but his leader steadied him with a hand to the shoulder. "One thing was obvious. There are those now who worship the blue figure."

"I told you Azrael should have been executed for his transgressions," Gabriel growled at Michael. "Look at how your soft nature has burdened us once more."

"That's not everything, I understand," Michael replied. Set's head swung around as he stared at the lead angel. "Perhaps the first horseman rides." The group squirmed at the thought. Set could sense

160

the whispers of prophecy and rapture gripping their chests. "If indeed this is true, then the problem with the Light of Souls is of most importance."

"Tell us more." Gabriel took Michael by the wrist. Set was surprised Michael didn't respond to the gesture with a sword.

"Come with me, brother," Michael said softly to Gabriel. He then looked at Raphael. "Do as we discussed earlier."

Raphael nodded. He pointed at the Assassins. "Wait at the table. I'll return shortly."

Set perched next to the round table. Boredom set in quickly as they waited. A large bowie knife spun on its tip in front of him, creating a sort of whistling noise as it drilled into the stainless steel table.

Hovering orbs provided a dim light, circling the table as if they were ticking around a clock. The powder white walls had soft green and blue undertones. The ceiling and floor were fully reflective.

To his left, Sif snored while slouched in a chair with her feet up on the table, crossed at the ankles. A large muted-yellow hood was draped over her eyes. Hermes paced nervously behind them.

"Why did you withhold information?" Hermes asked.

"Would you settle down? You're beginning to irritate me." Set snatched the blade. It disintegrated into a thousand particles of dust and merged together with his angelic armor. He looked over his shoulder, growling. "I said sit."

"Fine." Hermes stood in defiance, but only for a second. He took a seat next to Set and leaned close to whisper, "Why did they leave us? You think they're watching, waiting to see what we'll do?"

"I haven't the foggiest."

"We've done all they've asked for thousands of years. What could we possibly have left to prove?" Hermes asked.

"I don't know." Set raised his right eyebrow, staring holes into Hermes. This was as good a moment as any to pry. "What more could we have left to hide?"

161

"I wish for once you wouldn't talk around the subject. You're the one practically lying to the Archangels," Hermes whispered, his fists tightening as he adjusted himself to a more offensive position. "You've been hinting at things ever since we were put together as a team. I wish you'd just say it."

Hermes should have snitched about Set's withholding details of their Moscow visit, but something had kept him quiet. It was either something Svarog had said or the fact that Hermes suspected Set knew his dirty secret. Possibly both.

"You expect me to believe the heir of Olympus is dead?" Set's grin was menacing.

"I never said that." Hermes looked away.

That was a lie. Set remembered the day Hermes took his oath swearing she was gone as if it had just occurred. What could he possibly have to gain by lying about it now? It wasn't just a secret he was hiding. No, he must have been trying to divert attention away from something much bigger. It most definitely had to be something Svarog had talked about.

"You've never said much of anything." Set rested his chin on his propped up left arm, attempting to trick Hermes into thinking his guard was down. "You were the child's caretaker, were you not?"

"Why does that matter?" Hermes squinted.

"Could be nothing. Could be everything..."

Hermes lunged forward. A short knife manifested in his grip. He stabbed at Set's chest but was stopped in his tracks when three blades slid from around Set's wrist and hand. The two blades on the outside pressed against Hermes' jaw line, stopping right under the ears, while the middle blade prodded underneath the jaw, poking at his soft tissue. Hermes froze in place.

"The point is, baby sitter, that child was the cause for a whole lot of bloodshed. She should not have existed..."

"And what about your own boy?" Hermes said through his teeth, unable to move his mouth.

"Like I said, I took care of everything," Set replied calmly. "That was all independently verified, remember?"

"I've been with you long enough to know when you're lying." Hermes raised his empty hands in a show of surrender. The knife vanished.

"That goes both ways." Set opened his fist and the blades slithered back into his armor. "Remember that."

A door at the far end of the room swooshed open. Set knocked Sif's feet off the table, waking her. Raphael marched into the chamber followed by Uriel, who stood at attention while Raphael sat across from Set.

"This is an unexpected." Set sat up straight, pulling the chair forward and then folding his hands neatly on the table. He spoke to Raphael in a pompous tone. "Usually Gabriel or Michael handle these little conversations."

"They're preoccupied," Uriel said.

"Quiet." Raphael slightly turned his head, looking at Uriel with an irritated gaze.

"Still fighting like spoiled brats?" Set asked.

Raphael ignored Set's sarcastic tone. "I am sure you heard what has us riled up, no?" He slid his right hand under his left forearm and removed a crystal several inches in length. Inside the crystal was a pink vapor which swirled and raged like a storm cloud. Raphael placed it in the middle of the table. The crystals were a way for the angels to rift undetected by others, but sometimes they contained private information not meant for prying ears. "The informant in Moscow was of no use? I assume you silenced him."

"He didn't tell us much about what you'd hoped, no." Set grabbed the crystal and held it up to his eyes, studying the cloud. He glanced at Hermes, making sure he remained silent, and then looked at Raphael. "We let him live because he claimed to have been contacted by the missing Corners and others... including some descendants in the company of a female Angel-born." Hermes squirmed and cleared his throat. Set turned and looked at his banner mate. "Am I forgetting something? You look pale."

"No." Hermes shook his head. His smile said he was at ease. His wide eyes told a different story. "Continue."

"We let him live on the condition he bring us information about the other factions who have and were yet to visit. Were we wrong?"

"Very useful. Be sure to follow up post haste." Raphael snapped his fingers at Uriel. "Go ahead. On with what you've found."

"Souls wandering Earth have spoken of a being who can absorb them. They've seen it do so to others." Uriel paused as if contemplating. "We're not sure what to believe, as a soul's conscious understanding of reality is warped after death, but we can't ignore the rumors."

"And the fear is Azrael is back and pissed off. That's the rumblings I've heard, anyway." Set noticed Raphael scowl as he swallowed. Maybe there was some truth to the rumors. "Could he have disrupted the Light of Souls?"

"We considered that possibility," Raphael said, nodding. "But some among us are hesitant to..."

"Michael. Right?" Set grinned, unsurprised. The Archangels were a predictable bunch.

"There's no telling what sort of alliances the former Corners have made. Be careful of where you tread and how much you believe from this informant. Remember, he is a coward and a liar." Raphael seemed too adamant to actually believe his own statement. "The skirmish in the human city of Moscow has been settled, and the mortals are content with their explanations of aliens and government conspiracies. The need is not to remedy that but to stop it from happening further. If this is indeed Azrael, or a horseman as Michael believes, we need to quell the cries which call him a messiah."

"Not all of us think we should just let the old Corners be," Uriel said, ignoring Raphael's scornful glares. "We cannot allow them to think they can do as they please. After all, if one Corner thinks they can send a disruptive force into our protected realm without recourse, what's to stop the others?"

"Nothing, wouldn't you say so Hermes?" Set looked at his fellow Assassin, wearing a pleased expression. "You would have the inside track into Zeus' old faction, would you not? How big of a problem could that spoiled whore Maya be? Unless you see a reason you couldn't bring us by for a visit?"

"I can't think of any," Hermes said, clenching his jaw tightly.

"We don't want you venturing too far off the path. The most important objective is to find who is absorbing the stray souls, and if indeed it is Azrael returned." Raphael stood, clasping his fingers over the back of the chair as he pushed it in. "Your instructions are in the crystal. You leave at once."

Raphael snapped his fingers. The three Assassins were sucked into a pink blast of light and placed in the middle of a grass field. Large snowcapped mountains surrounded them on three sides and a slow-moving river cut through the field on their other side. Wind, fierce and crisp, nibbled at their noses. Set looked at the crystal. The pink storm inside produced lightning and fire within its clear shell.

"What does it say?" Sif asked, stepping over a pile of ox dung. She stood behind Set, trying to look at the crystal. "Why did you not tell them Svarog believed the man to be Death?"

"Would it matter if it was?" Set replied. "We're here now. Our mission would be no different. Why worry them with small things when clearly there are other issues to attend to? The mission remains the same."

"I thought the importance of information was for the Archangels to decide?" Hermes smiled, cockily swaying his head. "If Azrael has returned, destroying an Archangel is no easy task."

"I wouldn't expect it to be easy either way." Set let go of the crystal and it hovered in place. He gazed into it deeply as the storm cloud inside began to change its composition. It spoke to him and not the others—a message from his silent partner.

165

"Set," Hermes said, drifting in front of his commander, floating in the air a few feet from the ground. "Where are we to go?"

"The crystal will lead the way." Set looked up at Hermes and then over to Sif. Reality split open, causing the image of the mountains to twist and contort in Set's view. A portal formed and Set motioned for Hermes and Sif to head through first. "Let's get on with it."

CHAPTER SEVENTEEN

The Observer

Gabriel and Michael stood alone in an almost pitch black room. The only illumination came from hard light constructs formed over the control panel, shining upwards into their faces. Michael ran his hands along the various angelic symbols on the control panel. More streaks of light shot across the holographic display.

"You've still not answered me," Gabriel said while grabbing at Michael's arm. The Archangel's leader swiped the hand of God's former top messenger out of the way. "Look at me."

"I'm busy." Michael didn't give as much as a glance toward his brother.

"We get centuries of passive inaction, and now all of a sudden you decide you're going at things solo?" Gabriel snatched Michael by the robe and pulled him away from the flashing lights. "You don't just get to ignore me."

"No?" Michael's stare was collected and unrelenting. Gabriel's brow furrowed momentarily, obviously thinking better of his actions, and he let him go. Michael turned and continued to work, as if not giving it a second thought. "I need to focus."

"You're going back out there." Gabriel's muted laugh reeked of frustration. *This is unthinkable.* He waited nearly a minute—tapping his foot repeatedly, hands interlocked at his stomach—for Michael's response, but it didn't come. "I take your silence as confirmation. Just another of our laws to be broken."

"I'm rewriting them," Michael replied softly and emotionlessly. "The Light of Souls is down for a reason..."

"Let's fix it," Gabriel interrupted. His eyes scanned the holographic projection sprouting up around him. The tactile holographic objects manifested by the control panel moved out of his path as he walked towards Michael. He leaned in front of Michael to block his view. "Is your mind present?"

"It's not as simple as fixing it." Michael's shoulders sank under the burden. He sighed and rubbed the tired lines away from his face with the back of his hand. "If you wouldn't mind, I'd like to continue."

"Continue to do what?" The wheels were spinning in Gabriel's head. His eyes widened with the unthinkable realization. "You cannot be a collector again." Gabriel slammed his hand onto the control panel and typed feverishly to counter Michael's programming. Michael grabbed Gabriel by the wrists and shoved him back.

"I'm all that remains of the reapers." Michael's arms trembled while pinning Gabriel's arms above his head and into the wall. The herald of God tried feverishly to resist, but it was futile. Sweat poured down Gabriel's brow and webs of saliva connected his teeth. Michael's breathing labored yet remained steady. His eyes narrowed. "I collected souls before, and I did it for a long time. I can do it again. At least until the problem is found." He relaxed his grip just a tad but Gabriel tried to spring forward, so he tightened the reins once again. "I'd like to release you. Holding you here wastes my time and achieves nothing on your behalf. You can work with me, but you won't stop me."

"Fine," Gabriel sighed, nodding. Michael cocked his eyebrow before finally letting go. Gabriel straightened himself out as if embarrassed.

Michael returned to the panel and scanned his fingers over the lights. The room hissed with a release of air when Michael finished his programming. The black walls, which projected the vast nothingness of space in front them, opened. Michael raised his hands and cast them forward. The hard-light objects he created flowed out and into the cosmos. He positioned them at various spots among the galactic bodies by simply moving his hands.

"There were two of you last time, Michael," Gabriel said faintly. Regret and sorrow filled his eyes.

"I remember."

"You saw what it did to him..."

"What we did." Michael snapped his head around. Gabriel's lips sealed. Michael leaned over the control panel. His hands clamped over the edges. "The programming for the Light of Souls has been corrupted since nearly the beginning."

"How is that possible?" Gabriel scratched the back of his head, his brow scrunching as he looked ponderingly at the floor. *That would mean a traitor.* "I refuse believe it."

"You can see for yourself." Michael motioned to the control panel. "I don't think it was just Charon's massive rift overhaul or the figure stealing lost souls. If I'm guilty of anything, it's not keeping a closer eye on the small details, and resting on my laurels since the Last Great War."

"What you're alluding to simply cannot be," Gabriel whispered, looking around as he stepped closer to Michael.

"It wasn't impossible for Father's greatest and most powerful creation to rebel, or for his favored children to lose their way." Michael looked back out at the cosmic power of the universe. The galaxies swirled in unison, melding as their outer portions touched one another. Small cosmic explosions lit up parts of their view. Stars collided and then formed new celestial entities. It was like watching a billion years in the span of seconds. "Souls have been siphoned for eons. It's not just been recently. I'm happy for the Assassins to be on the hunt for this imposter, but the problem with the Light of Souls was written into the code long before this soul stealer arrived. We've been played, and there's no telling how powerful the other side has become."

"So you're leaving?" Gabriel stood in front of Michael, blocking his path out and into the Milky Way galaxy. The canvas on the wall before them zoomed in on a swirl in the center of the universe. "You reveal this to me and expect what?"

"There are souls who still need rescuing," Michael said, casting a trustful look at Gabriel. "They're still promised a home here, and no one else can do it. The one thing I can say for sure is that our Light of Souls and the artificial one which has been draining the lost are connected. If one has been shut down, the other has, and if we're this on edge about it then they certainly are. Their whole plan has been discovered and they know it."

"Who is going to find them?" Gabriel asked.

Michael smiled, placing a hand on Gabriel's shoulder. "You are."

"Why me?" Gabriel looked down in shame, unable to make eye contact with Michael. *I feel not worthy.* "With the way we've bickered since longer than I care to remember, what makes you still trust me?"

"Because you're still my brother," Michael said, stepping into space. His Aurascales manifested around his body. He turned and his eagle-faced helmet glistened in the sun. "And through it all, I still believe you to be the best of us."

Michael vanished into a solar flare and the room sealed shut once again. Gabriel stood alone in the darkness. He walked over to the control panel to analyze the work Michael had left behind: a code for Gabriel to follow. He lowered his hand to the control panel and a crystal popped out. Gabriel waved his hand over the crystal and it floated up into the air to meet his fingers. When he grasped the crystal, his armor manifested and absorbed the stone's data.

Sound your beacon to all realms but Heaven, the recording said. *Keep this secret. The call will rattle the Corners and root out the imposter. Keep a watchful eye on those around you. If they've alliances beyond these borders, they will be contacted.*

Gabriel fell to his knees. Tears collected in the corner of his eye. *Forgive me Father, for I've been spiteful and blind in my rage.* The scarlet flare of his aurascales turned into a deep merlot and then a bright vermilion. Gradually the luminescence of the armor strengthened. *Heed my call, oh brothers and sisters. Hear my trumpet sound. May the symphony of God almighty capture your hearts and overcome your thoughts. Be drawn home.*

The door to the chamber opened behind Gabriel. Raphael walked in with the remaining Archangels. Gabriel looked over his shoulder. His faceguard retracted and the aurascales returned to their normal hue and glow.

"Where's Michael?" Raphael asked with an uneasy look. "What were you doing?"

"That's privileged information," Gabriel replied, trying to move past him.

"We're privileged," Raphael said, nodding at Zedkiel and Chamuel. They stopped Gabriel in his tracks. A sheepish grin momentarily twitched across his face before his lips pursed. "More secrets?"

"Now we find ourselves in a predicament." Gabriel shoved the two out of his way and Uriel, his first lieutenant and heir to be herald, stepped in front of him. "You as well?"

"We've traveled too far to still be keeping secrets." Uriel cast his eyes away from Gabriel with shame pasted on his face. "Out with it."

"If that's the way it needs to be." Gabriel stood still, sighing. "He went to collect souls. As the last remaining reaper, he's in position to bring the believers home."

"Impossible," Raphael said through his teeth. "That is against the laws. You did something to him."

"As if I, or any we know, could." Gabriel pointed at the control panel. "Check the laws for yourself."

"Even if the laws were changed, he will wear himself thin." Raphael stepped away from Gabriel and paced anxiously. Standing next to the control panel to verify Michael's work, Zedkiel nodded at Raphael in affirmation. "There's no way he can do that alone."

"That's why he needs us to find this imposter." Gabriel looked at the group. They responded with their undivided attention. "We must ensure Set and the Assassins destroy this fake angel."

***

Gabriel's faith was shaken. Not shattered or even remotely chipped, but the foundation was slipping. He'd withstood his fair share of bumps and bruises over the past several thousand earth years, but he'd always taken them in his stride. Everything was supposed to be for the greater good, for 'Father's will'.

"How could he allow the Light of Souls to be corrupted?" He marched into his personal chamber. The lights activated as he made his way through the shifting halls.

Outside the windows of the citadel—the housing for angels where he resided—stood the grand palace of the Holy Host. The golden spire fence and energy shields that formed the protective perimeter were surrounded by a river of cyan fire. The path to Saint Peter's gate was empty, save for a few stragglers delivered by Michael's work. Those who guarded new Zion were noticeably bored. There wasn't much for them to do.

He stood in his armory. Large mechanical halos rotated. They were big enough to encompass an individual twice Gabriel's size. He stood on a catwalk and the twirling rings moved into position, spinning with him and the footway in the middle. A red light beamed from the center of the halos and his aurascales surged to the surface of his skin. He grimaced during the reversal of the process known as 'Deliverance.' It was a way for the angels to be shielded by their starstone without making physical contact since the aurascales had a way of forging too strong of a symbiotic relationship with their host.

"It could be any of them," he said aloud. "What if it was Michael?"

No, that would be impossible. I'd sooner blame myself. The list of suspects couldn't be too large, as the Light of Souls was only implemented after the last Great War though its conception began much sooner. *The number of logical perpetrators is likely less than twenty. How many remain alive and not imprisoned?* "If I accuse directly, they will become defensive and I won't find my answers."

The aurascales merged with the halo, leaving Gabriel naked. He continued down a flight of metals steps and stood in front of his starstone. The smooth slate-gray material against his skin harkened to a grittier time in their existence—a time when the aurascales merged directly with their bodies and were transmitted synthetically through their system.

"If one can violate the Light of Souls right under our watchful eye without Father stopping them, then what else can they corrupt?" he wondered aloud. "I can't chance that they've infiltrated the Deliverance."

The torso-sized starstone scanned his palm, glistening. Clamps and power cords that had been attached to the starstone unhinged, allowing it to float, and the billions of metal squares that interlocked to form the egg shape spread apart. The glow from its red core was blinding. Its powerful energy source was matched by very few. Taking a fluid form, the solid alloy adhered to his skin, merging with his subconscious and DNA. It was a cold, jagged sensation for every angel when they were reunited with their aurascales. The luminescent red gem in the center flared, causing his eyes to radiate red light in unison with its glow. The gem merged with his inner aura and vanished, his skin shining brightly before returning to its normal tone. The gray sentient armor turned red and sprouted its rigid, silver exoskeletal plating.

"The traitor will not have access to my power," he said, looking at his hand while the aurascales washed over his face and formed his tiger helmet. "By now the old four Corners must've received the sound of my call. Panic is surely setting in." He lowered and then raised his hands, palms up, and a holographic computer materialized from the floor up. Information on all of his kin, both past and present, displayed in the fizzing field of view in front of him. He sorted the angels in order of most likely suspects.

The first off the list was Azrael. *The Light of Souls was conceived after his banishment. I was there when he was locked away.*

Zeus and his comrades were the next to be discarded with a left-swipe. It was well known that Michael had defeated them all. Gabriel was assured of such as he was present for the battle, having killed many in Zeus' legion himself.

"It's possible Zeus shared information of the Light with others beneath him, but highly unlikely any of them infiltrated Heaven to insert their own code," Gabriel murmured to himself, chewing on an index finger while he rubbed his chin with a thumb.

Thor was dead. His head was delivered personally to the Archangel council by Sif. He was also a great opponent to the Light of Souls. It was largely constructed without his knowledge. Even though many in the Northern Corner still remained at large, it was believed with relative certainty that they lived on the outskirts of existence, beyond the rainbow falls.

"Loki was always a trouble maker." Gabriel brought up Loki's profile with a wave of the hand. His fingers moved, nearly throwing Loki into the slush-pile, but he hesitated. He enlarged Loki's picture. "No, you were crafty. Espionage doesn't seem like your cup of tea, but then again misdirection was your greatest asset." Gabriel swiped right and placed Loki in the suspect pile, which was still an exclusive list.

"There is something I'm missing." Gabriel looked out over his observation deck. His room was encased in a fortified glass sphere. He had a full-view of all of Heaven in any direction he looked. Directly below him was the rainbow falls, a swirling gush of fogged-light that no one dared enter. It was simultaneously beautiful and menacing for it held great sights but traveling through it led to unknown realms.

The monitors to his right shimmered and caught his attention. He typed feverishly over the lights, not blinking. *You're in my systems, aren't you?* He squinted and grinned. *You are fast, but I am craftier.* His fingers were a blur. He bit his lower lip, leaning over the panel, breathing with gleeful anticipation. "I have you."

The location of the hack was revealed. *It cannot be.* He stutter-stepped backwards. In the reflection of his breastplate, Michael's face shone brightly. "Michael is no traitor..." Gabriel ran his fingers over his head and pulled at his blonde hair. *Or is he?*

His eyes turned toward the monitors and soon his step followed. The holographic display suddenly shut off. He let out a frustrated laugh and looked at the floating halo in the armory. "Of course." He nodded. "You knew I would separate from the Deliverance to protect against enemy intrusion, thus you implanted the code in the crystal you gave me directly into my computer when I walked through my halo. Well played."

An orb of light appeared, formed by flickering lights in place of his control panel. He touched it and it shocked him. Undeterred, he tried again, this time with his armor fully manifested to shield his skin. Upon contact, a virtual display appeared over the eye-slits in his faceguard. Gabriel smiled.

"A secure and untraceable line, but why..." He froze in place, as if serendipity had caused him to take pause. "I was focused outwards. You mean for me to look within."

"Gabriel," Uriel said with surprise in his voice. He stood on his leader's catwalk, dressed in evening robes, and examined the scene before him. The empty space where Gabriel's starstone should be was of particular interest. "You've separated from the Deliverance?"

Gabriel's helmet folded into his shoulder plates and he turned around. "Your presence here is a peculiar one."

"I received this message." Uriel held up a crystal with pink mist within. "I assumed it was from you."

"Why?" Gabriel asked.

"It contained a message only we could know the answers to." Uriel tightened his robe and placed the crystal in a pocket. He looked at the ground with an embarrassed glow in his cheeks. "Pardon my intrusion. I shall leave."

"No." Gabriel's voice was firm. Uriel looked back with hope, but Gabriel's gaze held something different. "The information," Gabriel said, holding his hand up. "I'd like to take a look."

"It was an obvious misdirection. We are being played."

"But only one of us was in the game, Uriel. You were purposefully excluded." Gabriel walked up the steps, speaking with relative calm. "Tell me, when did you receive word?"

"The crystal?" Uriel seemed confused and slowly walked backwards. "It was in my quarters waiting for me when I retired for the cycle." His back foot slipped off the platform and Gabriel grabbed him by the robe. He pulled Uriel back onto the platform and steadied him before removing the crystal. "You don't think I fabricated…"

"I know not what to think; only we've experienced two rebellions in the past and I'm not beyond believing in a third." Gabriel looked at the crystal and it dematerialized, absorbing into his armor.

Information quickly scattered through his aurascales. The movement of his armored red scales slowed to a halt and turned gray. His exoskeleton became rigid and kept him from moving. All outside sound was muted and the vision through his eye slits turned black. He was trapped.

CHAPTER EIGHTEEN

Lian III

Lian moved away from Austin and gazed intently at the Progeny Lounge in order to memorize the surroundings. Tables made of reclaimed boat wood. Pheasantwood stools with leather cushions. Large oak barrels stood upright for use as cocktail tables near a stage. Walls and floors stained with cigar smoke. Her mind sketched a picture of Sanderson and his favorite habit. It was as if time stood still. She turned to Athena, whose platinum blonde locks were now familiar.

"When was I here?" Lian asked, but she spoke to no one in particular. She gazed wide-eyed at her hands as the several cuts she'd sustained during her vision at the pub healed. Her headache was gone. She no longer felt queasy, but instead more powerful than ever. It was as if the lounge was healing her and its energy surging through her. "My abilities... I can hear people think on the far corners of the earth. What is this realm?"

"It's not this realm that heals and works through you," Madame Patricia replied. Her hands massaged the shoulders of the small five year old boy in front of her. Her hands slid behind the boy's back and lightly pushed him forward. "It's your proximity to him."

Lian swiveled around and stood motionless, looking at the boy. Several memories flashed through her mind like a black and white super-8 film. She fell to her knees and extended her arms. After years of separation, could she finally be reunited with her brother? Austin stepped to help her, but Harold pulled him back.

"You're going to want to give her space, mate," Harold whispered.

"Jaden?" Lian asked through her tears, her voice hoarse. The child lowered his eyes and turned his head to hide. Lian folded her hands over her face while she sobbed. "You haven't changed." Her brother was almost exactly the way she'd left him. All the years they had been denied bubbled up in her throat and choked her words.

"I don't understand." Austin pushed past Harold and knelt beside Lian. His big arms steadied her while sorrow caused her bones to rattle. He kissed her cheek and whispered in shock. "Is that...?"

"Her brother? Yes." Madame Patricia nodded. Jaden ran to Athena and crawled into her arms instead of Lian's.

"He should be a teenager." The confusion in Austin's mind screamed out to Lian. Every question in his thoughts blurted out at once. He vocalized them. "Lian was abducted by the Agency when she was six. Jaden was just a few years younger. What happened to him?"

"He's never been outside this realm. At least, not since William Sanderson brought him here." Madame Patricia walked over to Lian and offered a hand. Lian's red eyes turned upward. She took Madam Patricia's hand and was led over to Jaden. The boy was timid at first, but eventually leapt into his sister's waiting arms. "All of our bodies are mortal in some way, yet time is relative. It affects us all, which is why my kind builds homes where the natural laws of physics are bent."

"You're not with Maya?" Jarrod cracked his knuckles, obviously still ready to throw down.

"Heavens no." Madame Patricia giggled. "Pardon the slight pun."

Lian put her forehead to Jaden's and smiled. She didn't know if she should kiss him or give a huge hug. To cry or to scream? To just close her eyes and breathe it all in, or to lament everything that'd been done to her? If she could've transformed into a hundred people to let it all out at once, she would have.

Her hands sifted through his hair and their eyes locked. There was a powerful bond between the two. It coursed through her blood.

An added sense of static was in the air, working its way in and out of everyone around them. The longer she held his gaze, the more his eyes reflected the energy she emitted.

His similarities to Azrael are striking; the black hair and beaming blue eyes... Madame Patricia's voice faded out. Lian turned around and cast a confused squint. The old woman was standing with her mouth closed and arms crossed, examining Jarrod.

"Did you say something?" Lian asked.

"Who, me?" Madame Patricia was thrown off by the question. The way her body remained steady told Lian she wasn't lying. "Just now? No."

"That's weird. I swear I heard... Never mind," Lian whispered, turning her attention back to Jaden, "Did you hear it too?" she asked him. Her brother grinned at her as if he knew something.

"Seriously, I don't get it." Austin stood up, scratching the back of his head, dumbfounded. "No, seriously. He's aged, what, maybe a day?" Austin asked, looking at Lian's little brother.

"What's not to get?" Madame Patricia circled Austin. "How many days passed when you were taken captive by Maya and her forces?"

"You're a special person, right? Like Jarrod, only natural?" Austin asked. "Aren't you gods?"

"Where you're wrong is I am no more natural than he." She nodded at Jarrod. "We've been called gods by those who search for words to understand us."

"Oreios didn't age," Jarrod said, standing toe-to-toe with Madame Patricia. Harold moved to her side. Jarrod glared at Harold, as if begging for a fight. "He said he'd been on the planet for ages. How does that work?"

"On Earth, your planet, yes." Madame Patricia nodded. "But where do you think you are now?"

Everyone turned to face Madame Patricia, silent.

"Earth, Heaven, Tartarus, Asgard and the other realms of the broken Corners, they're not all together and they're not some special dimension of existence. They're physical places with very specific laws and ways of subverting them. When you rift, you're not changing reality and time, you're slipping through the fabric of space." Lian only half listened to Madame Patricia speak. "You feel untethered and nauseous because your bodies have been ripped apart and then reconstructed to fit the laws of the new planet you're on. Your galaxy is but one of an infinite number. You didn't really think you were special, did you?"

"Well... kinda," Jarrod said sarcastically, shrugging.

Madame Patricia continued without hesitation. "Time has no effect on Oreios and his kind because he has no soul or version thereof. Ourea were strictly elemental and therefore can't decay, but go through changes of certain kinds. Time and space have no effect on them because when time and space cease to exist, so do they. Therefore, Oreios and his species are truly physically immortal until they are broken apart by a physical alteration. The human soul is a light that transcends the physical. The Ourea have not an afterlife, unlike mortals."

"Afterlife? Heaven?" Austin asked, squinting. Lian could hear in his mind as he tried to comprehend, but he was too jaded by the death of his parents to give the ideas the credence they needed to be understood. "You mean religious concoctions you just labeled as physically existing?"

"The great misconception of existence is to think myth and religion to be opposites of science. You think of them as black or white, truth or fallacy, when in reality they're the opposite sides of the same coin." Madame Patricia brushed past Jarrod and walked over to the bar.

Lian thought she heard an inflection in Madame Patricia's voice giving away the fear she was trying to mask, or had something else betrayed her?

Madame Patricia examined the glass of wine, tilting it side to side. She took a gulp and set it down with enough force to crack the stem. "We're the grooves between the two faces of a quarter, able to touch either side. What heads may do through experimentation and technology, tails does just as naturally as you breathe."

"If we're not on Earth, where are we?" Claire hyperventilated and bent over to collect her breath.

"We're at a point in space where a day here is, what, a year on earth?" Austin contemplated, looking at Lian as she tried to get Jaden's attention. "He didn't initially recognize his sister because to him they were separated yesterday?"

"It was twelve years ago." Lian touched Jaden's face. Her fingers glowed when their skin connected, as did his cheeks. He looked at her with a slight smile. "He's not but maybe a year older."

"Time on Earth moves thirty times faster than it does here?" Austin's eyes were wide with shock as his mind quickly did the math.

"God's time..." Jarrod whispered.

"Yes, it has been called that," Madame Patricia replied to Jarrod with a smile. "You've been here almost twenty minutes, which means it's already morning time where we picked you up. Believe me when I say this, there are places where time moves even slower than it does here, and there are beings capable of comprehending the static of it all simultaneously."

"How old are you?" Jarrod asked Madame Patricia and then looked at Athena. "And her?"

"I'm unquantifiable to you."

"You look like you're in your 70's." Jarrod smirked. "Seems pretty quantifiable to me."

"I'm flattered." Madame Patricia rolled her eyes and crossed her arms, countering his sarcastic tone tit for tat. "I look this old because recent struggles took a toll. My physical makeup is different than a human's, as is Athena's. Harold's is different still as he is something known as a half-breed. The three of us age at different rates to you. Athena has been here for eighty years…"

"Wow." Jarrod looked her up and down. Claire pinched him.

"The mind can only mature at the rate of the body. She's in her mid-twenties. Harold was born in the fifth century. Physically he is mid-40's…"

"And mentally some would say thirteen," Athena joked, holding back a smile.

"And she's unquantifiable," Jarrod added, pointing his thumb at Madame Patricia while turning to walk away. "What a crock. We came for answers, not a lecture."

"You're a speck of dust in a cosmic cube." Athena stood in his way. They connected eyes, ignoring everyone else. "To you, answers would be a lecture."

"Don't you want to know about yourself? William talked a great deal about you," Madame Patricia called, lifting her voice. Jarrod stopped dead in his tracks, cast his eyes down and looked over his shoulder. He shook his head and left. She continued despite his absence. "That's a shame."

"He's going through some things right now," Austin joked nervously.

"Athena, take Jaden to his room," Madame Patricia commanded while nodding to Austin's comment.

"What? No, I want him to remember me," Lian protested, pulling at her brother. Their grip on each other grew stronger, glow brightening. She'd just found him again and wouldn't let go. With ease, Athena pushed Lian onto her hind end and pulled Jaden away. Lian shoved her face into Austin's chest and wept. "Why…?"

"William had his reasons for splitting you two." Madame Patricia put a hand on Lian's back. She pulled her hand back quickly, as if Lian were a hot stove, and walked away. "You'll find you and I have a lot in common."

"I wish I could have just been normal." Lian pulled on Austin. Her tears soaked his shirt. He sat slowly on the ground and wrapped his arms tightly around her.

"Shh, it's gonna be alright," he whispered, rocking back and forth.

184

CHAPTER NINETEEN

Austin III

That last conversation didn't sit well in Austin's stomach. A sour note hung in the air, and it was more than just the bitter scent of pipe tobacco and wine stains making him gag. Since his parents were murdered by radicals in Lebanon, Austin had eaten more than his fair share of lies and secrets. The taste of them could no longer be choked down, especially when someone he cared so deeply for suffered because of it.

Sure, he was grateful for Madame Patricia and her people welcoming them into her realm for safekeeping. It beat the hell out of grunting it out on that god forsaken freight ship, or running from whatever might be hunting him and his friends. However, as he held Lian in his arms, feeling her shake with grief, he'd decided that Madame Patricia's casual dismissal of their questions and feelings wouldn't be tolerated.

"Don't say anything." Lian grabbed him. She had to be peeking inside his head again. "I was. Sorry. You were practically screaming your intentions."

"I'm tired of just falling in line. Nothing good can come of it."

"So you can see the future now?" she asked, but wasn't playful about it. Was it intended to be a slight? "No, it wasn't." Again, she'd replied to his thoughts.

"I'm here for you. I am. I know you're emotional because you just found your brother, but I'm serious when I tell you to stop snooping in my mind." Austin stepped away from her. If he didn't get his space, he might say or think something he'd regret. He tapped his head for emphasis. "What happens up here is mine and mine alone. You need to understand that." Her fingers slid up his back, between his hulking shoulder blades. She hugged him from behind, but he didn't care to accept the embrace. "You need to learn the difference between friend and foe."

"Those things were nearly the same when I was with Sanderson."

"You're not anymore," he replied. He waited for a retort. It didn't come. There was no way he could've really shut her up. "I would think by now you could trust me. My mind doesn't need supervision."

"You think that's what it is?" she asked laughingly. He raised an eyebrow. "It's not." She slapped his arm. "I just like making sure you're safe."

"Thomas Jefferson said you give up liberty for safety and you get neither…"

"That was Franklin," she replied, cutting him off.

"Whatever, it's been a long day." He rubbed his face and stepped between the tables. Claire was sitting with her chin resting on her hands, which were laid flat on the tabletop. "Don't you have anything to add to this?"

"Like anything I do or think has much of a consequence." Claire rolled her eyes.

"Shit, you two." Austin rested his hands on his hips. The self-prescribed haplessness in the room was almost tangible. He pointed at Claire. "You, buck up and quit moping."

"I'm not moping," Claire whined. She looked at Lian who smirked and nodded in agreement with Austin. "Whatever."

"And you," Austin added, pointing at Lian.

"Who, me?"

"Yes, you."

"What about me?" she asked.

"Stop snooping on the good guys and start working your magic on the unknowns. I don't want to stay around here any longer than we have to. I don't have a good vibe about this place."

"Is that one of your new spider-senses?" Lian giggled, casting playful flutters of her eyes toward Austin.

"Stop it." That shit was pissing him off. Madame Patricia really didn't give an answer as to why Sanderson had decided to separate Lian from her brother. Something wasn't meshing well and he needed all those he could trust to pull it together. "I'm just going to say what we're all refusing talk about: what the hell is wrong with Jarrod?" Claire's eyes vaulted up and Lian stood straight. He waited for them to add something to the conversation, but nothing came of it. "He's still our friend…"

"Is he?" Lian asked sharply. Claire shot her a look and Lian continued. "I didn't mean for it to sound like *that,* but we don't really know what we're dealing with. The Double-Helix would break down test subjects in a matter of months. It's been over a year for him. Maybe instead of physical decay it's warping his mind."

"He's still our friend. So whatever it is, we deal with it and take it on the chin if we have to." Austin stood rigid and squared his shoulders, expressing a dominant pose. The ladies were visibly unimpressed. "God knows he'd do whatever he could for us."

"I could try talking to him?" Claire sounded unsure, as if prodding for affirmation. Lian and Austin ignored her to banter back and forth.

"Austin, he nearly ripped your arm off," Lian chided.

"But he didn't. And he stopped a container from crushing me," he replied. She gave him a 'so what' smirk and cupped her hand behind her ear. That irritated him further. "You convinced Jarrod and Sanderson to walk into a trap while Charon and Argus launched a full scale assault. You then nearly beheaded Sanderson…"

"I was under Maya's influence, in case you don't remember." Her nostrils flared as she scowled and turned red.

"How's this any different?" He cocked a satisfied grin when the words slapped her face and sealed her lips. Immediately, guilt rooted out the happiness he felt putting her in her place. It wasn't like him. "I only wanted to point out that you of all people should know what it's like to not be yourself, and to have someone else fudging with your upstairs."

She nodded. "I've been a bitch."

"A massive one," he agreed.

Her eyes widened and her face went flat. "Let's not get too excited about that admission."

"I'm gonna hear about it later, aren't I?" he asked, but she continued to stare in silence. "Yeah. Dammit."

"None of this solves the Jarrod issue, or the lack of any real answers we just got," Claire said. The others looked her way and she sunk back in her seat. "Right?"

"Completely." Austin squinted at Lian. He was going to get answers from Madame Patricia, no matter what. Lian reluctantly waved him off.

Jarrod returned just as Austin was about to march off. He seemed out of it. Austin put his mission on standby, worried that the worst was about to happen. His longtime friend looked up, released a heavy sigh, and sat next to Claire to bury his forehead into her shoulder. Claire rubbed the back of his head and nodded at Austin that they were fine.

"Keep me posted on them," Austin whispered to Lian as he pulled her in close. She kissed his cheek and nodded.

He wandered through the building. It was immense—much larger than it appeared from the outside. It was strange how so many spacious rooms and hallways could be crammed into one tiny hut. Then again, was it really a hut or was that some sort of illusion to fool anyone who might try to sniff them out?

Austin approached a room at the far end of the hallway. Harold and Madame Patricia spoke quietly, oblivious to Austin's presence.

Curious, Austin pressed his back to the corner of the maple-panel wall and listened.

"He's not to be trusted," Madame Patricia said softly. "The others are going to push back. The changeling and powerless one should be easy to contend with, but the mind reader will be a handful."

"Why did you send for them?" Harold's whisper was more like a quietly forced grunt. "We could've easily just ignored them. Maybe they would've been caught and dealt with accordingly. The Assassins have a bounty on them. You know what that means, right?"

Assassins? Austin thought.

"You can't trust Svarog. He's a jilted coward."

"You just said we can't trust Jarrod either," Harold retorted. "You'll have to pick a side. At least cowards are known for spilling their guts."

"There are plenty of sides to choose." Madame Patricia took a sip of wine. Her eyes moved in Austin's direction. He pulled his head back and disappeared in the shadows before she could see him. "The age of revelation is fast approaching. It is best to juggle all sides until there are fewer to choose from."

"As far as the celestial clock is concerned, these are mere infants. What use are they?" Harold asked with a frustrated growl.

"Did you not see what those infants did in Moscow?" Madame Patricia giggled. "That was half of a legion's army laid to waste like a Sunday brunch. Imagine when the baby's appetite grows into a teenager. Will you be so quick to dismiss their side then?"

"The smart play would be to hand them to the Assassins and gain favor with the Archangels," Harold quickly replied. He spoke so low and fast that if it weren't for Austin's heightened sense of hearing, none of it would have been understood. "Don't let the children grow."

"You'll do no such thing!" Madame Patricia bellowed. Austin caught her jetting to her feet through the distorted reflection of several silver plates in a display case. "Jaden's kind is being hunted down..."

"Yeah, by the Assassins."

"Shut your yap until I am done speaking." Energy shot from her hands and a shockwave rippled through the air like a tsunami, scattering the furniture in the room. "This is not a forum for open debate. You will not speak over me."

"Yes ma'am." Harold leaned back away from her with his head down.

"The truth of the matter is that the woman detective that continuously snooped around where she didn't belong may have—unknowingly—been onto something."

"Emma?" Harold asked.

"Yes, now don't mention that bitch's name again." Madame Patricia raised her hands and the furniture realigned itself. "She was so fixated on the Ourea, that one girl, and Durga's gem, that she never thought to think why *that* girl. She was so busy looking for a religious reason behind it." Madame Patricia leaned over a chair and wrung her frustration out on it, snapping the wood in half.

"That's right," Harold said with pep in his voice. "When we was rummaging through her partner's belongings, Oreios said it was odd his kind would be up in this part of the world, preferring warmer climates. Emma..." Harold choked back the name when Madame Patricia glared at him. "I mean, that bitch said she was just looking for that type of religious fanaticism. She didn't think to broaden it to other kids."

"It was about the type of kid, not just the ritual." Madame Patricia and Harold went silent. Austin could sense his presence was being observed, so he turned the corner to get the inevitable over with. Madame Patricia appeared none too shocked. "Catch an ear full?"

"Plenty of it." Austin nodded. "Care to explain to me how Oreios was marching around here when he was supposed to be in custody? Did you break him out?"

"It would be a mistake to think a man like Oreios was being kept in custody without allowing himself to be." Madame Patricia grinned. She looked at Harold and continued their conversation. "There were other children being used in similar rituals. Children that shared similarities with the girl that female detective was fixated on. We need to find out more about them, and just how those Ourea were tracking them down. We do that, and we can protect Jaden from the man who is coming to get him."

"And who would that be?" Austin asked, standing as such that he demanded Madame Patricia's attention.

"An ancient one just like me." She looked at him with an unnerving force. "He's not the type to be trifled with."

"And you are?" Austin asked, squinting at her.

"That's beginning to change."

"What about the Assassins?" Harold shivered at the mention of their name. Austin was intrigued. The way Harold fidgeted meant he'd run into them before. "They're out there and they won't stop until they get what they're after."

"Have you learned nothing from history?" Madame Patricia asked. "You of all people should know what the Assassins are capable of."

"I do," he said, lowering his collar to expose three jagged scars at the top of his chest, just below the clavicle. "They killed my family when the Saxons came. The mark from that day reminds me every waking hour."

"You would hand us over to them?" Austin grabbed Harold by the shirt and lifted him off the ground with ease.

Harold growled through his teeth, "You know the old saying mate: if you can't beat them..."

"Then you try harder." Austin tossed Harold backwards. "You're no different than anyone else we've come across."

"Then maybe you should start to catch on," Harold replied, rubbing the back of his head and adjusting his clothes as he stood. "I'm afraid you've worn out your welcome. This realm no longer offers you safe harbor."

"That's not for you to decide, Harold," Madame Patricia snapped.

His breathing intensified. "You're making a mistake."

"Now you intend to tell me that I'm wrong?" She swiveled in place, folded her arms, and ground her teeth. Austin could tell she meant business. "If we're reexamining someone's welcome, maybe we should start with yours?"

"I've been like a son to you. I have followed you in everything, and this... You choose them?" Harold shouted. His hands were shaking, as was his jaw. His right eye twitched. "If you think Set and his cronies don't already have you in their sights, then you're the fool. The best thing to do is slap a bow on this lot. Everyone loves a good Christmas present."

"It's not just them you would be handing over, Harold. It's the collateral damage." Madame Patricia snapped her fingers and a pink vapor trail stabbed through Harold, dragging him into a rift until he was gone from their sight. She fell to her knees, holding back cries. "Harold, what did you make me do?"

Austin froze in shock. Even though he didn't trust Madame Patricia much more than he already had, he knew that whole expulsion scene wasn't for show. The anguish she held in her forehead, cheek and jaw was a dead giveaway of as much. If she could easily dispose of someone obviously so close to her, then what would she be willing to do to him and his friends? What was she really protecting? He had to know.

"He had a point," Austin said.

"He usually does, but that doesn't mean it isn't misguided." She stood and walked over to an unopened bottle of wine. The cork popped out and into her palm with just the wave of a hand. She poured two glasses and gave one to Austin. He didn't dare to refuse it.

"Don't get me wrong. I'm happy you chose us over him, but you're insane if you don't think he's running to these Assassins now.

Unless you killed him." Austin thought about it for a second. He was nervous to ask. "Did you kill him?"

"No." She sipped her wine. The volume in her glass suggested she had a thirst for it, but the slow, uninterested way she sipped it suggested it was the furthest thing from her mind.

"Who is taking Jaden's kind and how do we stop him?" Austin asked, drinking a good amount of the wine in order to brace for the answer.

"It's sweet you feel like helping, but really you don't have to." She smiled at him. "I'll be fine."

"I'm not doing it for you." Austin emptied the glass into his belly and set it aside. "If Heaven's real, and they've got these Assassins that have Harold that scared, they mean business. You shook them off like they were nothing. You threw Harold out like yesterday's newspaper. Why? What has you so worked up that the raging bitch I met when I first got here is all of a sudden sitting on her hands?" Austin took the bottle and poured himself some more. He was talking serious shit to a woman who could easily tear him apart with the snap of her fingers. More courage was in order. "I'm not in this to help you, or make you feel better or more at ease with the many poor choices I'm sure you've made over the years." He took another big swig. "I'm doing it because I love Lian, and her brother is incredibly important to her, as he seems to be to you. So maybe through this common goal we can get past the lies or the blatant omission of truth, air out our secrets and get something done."

"I like you." She smiled, drinking her wine.

"And I like this shit." He finished his second glass. "So, we cool?"

Madame Patricia tipped the bottom of her glass in the air, but kept her eyes trained squarely on him. She looked at the empty bottle and then cocked her eyes at Austin. He nervously awaited her answer.

CHAPTER TWENTY

Jarrod III

Everyone was frantic and talking over one another. The jumbled roar of their bickering raked across Jarrod's brain louder even than the voice that only he could hear. This was all wearing thin. Athena was barking at Madame Patricia about casting Harold from their realm. Lian was yelling at anyone standing close by, wanting answers about 'her kind' and asking 'why she and her friends don't just leave with her brother'. The only one who resembled anything close to calm was Jaden.

The boy sat in the corner, kicking his legs with his feet dangling several inches off the ground. The bowl of pudding on his lap held more intrigue than the constant arguing of grownups.

"Must be delicious," Jarrod said to himself, smirking. He folded his arms and leaned back in his chair. Jaden noticed him and mirrored the movement. "Chocolate?" Jaden nodded. Jarrod grinned. "My favorite. I like whipped cream on top. Ever had that?" Jaden shook his head no. "We'll have to change that sometime."

"Don't you have anything to contribute to all this?" Lian poked Jarrod's shoulder. He didn't bother acknowledging her. "I'm talking to you."

"No, you're yelling." Jarrod moved to sit by Jaden, pulled a quarter from his pocket, and spun it on the tabletop. He gently flicked it with his finger to keep it spinning. "The trick is to wait until the quarter is at the perfect speed and to lightly nudge it. Do it too hard and it'll fly off the table. Do it too soft and it'll fall flat. You try it."

"You can't be serious right now." Lian slammed her hand over the quarter and pushed it off the table. "We're being hunted. Did you hear that?"

"This is news to you?" Jarrod laughed sarcastically. "Seriously, when do we not have someone trying to bring us in for a science experiment, some douche trying to slit our throats, or some whore-mongering bitch trying to seduce us into joining her army? This is just another day at the office. You want me to get worked up over it?"

"Trust me, no one wants *you* worked up." Austin pulled Lian away from Jarrod's personal space. "Just, ya know…"

"Supposedly I don't know what I know, so you tell me." Jarrod shrugged and threw his hands up in the air like he was giving up. This was all getting old, and he wanted to break the cycle. He didn't trust himself, but he trusted himself more than he did Madame Patricia or anyone else who might be playing games. All options were dangerous.

It was time to part ways. His friends felt like they were walking on eggshells around him, and maybe they were. He couldn't really help that. In fact, he had his own demons that needed attending to. Certainly it wouldn't be a good idea to throw himself into a situation where the voice in his mind was in a position of influence. That was no way to help his new family.

"I still understand not why Harold was expelled," Athena said, pacing in circles. "He was our most trusted ally."

"I had the same question," Austin added. "Obviously Miss P. here is hiding something."

"I am ready for a fight." Athena smacked her left palm over her right fist. "Let them bring whatever force they want."

"The truth is Jaden wasn't the only one brought to me for safe keeping," Madame Patricia replied with a weary voice. She rubbed the tension from her face and spoke through her hands. "You were brought to me by an inside source. If your existence is revealed then there will be many brought into the light and whole realms of Descendants all over creation will die."

"So this isn't just about me and my brother?" Lian asked, as if offended.

"Sorry girly, but the world doesn't revolve around you," Madame Patricia said sassily. "You're here now. You're more than welcome to try things on your own, but you can't have your brother."

"As if you can stop me!" Lian yelled, Austin trying to restrain her. "Look at me, old woman. Do you know who you're messing with?"

"Do *you*?" Madame Patricia replied, the floor rumbling. "The many cogs in this machine are working overtime, and if one of them doesn't get cast out soon then they all break. Sorry to say, but that's you."

"You won't treat us like that." Austin stood in front of Lian and his eyes took a fierce shape. Athena stood in front of Madame Patricia. "Don't make me go through you."

"Have you lived a good life?" A static-charged purple glow slithered over Athena's body. Just as she and Austin were about to exchange blows, Jarrod jumped to his feet.

"Enough!" he yelled with such force that his skin turned blue. A blinding light beamed from his eyes and fingers, and the aurascales slowly swam to the surface of his skin. His voice was hollow. "The bickering ends. The secrets end. No more darkness."

"I see it," Madame Patricia said with a breathy voice. "The thing William feared."

"I see it every day," Jarrod replied, grinning.

"Perhaps one issue at a time?" Athena slowly stepped away from Austin and Lian with her hands up.

"Sounds like a plan." Austin nodded, pulling Lian away.

"Start with Lian's kind being collected," Jarrod said, pointing at Madame Patricia. "That is the most pressing issue."

"My kind are ancient beings. The truth of creation as you know it was a partial myth. The one you call God worked with us, the

Architects, to fashion a new place for the most powerful item in all of the many realities: the human soul. The ability to tap into its power can enable you to complete limitless feats." Madame Patricia walked over to Jarrod and stood toe-to-toe with him. "We are the most powerful beings known, but we tremble at the might of a soul. So you can see why Heaven would deem you worthy of assassination. You have to be put down."

"I said start with Lian's kind." Jarrod didn't blink as he leaned in towards Madame Patricia's face. "Get there."

"I am." She smiled. "Ra, a fellow Architect, is collecting those born with powers. I'm not talking about half-breeds like Maya or Harold. I'm talking about powerful individuals like Jaden and Lian. You see, the special abilities those like Harold exhibit don't come because of the angel in their bloodline. They come from the human side in them. Angels aren't the supernatural ones. They're bound by science. The human element is supernatural, but only when those traits are unlocked with comingling of bloodlines with angels. So when pure humans like Lian and Jaden are born, yet exhibit powers, it baffles us. Their proximity factor seems unique," she said, pointing at Lian and her brother. "The closer they are, the more in sync their abilities, and the more powerful they become."

"So why does this Ra want us?" Lian asked. "What does he gain from it?"

"Aside from the obvious collection of scarce resources, I don't know," Madame Patricia replied.

Jarrod could see she was lying. The same denial he used to see in the mirror was plastered over her face. Her glance in his direction asked him to hold it back. Why? He was not her puppet. Did she think she could control him? More games. Games were getting old. This wasn't a safe place for them to be. Just flat out lies and other ways to keep people under her thumb, that's all this debate was. A big spectacle.

Slit her throat. Put her head on a spike. The urge to punch through her ribcage bubbled and burned with Krakatoan force. No, that wouldn't solve anything. Who cared? It would feel good. It wasn't about feeling good. But who said things like that? The cycle needed to end.

"You do know," he growled. The veins in his arms radiated blue energy. The glow was reflected off their faces. Suddenly he felt himself unable to push it back. The only answer was to run from everyone. "You feel something… The truth about Jaden and Lian."

"They're unique, yes." Madame Patricia nodded.

"Tell us," Athena insisted. She took her surrogate mom's hand. "We can stop Ra."

"When Jaden and Lian are close, their bond amplifies my own abilities. Whatever they are, when they're together they're like Architects." Madame Patricia stared at Jarrod. "If I can sense it, then so can Ra. He must be collecting gifted like them in the hopes of duplicating the process. You see, he can't have her and her brother."

"So you'd give him me?" Lian asked.

"Yes. One is better than both," Madame Patricia replied bluntly.

"That might not be a bad idea," Austin said, drawing surprised and aghast looks from everyone around him, especially from Lian. "Trust me. It's not as bad as it sounds."

"Bait." She put her hands to her hips and squinted at him. "You're going to fish with me on a string?"

"You don't know what it is you're up against." Madame Patricia laughed boisterously. "Ra would skin you alive, and that would be just getting started."

"What if we find the other ones like her?" Athena asked. "We could get them before Ra does and return them to Madame Patricia for safe keeping. With Lian's powers and the research already done by that detective, how hard could it be?"

"Plenty hard." Madame Patricia sat at a table with her back turned to the group.

"We have something he's afraid of," Athena said, standing behind Madame Patricia. "We've got Jarrod on our side. Teach him how to control his powers and he can stop Ra."

"That's where you're wrong," Jarrod said. Everyone turned to him. "This can't be controlled. It sinks its noose into me tighter each day. You don't have me."

"Jarrod's right, you know," Madame Patricia added. "He's a different breed: simultaneously human and angel. When you were a child, Sanderson saw the raw power. Whatever your mother did kept you from learning to cope. By now, you're a nuclear bomb of pent up energy. Even if you wanted to control it, you couldn't handle it all at once."

I can, the voice in Jarrod's head said. Lian gave him a weird look as if she heard something.

"Jarrod?" she asked.

"You guys are on your own. There's nothing more I can do for you." Jarrod headed for the door despite the pleas from his friends to help.

"It's just as well," Madame Patricia spoke up, stopping Jarrod in his tracks. "With the Assassins on his heels, he'll be dead soon anyway. No sense in bringing that sort of heat down on the rest of you."

"You may think you're being a colossal cunt," Jarrod said, turning around, "but I couldn't agree with you more."

CHAPTER TWENTY-ONE

Jarrod IV

The wind howled up the hill causing the long blades of grass to bow at its command. A salty chill filled the air. The smooth, cloudy skies blocked out the moon and stars. There seemed to be no end to the black, lifeless water, and only the gentle stirring of the tide upon the sands lifted its voice. Jarrod's breath froze every time he exhaled. He rubbed his arms feverishly to warm himself as the stiff breeze along his skin numbed the shredding ache of the aurascales inside his body. When his efforts to warm up proved to be futile, he relented and allowed the aurascales to crawl over his skin to regulate his body temperature. They no longer prodded at him for release.

"There are no answers out there." Athena approached from behind. She noticed his aurascales. Hers also formed, seemingly as a precaution. Their heads remained uncovered.

"And they're in there?" Jarrod kept his focus ahead, pointing over his shoulder with his thumb at the Progeny Lounge. "This isn't my journey. Only thing I'll find in there is another version of someone else's truth."

"Time is relative, remember? Not truth." Her voice was soft, yet exuded confidence. Jarrod glanced at her, his eyes saying 'bullshit.' She continued. "A skeptic..."

"A realist," he said, cutting her off. "When you've been through what I have and seen what I've seen..."

"Oh, I am sorry. I did not realize you were the preeminent authority on sob stories and the universe." Athena crossed her arms, scowling at him while shaking her head in frustration. "Twenty plus years on Earth..."

"Twenty-three, now." He grinned, disrupting her train of thought in order to humor himself. Her nostrils widened. The residual ache of her cross-hook upon his chin reminded him to not irritate her too much.

"Whatever," Athena said, raising her voice. She stomped the ground and turned to leave, but stopped and looked over her shoulder. "I did not come out here to freeze my ass off."

"I'm sorry, wait," he laughed, grabbing her wrist. She pulled away, still marching. He ran to catch her and stood in her path. "I'm an asshole when I'm nervous. And frustrated... and sad, and sometimes happy... Pretty much all the time. Shit, I suck." Her eyes enlarged, leaning forward and awkwardly inspecting him. Jarrod leaned back to increase his personal space. She was being straight up weird. "What are you doing?" he asked.

"You said you were an asshole," she replied, smelling him. "Funny, you only half smell of feces."

"Wait, what?" Jarrod smelled his armpit. "No, I was joking. It's a figure of speech." Athena giggled, putting her right hand over her mouth. Maybe humor and jovial sparring weren't completely lost on her after all. "You're joking," he said, giving her fake applause. "Very well."

"I am not ignorant of sarcasm, metaphors or modern idioms." She stood rigid. Her tone and facial expression were serious. Even though the moment was light, Jarrod still got the impression she felt the need to prove herself.

"Of course." Jarrod nodded in agreement. "If you didn't come out here to freeze your ass off, then why did you come?"

"To get a look at you and your armor." She pointed at his aurascales. "I was told stories about you. Well, not you in particular."

"About who, then?" His words were quick, his heartbeat quicker. The eerie itch scratched and clawed at the back his mind the longer he powered the aurascales. He suppressed it.

"I am not so sure I am best qualified to tell you these things." She tried to avoid eye contact. Jarrod wouldn't let her. "Madame Patricia should be the one."

"I want to hear it from you." He put his fingers to her chin and moved her face up. His thumb rubbed the side of her cheek and elicited a smile. There was a force between the two attracting him to her. His aurascales wanted to bond. They tried persuading him like a devil on his shoulder. "Something about you says you're more honest than Madame Patricia. I don't know if we should trust her."

"Nonsense. She has always taken care of me." Athena shook her head, having none of that talk.

"It's just a feeling I have. You can't really help those." Jarrod stepped away and folded his hands behind his back. His heart still belonged to Claire even though there was a primitive allure about Athena. He knew there was another hand at work. He could sense it. "The more we work together, if that happens, then maybe I'll trust her more. But right now my gut says she's hiding something. My gut is rarely wrong, except on the occasions it says 'have that 17th deep fried taco'. In which case it punishes the shit out of me. Literally."

"Another joke." She smirked. "Crude humor and self-deprecation. Harold has taught me about that. Quite funny."

"Typically you're just supposed to laugh." Jarrod shrugged. The self-awareness of this chick was off the charts.

"You say your feelings persuade your rationality when it comes to the Madame, but there should be a line at which logic is transcendent." Athena stood by his side and looked out over the waters. The tone in her voice carried the sort of conviction radicals exude in their black and white views of the world. Jarrod knew there were only different shades of gray. Immediately, big signs urging caution when working with

Athena and the others flashed brightly in his mind. "Have you never closed your eyes and fallen into someone else's arms?"

"We did that in high school."

"I mean metaphorically." Her brows furrowed while her nose scrunched sideways. She didn't seem impressed.

"Yes. I know." He chuckled and folded his arms. "That just makes you dependant on someone else. If you really want to get by you need to brace yourself for the fall and learn to dust yourself off."

"But you would not need to fall."

"You always fall." His words shut her up. Not in a delicate, contemplative sort of way either. Her face was stunned. An awkward silence accompanied the salty chill. "You don't have to take it personally. It's just my opinion."

"What if someone was strong enough to lift you up?" she asked. "Would you have faith then?"

"If they were strong enough then what do they get out of lifting me up?" he replied.

"Maybe they are just with you in battle?" Her voice was stressed and agitated.

"Then fight by my side, not behind me to lift me up." He was done with the debate. None of what she said was going to change his mind. What did she have to gain out of trying so hard to alter his opinions anyway? "The people with the most hidden are the ones behind you. Why would I want them propping me up? If I allowed myself to count on them then I'd be helpless when I fell."

"What if there was no ulterior motive?" She stepped in front of him and lowered her head. She was tall for a chick—they were roughly the same height. "You would expect those not on par to stand as equal?"

"Better than using me as a shield. That does neither one of us any good in the end. Stand on your own feet."

"Why are you so standoffish?" She reached for his face and he jerked away. "We mean only to help. You should know you are uniquely in a position to help us and others. In turn we can help you."

"I don't need your help. And if you knew a thing about me, you wouldn't want mine. You'd want to run as far as you could."

"I'm a capable person." Her words struck a chord. Maybe that's what his aurascales were trying to relay. He may be powerful enough to destroy those closest to him, but Athena was more than capable of holding her own and knew what it was like to bear the burden of the armor.

"That you are." He nodded. "But I think at this point I'm better off solo. My friends are grown ass people. They can decide to stay with you or leave."

"But not to follow you?" she asked.

"Now you're getting it." He gave her a 'thumbs-up' and brushed past her on his way to the water line. He knelt and sifted his hand through the damp, clumpy sand. His armor shielded him from the jarring cold of the sea, but relayed to his mind the understanding of what he would be feeling with bare skin.

"You are either supremely arrogant or ignorant. It seems like a perfect combination of the two." She stood over him and shoved him into the water. He kicked himself off his back and stuck his landing. His wet hair hung over his scowl. "You are oblivious to what looms over you. There will be a time when you need someone."

"Tell me what's out there, then," he said, but he continued speaking before she could get another word in. "Oh yeah, that's right. That's up to the Madame to discuss. Only problem is, that old broad is playing her own game. But I won't be one of the cards in her hand."

The area around him grew bright with a bluish hue. His aurascales beamed. Athena's eyes widened and she stepped away from him. She raised her arm to shield her eyes from the glare.

"The lives of many who cannot fend or fight for themselves depend on us. We could use your help." She backed up and stumbled, but continued to crawl away from him as he pursued. "Your aurascales are raging. I mean you no harm."

"Why don't we work our way up to that part? Working together, that is." Jarrod snatched up her hand and pulled her off the ground. His armor returned to a neutral state. He hadn't meant to send Athena the wrong message by scaring her. In fact, he was sympathetic to their cause. The whole reason he joined the Army Rangers was to help those who couldn't defend themselves. He thought about what she'd said. He wanted to hear more, but first needed to have something answered. "You called them aurascales, why?"

"That is their proper name." She tepidly accepted his support in standing.

"That's funny, I thought we named them." Jarrod rubbed the back of his head, pondering. His thoughts began connecting dots he didn't think could be there. Jarrod thought back to when he was training to be a Double-Helix agent. Jackson had said Elliot named the armor. How could he have known they were called 'aurascales'? "Does the name Elliot Foster ring a bell?"

"No. Should it?"

"I guess not." The calm luminescence of their aurascales reflected off the rippling water. The radiance of her purple sentient armor caught his eye. "You look familiar. Not just your armor, but everything about you. Your eyes, your hair, even your face speaks of someone I could swear I've met before." He thought she looked like she could be related to Jackson. "Do you know Maya?"

"I have heard the name." She nodded.

"Are you like her, or are you like me?"

"If I had to choose, I suppose I am like you."

"You're a clone?" he asked. His words visibly shocked her. "It's OK, I know what I am. A lab experiment of something ancient. My mom always called me her little angel. I didn't think she meant it literally."

"I guess that must be a lot to comprehend. To not really believe you have a purpose, to think you are..."

"An abomination of mankind?" He sat down and picked up a smooth stone. His thumb glided over the surface of the rock and then he threw it into the water, skipping it over the waves.

"My existence started a war. Those who killed my parents called me an abomination." She sat beside him. "I was the heir to the throne Maya sat upon. I would have never caused the destruction she did, no matter what past transgressions the fates inflicted upon me. People are quick to excuse the behavior of mad individuals because of their tragic upbringing. I think some people are just evil and have no reasons."

"That's what scares me," Jarrod said, drawing stick figures in the sand. "I believe that too. Can't change human nature, right?" He looked at her and smiled. She stared into his eyes.

"It is not just human nature if we are equally capable." She leaned closer to him, looking at his lips.

"That's right. You aren't technically human." He didn't move his head, remaining still. Their armors flared as they leaned closer to one another. "So, we should just call it..."

"How about primal nature?" She moved over him, pressing her lips against his. Her hand stroked his arm and then moved to his chest. His aurascales reversed their flow and moved onto her fingers. After all, the aurascales Jarrod wore came from Maya and belonged to the Western Corner. They preferred Athena's DNA.

She's playing you. The voice in his head snapped him out of the trance his aurascales had over him.

"What are you doing?" He pulled his head back and twisted her wrist. His elbow forced her away and knocked her into the sand. Jarrod stood with his fists balled up. "You take me for a fool?"

She does. I'm all you really have.

"It is not like that." She flinched, covering her face when he stepped forward. He walked up the hill. She lowered her guard and pulled her knees to her chest. "It's not like that at all."

"Excuse me," Claire said, meeting him at the top of the slope, just outside the entrance to the Progeny Lounge. "I hope I'm not getting in the middle of anything."

"Claire. No." He tried to take her hand but she jerked away. She turned her head and covered her eyes, shaking. "Look, sweetie…"

"Shut up," she growled at him. When she uncovered her face, her eyes were filled with fury. "I get it. Really, I do."

"There's nothing to get…"

"Not anymore there isn't." Claire shoved him away and ran off, slamming the door behind her.

Athena was standing at the bottom of the hill watching on. The aurascales slid over Jarrod's face to hide his embarrassment. This cemented why he needed to separate from the group. The longer he stuck around the harder it'd be, and the more dangerous it would become for them. If only he had the wings to fly away.

CHAPTER TWENTY-TWO

Lian IV

Madame Patricia hugged the wall, stroking her hand across the grooves of the wood. Her eyes gazed longingly at her surroundings. She was moping. It could've been for show, but although it was hard to tell, Lian knew there really was something wrong. Initially she wanted to lend a friendly ear to help console the woman who'd long protected Jaden. Then again, what would she really get out of it? Madame Patricia seemed just as self-serving as everyone else they'd come across. Let her suffer.

Austin and Lian had regrouping to do. They were going to find and recruit Lian's kind before Ra could get his hands on them. Athena had agreed earlier to go with them. It was unfortunate Jarrod was going his own way, but that was probably for the best. The one thing she agreed with Madame Patricia about was him being a time bomb. Friendly or not, explosions are unforgiving to all in proximity.

She was exhausted. The group hadn't gotten any real sleep in days. The time lag didn't help. Whoever was out there on Earth, stealing kids away in the dark, was working at an advantage. Every second put Lian and her friends further behind. Even though they couldn't keep from yawning every three minutes, and their bodies ached just breathing, they had to push forward.

The candlelight to Lian's left reflected hues of orange and yellow off Madame Patricia's face and hair. It was obvious she wasn't going away until they said something. Lian nudged Austin. He shook himself from his sleep and propped himself against a sofa.

"Socks and undies," he said in a half-asleep stupor. He'd been drooling.

"Can I help you?" Lian asked Madame Patricia, shaking her head at Austin.

"I just wanted to make sure the accommodations are acceptable," Madame Patricia replied. "You don't have to leave so soon, you know."

"We're not rocking back and forth, and my stomach isn't upside down. This is the most comfortable I've been in weeks." Lian took a contemplative breath, thinking twice before allowing her question to find its way out. Her powers scintillated with her brother and Madame Patricia so close. "Do you plan on keeping Jaden?"

"You're his last remaining kin. The decision should be yours. I just want you to make an informed choice."

That was a surprising response. Completely counter to their previous argument. She must want... no, she needed something. But what? Lian approached with caution.

"I'm taking him with us. You know that, right? He's not staying." Lian stood to reinforce her position. She swore there was a mental signal coming from somewhere. She was inside someone else's thoughts. It wasn't Austin.

"If, after everything you've learned, that is the choice you make, I will honor and stand by it." Madame Patricia gave a conceding nod. "However, if you determine the most suitable place for him is by my side, I will honor your wishes just as I've done Sanderson's all these years. He isn't experienced like you are."

"Why would he want us separated? There wasn't much Sanderson couldn't conceal," Lian said, stepping forward. Madame Patricia quickly held a hand up, stepping back apprehensively. Lian furrowed her brow line, shaking her head. "Are you scared of me?"

"Not of you." Madame Patricia grabbed the door knob and attempted to close it.

"Excuse me," Claire said, barging into the room. She sat next to Austin's things and covered her eyes. While the attention was focused on her, Madame Patricia slipped away. "I don't even know what I'm doing here."

"Oh, girl-talk. I'm out." Austin practically jumped from his back and gingerly tip-toed to the door.

Get back here. Lian said, entering his mind. Like a dejected puppy, Austin hung his head and turned around. He sat next to Lian and she rubbed his head, boasting a large smile.

"I get it. I'm a dog. Good boy." He squinted at her, folding his arms. "Don't push it," he whispered. She quickly retracted her hand.

"I thought maybe we were headed in the right direction again, but I saw him with her." Claire pressed her head into her palms and spoke in a rapid, high-pitched whine. "I see you two and how you're able to just comfort each other with a simple look and I want so badly to just be that anchor for him... At first I thought he was just shutting me out to protect me, but what if this isn't really what he wants anymore?"

"I'm sorry, I don't follow," Austin said bewilderedly, pointing at Claire. "Did you catch that? Was that a frequency only girls can hear? I mean, I've got enhanced senses and all that still went right above my head."

"I'm sure it's not what you think," Lian replied while shoving her elbow into Austin's ribs.

"How can it not be?" Claire asked, still speaking at a frequency beyond male comprehension. "He was touching her face and it looked sincere."

"Seriously. Are you reading her mind to get this?" Austin asked.

Go away. Lian slammed the words into his head. Austin breathed a sigh of relief and left the room. Lian rubbed Claire's arm tenderly. "I'm gonna say something, and I don't want you to get offended, but man up. If you don't want to be seen as the powerless and needy one, then don't fit the stereotype. Austin and I are not you and Jarrod. You guys have a history far beyond what anyone else has so quit being a damn martyr and just talk to him. We're all going through stuff, and if he isn't strong enough to deal with his and yours, then maybe it's all for the best. But for the love of god don't come in here again and pine about shit you should be taking care of alone when my man and I are tired and getting ready to wear ourselves out even further. Sheesh."

"Tell me how you really feel," Claire said, wiping the tears from her eyes.

"Believe me, you don't want that." Lian uncrossed her arms and relaxed her shoulders. She took pity on Claire and stood up to give her a hug. "You're great in your own right. Everyone knows that."

"I do," Jarrod said. The girls turned their attention his way. He looked pitiful. Lian remembered the first time she and Jarrod really met. They were in the situation room at the Afghanistan complex, watching Austin and his group attempt to infiltrate Maya's forces. He looked helpless and lost as his best friend was seemingly murdered. The depression in his eyes and body now looked far more devastating than on that day.

"I'm going to give y'all some time." Lian squeezed Claire's hand and carefully inspected Jarrod as she walked by him.

"I'm solid." He nodded, obviously thankful Lian was being so careful with him.

She left the two behind. They had issues to work out. Actually, everyone did. The fact they were all willing to acknowledge those flaws gave Lian a sense of hope. Maybe at the end of all this, there would be a rainbow. Something, anything, to latch onto and offer hope for a brighter future where they could live peacefully.

She watched Austin and Jaden playing with each other and laughing up a storm. A storm; that's a weird way to put it. Storms brew when opposite forces mesh together in a sudden and drastic fashion. While those who came out of the storm were cleansed, it left the air forever changed. The sinking feeling in the pit of her stomach said they wouldn't all make it.

It was then that Madame Patricia's cautioning started to make sense. Jaden wasn't prepared like the others. If someone wasn't going to make it out of the ordeal, he'd be the logical choice. And if they were really going to use Lian as bait for Ra, it wouldn't work with Jaden around.

The pain ripped at her like a heart attack. He was so happy and just now getting used to her again. She wanted to take that away from him? Were these the types of emotions Sanderson had to contend with? When all the choices were bad choices, the only option was the one that minimized the damage. Feelings were better to damage than someone's life.

"What is it?" Austin asked her, smiling while he sat over Jaden and tickled him.

Her younger brother's soft, boyish giggle could melt ice. It was a sound she'd not heard since her family's last summer vacation together. Even then, it was barely a memory. There were times when Lian struggled to remember her mother's face, or the sound of her father's voice when he'd read to her at bedtime.

"Lian?" Austin persisted.

"Nothing." Lian feigned a smile. She didn't need to steal a thought from him to know he could see through that. It was no use denying it. "I think he should stay with Madame Patricia. She's right. It's what's safest."

"Are you sure?" Austin continued to wrestle with Jaden but kept his eyes squarely on his girlfriend. "If it's an issue of keeping track of him while we're out there, know he won't leave my sight."

"It's not." She shook her head and watched them play from a distance. Getting closer at this point and hugging Jaden would just make it harder to do what needed to be done. How in hell did Sanderson keep up his façade without cracking? Well, that was a stupid question. Scotch was the answer. "I need a drink."

"You don't drink," Austin said with a laugh, rolling onto his back as Jaden hopped on top of him.

"It's a good time to start." Lian smiled. Madame Patricia seemed to emerge from oblivion with two glasses of wine in hand.

"Someone said they needed a drink." She smirked Lian's direction, but seemed to have enough sense to keep her head straight and pointed away. It was a nice way of saying she knew she was right without rubbing it in. "I'll continue to guard him as if he were my own blood."

"I know you will." Lian took a sip of the wine. Hot damn was it bad. Her tongue curled and her throat burned. How could people put themselves through that? She tried again, and to her surprise it went down much smoother the second time. Perhaps she could get used to it. "It would be easiest with your help."

"It wouldn't." Madame Patricia seemed sure. "He'd feel my presence right away. The one thing you have in your favor—the element of surprise—would be wasted. The advantage you gain with me in tow wouldn't outweigh that. Get your kind back to me, and then I'll be my most useful."

"Feel your presence?" Jarrod laughed. He and Claire had entered the room but weren't holding hands. There was an obvious distance between them. "Like a Jedi? You're the Luke to his Vadar?"

"What is a Jedi?" Athena asked.

"Never mind." Jarrod slapped his forehead.

Lian and Jarrod exchanged looks. He must've been curious about the drink in her hand, while she wanted to know if he was with them. If he was with them, was he all in and able to cope? The best thing to do would be to keep him on the sideline until it was absolutely essential to bring him into the game. He nodded at Lian, as if reading her mind.

"Where will you go?" Lian asked Madame Patricia, turning to finally acknowledge her. Madame Patricia returned the favor in kind.

"There are ways to slip through the cracks unnoticed." Madame Patricia looked at Jaden like his mom used to look at Lian. "Obviously we can't stay here. But Jaden and I are ready."

"So are the rest of us," Athena said, stepping into the middle of the group.

Were they really? Lian had come around to Madame Patricia's way of seeing things, but she was still uneasy about it all. The storm was raging over warm waters and about to make landfall.

CHAPTER TWENTY-THREE

Anubis II

Could someone please shutoff the ringing in his head? Maybe his brains were mush. His jaw—was it still there? He couldn't feel it. Only one eye opened to take in the scene around him. There it was: the flickering jolt of sensation coming back to his face. It burned like the lashing he'd once received at the hands of Khnum. No. It was much worse. Anubis just wanted someone to put him out of his misery. Anything would do. Take the point of a blade and drive it through the temple.

"Are you lucid?" Khnum laughed, pushing Anubis' head up and back. "This is far worse than the beating I gave you. Do you remember it?"

Every day. Anubis couldn't even groan. His bones felt like sand.

"Let our guest be." Shiva sat in the commander's chair watching the slaves of the Southern Corner guide the Armada Cruiser through the vast emptiness of space.

Khnum acted as Shiva's de facto lieutenant by yelling obscenities at the people who were once his family. When one of them was deemed to be lagging behind on their duties, he quickly struck them to demand compliance.

"Why have we not opened the rift?" Shiva asked politely, yet didn't bother to look up from the piece of fruit he was delicately slicing. He slit the round fruit from pole-to-pole and then around the equator as if it brought him serenity. Anubis' jaw ached just from watching Shiva chew.

Khnum swallowed, noticeably shaken. Copious amounts of sweat soaked his back. "The systems haven't been used in ages – the programs must be rewritten. It helps not that we sustained large amounts of damage while leaving the event horizon."

"Excuses." Shiva stood. Khnum froze. Shiva walked past the nervous slaves and fiddled with the computer. Skanda, his son, entered. Shiva rolled his eyes at the presence of the new arrival to the bridge. "To what do I owe the pleasure?"

"Mother lies in the infirmary awaiting your arrival." Skanda stood to Shiva's six with his arms folded bashfully. His face was long and humble, yet held a reserved sadness, as if expecting this behavior from his father. "Could it be my fault she is in her condition? I should've gotten there sooner to deal with that old bastard."

"The fault is hers alone." Shiva kept swiping away at the light panel. His eyes didn't budge from their position, proving what Skanda must've already known: he didn't care. "Had she more skill and tenacity, Isis would've been captured or eliminated. Instead, she allowed herself to be maimed and Isis to jump across creation. If she expects me to act like a husband, she must earn it."

"Yet we allow the one who did that to her to live," Skanda said through his teeth.

Uncle lives? Anubis' breathing sped up. He was relieved to know he wasn't the only one left.

"Because you failed to retrieve the piece of the Forge from Horus," Shiva replied in a mocking tone.

"You let him get away first," Skanda barked back. Shiva drove a fist across his son's face, knocking Skanda to all fours. The Angel-born held an arm up to shield his face and closed his eyes. "Forgive me for my tone."

"Never forget your place. In the field, you are no better or higher than the rest under my command." Shiva pulled Skanda to his feet by the hair. "Respect and results are my only rules, and you've already broken one of them." His nose pressed against Skanda's cheek while he spoke calmly. "Don't push your luck by getting blasé with the other."

"Yes sir." Skanda nodded. Shiva released his son and turned his attention back to the viewing screen. Skanda looked over at Anubis and shoved a finger into his face. He growled. "What do you think you're looking at?"

"Skanda," Shiva said, causing his son to flinch. "You've no more warnings. I suggest you take leave. Stay by your mother's side like a good nurse."

A few of those from the Southern Corner chuckled. Shiva cleared his throat. Those laughing quickly muted themselves and returned to their work. Skanda looked around, snarling. Sobek was escorted into the bridge carrying a noticeable limp. Skanda reluctantly stomped out of the room, heeding Shiva's intense glare.

"What do we need with him?" Khnum asked. He bowed his head when approaching Shiva to make sure everyone knew he was humble. "A riveting example can be made of Sobek. Your son has a point, though he's unaware of it. We have Horus' cousin. Aside from Isis, there is none he values more."

"Perhaps a showcase will be made in due time," Shiva said. "As for now, Sobek can assist us by changing the codes."

"I'm well on the way to getting us into rift-space." Khnum stepped quickly and stood in front of Shiva.

"That's the problem," Shiva replied stoically. "You're still on the way. I'm quite fond of destinations."

"What d'ya want with me?" Sobek mumbled. He was forced to his knees. He caught a glimpse of Anubis and turned his eyes up. "Khali was nothing."

"She's more than capable of taking different kinds of poundings." Shiva smirked, stepped onto the platform and sat in the commander's chair. He swiveled the seat around to face Sobek. "I've been known to give her one on occasion. I think she'll be fine." Shiva folded his hands in his lap. His confidence was oddly inspiring. The charismatic tone demanded one hang onto his every word. If he weren't the enemy, Anubis could understand how some would follow such a figure.

"Right about now you are probably thinking your resolve will be unaffected by anything I can throw at you. You'd sooner lose a hand than give me what I want," Shiva said. One of his men pulled Sobek's hand forward and laid it across the podium that Shiva's seat was propped up on. Another of Shiva's cronies materialized a sword from their aurascales. "To go ahead and do away with that barrier in your mind, let's have off with it."

Shiva nodded and his pawn sliced through Sobek's arm a few inches above the wrist. His scream caused the fractured bones in Anubis' jaw to vibrate. Sobek curled to the side and crouched into the fetal position. The lackeys passed Sobek's hand to Shiva and he tossed it aside where it landed in front of Anubis.

"You may act as if you've nothing to lose, or you don't care what I do. Just know if that's the case, then I'll get rid of those options in the most gruesome way possible until I find something that gets you to comply." Shiva snapped his fingers and pointed at Anubis. His men dragged Anubis over the podium. A few strained gargles of pain rumbled out of his mouth as they moved him. They put a sword to the back of his neck. "You may act like your hand means little to you, but I'm sure you'll miss the warm embrace it offers as it strokes your cock at night. So tell me, Sobek, do you hold as little love for your dear nephew as you did your five fingered lover?"

"I'm yours to command," Sobek coughed. He rolled onto his face and screamed once again.

"Repeat it." Shiva stood, staring intently at Sobek. "Louder so everyone can understand you. Those among us who would be your brothers, sisters, and lieutenants desire your words. None more than your poor nephew here with a blade to his head."

"I. Am. YOURS." Sobek propped himself up on his knees and cried.

Shiva snapped his fingers at Khnum and had him pull Sobek over to the control panel. Sobek worked as fast as he could, occasionally glancing at Anubis to see if the sword still posed a threat. Finally, he stepped away from the control panel and fell to the ground. Those holding Anubis let him go. He rolled to his side, too weak to hold himself in a crouched position.

"Is it done?" Shiva asked with force.

"It is," Khnum said, breathing a giddy sigh of relief. "We await your coordinates."

Shiva pressed his palms together and slowly pulled them apart. A crystal with pink mist inside formed in his grasp. He raised an eyebrow to Khnum, telling the groveling traitor to step off. Shiva swiped three fingers down the light panel and a flute opened for the crystal. He placed it inside. The ship rumbled as a static force surged through the outer hull. A flare erupted like a pink star and opened the fabric of space.

CHAPTER TWENTY-FOUR

The Observer

Michael walked amongst the thousands of sick and dying, invisible to their eyes. Though his obligation as the last reaper carried him all over the globe, a plague gripping central Africa was the biggest consumer of his time. Every day, countless villages were wiped from existence by the ravages of what humans dubbed 'the rage'. His current stop in Burundi was no different.

The disease broke down human tissue until finally the body oozed itself into an idle state. During a person's last hours, their conscious brain would cease to function, and the primal cortex of their neural patterns would awake to aggressively operate motor functions. Several Red Cross volunteers had been murdered by dying villagers when wandering too close to their patients' bedsides. Even though the sick were too weak to walk, their aggression was so pronounced, so chaotic and exacting, that even a cat with the quickest reflexes stood little chance.

His every minute was spent collecting and absorbing souls for their return to Heaven for their judgment. After enduring the grueling pain and questioning of each soul's death, he periodically vocalized his understanding of the plight Azrael had faced before his banishment. Even though regret for Azrael's situation was plainly visible on Michael's face, he remained steadfast in his dedication to his 'Father's will'.

Maybe Gabriel was right about me being too far removed from my days as a collector to do any real good. Michael shook his head and scowled, showing real emotion for the first time since the Last Great War. *While I still draw breath, I will remain committed to the cause and deliver the promised.*

"You're weary." Raphael stood behind Michael while the Archangel Commander ran his fingers over the face of a dying woman and then down to her belly. A baby kicked his hand from inside the mother's womb. The woman's eyes bled and her skin opened with sores. Raphael moved to his leader's side, examining the woman. "The work of Pestilence?"

"Maybe." Michael knelt and closed his eyes. *I wish there were more I could do for you,* he thought of the unborn child. "This may be one of the horseman causing all this, or maybe we see the fulfillment of prophesies in everyday occurrences. The foretelling of Pestilence may be no more than a vision of what will happen, and not a physical manifestation of a literal being. We know not the whole of what was revealed at Patmos."

"A literal person or not, Pestilence and the other three will come to pass. Maybe some are physical, and others merely ideas, but nevertheless they signal another broken seal." Raphael turned his nose up from the rancid smell. His aurascales crawled over his mouth and nose only, blocking out the stench. "There's much going on in this world, Michael. Are we ready for it? Who will lead us with you gallivanting about?"

"I worry not. Father has his plans." Michael stood, intently watching the woman as she choked on her own blood. *The moment of her departure nears.* "You came to me for a purpose?"

"You spoke with Gabriel at the helm before leaving us behind."

"I did."

"What about?" Raphael asked, seeming to be more interested in the private conversation between the Commander and his right hand man than he should be.

224

The woman's eyes rolled into the back of her head. As if releasing pounds of pressure from her chest, she exhaled. Her soul took the form of a pale blue mist. In the hazy outline, she appeared healthy and rejuvenated. Michael touched the soul and merged it with his being. His eyes sparkled with blue light and his skin held a bluish hue. The pure, raw, and untamed power of the soul coursed through his veins.

Her life's regrets and love for the baby... He calmly breathed and leaned over the corpse to steady himself. *I understand your pain, but your consciousness will not overtake mine.* Michael stood straight and took in a deep, prolonged breath.

"It never gets any easier, does it?" Raphael asked with a furrowed brow. He stood beside Michael, who returned a steely gaze out of the corner of his eyes. "The energy of the soul working inside you boosts your mental and physical capabilities. The change is plainly seen by my eyes. I fear the emotional burden it places on your heart is far greater. That is why the Light of Souls is important—that is why you should not be here now." *You are as close to an unbeatable foe there ever was on the battlefield, yet the power coursing through your blood now makes you even more formidable. Who could possibly go toe-to-toe with a warrior overcome with the power of a soul?* Raphael took Michael by the wrist. "Tell me of your conversation with Gabriel..."

"What he and I spoke of is of little concern to you." Michael gazed intently at the kicking life inside the lifeless womb. The pushing against the mother's womb grew weaker. "I've tasked Gabriel with something important. I need you remain a figurehead at New Zion and make sure all are on task. The corruption in the Light of Souls needs to be repaired. If you feel you should be busy, perhaps starting there would be a good idea?"

"We should reactivate the portion of the Light that works and relieve you of this stress." Raphael walked behind Michael and then stood on the other side. He snapped his fingers, but Michael kept his focus. "This cannot be good for you. Let us help."

"The Light of Souls remains off. We mustn't chance another breach." Michael held his breath as the baby stopped kicking. He placed a hand over the dead woman's stomach. *The heart beats faintly.* "I trust you can relay those commands?"

"As always." Raphael bowed.

"So Gabriel's left?" Michael asked.

"He vanished without a word not long after you did," Raphael quickly replied, as though he wanted to prevent Michael from following up with another question. He didn't give Michael time for his thoughts to linger on Gabriel's supposed whereabouts. "No one doubted either of you. We all remain strong."

Michael nodded. A blue mist appeared. Inside was a blinding white force. It had no shape or form because it didn't live past the age of innocence. It was raw, untamed power. *A second chance at a life awaits you, my sweet darling.* Michael's hand trembled as it extended for the powerful soul.

"I've never seen an innocent soul outside its host before." Raphael watched with anticipation. It was widely rumored in Heaven among those who were not reapers that the energy from an innocent soul could shatter aurascales if one weren't prepared. "I do not wish to possess it, but merely bask in its almighty presence. The rush is exhilarating."

"It would seem as much to the uninitiated." Michael pulled his hand back. The glow of the soul grew dimmer. *It will cease to exist if I don't absorb it. I must be fair.*

Michael grabbed the soul and it merged with him. He crouched, holding his sides. His eyes exploded with blue light and the skin along his cheeks cracked. After a few seconds of immense pain, his body sealed, perfectly healed. His aurascales were radiant.

"I've work to do." Michael walked past Raphael and phased through the hut wall.

"As do we all." Raphael sneered and grinned slyly.

***

"Uriel, you traitor," Gabriel screamed at the top of his lungs, but his words were inaudible to those outside of his frozen armor. He flexed, trying to break free of the prison made of his aurascales. *My brother, why would you do this?*

Uriel and Gabriel were incredibly close. So much so, in fact, that their relationship was often questioned by others. Gabriel had remained steadfast on numerous occasions of the type of affections he held for his first lieutenant. The rules of Father's law were clear. His feelings had never manifested into anything other than a close brotherly bond, outwardly at least. The same couldn't be said for Gabriel's heart. He kept his emotions close to the vest. There could be something there, but any inclination otherwise would be pure speculation to outsiders. If Uriel wasn't the culprit of Gabriel's predicament, then the real perpetrator had used a well-placed guess to trick both messengers into falling for the trap.

"Maybe it was Michael," Gabriel reluctantly admitted. The pieces of the puzzle sure fit that theory. "No one knows me better than him."

A burning sensation surged through his bones. His aurascales once again moved, but this time they were forcibly withdrawn from his body. One would sooner have their bones ripped from their flesh than unwillingly relinquish their aurascales; nevertheless that was the situation Gabriel found himself in. His skin tore apart down his back and over his arms. The slate-gray cubes which formed his armor seeped into the porous metal floor. He was naked again, bleeding from several gashes. Only a necklace with a broken medallion attached covered any portion of his skin.

Raphael paced around Gabriel's head. The two were surrounded on all sides by lower level angels; mostly cherubs who'd recently undergone training to become guardians. They were in the judgment hall, the same place God had proclaimed Lucifer and his legion no longer welcome in Heaven and stripped them of their armor.

"And so, the story comes together," Raphael said in almost a proud tone. "The most resolute follower of God's word is nothing more than a traitorous homosexual."

"What? You have it wrong." Gabriel coughed and rolled to his side. "The truth, I seek it."

"Is that why you bonded directly with your aurascales? A ritual long since abandoned in the name of sanity and progress?" Raphael took Gabriel by the face and lifted him up. His aurascales reinforced his strength, enabling him to hold Gabriel without so much as a wince. "Why would one do such a thing? Do you enjoy the way the aurascales dictate to you and drive your compulsions? Did you not remember the anguish required to sever the bond?"

"I do, which goes to further emphasize my need to remain vigilant." Gabriel could barely breathe. Raphael's massive palm was covering his mouth and nose. "My actions were not taken lightly, but to protect against the Deliverance being used against me in the..."

"That's exactly what a guilty conscience would do," Raphael said, cutting Gabriel off. "Indeed, separating yourself from the Deliverance so that we are unable to sever your link with your starstone is smart, but damning given recent events. You weren't worried the traitor would take advantage of you, but worried we would come to find you were the traitor."

The other angels whispered amongst themselves. Gabriel looked panicked. "No. That's all a lie..."

"Michael is gone and he charged me with repairing the Light of Souls. I've come to find it was your code, Gabriel, which implanted the corrupted file," Raphael said loudly to overcome the roar of shock amongst the others. "Take a look for yourself." The room went dark and several hard light constructs moved into place, forming a monitor. The energy from Gabriel's starstone was like a fingerprint, unmistakably used to override the code in the Light of Souls, locking it in place not long before the second revolt. "The evidence *is* damning."

No. I don't believe it. Gabriel trembled. Raphael threw him to the floor, ripping the necklace away in the process. "There must be an explanation."

The others booed him, encouraging Raphael to continue with his inquisition.

"A code was hardwired into the Light of Souls. The promised have been siphoned since the beginning. We were all played!" Raphael roared with confidence. He walked about the group, slapping their shoulders and patting their backs, getting them riled up. "I see no other course of action than to lock you away like the first morning star."

"You can't…" Gabriel spluttered.

Raphael spoke over the Herald of God. "If you knew there was a fiend in our midst, you'd do the same."

Michael, you set me up. Gabriel fell onto all fours and raked his fingers across the ground. He quietly spoke to himself, "Why? I don't understand it. What advantage do you gain?"

"Speak up, for we cannot hear you," one of the other angels called out.

"Where is Uriel?" Raphael asked. "He stands accused as well."

Gabriel knitted his eyebrows and slowly turned his focus toward Raphael. "He's not among you?" he asked quietly. A light went off in his head. "Uriel is innocent. He took no part in my misdeeds."

"Even still, you show concern for him." A sword took form in Raphael's hand. He held the point of the blade to Gabriel's neck. "Give me not cause to end your life. Deliver your help mate."

Gabriel's chin jutted out and he sat straight and rigid. He stared through Raphael. There was a confidence about him. It wasn't resignation to fate. He had to know something. He took Raphael's blade by the hand and placed it against his own flesh.

"You've hated me because my faith has never broken. You must feel I've yet to be tested, but Father lays strife on my heart every day." Gabriel stood up, still holding the blade firmly against his neck. His hands bled. Raphael was shocked by the outburst.

"What are you doing?" he asked, panic in his gaze.

"You are playing them, Raphael." Gabriel narrowed his eyes. "Your mistake was leaving me no other option than to believe Michael has betrayed me. As I said before, my faith is unbreakable."

"We were played, Gabriel, not you!" Raphael shouted. His right arm shook as he held the sword in place. "We're wise to your game."

"What game? Have I not admitted guilt?" Gabriel smiled. He slapped the blade away from his body and wrapped an arm around Raphael's head to speak only where the two of them could hear. "I know what you are. Just tell me why."

"Because it was all a lie." A dagger manifested in Raphael's other hand. He stuck it into Gabriel's side and twisted. "And you were the strongest believer."

He pulled the weapon from Gabriel's flesh and attempted to drive it into him once again. The others restrained Raphael as Gabriel stumbled back and hit the floor.

"Death to him before he starts the third rebellion!" Raphael screamed.

An angel in unmarked aurascales approached Gabriel and helped him to his feet, moving him toward an exit. When the others noticed, they chased after them. The anonymous angel activated an emergency lockdown for the judgment hall and energy fields blocked off any route by which they could be followed by Raphael and his men. The duo made it to the end of the corridor. Gabriel couldn't take another step. The gash in his side had already begun changing color and the bleeding was constant.

"I'm afraid I know not your name in order to thank you." Gabriel labored to speak. He pressed his hand against the gash, soaking it with crimson. "Raphael's trademark strike."

"You are no traitor," Uriel said as the aurascales slid away from his face. His lips quivered with heartbreak. "You didn't write the code."

"How else could I keep them from blaming you as well, other than to fall onto the blade myself?" Gabriel replied, touching his forehead to Uriel's. His breathing stagnated. "Michael must be warned. Raphael will mislead the others in order to make him the culprit."

"How do you know he's not to blame?" Uriel clung tightly to Gabriel's hands, as if trying to pull him from death's clutches.

"Faith," Gabriel hacked, tapping his chest. "Souls are far too powerful to be contained by just any angel. Only one strong enough has use for them. Raphael will accuse Michael next until total command is his."

Uriel scooped up Gabriel and lumbered forward with fiery determination in his eyes. "I will not give up so easily." He looked at Gabriel, who slowly drifted unconscious. "The aurascales will heal you."

"Mine... are gone." He dozed off, yet still drew faint breath.

Uriel powered into Gabriel's personal quarters. The lights activated, responding to Gabriel's presence. Uriel marched for the halo in his friend's armory and laid Gabriel down in the middle of the catwalk.

Uriel soared to the far end of the room, where Gabriel's starstone used to rest. "I too removed myself from the Deliverance to bond with my star." He looked back at Gabriel and nodded reverently. "I now I give it to you."

Uriel swiped his hand across the control panel and the large slate-gray rings rotated around Gabriel. Uriel ran up the steps of the platform and stood on the opposite end. Static light crackled and tore into him. His skin split apart along his face, legs, abdomen and back, light erupting from his eyes. The aurascales flew off his body and flowed onto Gabriel. The armor pierced into his wounds and sealed them shut. Uriel fell face-first onto the platform while Gabriel slowly pushed himself to his knees. After a few laborious minutes, he crawled over to his friend's side.

"Your sacrifice was not necessary." Gabriel hugged his brother and squeezed tightly.

He turned his head when the walls in his chamber shifted. Someone was here. Gabriel stood to face his prosecutors, and sure enough, Raphael, along with several other angels, walked up the platform of Gabriel's armory and observation deck. Through the glass dome, the rainbow falls erupted with unusual activity. There was no place among them for shadows to hide.

"You stand before us in your friend's armor?" Raphael questioned, his aurascales beaming. A short sword and shield materialized in his grasp. The other angels followed suit. "This is not too unlike the scene that unfolded when you led the charge against Azrael. He stood before you and the others in his full armor, and you questioned his motives."

"That was different…"

"How?" Raphael jumped and landed in front of Gabriel with a thud. A few of the other angels soared across the dome and landed on the other end of the catwalk. Gabriel was surrounded. "Oh yes, it was very different. Azrael rebelled out of love for humanity. His tender-heartedness saw him expelled. That grated at you, didn't it? He was able to inspire a second war all because he was kind and loved. But you, the great messenger of God, the Herald of the all knowing, you were knocked down a peg. You've always looked down on the humans, and so you impregnated the code with a disease."

"I did, and I've used the trust of Uriel against him and stolen his aurascales," Gabriel said, stepping away from Uriel and toward Raphael. "And I will now use the power of the Light of Souls to destroy you."

Raphael's tongue was stilled. His eyes twitched as he searched for words. Confused, he said, "You will have to destroy us from exile." He nodded at the other angels, giving a silent command.

"I am one of the original Archangels." Gabriel's flaming sword exploded with power. "Do not push this any further. You will not like where it leads."

Those Raphael commanded engaged. Gabriel deflected a strike to his right. Raphael's wings sparkled, expanding as he lunged forward. He kicked Gabriel in the chest, knocking him off kilter. A lucky slash caught Gabriel across the tiger helmet and a beam of light protruded through the gash.

A spear thrust into Gabriel's shoulder. Another's mallet went across his shin. They all attacked at once, bringing him to the floor. The eye slits in his faceguard burned crimson and the aurascales vibrated so quickly that they began to sing. He jumped up, slinging the cherubs off.

Gabriel took Raphael by the throat, jabbing his stomach repeatedly. He threw the traitor toward the bottom of the observation dome, but Raphael simply flapped his wings and hovered back toward the catwalk. Gabriel stumbled about woozily.

"Do you feel the poison running through you?" Raphael swooped through the air, knocking Gabriel off the platform like a wrecking ball and onto the glass landing twenty feet below.

Raphael followed, landing on the splintered glass. The massive celestial waterfall of light was in full view. The edge of eternity stood in darkness at the end of the rainbow falls. Only the most prestigious were afforded quarters endowed with the awe-inspiring view. It was also forbidden for any to journey through. The exit on the other side was a great unknown. One might find themselves slipping through the fabric of history.

"You know not what you do." Gabriel tried to sit up, lethargically raising a hand.

"But I do." Raphael knelt to bludgeon with an open palm. "They've all seen the code for themselves. While they're focused on the Light of Souls, I have the real prize." He held up the necklace he tore from Gabriel's neck. A broken piece of the Forge was attached to it. "There can be no third rebellion when the first is yet to be decided."

"No," Gabriel protested. His aurascales retreated from his face and skin to hide inside the body. Blood seeped from his mouth and nose. "You can't set him free."

"You will die, traitor!" Raphael shouted. He slammed Gabriel's head into the tempered glass. He whispered, "Imagine the power he'll contain when he absorbs all the souls I've been siphoning for eons."

Gabriel's aurascales suddenly surged into action. They sealed his wounds and spread across him to form a protective egg shaped cocoon. A pulse of energy knocked Raphael away and destroyed the glass floor. The traitor regained his balance, hovered midair, and watched helplessly as Gabriel's cocoon vanished through the rainbow falls.

He soared back into Gabriel's armory, landing on the catwalk. The others gathered around. Uriel awoke from his separation with his aurascales. Raphael's frustrated and disappointed scowl seemed to bring light to Uriel's hopeful face.

"Where's Gabriel?" Uriel asked, pushing the others away for space to breathe. Raphael knelt beside him, looking down his nose at Heaven's new highest ranking messenger. "Tell me," Uriel pleaded.

"He fell into the darkness, imprisoned like Azrael." Raphael stood, turned his back to the others, and marched off with determination. "We've much to do. We need to ensure the betrayal ended with Gabriel." He stopped and looked at the others. "After all, what would a messenger, someone incapable of harnessing the power of souls, want with the Light?"

CHAPTER TWENTY-FIVE

Horus IV

The land around him was desolate. It had been laid to waste by a riptide of solar magnitude and sucked back into the epicenter. He knew as much from his lessons with Sobek. The sand dancing in the wind like cautious paint strokes of rusted brown, in an impact zone a few miles in radius, was a telltale sign that a starstone had imploded. It must have been a weaker starstone, likely from a muse.

He'd studied guardians losing their lives on the battlefield, desolating mountains, shifting rivers and creating lakes when their starstones were destroyed. There was a famous battle in a place that was once called Babylon, which he'd rigorously investigated for a report at age twelve. A human army led by Alexander the Great had procured a starstone from an angel in the Western Corner, thought to be Poseidon, but its power eventually turned against its wielders and wiped out both armies.

The most recent—and most famous—instance of a starstone releasing its ominous power was when Zeus fought Michael. The two raged in a battle that spanned a solar system. When Michael finally defeated Zeus, the latter's starstone imploded and decimated an entire planet, turning it into an asteroid belt between Mars and Jupiter.

Horus sought the being known as Death. He'd spent several Earth months seeking him and had finally made it to the place rumored to be Death's home, but it was destroyed. There had been a battle of some kind, and an angel or a being in possession of a muse's starstone had lost the fight. The resulting blast had wiped out a town in central Texas. After months of extensive research, Horus finally met a dead end. Maybe this Death perished in the starstone's implosion.

He sifted through the fine dirt and scooped up a handful, opening his fingers and watching it blow away. His hawk-mask formed. The armor alerted him to the presence of human authorities. He heard the sound of aircrafts approaching, though they were still specks along the horizon.

Horus returned to his shuttle. It was a smaller aircraft, built before the Pride Rebellion. It could carry only three passengers. The front windshield slid back into the frame, allowing him to hop into the pilot's seat. The glass covering swooshed shut and the systems slowly powered up.

"Hurry along now," he said, trying to shift energy from the life-support, which he would only need for space travel, into the propulsion system. "You've got a few more flights left in you." He tenderly rubbed the control panel.

In front of him were hundreds of rusted knobs, switches, and levers. The modern comfort of a hard-light control panel was nowhere to be seen. It was an ancient shuttlecraft known as a 'Spear', dubbed so due to its elongated design with a pointed bow and rounded stern. It was an echo of technology long abandoned by the angels from when they held fortresses on the planet. Luckily for Horus, he was able to find one via old maps his father had once had.

Osiris had marked every location where the Southern Corner took up residence. All Horus had to do was dig through a few ancient cities and uncover the Spear. That was important for him to do, as it allowed quick travel across the globe without using the power of his parents' melded starstones.

The levitators kicked on. They sucked air from the top of the shuttle through twenty slits on both the port and starboard, and forced it underneath the craft through six turbines to give him lift. He pulled back on the rear propulsion and a stream of blue and purple fire shot him forward.

The wasteland below quickly turned into rolling hills of grasslands. The shuttle's cloaking device activated before he could be spotted by human eyes. Soon there were thousands of homes filling the landscape, and cars piled on the highways and in parking lots. He plotted a course for his base of operations: Kom Ombo, where his mother and Uncle Sobek used to interact with the humans they guarded, back before the banishment of Azrael brought a change to the angelic order.

It wouldn't be accurate to say frustration was slowly setting in. Horus was long past that point. Desperation would've been a more fitting description for what he felt every waking hour. The only solace he found was in time-dilation—the fact that while several arduous months had passed for him, likely only a few days had elapsed for his mother, cousin, and uncle. Still, whatever use their captors had for them would eventually come to an end. He only hoped his timeline would advance quickly enough for him to garner support before his family became nothing more than history in theirs.

His belly rumbled, not immune to the effects of operating in a different flow of time for prolonged periods. At first, his internal clock worked at the pace of his old realm. Several weeks went by and he ate only a handful of times. By the time two months rolled around, he'd completely adjusted. His normal twice-a-day feeding schedule was replaced by the traditional human cycle of three times a day.

While at Kom Ombo, he discovered stashes of gold and precious jewels. He exchanged those on the black market for human currency, which happened to be Euros, and from there converted the cash into anything that might be useful, including US Dollars and British Sterling.

He rummaged around under his seat and pulled out a bag of peanuts. It was empty, so he discarded it into the growing trash pile in the seats behind him. They were filled with chip bags, burrito wrappers—one of his new favorite meals, despite the odd color it left his feces—along with soda and water bottles.

"I must stop. Is there a taco place nearby?" he wondered aloud. His computer hacked nearby wifi signals. "A hundred results in the next twelve miles," he said with glee. "I like this place."

The Spear dove behind some trees, far from prying eyes. The front hatch opened, sliding back and locking into place, and he exited. His aurascales vanished, leaving behind his frayed beige cloak with bamboo toggles and dark pants. The Spear faded, blending in with its surroundings until it was invisible. He pulled the hood over his head as he approached the fast-food restaurant.

"Yes, I believe supreme nachos and five burritos are in order." The smell made his stomach kick with excitement. While in line, he noticed several customers had their faces buried in their mobile devices while a radio played in the kitchen. The workers seemed more interested in what the voices on the radio had to say than making food.

His ears caught the sound coming from a tablet of a customer sitting near the door. The woman was watching video about a freight ship that had run ashore in Wales the day before, and how local authorities suspected the event had something to do with the alien invasion in Moscow and insurgency in London. Horus peered over her shoulder just as the video turned to an interview.

"It was the alien from those Twitter videos in Moscow. The same ghoulish face and blue eyes… Everything," the ship worker said, visibly shaken.

Horus jetted for his shuttle craft, sprinting through traffic. A few kids were playing in the park when the shuttle de-cloaked. They dropped their bat and gloves and looked on in awe. Horus' aurascales sizzled to the surface of his skin and his faceguard took shape. The kids scattered, screaming.

In his mind, he could think of only the half-breeds he'd recently spoken with about the Ourea and their battle that split England in two. He tried to recall their names. "Harold," he mumbled to himself, sure that was the pudgy man's name. He set a course for England once again.

***

Rain fell on the concrete jungle like chum into the raging sea. The clouds blotted out the full-moon, which only acted to attract ravenous nighttime beasts of the underworld. There were no friends for him among those gathered, and everyone around him knew it.

Horus was a marked man. Those gifted with the sight to see faces beyond the flesh knew there was something off about him. Nothing close to human, half-breed, or changeling, but not quite angel either. The demons were what he really had to watch out for. In small bursts, groups of two to five, they were manageable and mostly kept to themselves when dealing with beings of a higher power. When their numbers swelled like locusts in the eighth plague, they acted like hyenas. They fought in groups—cackles—and once the first punch was thrown they'd call for reinforcements.

When the numbers were in their favor, demons could take out someone much stronger than themselves. Of course, tonight, Horus was the alpha lion. Though they took a passive interest in hunting and fights in the jungle, alpha lions weren't ones to back down when the pride was at stake. They could take their fair share of licks in a skirmish, but they always thinned out the clan enough that the few remaining hyenas thought better and fled.

Horus had last visited England two months ago, working his way west from Afghanistan, trying to better understand the events that had forever changed the realm. At that time, he met a half-blood by the name of Harold. The descendants ran with a group that often met at a place called the Progeny Lounge. Though Harold had a reputation as a strong and steady force in the underground community, Horus found him to be little more than a drunk unwilling to cooperate. Harold admitted he'd fallen out with his master for a reason he wasn't willing to disclose. Travel to her realm wouldn't be permissible for him anymore, nor did he care to draw a map and leave a key. Tonight needed to be different.

"You don't belong here, abomination," a demon snickered as Horus passed by. He lowered his brow-line and glanced at the group of seven playing pool. His eyes didn't linger for long, as he did not wish to draw attention. "Yeah, keep moving you freak," he heard them laugh, but let it go.

Things had become deplorable since the last time he'd visited the establishment, which had been nothing more than a small pub in the English countryside. Now it was more like a gateway to a different dimension. The patrons on this night were more like those found in big cities like London or Prague. Previously, there was an even split of human, demon, and other paranormal guests. This time, it was mostly demons and changelings. There were plenty of Satyrs, Centaurs, Goblins and more as well. What attracted them here?

"You look lost, choir boy." A slender, sultry vixen moseyed over. Her shoulder length, multi-colored hair was purposefully cut into uneven spikes at the ends and covered half her face. Tight leather pants accentuated her figure. She was a demon. "I must say, I haven't come across the likes of you before."

Horus didn't want to acknowledge her in case he drew the ire of other demons in the pub, nor did he wish to blatantly ignore her lest he offend her. It was a tricky line to tread.

"C'mon sugar, I don't bite… too hard." She slid into the booth and leaned over him. She was powerful enough to have angelic sight and see what he wasn't, though she was too young to know what he was. That was a dangerous combination for the both of them. "The name is Tunrida."

"I didn't ask," he replied. "Not to be rude, but I didn't invite you to sit with me either."

"Waiting for someone? No?" she asked. He raised an eyebrow at her and kept silent. She giggled. "If you're stand-offish because there's a demon in this shell and not a soul, then that is kind of rude… Unless this shell isn't your type of thing, in which case I can rent another for the night and let you play with it. Man whores are more common nowadays, if that's what you're into."

"I am waiting for someone and it would be impolite to cut short a conversation with you upon their arrival. Nor would it be any more acceptable to neglect them in order to finish out formalities with you." Horus looked at her and she cast an air-headed, blank eyed smile while licking her lips.

"You're cute," she laughed, rubbing his head and messing his hair. "You can be done with me whenever you'd like."

"Tunrida," the demon at the pool table grumbled. She looked his way and he stomped his feet. "You shouldn't fraternize with him."

"It's my night off, hun, I can frat all I'd like with whomever." She flashed her middle finger, stuck her tongue out, and looked back at Horus. "Where was we?"

"Your night off?" Horus asked. If Tunrida knew the other demons in the pub, then they likely worked together. And if it was their night off, then why were they so far outside the urban areas where they thrived and were made less of a target for angels? "Kind of far from civilization, aren't you?

"I'm in the city all the time. It's a never ending rat-race." She held two fingers up for the bartender and two stiff-whiskies were placed in front of them. "But out here in the countryside, I can just relax. Also, the human pickings are a lot less crafty out here than their city counterparts. It's more fun ruining their innocence." She giggled and leaned into him, resting her head on his shoulder. "What about you, hunk-a-luv? What's got ya out this way?"

"I'm meeting a friend. Remember?"

"What are's ya anyway?" She leaned back and looked him over. "I can't quite make it out."

"I'm just an abomination…"

"Aren't we all?" She laughed loudly and dug her elbow into his side. Her hand slid up his leg and onto his crotch. "You like that?"

The placement of the hand was enjoyable, but not the person the hand was attached to. He squirmed out of the way. "That wouldn't be very chivalrous of me."

"Oh please, you make me blush." She straddled him and wrapped her arms around the back of his head. "This meat suit has been scored on more times than Man-U with Wayne Rooney trying to play defense. It don't hurt me none."

"What does that even mean?"

"Never mind." She licked his cheek and whispered into his ear, "Seems your friend is late. Perhaps I can help you find them after…"

From what Horus grew to know of Harold, he was a creature of habit. If he wasn't going to show, then something had changed for him. A long night was likely in store, but that didn't mean he cared to spend it with a demon whore grinding against him.

"I need to make a call." He stood from the table and walked towards the back of the establishment. Near the rear, just past the restrooms, was a sauna area. It hadn't been there before. Curious, Horus decided to check it out.

The air was stifling and he could barely see his nose through the steam. The water in a trough to his left bubbled with volcanic power. He leaned over the long and narrow wooden bucket, examining the dark, murky water being used to bathe in. The water shimmered when he got close, and a whispering murmur escaped the bubbles.

Come. The voice was breathy and reserved. *Find what you seek…* The voice faded in and out. He could hear it only when he breathed in the steam that broke free of each bubble.

"You care to have your fortune told?" Tunrida asked. Horus spun around and she was unclothed, leaning against the wall, with only a towel covering her from her hips down. "Or was it just an invite?"

"I'm unfamiliar with this place," he replied. His mind felt off. Lethargic. Scatterbrained. Everywhere yet nowhere. Why was he here, again?

Tunrida took his hand and escorted him further into the bathhouse. "We'll see if the wise one is willing and available to see what lies ahead for you." She skipped along, tugging his arm. He stutter-stepped forward and went cross-eyed. "Oh, shit, there's a line."

Horus swayed in a circle. His hazy vision was able to make out two or three changelings waiting in line for the stall at the end of the room. When they reached the final stall, they would turn and face away from the half-open door.

The more he inhaled the steam, the stronger the urge his aurascales placed upon him to release them. He was in the den of demons and releasing his armor would set them all off. In this state, he was in no place to take them on.

Like a bolt of lightning, a memory snapped through his brain. "Bagiennik," he could hear Sobek proclaim. What were they again? Early forms of spirits created by Lucifer in his attempt to duplicate the human soul. Essentially, they were failed demons entrapped by water and only able to possess their prey when inhaled. They were raping his mind.

A Satyr climbed into the second to last stall and peered over the divider. Tunrida nudged Horus. "Watch," she said, nodding at the Satyr. A vat of lava-hot water was thrown over the Satyr, melting his skin. He hit the ground and kicked in circles. His friends scooped him up and dragged him away.

"He doesn't like to be looked at," Tunrida said, pulling Horus to the front of the line when the Satyrs moved along. She turned him around and rubbed his face. "Bannik is wise and old. He can see into many a creature's essence, know their struggles, and see what lies ahead."

"No, I'm fine, really." Horus tried to walk away, but his muscles refused to listen. The mist was in his mind. Tunrida grabbed his face and pulled him in for a long kiss. Her tongue worked into his mouth and rubbed against his teeth, a sensation he found odd yet was reluctantly attracted to.

She pulled his head back by the hair. His eyes opened and peered into her sparkling red gaze. "Relax, my hunk, and let Bannik read you."

A pair of gnarly hands with long, pointed fingernails crawled up Horus' back. There was a forced wheeze about the nasally breathing. Given the angle of the grasp, Horus knew Bannik had to be several feet shorter than him.

The hands crooked up between the shoulder blades, back down, and around the waist. Bannik pulled Horus' shoulders backwards and relaxed his arms, taking the cloak off and throwing it to the side. He then tore away Horus' puffy white shirt, splitting it all the way down. The fingernails lightly dug into his muscular back, and Tunrida ran her fingers through the hair on his chest.

"Such a man." She stood on her tiptoes and hovered her mouth a mere inch from his, smelling his hair. "Such a warrior."

"There is much pain," Bannik croaked, digging further into Horus' flesh. It hurt, but his body refused to move. "His heart is void. Suffering," Bannik cried in a high pitched staccato. "What he seeks he finds only in death."

"So he fails?" Turnida asked, rubbing her face along Horus' belly as she knelt.

"Death is what he wants," Bannik replied, pulling his fingers from Horus' back. Blood trickled from the wounds and he licked it off. "His eye is all seeing, yet knowledge and wisdom will only come once a great pain is inflicted, and another revealed. Heaven's elite will stand opposed."

"I knew you were a good one." Tunrida laughed maniacally as she undid his belt. "Anyone who stands against Heaven is worth an alliance."

"There is power in this one, I feel it." Bannik's voice trembled as he spoke, breathing in. "He is descended from angels. The son of great power."

Tunrida pulled away. "What?" she asked.

"The aura within," Bannik said. Horus' armor surged to the surface. "This Angel-born will be a vessel for us. I see it now."

"An Angel-born?" she asked, shocked. Tunrida stepped back and scrunched her eyebrows. The steam swarmed around Horus, choking him. He coughed as it forced its way inside his mouth. "Who in Heaven stands opposed? You said he finds death. Are you being literal or figurative?" She was panicked, as if she knew something.

"We see only glimmers in the abstract. The words are what they are." Bannik's voice roared as the steam all vanished inside of Horus. He could feel his hands and feet, yet no longer instructed them. There was a great burning in his chest as he stepped forward. Bannik's previous host lay dead on the floor. "Now we have true form."

"You're going to have to let him go," she said with trepidation. "The boss has need for certain plans to go accordingly. Does he stand against the Assassins?" The body of Horus closed its eyes and smelled the air, finally nodding to the question. "Leave him at once—you know not what you mess with."

"It's ours now." Horus' body smiled and grabbed Tunrida by the neck. It slowly squeezed her until she was on the brink of unconsciousness. Suddenly it released and fell to its knees, letting out a horrific scream. The steam poured out of its mouth.

"What was that?" Horus breathed in and coughed. His aurascales had forced the water demons from his body. He could taste blood on his tongue. The steam gathered together, taking the form of a dragon.

The body Bennik had used as a host reanimated and shrieked. A shield materialized over Horus' left arm and the dragon attacked. The beast dissipated in a plume of steam and regrouped behind him. Horus scooped Tunrida up and ran for the rear of the building. A cross-bow of light scintillated over his wrist in place of the shield and blasted a hole through the back wall. Cold air surged into the bathhouse with tsunami force and bludgeoned the dragon. Horus turned to see Bannik screech and run away.

The rain had slowed to a lazy drizzle. He knelt in the muddy creek and laid Tunrida over his lap, moving the wet strands of hair out of her face and caressing her cheek with the back of his hand. The sound of a gathering demon cackle on the opposite side of the building built into a howl. His fingers swiped along the wrist pad and his shuttle soon swooped in over head. It decloaked and lowered to the ground, hatch opening. He tossed Tunrida inside, hopped in the pilot's seat, and sped off into the early morning sky before the stalking clan of demons could swarm him.

CHAPTER TWENTY-SIX

Set III

Svarog was dead and Set didn't know who was responsible. That meant it wasn't one of his allies. To further his anxiousness, word had spread to him that Gabriel had enacted the 'Song of Father.' Since Raphael didn't alert Set of the impending call by Gabriel before sending the Assassins on their mission, it was likely nothing more than a ploy to coax the traitor into showing their hand. Hopefully, Raphael had been coy about the whole thing. Set had no other choice than to continue with the plan. If Raphael had blown his cover, then Heaven's guard would've already descended upon Set and the others to arrest them.

The trio waited on the rooftop of a Hong Kong skyscraper. To their left, Kowloon Bay reflected the many colors of the night time city skyline. The flashing neon lights were a formidable opponent to the radiance of their aurascales. Hundreds of naval vessels stretched out over the horizon. The humans were preparing for something to happen; they just didn't know when it would take place or who would be the opposing force.

Sif and Hermes sat with their backs resting against a large air duct. Behind them the enormous ventilation system rattled. Set was perched on the edge of the roof with his feet dangling over the bustling city streets.

"They're late!" Hermes yelled out. He never missed a chance to dickishly nitpick at the smallest details. "What are we even doing here? I don't believe this was the destination in the crystal."

"See for yourself." Set tossed Hermes the crystal and jetted to his feet.

"What are we looking for?" Sif asked, her leather cloak sliding along the ground behind her feet as she walked circles around Set. "This seems a strange location. We will not find much up here."

"Not a what, but a who," Set replied. For the moment, the less he said the better.

"It doesn't speak to me," Hermes said, throwing the crystal back to Set with force. Set caught it without looking, which pissed Hermes off. "We never finished our conversation."

"I suspect when our guest arrives, you'll not want to." Set squinted imperiously, causing his fellow Assassin to shrink back.

The hot magenta flash of a rift opening to Set's right matched the flare of the digital billboard advertising a casual sex dating site. An overweight half-breed with a scruffy beard, escorted by a group of demons, approached Set.

"Finally, you arrive. Could you graveling, repugnant fools be any more irritating than you already are?" Set chided the group of a dozen demons. When one of them attempted to speak, he cut them off. "Hold your tongue or lose it. I don't care to hear your excuses. They would be only lies anyway, as that's all your retarded kind is capable of."

"We don't have to listen to this." One of the demons spit on Set's boot. "They can do their own footwork."

"You intrude on my patience by thinking yourself worthy of speaking to me." The three blades elongated around Set's left hand. In a quick blur, the serrated edges sliced through the demon's neck and returned to their resting position. The arrogant demon's head hit the ground, followed by his body a few seconds later. "Anyone else?" The other demons stepped away from their friend's twitching body. Set nodded at the plump half-breed, who was none too happy to be in his situation. "Half-breed, you've ninety seconds to get to the point."

He cautiously opened his mouth, speaking with a British accent. "I spoke to Svarog..."

"Were you the last to see him alive?" Set interrupted.

The half-breed struggled to talk, grabbing his shoulder. The gesture was irritating. Set tore away the shirt's collar, exposing three slashing scars just below the clavicle. The blades elongated from over his wrist, matching the marks, and the man squirmed.

"You remember the sting?" Set leaned over the prisoner with a chilling smirk and breathed down his neck. "Yes, now you're familiar. We're forever connected, you and I. The refreshing cool of your parents' blood on my hands is in my mind like yesterday's memories."

"Are you going to let him speak or torment him further?" Hermes asked, agitated just as Set expected.

"That depends," Set replied.

"On what?" Hermes asked.

"Whether or not you'd like to speak in his stead." Set held the blades up to the prisoner's throat, which seemed to bring relief to Hermes' face. "You'd have me take his head?"

"He's the reason we're here, right?" Hermes relaxed and sat down. "If you want to kill Harold, then have at it. Make our job that much more difficult."

Set nodded. "You would like that." He stopped walking midstride and Hermes' face fell. The half-breed's name was never mentioned. Set could tell Hermes knew he'd given away his hand, but decided to momentarily let it pass as if it had gone unnoticed. There was a nervous silence.

"Do we still get paid if you kill the prisoner?" another demon asked. Set sighed heavily, emphasizing his annoyance with the question. "I'll shut up."

"That would be in your best interest," Set said through his teeth and looked at the half-breed prisoner he now knew was named Harold. "Ninety seconds, half-breed," Set reminded him.

"I have information on the remake you seek," Harold stuttered. Set's curiosity was piqued, so he smiled. Harold asked, "Do I get more time?"

"You can spend it, but your words must earn it. If not, I'll seek retribution for the debt in the form of blood." Set towered over Harold and forced him away from the other Assassins who were now standing at attention. "Get on with it."

"I've seen him, met him, and guided him to another realm. I can give you his location, but I ask for certain reassurances."

"Of course you do," Set replied sarcastically. "We are but genies in your care."

"I, uh…" Harold swallowed. His jugular pulsated with trepidation. He rubbed his hands together and wiped the sweat off onto his pants. "He resides in the realm of Danu, an Architect…"

"Yes, I know who Danu is." Set rubbed his face, agitated.

"Danu?" Hermes asked. The mention of her name seemed to chill his blood. That probably meant Athena was in play. "I don't understand."

"No?" Set asked, sure by Hermes' forced ignorant tone that he did. "One of the original seven to create existence, and she doesn't ring a bell? Danu, Ra, Chronos, Odin, Durga, Nüwa and the All Mighty Father himself, God. Of course, we all know who got the lion's share of credit."

"God is the only creator we know. To say otherwise is treason," Hermes said.

"Please, you can cut the crap. We both know we're past that," Set replied. It was time to gamble. If Heaven's guard wasn't descending upon them, then Raphael had control on his end of the board. "Danu being involved doesn't so much complicate things, but make them interesting."

"So you can't track him there?" Harold asked, somewhat relieved.

"The only question, really, is what does an Architect want with a remake?" The interrogation was lacking flare and Set wanted to provide it. He tossed Harold across the roof. The half-breed rolled to the very edge. He pushed up but Set's feet were already at his head. Set lifted him off the ground and held him over the drop. "You're out of time. Earn more. Fill in all the blanks."

Hermes sat forward. A knife slid into his grasp. His eyes honed in on beads of sweat forming on Harold's brow line. Sif steadied him. Their gazes connected. She shook her head. Hermes relaxed.

"Is there something you'd like to keep him from saying?" Set asked Hermes. The subordinate Assassin didn't respond.

"There's a child. A young boy in her possession for over a human decade," Harold choked the words out. "The remake and his followers sought Danu. The boy is siblings with a friend of the remake."

"A boy?" Set pulled Harold in close and glared into his frightened gaze. There was only truth in his eyes, so he tossed Harold back onto the rooftop. "What does that information do for me?"

"The boy is a new kind of powered human. Another Architect is hunting them." Harold looked over at the demons, who seemed rather scared of the topic. "The boy's sister and the remake want to save the hunted from this other Architect, Ra." Harold coughed and rubbed his chest. "These demons are corralling the gifted at Ra's behest. Follow the trail of gifted and you'll find your remake."

Set rubbed his chin. "This is interesting."

"What is?" Hermes asked. His weapon disintegrated back into the aurascales. "Your treason?"

"I'm no more treasonous than you." Set twisted Harold's arm under then up, snapping the shoulder and eliciting a blood-curdling scream from Harold before throwing him at Hermes' feet. "Kill him and take me to Danu, and I'll let you live."

"I won't murder an innocent man. That's not our mission."

"No one is innocent, that's the great revelation of it all. No?" Set laughed, shaking his hips as he walked flamboyantly toward Sif. He took her by the hand, twirled her around, and dipped her to the sound of the Waltz in his mind. "Prove yourself worthy of the new order."

"You're insane," Hermes grunted.

"And yet you follow me, so what does that make you?"

"I don't know who Danu is, or where she's located!" Hermes yelled.

Set skipped forward and Spartan-kicked Hermes through the sky-scraper's massive air-conditioning systems. "You will not raise your voice to your master!" he yelled.

Sif flinched, as if wanting to help Hermes. Set gave her a 'mind your own business' glare. He jumped through the fire and landed on Hermes' chest. His knee drove Hermes through the roof and the top few floors of the building. Those staying late for work scattered like roaches from the light. Crossbows of energy assembled over Set's wrists and he disintegrated the people one by one, to Hermes' protests.

The former warrior of the Western Corner attacked. Set grabbed the jab and struck an elbow to Hermes' throat. Cross. Cross. Forehead ram. He followed with a barrage of blows, finishing with a spin kick and jumping hammer fist.

Hermes had always been the inferior fighter. In fact, there were few who could match the technique and ferocity of Set. He picked his subordinate up by the shoulder plates and flew back to the roof. Sif, Harold, and the demons waited like lapdogs for their return.

Set swayed in the breeze, slowly lowering to the roof. He dropped Hermes next to Harold and folded his arms.

"I've proven myself time and again." Hermes crawled away from Harold. "Together we've slaughtered the remnants of my Corner's half-blood descendants by the millions. We hunted children and the mentally challenged. At every instance, I've never backed down."

"And you'll do it again because I command it, lest you have something to hide."

"Athena is dead..." A knife slid into Hermes' grasp. He cried as he put the blade to Harold's neck.

"You've claimed that fallacy long enough." Set was eerily calm, despite the attention his little outburst had attracted from the local human population. "It would make sense for you to hide Athena with Danu. The Architect was the one who assisted Zeus in creating the Ourea. If you admit now that you've lied all these years—that Athena does indeed live—then this half-breed's life may be spared."

"It's OK," Harold whispered. He lunged at Hermes, almost pulling the knife into his own gut. Blood soaked through Harold's clothes, flooding around Hermes as he knelt, shaking from sorrow.

"Tsk-tsk. You are a cold one, Hermes," Set crowed, taunting while sarcastically shaking his head in disapproval. He whistled at Sif. "The first of them who caves with information lives." The demons cowered while she quickly eradicated them. Set knelt by Hermes. "Either you'd kill this man to keep false pretences, or you're truly—at heart—the slayer of children and invalids you claim to be."

"Being charged with the duty of an Assassin is supposed to be penance, not taken lightly. Instead, you joke and revel in the pain we inflict on otherwise innocent people." He laid Harold's head down and placed two coins over the eyes. "You were born for this life, Set."

"It certainly feels like it." Set offered a hand to Hermes and pulled him up. By the time they turned around, finished with the conversation, Sif had murdered all but one piss-stained demon. He looked at Sif with curiosity as she remorsefully slung the blood from her swords. "I guess everyone has their secrets," he chuckled and her eyes shot up to him, afraid.

"Perhaps words you should take to heart," Hermes added. "We should head back to the Archangel's council. They need to hear about the current status quo."

"This changes nothing about our mission." Set walked to the edge of the roof, pretending not to notice Sif and Hermes exchange contemplative looks. Neither was fully aware of his plan, but it was time to scatter a few breadcrumbs. "We're to draw out this imposter who wears Azrael's colors..."

"And then kill him?" Sif asked.

Set didn't bother to answer the question. That part was vague on purpose.

"You intend to let the monster out?" Hermes asked. It seemed he wasn't as dense as Set assumed.

"That was my plan, yes," Set said matter-of-factly.

"What is it?" Sif asked.

"The start of tribulation," Hermes replied. "The horseman, Death."

"I'm going to let you in on a little secret. A great opportunity, if you will." Set turned to face his fellow Assassins. "I've grown tired of fighting for a lie. Have you not? What happened to the four Corners, to Azrael and all before them was unjustified, yet a higher being decided otherwise. Do you not wonder why?"

"You've not learned anything all these years," Hermes snickered.

"I'm just like you, brother." Set gazed at Hermes, not joking or grinning but wearing a serious, stone-cold expression. "I still serve the one I swore an oath to despite his absence. Don't you?"

"I'm not sure I understand. Didn't you kill Osiris?" Hermes swallowed nervously. Set could tell this line of talk made his stomach uneasy. "Michael and the others will stop you. Father guides them."

"Do you not find it curious that I act on my own volition and there is no one here to tell me otherwise? Where is the Armada to wipe me from existence?" Set jumped up, cupping his hand over his left ear, pretending to listen for footsteps while he mocked. "See, there's nothing. I'm either divinely inspired, acting on Father's accord, or he knows not what I do because he is a fraud. Free will granted by a powerless god, or predestination, what have you Hermes?"

"It does nothing to explain why you had me kill him." Hermes shivered, pointing at Harold. He gaped at Set, his eyes watering. "How many more will die this time?"

"You showed no remorse when we snuffed them out during the French Inquisition, the fall of Rome, or the Saxon invasion. The only difference now is that your master's precious Athena is at stake." Set gently laid a hand on Hermes' shoulder and spoke solemnly. "So, this I offer you one last time, are you with us or against us?"

The jagged blades slid down Set's arms. His stare was piercing and his breathing smooth. Hermes tried to make eye contact with Sif, but her head was turned away, offering no support. Set was ready to stab him.

"I am with you." Hermes closed his eyes. When Set let him go, he slowly looked up to his superior's smile. Trembling, he reaffirmed his position. "I am with you."

"I know." Set nodded. Having practically confirmed that Athena lived, he decided to drop the subject. The threat of her discovery, along with Set's superior physicality, would keep Hermes in line. He approached the last demon. "Lead the way," Set commanded.

"Where to?" Hermes asked.

"There's only one demon with the cojones and tact to corral the likes of gifted children and sell them to an Architect." Set rubbed the demon's shoulders. "Back to Beelzebub, please."

CHAPTER TWENTY-SEVEN

Austin IV

A platoon of feet stomped through puddles in the broken concrete, giving chase. Three helicopters moved through the sky, their rumbling vibrating through the floor. The nighttime chill pressed against his lungs. The girl they'd found—Paula, one of the first of Lian's kind they'd actually secured—labored to breathe. Austin took her hand and dragged her along. They had to keep up with Athena, and holy hell she was fast. A searchlight poured in through the tower of broken windows. Had they been seen?

Austin ducked behind a stack of long-forgotten bricks. The abandoned industrial warehouse echoed with the sound of rotating blades and soldiers descending from the sky. "Fan out," was the order he heard through a gunman's com-link, thanks to his enhanced hearing.

Paula was red with exhaustion, and her dark brown hair was soaked from the rain falling through a hole in the roof above them. The splatter of water rushing through the fractured roof diffused any noise they made.

How many are there? Austin asked Lian through his mind. He knew his girlfriend would be listening in on his thoughts, and patiently waited for her reply. *Something must be wrong. More than ten seconds and still no...*

Eight on your level, ten below, and another twenty-five on the ground floor and building across the way, she replied. *They know you're behind the bricks, but they're busy setting the trap. I'd move.* Lian seemed rather calm about the whole thing. *Of course I'm calm. You got this.*

Paula is freaking out. Austin rubbed her back in order to comfort her. He faked a smile but it seemed to comfort Paula. *She's gonna crack under pressure.*

Hold on, Lian replied.

Paula's body went rigid and her jaw snapped shut. Her eyes rolled back and then forward. She smiled at Austin with a certain cockiness about her. "You don't recognize me?" she laughed.

"You didn't." Austin was part impressed and part disappointed. Lian may have the power to commandeer a person's consciousness, but that didn't mean she should. It wasn't worth arguing about at that moment. "I assume you have a plan."

"We go up," Paula, or Lian in Paula's body, said. It was strange hearing Lian's words come out in a posh British accent. It was even weirder to see Lian, who was a slight whisper of a woman, maneuver around in a plump teenager's body. She tried to climb up the stack of bricks. "Oh my god, this is hard. My chubby fingers can't grip."

"She can't hear you say all that, can she?" Austin asked, putting his hands around Lian's temporary hips.

"Of course she can," Lian said candidly. "You're turning her on the way you're grabbing her. She's never been touched like this."

"Eww, gross," he said under his breath.

Austin looked up through the hole. It was almost thirty feet above them. His muscles grew as he shifted his body to lie somewhere between beast and man. He squatted and then jetted into a standing position, heaving Paula with all his might. In a fluid motion, he shifted into wolf-form and sprinted up the stack of bricks. The laser-guided barrels of the soldiers closing in turned his direction. Flashes of yellow and orange lit up the night.

He grabbed the ledge, reaching the next floor before Paula reached the crest of her flight, and lowered his right hand to grab her wrist. Austin flung her over his head and she landed on the roof with a splash. A few rounds tore through his left shoulder and chest. They were clean hits, going straight through. His grip on the roof slipped, and he crashed through the brick pile, tumbling to the ground. The platoon closed their ranks.

"Go," Austin yelled while looking up at Paula's distraught stare, knowing it was Lian who held her back. "I'm serious. Leave…" Several hooked-lines dug into his flesh and sent enough voltage into his muscles to paralyze him. He seized, unable to fight the jolt.

"We have the first target," a voice said. Austin couldn't open his eyes to see who it was. The stinging surge relented, allowing him to draw a single breath before starting back up. His face fell into the pooling rainwater.

Austin pushed up. His elbows rattled. It was all he could do to prevent his bones from breaking as he forced his muscles to fight against the tasers. A single military grade taser—the kind being used against him—was capable of bringing down an elephant, and there were four hooked into his flesh. He'd seen it firsthand once when he first joined the Rangers. The other men in his unit did it for sport. The pain was beyond description. Still, he pushed to his feet and roared with the force of a stampeding heard.

A streak of purple whizzed through his vision. Deafening gunfire overtook all other noise, but it was not aimed in his direction. The men around him screamed and shouted for help. Their pleas came to an abrupt end, snuffed out with gasps for air. He ripped the lines from his body while the others were distracted and fell to his knees, lethargic.

"Need a hand?" Athena asked, grabbing him under the arms and lifting him to his feet. The silver-plated helmet collapsed into her exoskeleton's shoulders. Her platinum blonde hair was dry. Not even a drop of sweat from the constant running, or nervous perspiration, could be found on her face.

"I had a handle," Austin panted with a tired grin. All around him men were sprawled out either dead or unconscious. She wrinkled her nose and folded her arms, with a 'yeah, OK' gleam in her eyes. "I hate you," he coughed, stumbling over to the stack of bricks. He looked up and Paula was gone. "She took my advice."

"You told her to run. Why?" Athena needed to be clued in on who was the real pilot of Paula's body. Austin chuckled. "It is not funny," she insisted.

"You laugh at me and me at you. Relax." Austin patted her shoulder and motioned for her to follow. "Lian was in her brain. She'll be fine. Now, you mind helping me up there?"

Athena put her hand under his backend and threw him like a shot-put. He landed on the roof and rolled forward. By the time he'd gathered his bearings, Athena was already standing beside him. Austin looked around, but they were the only two up top. A helicopter was coming their way. The sound was unmistakable.

"We need to get moving. We're gonna have an eye in the sky on top of us."

Sure enough, two aircraft emerged behind them. Their searchlights glued on Austin and Athena. He took off running, but Athena turned to face the helicopters. They opened fire. A shield the size of her body crackled with static as it materialized around her arm. It easily deflected the machine gun fire.

Austin reached the end of the roof. On the bottom level, there were more men than he could count and numerous armored vehicles. The unfinished apartment building across the parking lot was a little more than forty yards away. He spotted a few snipers taking position.

This type of military response was unheard of. The only agency capable of putting together a team like this, this quickly, was Sanderson's. He was gone. Was Elliot in charge now?

He turned around. Athena continued to deflect machine gun fire. The second helicopter swirled around to her six. It had a kill shot. Before he could open his mouth to warn her, a chrome aircraft in the shape of an arrowhead seemed to materialize out of thin air above both helicopters. It was like it teleported out of nowhere, invisible one moment and there the next.

260

The helicopters took evasive maneuvers, but the arrowhead was too nimble. Green charges of circular fire spit from the tip of the vessel and engulfed the first helicopter in flames.

The second helicopter released a missile at Austin. He froze. Athena jumped in front of him and raised her shield. The impact tore a crater the size of a train car into the warehouse and blasted them both forty feet into the unfinished apartments across the parking lot.

Athena—holding Austin in her arms—tumbled across the concrete floor and through support columns like a well-hit groundball. They reached the end of their roll and she stumbled to her feet with several sections of her aurascales torn to shreds. In the brief moment it took her armor to repair, he could see she was bleeding pretty badly.

"Can you make it?" he asked, draping her arm over his shoulders.

"Of course," Athena replied, determined. She pushed away from Austin and her armor erupted with light. Two swords a little shorter than the length of his arms formed in her grasp. They were standing next to a staircase that had yet to be closed off. A large group of gunmen snaked their way up the steps.

"What was that thing?" Austin panted, hunching over onto his knees to collect his breath. "It looked like an alien ship."

"I don't know." Athena stared down at the bottom of the stair shaft.

Lian, where are you? Austin scrunched his eyes closed and clenched his fists. When she failed to reply, he feared the worst. "There are too many people around and I'm hurting. You need to go."

"Would your friends leave you behind?" she asked in a robotic tone because of the armor over her face. Austin shook his head no. "Then I shall not abandon you either." Athena looked over the railing and twirled a sword in her hand. "The fastest way from one point to the next is…" She looked in his direction. The glowing eye-slits in her faceguard beckoned him to finish the statement.

"… a straight line?" he asked.

"Indeed." She nodded and jumped over the side of the railing. Upon landing she punched the ground. A charge of static energy erupted around her, rendering the many soldiers in her vicinity inert.

"Show off," Austin mumbled. He leapt over the railing and landed a few floors down. He repeated the process, jumping from floor-to-floor, until he reached the ground level. By the time he landed on the bottom, Athena was already well on her way to clearing the area.

Two men snatched Austin from behind. The first pulled an iron rod underneath his chin and leaned back. The second grabbed for his feet. The eyes of their masks were blacked out, as if what lingered inside weren't human. Austin kicked one in the face and swiped his paw at the assailant to his back.

They released him. He rolled along the ground, avoiding a bash of the rod. The blunt weapon rattled in its wielder's hands. Austin struck the man in the gut, pulled the rod from his grasp, and knocked it across the foe's facemask, crushing the plastic headgear. He turned to face the second enemy when a body soared through the air and collided with the adversary, crashing them both into the wall. Athena tapped her wrist as if they were late for dinner.

"Now you're just showing off," Austin huffed. Athena nodded in reply.

A large, armored vehicle crushed through the wall along the street front. Each side of the vehicle had three tires twice as wide as Austin's torso. Attached to the front was a battering ram which resembled a snow plow. Above it were two turret guns.

Bullets three fingers in width tore through the air. Austin ran for cover, but Athena was taken off-guard. The rounds swung at her chin like a heavyweight boxer. She skidded across the ground unable to balance or manifest a shield. The sheet rock collapsed around her as she lay motionless.

"Athena!" Austin could barely hear his own scream above the turret fire.

The colossal vehicle rolled forward, breaking through walls. Austin lowered his shoulder and burst through dry wall, tearing through studs and plumbing to clear a path. The rounds ripped after him. He barely outpaced their chase.

Austin circled around, trying to sneak up on the tank-like vehicle he dubbed 'the crusher.' He leapt through a window and rolled into the street. Several laser lights locked on to his chest. Snipers were everywhere with helicopters above them.

A streak of lightning belted through the black clouds. Its light shimmered, as if being refracted through a prism. The arrowhead appeared once more. Green balls of plasma fire eradicated several of the snipers. The crusher rolled out into the street, firing a missile. The arrowhead turned sideways on its axis without losing any altitude. The missile destroyed a helicopter that was lowering in for a strike. The arrowhead spit plasma once again. It melted through the crusher, slicing it in half. The two sides of the severed crusher fell open like an old book.

The remaining helicopters sped away but the arrowhead chased after them. They didn't get far. The rumble from the explosions and crashes shook the remaining shattered windowpanes from their perches.

Austin returned to Athena. She slowly stumbled out of the building and collapsed to her knees next to the wrecked crusher. A survivor crawled out of the vehicle with a leg singed off below the thigh. The wound seemed to have been cauterized by the blast. Athena twirled a sword around her hand and shoved it through the back of the man's head, pinning him to the ground.

"I like you not," she grunted.

The arrowhead hovered behind Athena. It stayed in place for what seemed like an eternity. A search light shone over the two, blinding them. They raised their hands in a show of surrender. Could this be the Assassins come to kill them?

Suddenly, the arrowhead craft spun out of control. The searchlight was punctured, and Austin could see the reason for the commotion. Jarrod, dressed in aurascales, had landed on the aircraft and begun tearing it apart. He punched through the bow of the craft and it took a steep nose dive toward Austin and Athena.

The two ducked into the building as the craft skidded along the street to a stop. Jarrod landed with a thud, digging his left knee and right fist into the concrete. He looked at Austin. The blue eyes of his ghoulish helmet were piercing. Austin didn't know who to be more afraid of at that moment: the unknown visitor from the sky, or his best friend.

CHAPTER TWENTY-EIGHT

Lian V

She needed to run faster. It was difficult. This Paula girl was so out of shape that it was all Lian could do to not choke on air. Her feet were clumsy. She stumbled forward and slid across the roof, tearing the skin on her forearms away. Lian rolled side-to-side and was finally able to move to her feet.

While her body struggled to crawl down the slippery ladder, her mind fixed on Austin. She tried to read his thoughts, but her power and focus was spent controlling Paula's motor functions.

How far can I really get in this body? Lian couldn't make it more than twelve steps without sucking in air. Two hummers sped her way.

Ahead was an alleyway. Grabbing her chest to hold the stabbing pains at bay, she labored forward. Several tin trashcans, piled high with slop, toppled over in her wake. It wouldn't take a hound dog to track her down.

The hummers screeched to a halt and several soldiers pursued her on foot. Lian hobbled on, able to see a river ahead. Maybe she could get Paula to a boat and somehow row across to the heavily wooded park on the other side. Who was she kidding? If this body didn't suffer a heart attack mid-row then she would probably fall off balance, turn the boat on its head, and then drown.

"Got you." A soldier grabbed her, struggling to lift her off the ground. He grunted, "Got. The. Second. Target." It sounded like he was about to have an aneurism.

Lian elbowed him in the nose and waddled a few more steps before her feet gave out and her face plopped into the mud. She rolled to her back and held her hand up, trying to will the soldiers with her mind. Nothing happened. They smirked at her.

"That's right," she said, heaving. "One mind… at a time."

"I think that fat little cunt broke my nose." Blood seeped from between the soldier's fingers as he pressed his hand against his face. He unholstered his pistol and aimed it between her eyes. "I'm gonna smear her brains along the asphalt."

Two of the other four soldiers restrained him. "Stay your weapon, grunt," the leader said. Lian looked him over. He was pretty buff and in shape, at the level Austin was before his animalistic augmentation. "Boss wants 'em whole, remember?"

"Where are you taking me?" Lian asked. Two of the men labored to help her to her feet. "I have a right to know." They weren't going to answer, and she was incapable of prying into their minds while inside Paula's. She briefly thought about trying to run again, but knew she wasn't getting anywhere with those legs. Then she had an idea.

She grabbed the C/O's arm and transferred her consciousness from Paula into him. When her eyes rolled forward, she was staring back at Paula who was shaking and nearly on the verge of peeing herself.

"Let me go," Paula cried, biting one of the men.

The soldier raised the blunt end of his rifle in order to strike the back of her head, but Lian pushed him back. "We can get more cooperation with kindness," she said.

"Since when is that your M.O., sir?"

"Since now, maggot." She slapped him in the back of the head. *OK, maybe that last part was a bit much. A little less Full-Metal and a little more like the real deal.* Lian knelt and took Paula's hand. "Listen girl, you need to relax and come with me." She winked at the teenager and received a knowing nod in reply. Lian looked at the man who she now knew to be the Sergeant. "Lead the way and inform central command we have the target and that we can back off from the others."

"Don't you remember, sir?" the Sergeant asked. "The mission was to bring them all back, dead or alive, for testing. The reserve units are pulling in as we speak now that we've acquired the primary target."

"Right." Lian nodded. She searched the Lieutenant's memories to find out what that meant. She found it, and it wasn't good. Whatever she was going to learn about this operation, and the people who wanted Paula, it had to happen fast so she could return to her body and warn the others. "We need to get a move on."

They loaded up the hummers and took off. Was this the right play? Her friends were more than capable of handling themselves, but they really needed to know who they were dealing with. If Ra wasn't doing his own dirty work, then the information she'd garner undercover would help her friends out a lot more than alerting them to something they could fend off.

Paula fidgeted with her thumbs. Lian laid a hand over Paula's and nodded reassuringly. The teen breathed a heavy sigh and nodded. The hummer stopped. A CH-47D waited for them with open arms. Lian recognized the model from her time working under Sanderson. The soldiers hunting Lian's kind were, in fact, under the agency's command, but how did they go from mimicking angels to human trafficking at the behest of renegade Architects?

Lian saw Hershiser. He was coordinating the entire effort. On one hand she felt relieved to see him, knowing from her time with the agency he was a smart and sensible person. Yet with the bodies piling up in the wake of Moscow, was he Elliot's new number one lackey? She had to find out.

"Hershiser, sir," she called out and approached the soldier she'd often mind-melded with for the most sensitive covert missions. There was something off about him. A bulge on the right side of his neck was disturbing to look at. She tried not to stare.

He looked her way. "What is it, Lieutenant Kennison?" he asked.

Lian wanted to get close enough to touch him since she couldn't make the leap from her current body to Hershiser's. "We found the primary target…"

"I know, and?"

"I caught a glimpse of the other ones, sir. I fear our forces would be wasted." Lian made it to the stack of crates Hershiser was leaning against but he moved. She followed like a lap dog. This Kennison fellow didn't know much about Paula's purpose. The answers were in Hershiser's head. She knew it. "If we withdraw now we can prevent casualties."

"Really, you saw them?" There was an arrogant flare to his tone that didn't belong there from what she recalled. Of course, people could change a lot over the course of two years. He seemed more like Elliot Foster than Shawn Hershiser. She assumed a close bond had formed between the two.

Never mind that. Touch him and call everything off.

Hershiser stepped out of her path. "So you know that we can't very well fly away without bringing down the men responsible for Moscow?" They knew it was Jarrod and Austin. Her friends were in more danger than she thought.

Touch Hershiser and end it.

He snatched her wrist. "Trying to give me a pat on the back?" He laughed. "What do you expect, Lian?"

"How did you know?" She tried to tug away but his grip was strong—too strong for a human. His eyes went black and they shared consciousness.

Pain. Burning. Eons of lies. Lian had experienced this tone of voice before. The entity possessing Hershiser was the same as was previously inside Elliot. He'd switched one body for the other. Hershiser was dead. The pain of his neck snapping surged down her spine.

She saw Paula and others being shipped off. A man with charred flesh took them. In turn he gave to Hershiser a rejuvenated starstone:

the one Maya had, the one that destroyed Jarrod's hometown and killed Sanderson. Ra would reignite the starstone for Elliot, for Hershiser—no, for Beelzebub—just as he'd done with Zeus' starstone. From there, Beelzebub would resume the Double-Helix with a different catalyst.

"Azrael," she screeched. The name burned through her. Another plan raped her mind. The word 'sundown' was stuck. Every thought zoomed through her mind at once. She couldn't return to her own body. Beelzebub had her trapped. He let go and she hit the ground.

"Arrest Lieutenant Kennison," Hershiser—no, Beelzebub— ordered.

When the men grabbed her, she leapt from one body to the next. Beelzebub's eyes remained fixed on her. Her consciousness took up residence in the soldier behind Paula. She removed her sidearm and put it to Paula's head.

"Don't make me pull the trigger."

Beelzebub shrugged. "There's more where she came from."

Paula peed herself. "P–please don't kill me."

There was no way for Lian to rescue Paula. Having seen Beelzebub's intentions, she couldn't very well let him have her, either. The choices shredded her heart and Beelzebub knew it. That cocky, shit-eating gleam in Elliot's eyes was present in Hershiser's gaze. He didn't think she had the guts. She needed to prove him wrong. Lian pulled back on the trigger and smeared Paula's brains all over the helicopter. The other soldiers advanced but Beelzebub called them off.

He plodded toward her. "I always knew there was a ruthless fighter in you, Lian." He smiled, pulling his hands from his pockets. "You were the most special of them all. Sanderson knew it. Your father knew it. Ra knows it."

"Don't move any further." She aimed at him but that didn't sway him. "I mean it."

"That won't do a thing to me." He unsnapped his shirt and displayed several bullet wounds in the chest. "I run on a different motor." He raised a hand, fingers curled, and the gun flew from her grip and into his. "You see, I'm a demon inside. One of the first. My power is much greater than others'." Beelzebub squinted and Lian froze. The bones inside the soldier's body rattled and snapped. He made a fist and she could feel the internal organs rupture, yet her mind remained trapped, feeling everything. "I can contort you all night but I have other places to be." He lifted his hand and she levitated. "Until next time, old friend." Beelzebub's fingers spread like an exploding star and the body tore apart, flying in several directions.

CHAPTER TWENTY-NINE

Jarrod V

Jarrod battled relentlessly with the unforgiving power of a riptide. His vision had blurred until all he could see was the adversary in front of him. The primal instinct for destruction, emphasized by the foreign voice in his mind, was a force neither he nor his opposition in green and pink aurascales could match.

Jarrod sunk a roundhouse into his hawk-faced foe. His fists were a blur. Each strike flowed into the next. His autopilot aurascales dictated the next attack. He dislodged the opponent's weapon, kicking him through a building and into heavy traffic.

Commuters of the early morning rush hour swerved to miss the two fighters. Jarrod tackled his rival with a shoulder, shoved him into the ground, and dug a trench in the road. A cargo truck barreled forward, unable to stop. Jarrod leapt backwards in a crescent motion, avoiding the vehicle. His enemy wasn't so quick. The 18-wheeler compressed like an accordion as it hit the figure. The tail end of the truck lifted and it fell on its side.

"Have you had enough?" Jarrod howled. "You won't hurt my friends."

Traffic came to a standstill in both directions. Smoke rose from the toppled truck's engine. The wreckage rattled as the man underneath pushed free.

It's time to finish him off, the voice inside Jarrod's head urged. But why? The fight was all but over. There wasn't a need. *You can't take that chance.*

"Question him and find out who he is," Jarrod insisted. The exo-armor retreated from his face and he pulled his hair. His skin had a bluish hue to it, glowing from within his veins. He noticed the shocked, frightened, and hurt people all around him. This wasn't the place for a fight. The only thing he'd achieved was to draw more attention to him and his friends. "You've gotta get outa here. I can't listen to you anymore."

You're a fool. I'm your savior.

Jarrod looked up and was viciously cracked in the face with a fist.

***

"We don't talk much about home anymore," Claire said, sitting on a chair, staring out the window with her chin resting on the windowsill. Her breath fogged the inside of the glass while the outside continued to weather the brunt of the storm. "Not really where we're from, since there's nothing to go back to, but where it'll be, if that makes sense." She looked longingly at Jarrod, who lay on a stained and torn sofa. "Everyone wants a home."

That was a pretty pointless discussion. Jarrod had already resigned himself to the road. Keeping his mind busy kept other things from influencing him. *Don't go there. Think of something else.* He wiped it from his mind.

"What was the other side like?" she asked, insisting on filling the nervous silence.

"Other side?" He wasn't sure of the question.

"I figured you're not one for talking about sentimental crap, so we should keep it business." Claire leaned back in the wooden chair and it creaked.

The rain relented briefly and the moon poked through the clouds. Light washed over her face, illuminating her eyes, reminding him just how beautiful she was. There was a time when she was all that got him through the night, thinking of returning to her, the warm hugs and smooth kisses on the cheek while he rested. She deserved more. More than he could ever give.

She shrugged with a sigh. "That's fine."

He assumed she was talking about the alternate realm. New Troy, it was called by Charon. It was a desperate place; musky, cold, and devoid of hope. A realm where candlelit homes and water churned mechanics went hand-in-hand with advanced computers and god-like powers. The people were oppressed by a hard-fisted rule, forced to comply by lashing or worse. It was the future of their planet, but it would do no good telling her that. Home, like it or not, would soon be obsolete for everyone.

"I'd never seen forests so thick." He stared at the ceiling. There were holes in it, making the cobweb-laden plumbing of the next floor up visible. "I remember looking out over the still waters, feeling the gentle and inviting breeze on my face, and all I could think was: this place isn't frightening." He sat up, glancing at Lian's body while she mind-melded with the girl they were rescuing. "The pine and cedar trees smelled so sweet—I could taste them in the air. It was strange, yet there was comfort in it. Something had to've been different with gravity or what not. Up-down-left-right-under-and-over, it all had no definition. And that was alright."

Claire sunk back, deep in thought, her foot grinding into the floor pensively. He was sure a steady diet of fingernails would follow.

"In a lot of ways, it was like it'd been through a reset. Or maybe it never started the game to begin with." He knelt beside Lian, checked her pulse, made sure she was still breathing, and then stood in front of Claire. He turned her chin up and rubbed his fingers along her cheek. She squeezed his palm between her face and hands. "That place and here fit together perfectly like… like jagged blocks. We have inspiration that they lack, but what we fail to understand they've always known. I can…" He tapped his chest, searching for the words. "I can feel the two coming together. All around us, in the air, everywhere and nowhere, all in sync as the cycle creeps towards something inevitable. And you know what I want to shout?"

"What?" she asked as if she didn't really want to hear the answer.

"That I'm OK with it… and that's not OK." He pulled her in close and turned his gaze out the window.

A distant explosion rumbled through the building. Claire jumped, pulling on his shirt. He ran into another room. A helicopter had crashed into a warehouse. The flames reflected off his face. An arrowhead-shaped aircraft became visible and then disappeared. He squeezed his fists and the aurascales slowly washed over his skin.

"Please stay," Claire urged. He turned around. She leaned against the doorway with a desperate fear shining through her eyes and skin. "Don't leave us."

***

Jarrod crashed onto a roof. The hawk-faced enemy landed on him, driving downward with his knees almost immediately. They broke through the ceiling and the dilapidated building—which had been hanging together by a thread—toppled inward with them inside.

Jarrod punched through the rubble, dust flying off his armor as he stood. That last blow had packed a wallop. The avian bandit was nowhere to be seen. He heard something stir behind him and his eyes crept over his shoulder. He took a section of concrete encased rebar and swung it. The concrete exploded into pebbles, but the impact knocked the soaring assailant through a still-standing wall.

"He can fly?" Jarrod stumbled out of the debris and outside. People watched the fight from atop an overpass while others hung their heads out of their condos and duplexes. Jarrod and this new foe had torn through the city, neither really gaining the upper hand.

Stay vigilant.

"I know what to do," Jarrod griped. He turned to the spectators. "If y'all people knew what was best for ya, you'd leave here." They continued to snap pictures and make calls. Police sirens grew louder. His armor erupted like a solar flare. "I said leave." The onlookers scattered.

"You are not without honor," the mechanical voice proclaimed, sounding like it was broadcasting out of a loudspeaker. It echoed down the residential street lined with tricycles, white picket fences, and tire swings. There was no way of knowing its origin. "But you are not the hope I seek. Instead, Death incarnate. I was foolish to think otherwise."

Jarrod was plucked from the ground and dragged into the sky by his shoulder plates. The winged fighter flew straight up and then slung him down. Jarrod tumbled end-over-end until he finally righted himself. The aurascales formed a layer of skin between his arms and legs, like a flying lemur. His enemy wasn't done.

A crossbow of light materialized over the foe's wrist and he blasted holes in Jarrod's armor. The wing suit vanished and he bounced twice off the ground before crushing the hood of a parked car.

Police surrounded the street. The avian bandit hovered a few feet off the ground with his crossbow still fixed on Jarrod. The faceguard slid back, exposing his tan skin and curly hair.

His eyes narrowed. "You wear Azrael's colors, yet you are not him. I'd like to know how."

"Yeah, good ol' Azrael," Jarrod croaked, rolling forward and falling face first onto the ground. His rickety knees barely worked. "I keep hearing that I bear a striking resemblance, and as much as I'd like to, I can't seem to escape his name." He squinted at the flying foe. "You know a lot about me. Who are you?"

"I am Horus, Prince of the Southern Corner, and guardian of my people."

Jarrod nodded. "Horus, yeah, I took a semester of mythology."

"Stop. Land. Put the… glowing weapon down and your hands behind your head," the police insisted over the megaphone.

Jarrod nodded their direction. "I'd prefer no one else get hurt, but I can't promise that unless you leave me alone or kill me."

"You mean to do them harm?" Horus shouted, gliding forward slightly.

Jarrod shook his head, biting his lip. His hands trembled. Someone near him had evil in their soul and he knew once he snuffed it out, he likely wouldn't be able to stop there. His lips quivered as he fell to his knees.

"I said kill me," he shouted. His eyes erupted, as did the urge to cleanse. "You don't know what it is inside."

Neither do you.

"I said shut up," Jarrod cried, picking up the car and slinging it at Horus.

***

"You don't know what's out there," Jarrod said, relaxing his muscles. The aurascales held back, momentarily. He took Claire's hands. "What are you afraid of?"

"I'm not sure anymore." A tear slid down her cheek. "Losing."

"Like a contest?"

"In general. Everything." A wise yet fearful glimmer was in her eyes. Like she knew what they both weren't talking about. None of them talked about it. Their silence around him was annoying. "Losing this world, losing the family I have left, losing you out there…" She paused and touched his head. "And in here. I'm powerless to help any of you, and right now I feel selfish to ask that you be here with me instead of helping the ones we love, but dammit, at some point don't I rank?"

"You always rank…"

"Oh, please," she scoffed. "Like when you joined the army to look after Austin because Mrs. Hanigan made you promise? That was noble, yeah." She rolled her eyes and let out a frustrated grunt. "Ugh… Sometimes I think the choice for you to leap is easy because you know I'll always be here when you get back. But what if I'm not?"

"I'll protect you." He hugged her tight and kissed her forehead. "I won't let anyone hurt you."

"I'm not talking about if I die, Jarrod."

He leaned back. What was that supposed to mean? "You're saying?"

"I just want to spend whatever time this world has left being happy. We got Lian to where she wanted to go, and Austin loves her. They're in it together." She looked at him, crying. "And I don't feel like you're in this with any of us. So where will home be, Jarrod? Our friends are fighting for theirs. What are you fighting for? Because I need to know if I'm a part of your home… if any of us are. If I'm not then I won't continue to fight for you to be in mine, because history has shown me enough to know when it's a lost cause."

"I don't, uh…" He pretended to not understand what she was talking about, but it was pretty clear. Another explosion rattled the windows behind him, rumbled through the floors, and shook dust from the ceiling.

She didn't even flinch. "In case the message is lost in translation, I'm saying if you go out that door—abandon me in this dark shithole to look after Lian's idle body alone—I won't be here for more than five seconds after she wakes up." She slung his hands off hers and pushed him away. This time, his silence was suffocating. She nodded. "You can be selfish sometimes. It doesn't always have to be about someone else."

If you only knew. Jarrod was dying to tell her that. Maybe it was unfair to keep secrets and not allow her to be brave enough to handle the truth. But whatever time was indeed left for either of them, it was best if she didn't waste hers waiting for him to get better. He wasn't going to. He was too dangerous for her to be around. "I have to go."

"You don't." She shook her head. "But you will."

***

Jarrod pulled shards of rebar from his shoulder. A pale blue light hovered over his wounds, keeping them sealed so he wouldn't bleed out. The light turned rigid. More aurascales slithered over his body, keeping his armor whole. He slowly stalked Horus, taking well measured steps towards his foe.

He stood on Horus' wrist and pulled the sword away. The Angelborn crawled backwards and manifested a shield. Jarrod struck, lodging the blade into and through the shield. The sword missed Horus' head by mere inches.

A trio of helicopters soared over head. The aircrafts unleashed hell upon the fighters. Jarrod sprinted away, zigzagging so quickly through back streets and alleyways that soon he was just another body in the bustling city. The sun replaced streetlights, and his aurascales vanished. The wound on his shoulder bled through his clothes. Passing by an apartment complex, he grabbed a few new shirts and jackets from clothes lines and redressed. He pulled a leather hood over his head and zipped the coat up.

Who runs from a fight? the voice taunted. He ignored it. *You're butt hurt.*

Despite the carnage on the other side of the city, the people seemed rather immune to it all. The busses ran on schedule and kids walked to school. It was like the rain had washed everything away. It didn't make sense. Was this the new normal?

People are lazy. They condition themselves to accept an inconvenience rather than fix it.

A red double-decker bus rolled up and he got on. He searched his new pockets and found enough spare change to buy a ticket. He lowered his head, walked up top, and sat in the back.

Horus tore through the bus, grabbed Jarrod by the head, and flipped him backwards. Jarrod rolled to a stop and tried pushing off the ground. Horus stomped on Jarrod's back, pinning him. His hands clamped around Jarrod's neck, squeezing. Horus pulled backwards with all his might, trying to snap Jarrod's spine.

"Do. It. Already," Jarrod urged, clenching Horus' wrists. "Rip my head off." He fought back against his aurascales, but they had other plans.

The voice in his head grew desperate, his life nearly extinguished. Then it felt something. Horus' soul, or an aura very similar. Jarrod, or the voice inside, laughed: the advantage was theirs.

A blue flare erupted. The blinding light drained from Horus. Jarrod could feel him grow weak. Horus' aurascales merged with Jarrod's, and the color of his skin faded until it was a sickly yellow.

Jarrod broke free of Horus' grasp and stood over the prince, choking him with one hand. Just as the voice inside Jarrod's mind grew to dominate, Jarrod decided he'd had enough. He released Horus before absorbing his life force.

No. You can't! the voice screamed. Jarrod hunched over, trying to shove the entity back into a box. *You will regret not finishing him. Devour them all and we can leave this place.*

"I won't," Jarrod growled. He grabbed Horus and returned the aurascales he'd stolen. "I'm dangerous to everyone and this is the only one who can kill me."

Horus looked at Jarrod, confused. His breathing steadied. He pushed against a light post and stood. "What are you?" he asked.

"I don't know." Jarrod covered his face sat on his feet. He looked at the sword forming Horus' hand, nodding in approval. Having nearly killed Horus by absorbing his essence, he'd seen inside and knew he was a good man. His friends would be in good company. "Do it," he begged.

Horus lifted the sword. Athena knocked him out from behind. He hit the ground, out cold. Austin pulled Jarrod to his feet.

"C'mon, we don't got much time," he panted, dragging Jarrod. Athena slung Horus over her shoulder. "Lian's awake. She's got bad news, and Claire is gone."

Fate lets us live.

"While it can," Jarrod whispered.

I fight for survival, Jarrod, said the voice. The sound pushed his brain against his skull. He couldn't breathe. Darkness crept over his vision like the time he'd nearly drowned. His grip on his shell was slipping. *What do you fight for?*

CHAPTER THIRTY

Jarrod VI

Lian prodded Jarrod with her foot. She stood over him with knuckles on her hips. "Wake your ass up."

He tried sitting. His ribs and legs felt splintered. Through his hazy vision, the fire-orange sky loomed over a burning village. A gigantic wall circled the horizon. The people's cries drowned out Lian's voice. Her lips moved and he heard nothing.

"The people." He pulled himself up and stumbled before gaining control of his legs. He bumped into Lian who steadied him. "You have to speak up." His eyes turned to the town. A boy was crying for help. "Can't you hear that incessant shrieking?"

Jarrod sprinted down a hill and Lian followed. The smell of burning flesh overcame him. God, was it potent. He stopped. The flaming house loomed tall like an executioner. Lian put her shirt over her face and tugged on his arm.

"Wake up," she insisted. He was relieved to hear her. The aurascales crawled over his body and he continued despite her words. "Come on."

Inside, the roof had caved. The heat had no effect. The aurascales coddled him and flushed his blood with adrenaline. "This has happened before, I swear."

"This isn't real," Lian said, standing next to him, sweating. Jarrod scooped her up and jumped outside. Her face was smeared with wet, black ash. She rubbed it off and showed it to him. "See, I'm fine."

"You're gonna get hurt," he yelled. A screaming child snared his attention. "I have to go."

Jarrod leapt into the home once more. It crumbled and slid towards Lian like a river of lava. She crawled backwards, eventually jumping to her feet and scurrying out of its path. To her right, three devious-looking horsemen sat on their sickly animals. Black hoods draped over their heads cast shadows on their faces.

The horses' pounding strides thundered against the ground. They were nearly on top of her when Jarrod sprang to the rescue. He knocked the spooky individuals to the ground. They attacked in unison, but were easily gutted. They fell to the ground and evaporated into blue mist. Jarrod lent his hand to Lian and lifted her up. The armor retracted from his face.

"It may not be real, but it's no less dangerous," he said, walking away.

She followed. They stopped at a child with charred flesh. Lian covered her mouth, trying not to vomit. Jarrod pulled a handful of the boy's crisp skin away, revealing the face of the child who cried for help.

"Is that... you?" she asked, in awe.

"It was." Jarrod nodded, still cleaning his younger version. "This is all I dream of anymore. I must've been here a thousand times." His eyes looked up at the brimstone-filled sky, crackling with lightning. "This part isn't a dream. It's the convergence of memories that aren't mine."

"Can you wake up?" she asked, pressing herself close to him. A crack formed in the giant city wall and portions of it crumbled. "You're in London. You've passed out and are lying on a sofa."

"This must finish."

"We didn't bring you back alone," Lian said. Jarrod was intrigued. "Do you know who the man piloting that... spaceship was?"

"He's Horus." Jarrod looked at the boy, who'd started breathing again. "In his thoughts—when I nearly killed him—he's what they call an Angel-born, with a soul or essence like ours. I could feel it and nearly consumed it. His memories are now in my head too. Is he awake?"

"He's alive, but recovering slowly from that wallop Athena gave him." Lian stood over his shoulder and watched as the boy awakened. "Does he mean us harm?"

"Horus or the boy?" Jarrod asked.

Lian giggled at Jarrod's question. "Horus, of course."

"Horus, no. He's like us. Lost and trying to unite his family." Jarrod stood and wrapped his arms around Lian's head so the sonic boom of what came next didn't deafen her. The aurascales covered his head. "The boy, on the other hand, he's the voice I hear. His name is Ryan, and I think he's the rightful owner of my body."

Lian looked up at Jarrod, confused. A blinding flare exploded in the sky. The sonic wave tore the landscape apart. She sat up straight—back in the dingy apartment—screaming her lungs off.

"You're fine," Austin reassured her. "What happened?"

Her eyes shifted over to Jarrod. He sat, staring at her while Athena stood next to him with her armor beaming and sword in hand. Jarrod flinched at the sight of the weapon, rolling out of the way. Athena was on edge, engaged. The point of her weapon pressed against Jarrod's heart.

Lian sprang forward and stood between the two. "He's OK. I've seen it." She pushed hair out of Jarrod's face, revealing his lost eyes. "I don't get it."

"What happened?" The last thing he remembered was blacking out to the voice in his head trying to suffocate him. Slowly, his body was becoming less and less his own.

"Can you remember your dream?" Lian asked.

"What dream?" Jarrod pushed away, his hands shaking. He imagined putting his head into Claire's embrace. It was for the best that she'd left.

"Who's Ryan?" Lian asked.

"That's Jarrod's last name," Austin responded.

283

"No, the boy Ryan. The one inside your mind. The voice you claimed drives you mad." Lian pulled on Jarrod in a rage. "You have to remember, dammit. You've nearly killed us all because of the shit you've kept to yourself. Tell us."

"You're the one out of control." Austin yanked her back.

"Don't touch me." Lian finagled a way out of his grip and held her hand up. He crumpled over, in pain. Alarmed at her own actions, she stopped. She knelt, too tepid to touch him. "I'm sorry."

"Look at who's the monster now." Austin pushed her away.

"I'm done." Jarrod moved for the exit.

Give the bitch a psychotic breakdown, Ryan laughed as Jarrod walked away. *Only I know what you are. Only I can understand you.*

"I heard that, Jarrod." Lian stood, glaring at him. "Or should I say, Ryan."

A small tear collected in the corner of Jarrod's eye, and a smile formed. Could someone finally understand?

"You can?" he asked. "It's not just me?"

"I don't know how I can hear him, but I can." She motioned for him to sit. To the loud protests of Ryan inside his brain, he obliged. Her fingers crawled along his temples. "Jarrod, I want you to think of a number."

41, Jarrod thought.

"Any time now."

"I already have," he sighed. He tried to stand but she pushed him back down by the shoulders. "We've been through this. You can't read my mind. I don't have a soul."

"I can't read Athena's mind either, but that doesn't mean you can't drain her essence." Lian moved around the chair and stood in front of him. "This Horus you fought with—he's an Angel-born just like Athena. In your dream, you said you nearly killed him by draining whatever passes for a soul inside him."

"We have not a soul," Athena said, still gripping her sword tightly. "What you're describing is impossible."

"It's not impossible," Lian contended.

Kill the bitch. She's messing with your mind, Ryan demanded. Lian's eyes went wide, afraid.

"Don't worry. I'm not going to," Jarrod chuckled. "I can control some things."

"That's much appreciated." Lian let out a relieved breath.

"How do you know all this?" Austin asked, pulling a chair over to sit behind Jarrod. "Who told you?"

"Jarrod did." Lian and Jarrod stared at each other. Her hands shone brightly as she touched his head. Her eyes rolled back. The veins in Jarrod's face rose to the surface. Lian pulled back, in pain. "There's a soul in there, Jarrod. You're human after all. I can feel it, but it's fighting against me. I'm not strong enough on my own to overcome it."

"I'm not human." Jarrod had already come to terms with being something else. He didn't want to accept a new path.

You're a freak, Ryan taunted. *She knows it. You should be the one locked in here.*

"Don't listen to him, Jarrod. We all love you. We're going to help you through it." Lian tenderly rubbed his hand. "I can get inside. I know I can."

You're too weak, Ryan laughed.

"Maybe I have answers," Madame Patricia said. Everyone turned, surprised to see her.

"I called for her when we came across the Spear," Athena said.

"The what?" Austin asked.

Athena rolled her eyes. "The spaceship."

"You read my mind and the secrets locked in my subconscious," Madame Patricia said to Lian. "Since then, I've been going through a period of self discovery to find out what those hidden truths were."

She held Jaden's hand and cautiously approached. "The reason William separated you two is because your powers strengthen exponentially when together. Apart, you're half of what you can be.

That's the exact reason why the Architects agreed, in our treaty, to go our own ways. Our powers grow unstable when we're in the prolonged company of others like us. That's why you and I, and Jaden, melded as one when the three of us touched. You and Jaden... Together, the two of you are an Architect."

"What am I?" Jarrod asked. It was time to stop bottling things up and seek help. The anger of what Sanderson and his mother had done could no longer dictate his actions. "I'm ready to find out. I thought I was strong enough to handle things on my own, to fulfill my own purpose, but I know now that I have to place faith in others." Jarrod grabbed Lian and Austin by the hands and squeezed. "If I were to do anything to the ones I love, then what would be the point of living?"

Oh please, let me play the world's smallest violin, Ryan huffed, his words eventually turning into a full-on laugh. Jarrod's eyes flickered and he rocked back and forth. *The time for child's play is over.*

Jarrod collapsed onto the floor, foaming at the mouth. His desperate eyes fixed on Lian.

"What's wrong with him?" Austin moved out of the way so Lian could kneel by Jarrod.

"There was a child in his dream. A child Jarrod claimed was named Ryan. He said Ryan was the true owner of his vessel." Lian placed a hand on Jarrod's back, speaking to Madame Patricia. "I can hear Ryan thoughts. There's two personalities..."

"There are two halves to Jarrod." Madame Patricia escorted Jaden to Lian's side. "Sanderson told me about Ryan, a clone of who I know to be Azrael. Sanderson merged the cloned DNA into the dead embryo that was inside his wife, reigniting its life. Supposedly, the powers and connection Ryan had to the many realms was uncanny. The boy was scared and too powerful for his own good. Sanderson believed he'd died along with his wife in a house fire..."

"I will destroy all life for what they did." A blue shockwave surged from Jarrod's body and threw them all back. Ryan was taking control. It was he who spoke.

Jaden grabbed his sister's hand and covered her mouth to keep her quiet.

Ryan continued to scream, "I hear you speak of my mother, but the bitch was nothing of the sort. Instead of helping me control what I was, loving me despite my destiny, she locked me away and let Jarrod roam instead. Not anymore. The wall is down for good and Jarrod will burn while I'm free."

Athena grabbed Ryan and tossed him backwards. He rolled to a stop. Athena lunged, driving the point of her blade towards him. Ryan flicked his hand up and Athena went rigid. Her aurascales vanished. Blue flames circled her frame as she levitated unwillingly. Her eyes shone with pale blue light.

"That's not a soul I feel." Ryan squinted, unsure what to call it. It felt good, making him powerful. He tried touching Athena, but Jaden intervened.

A white energy flowed from Lian's eyes. With her brother, she entered Ryan and Jarrod's collective mind and searched for the wall Aunt Liv had created.

"Wait," she said, holding her brother's hand. "The dream he always has. We need to find the burning child."

"I hear you," Ryan shouted. The ground shook.

Reality in Jarrod's mind shifted. The dream world he was stuck in every night came to form. There were two Jarrods, stuck in a deadlock. Jaden tugged on Lian, pointing at the wall. While the duplicates fought, the wall fractured.

Lian lifted her hands and large boulders pieced the barrier together, sealing the cracks. One duplicate flickered and the other overcame it. Ryan vanished. Jaden released Lian and they exited Jarrod's mind.

Jaden laughed and walked away from his sister to sit in a corner of the room. Austin and the others gaped at Lian, looking for answers.

"Did it work?" she asked, groggy. They remained dears in a headlight. She squinted at Jarrod. "I hear nothing."

"That doesn't mean it failed," Austin reassured.

Jarrod's eyes opened, but instead of a tired fear overcoming him, there was a sense of relief. He smiled at Lian, breathing heavily.

"Jarrod?" Lian asked, crying. She crawled to him and sat on his lap.

"I'm OK," Jarrod said softly, rubbing her head. "I don't hear him."

"For now, yes." Madame Patricia brushed herself off. She looked at Lian and Jarrod. "But for how long? Until you learn to merge your human soul with your angelic aura, you're a danger to yourself and everyone else."

"Human and angel?" Lian asked. She thought about it for a second and finally nodded. "The boy Sanderson knew was human and angel. When Aunt Liv could no longer keep Ryan under control, she split the two halves, locking the unstable soul away and creating the personality of Jarrod to control his angelic side." She smiled at Jarrod, amused at the answer. "I can't read your mind because you're an angel."

***

Horus—hands chained—flinched when he noticed Jarrod standing over him. The room with broken floorboards was barely large enough for a twin size mattress. Jarrod remained silent but vigilant, etching a note into the wall. His armor was gone, but he knew Horus didn't pose a threat.

"Thank you for sparing me." Horus sat the book he was reading onto the pillow. "You could have easily not."

"It's not that easy." Jarrod was short on purpose. He wanted to see how Horus would react. The twitch in his guest's eyes said he believed otherwise. "Well, killing you would've been simple. Living with it, not so much. I don't like what I am more than anyone else."

"And yet there you stand and here I sit." Horus lifted his chains. "Clearly there is something trustworthy about you."

"I think they figure cuffs are useless." Jarrod smirked, finding Horus' dry sense of humor entertaining. "It's probably better to not ruffle my feathers, or get me anxious. I've got this Jekyll and Hyde thing going on."

"I noticed," Horus quipped.

"You understand the reference?" Jarrod was caught off guard.

"I lived in space, not under a rock. We procured human literature from time to time." Horus flashed the book he was currently reading. "Hamlet is one of my favorites."

"Is that because the son takes over for the father? Avenges him?" The memories he'd absorbed from Horus had grown more poignant since Lian had helped quiet Ryan, as did the memories of past souls. "I hope that didn't seem too forward. I know how the memory stings. I figured we'd be transparent, given how well we know each other."

"The story always had a familiar sense about it. I don't know why. I found Claudius' betrayal of his brother cold and unthinkable." Horus shrugged, standing from the bed. His fingers roamed over the book's edges. "Hamlet's mother is like my own. She's unaware that I know the things she did to keep me safe... to keep herself in power. No, she didn't bed my uncle, if that's what you're thinking."

"I wasn't." Jarrod shook his head. "The others don't know if you're a friend or foe. I told them who you were. Madame Patricia and Athena recognized the name, but they aren't telling me why. I didn't clue them in that I already understood the significance."

"Did you say Athena?" Horus asked, shocked. "I was told she was—"

"—Dead?" Jarrod nodded. "I know. The two of you were to be married. Kind of like fate that you're here, with us."

"With you, too." Horus furrowed his brow and folded his hands. "Seems destiny has a way of making itself go full circle, despite how hard we fight against it."

"I'm hoping that's not entirely true." Jarrod thought about something his mother once said. How she was afraid of what he'd become, but the world would need to deal with it. He didn't want the world to deal with it. He didn't like surrendering to fate. "I'd rather believe in free will. Worst case scenario, I'd sooner put faith in random chance."

"A trillion decisions, coincidences and occurrences had to take place for you and me to stand here together, at this very moment in time and space. The knowledge and love that spawned your birth had to age in perfect symmetry with my growth in the time warp of a collapsed star, so that whatever galactic force saw you on that street the instant I arrived could bring us together." Horus smiled, laughing under his breath. "If that's not masterfully constructed chess maneuvering, then I know not what is."

"You forgot Athena." Jarrod smiled. "Your child bride. Care to meet her?"

"I suppose." Horus sat on the bed. "Bring her in."

"No, I meant, would you like to *GO* and meet her." Jarrod pointed at the chains. "This is all a little overkill."

"How can you be so sure?" Horus asked.

"Because you need us to rescue your family." Jarrod unlocked the cuffs and they collapsed into his aurascales. He nodded for Horus to follow. "I know about that too."

"Why would you do such a thing?" Horus followed as if walking on glass. His voice was nervous. "That is the wrong question. I should be grateful."

"I know what it's like to leave your friends behind, failing your family and the ones you love. I don't want you to feel that." Jarrod pushed through the door and into the main room of the apartment. The others waited. They were uncomfortable with the plan and showed it. "Everyone, this is Horus. His cousin is a prisoner of war and his mother held captive by traitors with ill intent. We're going to save them."

CHAPTER THIRTY-ONE

Lian VI

Lian kept her watchful gaze on Jarrod, continuously scanning his head for signs of Ryan. Even though Ryan was absent, the plethora of other voices clamoring for power in his absence gave her pause. Jarrod shot her a squint.

"Can you focus on what's being said?" he asked Lian, referring to Horus' speech. The others were enamored with the space prince.

"None of that will matter if you come unhinged," Lian whispered, turning her eyes to Horus while she spoke. She leaned close to Jarrod. "What about all the others who are stirring around in there?"

"They're echoes, not conscious thoughts. I can handle them." Jarrod looked down at Lian, nodding. She wanted to believe him, but had doubts. He sighed, irritated. "If you're not convinced I can do this, then lock everything into a safe and drop it in the ocean. Make me a vegetable."

"Don't think I won't, just because you're my best friend." She prodded him with an elbow, turning her attention to Horus.

"Where are they now?" Austin asked Horus about Isis and Hathor.

"The rift should have delivered them somewhere on Earth," Horus said, rubbing the stress off the back of his head. "I need to reenergize my starstone in order to locate them. Anything built under the Southern Corner star will have a connection."

Madame Patricia was wary. "I'm sorry, but we can't permit..."

"Of course you can," Jarrod interrupted her. She sneered at him in return. Lian was shocked he would make such a commitment without consulting the others. "What do you need?"

"If I could only borrow the power of another starstone." Horus' eyes were filled with hope. "I should be able to reignite my aurascales."

"Hold on, Jarrod." Austin grabbed his longtime friend by the wrist. "We can't offer up things that aren't ours."

"You're right." Jarrod nodded. "I mean, we can debate what takes precedence when the clock is ticking. But we know there's more going on out there than what we can handle on our own. I see a way to build our alliance and tip the scales in our favor. There's a game that's been played since creation first sparked. We're just now getting onto the board. So, if you have any other suggestions on how to catch ourselves up, I'm all ears."

Lian was happy that Jarrod was finally showing flashes of the cocksure soldier he'd been when she'd first met him. Slowly, he made her a believer. No one else was sure. The room's silent doubt stunted the flow of debate.

Jarrod looked at each of them, hoping to find affirmation. Athena narrowed her eyes, shaking her head with defiant determination. Lian could hear that Austin was torn. She couldn't take her eyes off Jarrod. When his gaze fell to her, she smiled. That same honest look he'd displayed when offering himself for the Double-Helix sparkled in his eyes. It was a hope she'd not sensed in him since Sanderson died. That was all the convincing she needed.

"He's right." Lian nodded. The others rolled their eyes, so she knew a case had to be made. "I don't have eons of knowledge and fighting skill back up my judgment, an inner beast to take over when cornered by the enemy, or the ability to construct worlds. But what I do have is an intimate knowledge of Jarrod's heart, despite the lack of connection to his mind. I've had my doubts and concerns. But I trust him with my life."

Before anyone could argue against her, she steered the debate. "How does it work?" Horus was shocked by the question. She nodded but remained stern. "You want us to trust you? We need transparency."

Athena offered her hand to Horus. The two exchanged a look of understanding. A static charge surged through Athena's hand and swirled around Horus' arms. His green and pink aurascales bubbled to the surface of his skin. His shiny silver armor grew from the fluid green and pink swirl, hardening. The hawk mask stretched over his face and his eyes glowed with green light. All of Athena's armor vanished as she transferred any reserve power into Horus' starstone.

"I too believe," Athena said, catching her breath.

Horus swiped his fingers over the back of his wrist. A cone shaped light sprouted over his forearm and a map of far-reaching constellations took shape in the hard light constructs. Hundreds of fuchsia, cypress, and mustard flickering dots overtook the spheres of blues and tan. Jarrod was drawn to the figures, almost in a trance. He stepped towards the map, but Lian tugged him back.

"This is strange," Horus said, almost in a panic. His fingers sifted through the light, sliding the image on all axes. "The green dots are others like me, powered by a Southern star. The yellow ones are our ships. This large one is our fortress, but it lingers in a place I don't recognize."

"What about your mother's escape pod?" Lian asked, pressing the issue to keep Horus focused.

"It's vanished." Horus replied. The light map dissipated and he hung his head. Austin patted his back, trying to restore confidence in the new ally. Horus extended his arm and the light reappeared. "I remember the sector we were in. If I can acquire another chariot, I can head out there and find it for myself. Maybe the problem with my map is a proximity one."

"A chariot?" Austin wondered aloud.

"A jet that can fly in outer space, like the one Jarrod tore apart," Athena replied. "How did you get your hands on the previous chariot?"

"When the Four Corners were intact, they built hideouts, gateways, and slipstreams all over the planet. If I retune my locator to find them,"—Horus held his tongue between his lips as he focused—"I can simply find another and leave. There."

The holographic map reshaped into an image of Earth. On the surface of the rotating sphere, yellow and pink dots were sprinkled all over the map. This time, it was Lian who was infatuated. She pointed at the dots, calling out the locations.

"The pink dots, are they rifts?" she asked. Horus nodded in reply. "Look here, it's Stonehenge, and here is the Bermuda triangle. That one is the rift in Afghanistan that we took to New Troy."

"There are others in South Africa and on the Pacific coast of South America," Austin chimed in. He pointed at a black spot in northern Mexico. "What is that?"

"I know not." Horus shook off the question, seemingly more concerned with finding a way to Isis. He pointed at several clusters of yellowish dots. "This is where I found my previous ship, Northern Africa. What are these locations?"

"The others are New York and Paris. Likely museums with exhibits." Jarrod pointed at the dots. "It would probably be easier for us to rift to an off-the-grid locale in Egypt and search for a chariot than to fool around in a crowded city. Plus it would help mitigate collateral damage."

"Agreed." Horus retracted the light. "When can we leave?"

"We can't rift anywhere," Athena cautioned. "Without a coded crystal, Heaven would locate us."

"Wait, I have one." Horus patted his pockets. "It must've been left in the Spear."

"You got what you needed," Madame Patricia said in cold tone. She tugged on Athena. "It's best we be on our way."

"No." Athena pulled away. "I was under the impression we were on the same page?"

294

"You were wrong," Madame Patricia snapped back. "This will be entertained no longer." She looked at Lian. "If you wish to stay with your brother, it would be wise to agree. The things we deal with are far larger than a reuniting a random Angel-born with his mommy."

"Excuse me, but are you barking orders?" Lian asked, ready to slap her.

"Call it what you will, I make no apologies for the tone of my voice." Madame Patricia leaned in close to Lian's face.

Oh, a cat fight, Austin thought, a little too excitedly. Lian scowled at him. "Right. Totally wrong."

"I would if I were you," Lian said to Madame Patricia, making a fist.

"Y'all can stay and fight if you'd like," Jarrod interjected. He prodded Horus. "We'll head on our way. You don't need me anymore."

Madame Patricia and Lian spoke in unison: "No."

"Why?" Jarrod asked, gawking at both of them. "My mind is made up. Either you two start making some decisions, or I'm bolting."

"What's the real reason you want to leave?" Lian asked, stomping her foot. Her lungs decompressed a thousand pounds of stress. "You know why we can't let you go."

"I won't hurt anyone," Jarrod replied.

"But you're afraid you will," Horus added. Everyone looked at him. Jarrod went white and silent. "I could hear your voice in my head when you nearly drained whatever lingers inside me. You begged me to kill you, afraid you'd kill everyone."

"Not just everyone." Jarrod knelt and rubbed his face. He glanced at his friends, solemnly. "The people I love the most. It's bad enough knowing I can't save them; it's even worse knowing I might be the one to destroy them. The only way I can't harm anyone is if you dump me on a desolate planet. It's the only place where I can't possibly drain someone's soul and unleash Ryan."

"So you were going to help rescue Horus' family and just ask us to leave you isolated?" Lian asked, realizing how insulted Jarrod must have felt when they didn't trust him. The shoe was now on the other foot and it stung. "You're the key to it all, Jarrod. There's no hiding from fate. They would find you."

"Who?"

"Heaven," Lian said, "and their Assassins."

"The Assassins?" He looked up, smirking as if not believing it.

"It's true." Horus stood beside Lian. "The Corners have been abuzz with news of your arrival. A middle-guard angel who made his home in Moscow told us of you. He mentioned that the Assassins sought verification of your existence. Believe me, when an Assassin leaves a deserter alive, it's because they received information far more valuable than a random coward's life."

"So why am I valuable?" Jarrod walked over to Madame Patricia. She was the only one with any sort of answers. Her face was pink with shame. When she didn't answer, he said, "Then keep it a secret. After all, it's been secrecy that's given us our good fortune so far, no? Let's just continue the tradition."

"The four horseman of the apocalypse are the scourge of prophecy that no man, angel or otherwise, can stop." Madame Patricia took in a deep breath. "It was always a debate if the horseman were literal or figurative. Perhaps they're a combination of the two."

Jarrod snickered, anxiously rubbing his arms. Everyone apprehensively stepped away from him. Noticing they were on edge, he relaxed his tense body language.

"I know." He nodded in reply to Madame Patricia. "I've always known. The horsemen in my dream. I can overcome the others, but not without fulfilling the vision and becoming the last."

"You have prophetic visions?" Athena asked. "What else do they say?"

Jarrod hesitated. Lian decided to alleviate him of the burden. "That only Ryan can keep us all alive."

CHAPTER THIRTY-TWO

Set IV

The rift closed. Those nearby were stricken with fear, as well they should have been. Beelzebub had been a busy bee and Set was none too happy about it. Then again, transparency never was any demon's strong suit. Still, he expected more from Beelzebub. He'd wormed his way into the top ranks of his species long ago and completely understood the arrangement with Set and his allies.

Set held a hand up, halting his two compatriots. He half expected some sort of snickering from Hermes, but none came. Maybe he finally knew his place. A few of Beelzebub's lower-levels marched on an intercept course with Set. What did they really think they could do? When he took a second to count their numbers, he found that a few dozen approached. That would be little more than a handful.

"I didn't realize I'd be such an honored guest," Set mocked, bowing to the cackle.

"You're not on the schedule."

"Au contraire." He smirked. "I've a standing reservation." A metallic sphere slid into his palm. He kicked the lead demon back into the core of the group and released the device. It spun so fast while emitting its white energy that it appeared to be completely still. It erupted, sucking many of the demons from their meat suits. The ones it didn't, Set attacked.

He chuckled. It was like brutalizing invalid kids at St. Jude's. A severed arm here. A fractured spine there. One demon had his face crushed in by his knee. They used guns, but weren't able to get a lock. Set's jagged wrist blades split a gunner in half.

"I'm here," Beelzebub called out. With his hands forced into his coat pocket, he teetered back and forth on his feet, shrugging. "To what do I owe the pleasure?"

"The descendant you offered let a little more slip than I'm sure you cared for." Set jammed his blades through a pleading demon's head while walking towards Beelzebub. "Have anything you'd like to admit?"

"Forgive me Father, for I have sinned. It's been, I don't know, three thousand or so years since my last confession," Beelzebub laughed.

Set grabbed him by the neck and lifted. "You think you're amusing?"

"A little," Beelzebub croaked. He tapped Set's hand in submission. "I'm good."

Set pulled him closer, eyeing him. "You sure?"

Beelzebub flashed a-thumbs up and Set threw him several yards into a truck. Beelzebub coughed, readjusting his suit as he stood. He nodded. "You regained your form."

"Never lost it."

"Of course." Beelzebub nodded, still rubbing his throat. "So which one of the sniveling retards I sent to escort that half-breed pissed their pants first?" He looked over to Hermes and Sif who were standing guard over the demon who'd confessed Beelzebub's plan. "Right. Mind if I teach him some manners?"

Set shrugged, indifferent.

"Oh, Danny boy," Beelzebub whistled. The demon informant looked up, shaking his head. He slunk behind Sif who pushed him forward. "Be a good chap and hurry along," Beelzebub tormented. "That's it."

Danny shuffled his feet, head down. "Sir?"

"It's not that I don't like my friends here stopping by for a visit." Beelzebub motioned to the Assassins, pulling his subservient in close. He whispered, "It's that I don't like them coming for a visit."

His hand moved up the back of Danny's skull, tearing into the skin. The demon screamed. His body contorted to the chorus of splintering bones. Beelzebub snapped Danny's head back, breaking the neck. The demon shivered on the ground, trapped in the body, in agony.

"Some fates are worse than death." Beelzebub tapped Set on the shoulder as he walked by. "Do come."

Set followed. "What's with the large military presence? The British government is fine with having American forces in the homeland?"

"You know I've an arrangement with the queen…"

"I'm sure," Set interrupted, clearing his throat. He crossed his arms. "A new breed of gifted… Have you been making them?"

"I've been helping them realize their potential earlier than usual, if that's what you're asking." He rifled through a mini-fridge, removing a beer. He offered one to Set, who seemed disgusted. "Yes, I am too. It's this body though." Beelzebub popped a can and guzzled. "He liked the cheap shit. Slowly, I've been refining his tastes."

"You're stalling."

He smiled slyly. "Can't blame me for trying."

The wrist blades shot out. Set remained still. "I can do other things."

"Maybe you'll be a little less annoyed when I tell you he's here." Beelzebub wore a satisfied gaze. Set moved forward, intrigued. "Your mission, right? Death."

"Where is he?" Set loomed over Beelzebub, irate he'd not alerted him. "You weren't going to tell me. Why?"

"I need more time."

"Your plan is secondary to whatever we've got in motion." Set hacked Beelzebub's arm off, just below the elbow. No blood gushed as his heart no longer pumped.

Beelzebub held his other hand up. "Please, I still need this body. My work isn't done. Even in a rage, you understand assets."

"Why are you working with Ra?" Set kicked Beelzebub onto his back and stood on his chest. A few ribs popped as he leaned with more pressure. "What do you mean you're helping this new breed realize their potential?"

"The ones promised to lead in the end days," Beelzebub grunted. "Please..." Set stepped off. Beelzebub wheezed. "If I help them reach maturity early, he takes them. Some of them have already matured... The powerful ones blossom early."

"What does he want with them?"

"Does it matter?" Beelzebub slowly stood, examining his severed limb. "How am I going to explain that?"

"It matters to me!" Set yelled, raising a fist.

Beelzebub cowered to his knees. "It's not what he gets but what we do." Set narrowed his eyes. Beelzebub continued, "We found a portion of a muse's starstone. In exchange for the gifted, he'll reignite its power far beyond its original capabilities. With it, we duplicate Azrael as we did Zeus. Maybe even recover his piece of the Forge."

"You'll risk waking him."

"When we get that far, you'll be my first call."

"I don't like it." Set shook his head. There was a piece of him that refused to admit it wasn't a bad plan. Ra had his way sodomizing young ones, Beelzebub continued wreaking havoc. The less promised when tribulation rolled around, the better.

"How many pieces of the Forge do you have, anyway?" Beelzebub asked snarkily. Set didn't acknowledge the question with so much as a look. They both knew the answer. "You're no worse off. The way I see it, we both know this muse-starstone I've got belonged to Aphrodite. We can sense it. That means Maya is no longer ruling her people, and the piece of the Forge she possessed is in jeopardy. Shiva is taking his sweet time acquiring Vishnu's, and you let Osiris' wife slip between your fingers with his. That leaves Thor's, which is off the reservation. Azrael's, and we both know where he is. Gabriel's, and then, finally, Michael's, and good luck prying that from his hand…"

"I'm working on it." Set bit his finger, contemplating.

"Yeah, you seem to be doing a real good job of it."

"Your tone," Set warned.

"Face it, we need each other equally. Sure, you could take my head and trap me in one of those little devices of yours. Then what?" Beelzebub asked. "Who do you get to do what I can do? You want Jarrod—that's Death's name, by the way. Your mission is to do whatever with him, and then what? Hurry to collect the pieces of the Forge?"

Beelzebub didn't see that those two things were mutually exclusive. To get all the pieces, Set needed to complete his mission. Then again, his personal goal was to prevent tribulation. Killing Jarrod would be the easiest way of delaying it.

"Where are they?" Set asked.

"I can help with that." Tunrida stumbled into their conversation. Beelzebub held her up. "I met an Angel-born. He took me in his spaceship."

"Did he probe you?" Set bit his lip, unable to help himself.

"I wish." Tunrida stared longingly into the sky. "He's strong. He rejected the water spirits."

"I wish you wouldn't frequent those bath houses," Beelzebub said, stroking her face. "Leaving the city is dangerous."

"Yes, you could run into the Assassins." Set walked around her.

"Dad, don't worry," she replied to Beelzebub. "I'm fine."

"You don't look it," Set pressed. "What happened?"

"I was going to tell you that…" Beelzebub started.

Set interrupted. "I was asking her."

"His name was Horus and he finds death." She shivered, pulling on Beelzebub's sleeve. Set exchanged nervous looks with the elder demon. "I was hoping Bannik meant actual death, but when we soared through the city, and those hollow blue eyes landed in front and ripped through the windshield, I knew Bannik spoke of the actual Death."

"My nephew and Death?" Set asked under his breath.

Beelzebub pursed his lips. "It seems your unfinished past is catching up with us."

"I'll fix the problem."

"You better." Beelzebub squinted angrily. He looked at Tunrida, coddling her. "Anything else?" She shook her head and he pulled her into his clutches.

"Which way?" Set asked. "If he's tearing into spaceships, there must be a scene."

"That's how I got away." Tunrida tried to sit up. "When Death brought us down, he pulled Horus from the shuttle. I escaped while they fought."

"That was the ruckus I was going to tell you about," Beelzebub said.

"You need to leave and stay far away," Set implored, pulling Beelzebub to his feet. "If they're attracting attention to themselves in a squabble, other forces are going to be alerted. I need to quell the issue before it gets out of hand and Michael comes poking around."

"Who's in charge up there?" Beelzebub asked, grinning. "Do I smell a coup?" Set just stared, making Beelzebub giddy. "Who was the first to go?"

"Just leave." Set pushed Beelzebub away. He turned to Tunrida. "But I'll need her to come with me."

"Impossible..." Beelzebub went silent, shrinking away. Set's eyes showed that he meant business.

"Take me." Set offered a hand and pulled Tunrida to her feet.

***

The area was decimated. The Assassins and Tunrida weaved through the local authorities, blending in. To their left, an apartment building under construction was torn to shreds, and to the right a warehouse was in ruin. Through the center of the avenue was a crater leading to a crashed ship.

Set looked it over from a distance. It was a Spear. Those hadn't been used in over a millennium, abandoned long before the Pride Rebellion. How did Horus get his hands on one of those?

"Why here?" Hermes asked Turnida.

"He had a lot of questions about what we demons were doing. I was afraid he'd kill me, so I told him." She sat against a wall behind the huddled onlookers. "Part of my team was responsible for tracking down the chosen. My mental connection with the other demons alerted me to what was happening. For about a week now, these groups of unknowns have been interrupting our hunts. We didn't know it was Death and his friends until last night."

"That's what brought your father in." Set nodded. The Spear would have more answers. "Stay put," he commanded.

"Yes sir," Hermes complied, drawing a grin from Set.

Set activated his aurascales and went transparent. He slipped through the investigation scene unnoticed. The Spear's systems activated when he approached, putting the nearby humans on edge.

He walked into the building that the ship had crashed into and de-cloaked. The navigation systems were still active. All power had been rerouted to there. Horus grew to be a crafty one, evidently. One of the nearby human officials stood motionless, pissing himself.

"If you don't scream I won't have to kill you," Set advised calmly. The men and women nodded, minding their own business. He crawled into the Spear and messed around. "You've been to Kom Ombo. You learned your history well."

Set removed a crystal from the rift-system. The information inside was still intact. He was curious to see where it led back to, or instead he could use it to find Horus' current location. Since there was no telling what he'd find rifting back to wherever Horus made the crystal, he decided to use what little energy remained to find him on earth.

A plume of powder fell over his head. He looked up, staring holes through the woman who'd stumbled.

"Please, excuse me," she pleaded.

He released a heavy sigh, shaking his head. Set stepped out of the Spear and went invisible. He arrived back in front of the other Assassins.

"What did you find?" Hermes asked.

"Return home, Tunrida," Set insisted. She sprang to her feet and ran. He removed the crystal. "We get one shot. Let's make use of it."

CHAPTER THIRTY-THREE

Isis III

A jostling yanked Isis awake. The rush of what seemed like a dozen spikes sliding into her head made her eyes feel like they were going to pop from their sockets. Again, her surroundings rumbled. Everything was hazy. One of her eyes couldn't focus. The other didn't work at all.

A female voice spoke to her, but everything was jumbled. The woman continued to squawk. Isis couldn't think of a reason why the faceless voice would be so agitated with her. It didn't make sense. Nothing seemed right. *Where the hell am I?* The main concern in her heart was Horus' wellbeing.

Isis slowly tuned into Bastet's voice. She was grabbed and jerked from her resting position. "I hate asking twice," Bastet said, voice raised. Isis still couldn't see her.

"Forgive me. My head…" Isis stuttered. "It hurts."

"I could end your suffering," Bastet growled.

"That is not what master ordered," Taweret chided. At least that was who the lumbering voice sounded like. She *was* a rather masculine woman.

"Bastet, please. She's not to blame," Hathor pleaded. Someone delicately stroked the back of Isis' head. She assumed it was Amun's daughter.

The floor wasn't rumbling. It vibrated with a dissonant hum. She could smell those around her, suggesting cramped conditions; were they in a chariot? If they were on a shuttle then where was the Armada cruiser?

"Where are we?" Isis asked, panicking.

"The better question: where are we going?" Hathor whispered to Isis.

She didn't know? It was hard to believe Amun hadn't told his daughter of their destination.

Isis finally processed a sliver of light, seeing outlines but not much more. There were five other individuals in the chariot with her. Bastet, Hathor, and Taweret were three of them. Who were the other two? The way Bastet and Taweret spoke, it was unlikely Amun was with them. However, if Hathor was among the group then the two other silhouettes were probably Amun's wife and son.

"So Amun didn't completely leave you to ruin?" Isis mocked Sekhmet, who was well aware of her husband's lustful affections for Isis. Just how much wasn't clear. Even still, Amun was a hard man on his family. It pleased Isis to prod Sekhmet, if only to comfort herself. "Is your son still a drooling mess? I can't see him, but I hear a murmuring retard. Served him right."

Isis, of course, referred to the time Anubis beat Hapy to a pulp. The battering was so intense that Hapy's eye-sockets were crushed, his skull was fractured, and his brain swelled to twice its normal size. Many of his cognitive abilities never recovered. It was widely known Hapy deserved what he got, having tricked Anubis into a compromising sexual position with an animal, a jackal.

"You've no retort?" Isis asked. Sekhmet's silence wasn't surprising. Amun had savagely trained her to know her place. "Just as well. No telling where or how he'd stick you for speaking up. Well, the how wouldn't be hard to ascertain."

"Enough of your words," Taweret yelled from the pilot's seat. "Bastet, come." She sounded concerned. Were they lost?

"I've always held a certain fondness for you, Hathor," Isis whispered, taking the Angel-born by the hand. "Do tell, where are we headed?"

"I was hoping you would know," she replied tepidly.

"Quiet, you two, or we'll launch you in the chute," Bastet yelled.

"If that were true, Bastet my dear, you'd not have hauled me along for the ride." Isis giggled, resting her hands behind her head. Her eyesight slowly progressed.

"That one upset her." Hathor continued stroking Isis' head while it was on her lap.

After a few hours of blindly cruising through the cold of space, Isis regained her vision. It was well-timed and fortunate because her captors had grown increasingly anxious with the prospect of being abandoned and left for dead. She was frequently on the receiving end of nasty snarls and evil glares, and had to be able to defend herself. Even if Horus was in possession of her starstone, her ability to move quickly in close confines enabled the use of the surroundings to her benefit. One such strategy could be to pull the release for the back hatch and kill everyone. The fact that Isis had a way to ensure mutual destruction kept Bastet and Taweret in check for the sake of self preservation.

Chirping noise from the shuttle's relay beacons alerted them of familiar tech nearby. Isis was overcome with hope and trepidation. On one hand, she had a way out of this space coffin. At least being with Amun meant her body and their relationship afforded her a tiny bit of clout. Then again, if Amun had orchestrated the destruction of her Corner and set up a throne elsewhere among the stars, what need would he have for her other than as a sex slave? Perhaps death would be a better fate.

"There's nothing but emptiness out there," Bastet groaned.

Isis leaned forward to catch a glimpse of the monitors. There was a section in space void of any light. The stars on the black canvas dared not venture there, yet were sporadically placed along the perimeter of the darkness.

"What we seek is there in the void," Isis said. Bastet motioned to throw her back into the seat, but Taweret steadied her friend. Isis leaned into the cockpit. "The Giver of Day," she said softly, as if cold realization was overcoming her.

"The one father spoke of?" Hathor asked, joining Isis hand-in-hand. "The Burned man's realm?"

"The Architect." Isis nodded. She reached for the controls, but the others pushed her away. "You lot are crazy. You know not what you do." She turned and frantically crawled for the rear hatch. Suffocating in space and having her body explode and rupture from within was a far better fate than what was in store if they continued on this path.

Just as her hand touched the hatch lock, a club struck her and knocked her out.

***

Isis sat up. What was this place? Was she blind again or were the lights off? Her clothes were different, that much she could feel: a lacy dress made of soft fabric. Remnants of a time long abandoned on a planet once called home, crafted by those seeking her guidance.

She slid along the stone floor. She hadn't felt something of this composition in ages. It was as if it'd been super-heated then slowly cooled and smoothed to perfection. Gaining traction was impossible.

Where the hell am I crawling? She moved in a random direction. There was no telling if her guess was correct. Something had to be done. Anything. Inaction was the wrong action.

Sounds of life, echoing through the black, encouraged her. Her head bumped into a wall. A dead end. Yet sounds of others talking through the stone encouraged her to pound the wall until her flesh broke raw.

It was useless. The good news was her eyes probably worked. The bad news was imprisonment for the foreseeable future. Exhaustion soon set in. Suddenly the wall lifted and she fell onto her side. The light was blinding. The extended stay in the darkness had warped her eyes. A hand lowered and she took it, not seeing much of a choice. It was Amun. His musk was unmistakable.

"My lovely Isis," he said, kissing her hand. "I've longed to see your face."

"I didn't get that impression when you bashed my head into the floor, stealing that girl away." Isis doused her words with sarcasm, but only drew a chuckle from Amun. "Where is the child?"

"Making herself comfortable among her new surroundings."

Amun escorted her into a brig of sorts. Carved into the rock were several inlets barely the size of her closet. A radiant barrier of black fire blocked any escape from the inlets. The prisoners were all children— none older than a teenager. Boys were to the left and girls to the right. Isis understood. The kids were like trophies rather than prisoners. Each was well maintained and didn't lack creature comforts such as chocolates or toys, though none were free. She finally saw Rashini. A clearer picture took form. All the children had to be like her. But what was that? How did it coordinate with Amun and Ra?

"Are you OK, child?" Isis asked Rashini. The girl sulked into the corner, continuing to comb her doll's hair. "Precious little one, all will be OK."

"You make promises you cannot keep." Amun's large hands wrapped around her shoulders and massaged. He breathed down her neck. "I wish you didn't make it so difficult for the two of us. Things could've been simpler."

Isis looked down the corridor. The empty cells far outnumbered the occupied by at least four to one. Whatever Ra and Amun were planning, it was still new.

"Tell me, Amun, why Ra? What do you get out of this alliance?" She turned, pressed her chest against his, and stroked his frizzy beard. He seemed pleased with her posture. "Did you come to him before or after my refusal to marry? Was our arrangement never sufficient?"

"It'd be a lie to say you didn't satisfy certain desires, nevertheless I always yearned for more." He pulled her along, walking past the empty cells. Isis tried to keep count, but there were too many and their pace was too quick. "The idea of the Architects intrigued me long ago. The seed planted in my head during the Pride Rebellion. Before Osiris' death, I ventured to find these beings... to consult with them and consolidate power. What I found was the startling truth that we'd all been lied to, Isis, from the beginning. Lucifer had more justification than previously thought."

"Lucifer, a hero?" Isis scoffed. The sickening twist in her gut worried her—maybe it was true. A lot was adding up to that conclusion. The memories in her mind she swore weren't hers. The lies about infertility of angels. The rage and massacre of the Angel-born. Why would God go to such lengths to stifle freewill for her kind? Were they really second class to the humans?

"I know the wheels are spinning in your mind..."

"Why Ra?"

"The power at the center of our starstones—the glowing gem which fuels our energy and regenerates our alloy—was his design." Amun pushed through a gate and out onto a terrace overlooking nothing but blue sky above and clouds below. They were inside a mountain, but where? "They say angels are born of light and forever linked with the stars, and when ours fade, collapse in the cold, unrelenting embrace of space, so does our life force. Where do we go? Nowhere. We cease to be because we've not a soul capable of transcending space-time. Ra reinvigorated my starstone. Ra is the sun of our solar system. We revolve around his true power. I deliver what he wants, in this case specific children, and he gifts me with more power."

"Why doesn't he just take the children for himself, or use his own powers to fight against God and unite with the other Architects? Yes, I know there are many."

"The Architects are not warriors, nor do their powers last long beyond their realm." Amun gazed at the multitude of suns in the sky with reverence. "He and I shall unite our lineage and become one: Amun-Ra. When the galaxies align and tribulation nears its end, passage between realms will no longer weaken our power. We will keep tribulation from happening."

"Then what, when you've stopped the end?" she asked, already knowing the answer. One tyrant would be replaced by another. Hordes of innocent lives would be enslaved in the name of vengeance, or slaughtered. She remembered the words of her sweet Osiris: hope lay with the Angel-born.

Hope was a fine concept, though it seemed all of it had dried up.

CHAPTER THIRTY-FOUR

Anubis III

lank-Clank-Clank

Anubis opened his good eye, pulled from his sleep by the noise. His torso burned as if ropes of steel wool were yanking his bones in opposite directions.

Clank-Clank-Clank

Blood dripped from a fresh opening in his mouth and formed a puddle between his legs. Teeth collected like a small chain of islands in the sea of red at his feet. His head swayed like a pendulum. A plethora of footsteps hammered around him. Pee dripped down the man's leg to his right, forming a rival ocean next to the blood.

Clank-Clank-KaClunk-Psshtt.

Chains rattled. A steel cage opened. It took four men to drag Anubis behind the group of prisoners. Skanda cracked a whip.

At first the scintillating light blurred his vision. The surroundings took shape as his eyes adjusted. A mess hall of gold, silver, and fine gems greeted him. Jade carvings melded into the gold floor resembled lotus flowers, waterfalls and constellations. Marble columns of cream and salmon were adorned with large, gleaming sapphires, emeralds, and rubies, all carved to resemble stars. Ginger and cinnamon incense made Anubis lethargic and numb. His face no longer felt like shattered glass.

All prisoners were commanded to halt and face a throne atop a pyramid of golden steps. Seated above for all to see was a hooded figure, gangly and misshapen. The man's frilly purple and white robe covered all portions of his body except for his lace dressed hands. Shadows blanketed his face.

"Lord Vishnu is so majestic," Anubis overheard one of the girls behind him swoon.

He looked at this supposed Vishnu. The odd sight was not what he'd expected, especially given the way those in his Corner talked about him.

A group of five teenage dancers—boys and girls—performed to the rhythm of tambourines, hand drums, and bamboo sticks, and the melodic mix of sitar, sarangi, and tambura. Their graceful jumps and arm waves were exact like a crane. Their routine was evocative of a martial arts exercise, yet it was open and accepting like a mating ritual.

They danced in a line, curving between one another, gyrating their hips, bending backwards to reveal their intimate parts, disrobing and fondling each other during the sleek movements. Despite the sleazy and pleased expressions of the many subservient angels under Vishnu's command, the Archangel himself remained still and relatively unimpressed. He nodded with his index finger, as if saying 'move on with it.'

"Welcome to Swarga Loka. Today, we honor our god, Lord Vishnu, the supreme purveyor of truth, the light of destiny, and fulfiller of wisdom and prayers," the attractive woman to Vishnu's right proclaimed. Anubis recalled his lessons. She must've been Lakshmi, Vishnu's primary consort. She stepped forward and blew through a conch shell. Those below touched the ground with their foreheads. She chanted quietly, building up into a thundering roar. "Om Vishnave Namah."

The group followed suit. The crowd tapped their hands on the floor, sounding like a frenetic snare drum. Vishnu nodded. Lakshmi took his Gada and pounded the floor five times. The crowd went silent as if no one dared breathe.

Vishnu stood and Lakshmi disrobed him, revealing his bare form. His skin was a combination of dark brown and a sickly looking pale blue. Many scars and lesions littered his body. Calloused boils formed rough patches over his back, stomach, legs, and bald head.

His original arms were mismatched. One was muscular and sleek; the other thin and miniature, almost as if it were cut from a tinier individual and sewn on. It grew from a mangled mesh of skin just above the bicep. Nearly a dozen other limbs grew from nubs along his ribs and thighs, even along the base of his groin.

The five teenagers formed a semi-circle at the bottom of the steps. They knelt, rigid and motionless, with their eyes lowered. Their upper bodies were bare. Vishnu walked among them, groping the breasts of the girls and rubbing against the boys. He made them stand. Lakshmi removed their skirts, revealing their freshly trimmed and waxed figures. She bent the first girl over for inspection.

Vishnu groped the girl's buttocks, at which point Anubis turned away. Skanda forced his head around, but Anubis closed his eyes. The girl groaned. Anubis glanced as Vishnu slid his hand out of the girl and moved onto the next teenager. The boy grimaced and bit his lip to suppress his grunting. Vishnu shook his head. The boy knelt and the process was repeated for each dancer. Finally, the second boy met Vishnu's approval. The others dressed and backed away slowly.

Shiva and one of his lieutenants carried a chaise lounge into the middle of the floor. The crowd swayed left and right. The women hummed and the men chanted. Lakshmi escorted the chipper teenager over to the chaise and bent him over with his ass raised. He called out for his parents, and they returned his seemingly happy words with cheerful applause of their own. Lakshmi poured a liquid into the boy's mouth and he immediately went limp, but still cognizant.

"What the fuck is this?" Sobek murmured. Anubis turned left. His uncle knelt not far away.

"Shut your mouth old fool or I'll have your head," Skanda whispered, spitting into Sobek's ear.

A few servants powdered Vishnu and massaged his body. He nodded and they stopped. He circled the boy. Only the teenager's eyes moved in acknowledgement. Lakshmi spit on her hand and stroked Vishnu until he was aroused.

Anubis couldn't bear to watch, on the verge of tears. He just wanted to go home. The cold and inhospitable surroundings of Amun's Armada cruiser were far more welcoming than whatever this was. For several minutes he scrunched his eyes shut, listening to the boy groan in pain while Vishnu wheezed and hacked.

Finally, Vishnu decompressed with an elaborate moan. Thinking the ordeal over, Anubis looked up only to find Lakshmi slice into the boy's skin and choke him with a garrote wire.

Vishnu conjured a starstone. The boy's soul left his body and merged with Vishnu's starstone. His skin illuminated with a pale blue glow, drowning out his natural dark pigment, and split apart while his sores oozed. He moaned with delight. Shiva dragged the chaise away with the dead boy on it.

The wounds and gashes on Vishnu sealed. Several of his nubs elongated. One sprouted a hand with three fingers. The crowd rejoiced.

"Your worship and the boy's sacrifice honor Lord Vishnu. The galaxy rewards our faithfulness," Lakshmi proclaimed. She clapped while servants dressed Vishnu and escorted him up the steps, supporting him as he walked. Lakshmi spoke again, "What is the word from the Southern Corner? Shiva, what have you before us?"

"This is repulsive," Khepri said. Anubis was relieved to see that he, too, was alive. "What kind of demented cult have they become? Khnum was truly ignorant."

"Quiet, fool," Sobek mumbled.

"I bring god Vishnu an offering. The last remnants of the Southern Corner, to be executed for his glorification, sold into slavery to replenish his holdings, or broken by our whips and ingrained into his service." Shiva nodded at his son. Skanda kicked all of the prisoners flat on their faces. Khnum cleared his throat, getting Shiva's attention. "There is one I wish to exalt, your Excellency. A man without whose assistance our task would've been much greater. He honors my Lord with the highest of gifts: his service. He wishes to be placed under my foot."

"Bring him forward," Vishnu said with a raspy voice. Khnum knelt beside Shiva. Vishnu waved his hand, bored. "Yes, very well. Permeate his starstone and change the color of his banner. What else have you?"

"Several women and young ladies who would make excellent sacrifices to bestow further gifts upon your body." Shiva stamped his foot and the ladies were dragged by their hair and placed at his feet. One of them was Khepri's mother. He struggled to remain still.

"Do not give them the satisfaction of knowing they torment you," Sobek urged.

"Their scents interest me not. They shall be sold." Vishnu turned his nose up. "Have you any Angel-born warriors?"

"We have." Shiva tapped Khnum on the shoulder, nodding at Anubis and the others.

Khnum introduced them one by one. Each was offered a choice: change the color of their banner and fight under Vishnu, or be sold into slavery and live out their days in the fighting pits. Many chose to worship Vishnu, just as their supervising officer Khnum had chosen. Very few, including Sobek and Khepri, refused and were dragged off to be sold.

Anubis shrugged Khnum off. It took six men this time to drag him to Shiva's feet. Vishnu was curious, sitting forward and pulling his hood back. His eyes ravaged Anubis, almost as if he recognized him.

"Your name?" Vishnu commanded. When Anubis refused to speak, Vishnu clapped his hands. Khnum kicked Anubis in the ribs, causing him to spit more blood. Vishnu grinned, enjoying the sadistic beating Khnum continued to rain down. "This will end when the words are uttered from your lips. Your name."

"Anubis," he said, finally relenting. He could barely speak. Khnum threw him to the ground. "My name is Anubis."

"Yes, I knew you looked familiar." Vishnu smiled. "You were the first Angel-born, were you not? Your father Set—brother to Osiris—was the first traitor of his people. His dishonorable blood flows through your veins. I assume that accounts for the ghastly color of your skin."

Anubis shook his head. That wasn't true. There was no traitor in his blood. "My father… is dead."

"The innocence in your voice is both arousing and humorous." Vishnu leaned back and crossed his legs. He snapped his fingers for a drink. A crystal flute filled was presented to him. Lakshmi held the beverage while he guzzled. Streams of white drenched his throat and chest. "You believe me not? There are no lies spouting from my tongue. To suggest otherwise is a sin. I am divine truth. Your father, Set, murdered the great Osiris and delivered the head of your mother on a platter to Heaven's gates. Concerned more with his own hide, he now serves as a groveling slave to Michael and his cock-sucking brigade." Vishnu's cackling hack echoed. Anubis seethed with anger. "He's an Assassin, performing lapdog duties the Archangels are too pretentious to do themselves. You're gray because your father is dishonorable."

"This cannot be," Anubis sobbed. He snarled at Vishnu. "You're as divine as my ass." He wanted to rip the throat off that grotesque and malformed psychopath with his bare hands. "Cast me into the pits with my kind so that I may annihilate all in my path, imagining your head upon their shoulders."

The crowd gasped. They waited to see how Vishnu would respond. His jaw snapped shut and his eyes narrowed with fire. Just as it seemed he was about to speak, he erupted with laughter.

"Very well." Vishnu stood, holding his hand up to keep the servants at bay. He marched down the steps, alone. His Gada with a diamond shaped head followed suit, thumping each step as it trailed behind. "You think your situation couldn't possibly be grimmer, but you've yet to learn true misery."

With his one good arm, Vishnu lifted the weapon and swiped it off Anubis' forehead. Anubis hit the ground. His vision momentarily

318

flickered. Vishnu went for a follow up strike to crush his prisoner's skull, but Shiva spoke up.

"Would be a shame to extinguish such a physical specimen before exhausting all resources to reprogram his allegiance. Think of the power he would fight with under your banner if he were to be turned," Shiva said, drawing Vishnu's attention. His lord nodded, probing for more information. "In all of your great wisdom and reign, I have never seen you make a final decision without first exploring all options. It's what makes you the powerful and just lord we all would die for. Allow me time to teach this blasphemer the truth of your all-mighty stature, bending him to your will and command. I will make a great warrior of him in your honor. If not, we will cast him to the pits for a good show, and eventually I will face him in combat, push him to his breaking point, and allow you the honor of execution."

Anubis' sight flickered again. The sounds of those talking around him grew faint.

"You've my blessing," Vishnu said with a yawn. "Take him from my sight. I grow tired of this court. I retire to my quarters."

"As you wish," Shiva replied and took Anubis by the feet before he passed out from the pain.

CHAPTER THIRTY-FIVE

Madame Patricia II

She meandered through the open market with Jaden close by her side. Jaden held his fingers over his nose while passing a fish stand. She teased him by lifting a carp and offering it, laughing when he faked a gagging sound.

She smiled. "What will you have then?" He pointed over at a chocolate shop on the corner of the crowded Swiss street. Large snow piles were stacked next to the shop windows. "You need something healthy. You're a growing boy."

In fact, he was growing. They'd spent less than a day back in the human realm, and already Jaden was half a year older. His body compensated for lost time. It was the same for her, though her physiological makeup was better able to counter the warp.

"Let's get some fruit and bread. Then we'll see about chocolate, if we have time."

Madame Patricia sifted through the fruit. There wasn't much of a selection, given many trade routes were closed as a precaution since last summer's event in Moscow and the other in London just yesterday. She jerked when the flames roasting chestnuts to her left inexplicably went out and came back on seconds later.

Her mind immediately leapt to conclusions. *It can't be him.* She pulled Jaden closer to her anyway. She gave the clerk a few coins and thanked him for the fruit. Denial wouldn't do any good. Ra must've been close. She had to remain alert.

Again, Jaden pointed at the chocolate shop, tugging her arm.

"Not right now," she insisted. "We must get back." He tilted his head to the side and opened his eyes in a sad, puppy dog sort of way. "Alright."

The top layer of a snow pile melted, forming a trickling stream into a nearby gutter. The snow on the awning evaporated. The shop across the street had all of its snow. She panicked. *Where's Jaden?* He stood unharmed, sampling chocolate.

"Honey, try and stay close, OK?" She approached Jaden and all of the candy and chocolate in the display cases melted. The room was a sauna. The man behind the counter stood motionless and hazy eyed. They'd been found. "I thought we agreed to never meet again."

"Did you think me a fool?" The hissing sound of Ra's voice slid across her back. Her fingers clung tightly to Jaden. Smoke snaked through the air, forming a rigid outline before turning solid. He placed his ironclad gloves on top of the display case, rattling the glass. "Your surrogate daughter and her friends work against me."

"She's left the roost." Madame Patricia stood between Jaden and Ra. Both of the Architects glowed as their powers fed off one another. "What they do, they do without my consent."

"Indeed," Ra chuckled. He turned into smoke and passed through the display case, reassembling next to Jaden. He knelt to the boy's level. "You like the mask?" Jaden nodded. Ra turned his head and sighed. "You wouldn't like it if you had to hide behind it. Do you like hiding?"

"That's enough," Madame Patricia replied, stern. She moved Jaden behind her once more. "There's nothing for you here."

"Don't be like that." He stood. "You don't really know what I want, not just for me but for us. It was a purity I felt when we were last together, intimately. We can have that again."

"If I refuse?"

"Your boy here is like us, as were those your surrogate kept from me. Debts need to be paid." Ra moved his hands close to her face. Heat radiated from them. She moved and slapped his hand away. "There are others like him. Able to use their powers, yet not confined to a gem like us."

"What do you want with them?" she asked. When his head snapped up in a curious fashion, she knew she'd let on too much. "I, too, figured it out. They don't deserve to be collected like trophies."

"They deserve to be treated like precious gems because that's what they are." Ra's chest rumbled with a suppressed laugh. He offered his hand. "Care to join me and see?"

"Not really..."

"It was a rhetorical question." He removed his mask, revealing molten red flesh covered with crispy-black patches. His scraggily hair was thin and singed. He grabbed Jaden who screamed in agony. The crisp flesh on Ra's face was replenished and made healthy, sealing in the gooey red lines. Long black hair grew thick, down to his shoulder blades. His eyes remained yellow like the midday sun. He released Jaden. The boy fell to the ground. "I don't wish to keep my guests waiting."

Pink vapor trails spiraled together, forming a swirling portal between realms in time and space. Madame Patricia, with Jaden, stepped through. At first her bearings were off. The light of his realm was so intense she could barely open her eyes. Ra snapped his fingers. The light fell back to a comfortable intensity.

"You will get used to it." Ra pushed through a set of doors leading to an underground cavern carved into a mountain. It was his home.

"How long do you plan to keep us?" she asked.

"You can leave whenever you want." Ra turned, walking backwards. "The boy gets a lifetime sentence."

They passed a chariot with carvings in a Southern Corner dialect. She recognized the design from long ago, in a memory unlocked by her proximity to the siblings. She wondered if Ra had uncovered similar hidden memories since encountering their kind.

"You have visitors from the Southern Corner?" Madame Patricia asked, following Ra down a long corridor. The hallway opened into a dining hall. Four fireplaces, each on a separate wall, illuminated the room along with candles placed all around. In the center of the room was a U-shaped table, big enough to seat nearly a hundred guests. "Plan on having a ball?"

"I always do." He clapped his hands and a few butlers approached. Their eyes were melted shut. "Retrieve our guests, both honored and forced alike. I'm famished."

Ra gestured for Jaden and Madame Patricia to sit near his large seat at the cross section of the table. They obliged. Two butlers pulled their chairs back. On the far side of the room, she recognized Isis approaching the table. A slew of children, none older than teenagers, spilled into the dining hall behind her.

"Danu, please allow me to introduce you to the lovely Isis. Wife of the fallen Osiris, former queen of the now defunct Southern Corner." Ra took a sip from his chalice and nodded for Isis to sit. "The cute young lady to her left is Rashini Nambitu. The child of the dead bastard who lost Durga's gem. I had to pull together quite a few resources to resurrect those Ourea cunts and hire those wretched Islamic radicals, only to see her incompetent father lose the damn thing. You may be wondering why she and the other kids are here."

"It crossed my mind," Madame Patricia whispered.

"Rashini," Ra said, clearing his throat. The girl went rigid, closing her eyes in fear. He slammed the table and she looked at him. "It's polite to look at your elders. Now, welcome our new guest Jaden here with a hug. You two have a lot in common."

Rashini looked at Jaden, crying. Isis touched her shoulder in a calming manner. The girl approached Jaden and he stood. They hugged one another. Their skin illuminated with a transparent glow and they fused together with blinding force.

"Enough," Ra commanded. Rashini stepped away from Jaden and returned to her seat. Ra smiled. "Did you think the boy and his sister were only special with each other? No. There's a whole fleet of these new Architects out there who are powered by souls and not gems. They work together and the more in their collective the more powerful they become."

"Still talking of Architects, gems, and souls, my darling?" Hathor giggled, approaching the table from behind Madame Patricia. Her flowing lace dress slid along the floor. Her hair was rolled up on top of her head. She kissed Ra while running her hand over his face. "You are a handsome devil, aren't you? Just know I loved you before you regained your looks."

"How fortunate you are for this arrangement by your father," Amun said. Madame Patricia recognized him from her meeting with Ra at Beelzebub's club. His long fingers snaked over Hathor's shoulders as he moved past her with his wife in tow. His son Hapy sat to his left. "Another Architect graces us with her presence. With whom do I have the honor?"

"I am Madame Patricia..."

"No," Ra yelled. Everyone jumped in their seat. He laughed. "My apologies. I just get so worked up and flustered when excited with future promise. Please, Danu, shed that horrible moniker and embrace who you are. You're among friends."

"Forgive me." Madame Patricia nodded. Jaden's hand clung tightly to hers. "I am Danu, the Architect of Earth. I parted the seas from the sky, and the sky from the land. I am responsible for ensuring the sanctuary of all of God's chosen creations."

"How marvelous." Amun applauded pompously. His wife reluctantly followed suit. His son remained unmoved. "Please forgive the attitudes of my family. They're having a hard time coping. I didn't want to leave our home, but certain individuals lacked proper motivation to see things my way. Ra understood the whole ordeal."

"I don't follow." Madame Patricia shook her head.

"He means he's a traitor, rapist, and adulterer. And now he's whoring his daughter out to this mad man," Isis snarled. She pushed her food away. "I'm not hungry."

"I'll provide you with all the nourishment you'll need later this evening." Amun glared at Isis. His wife looked at the ground, somber.

"Your woman seems none too pleased with such talk," Madame Patricia said, poking the meat on her plate with a knife.

"Yes, my poor, unfortunate wife, Sekhmet." Amun twirled her hair around his fingers and then yanked her close. "She pleased me once, gracing me with my beautiful daughter Hathor. I endured a second time, resulting in this retarded bastard you see at my side..."

"He wasn't always so," Hathor interjected. "If it weren't for the beating Anubis—"

"Quiet, daughter." Amun glared at her.

"I'll remind you she's no longer your daughter, but my consort to be had at my discretion," Ra said, calmly eating his food. "A bargain you readily made for safe harbor when you were unsuccessful at securing claim to the Southern Corner's throne. You'll acknowledge her with respect."

"Of course." Amun nodded. "Yes, that dumb nephew of yours, Isis. He gave Hapy such an uncalled for beating that it left him with permanent damage to the mind."

"Uncalled for?" Isis laughed, slapping her knee. "Now you play the jester, Amun. The stories told say Hapy rightfully got what he deserved. Beside, you had Khnum repay the deed to Anubis tenfold with that lashing. You later forced him to wear the mark of a jackal as a reminder for his deeds. I'd say both Hapy and Anubis were more than punished for their actions."

"What do you have to say of this, Sekhmet?" Madame Patricia asked. "To see your husband hold affections for another woman who despises him?"

"She knows when to keep her mouth shut, and when to open it," Amun chuckled. "For me to insert my cock."

"Count yourself lucky she doesn't bite it off." Madame Patricia smiled, drinking from her cup.

"There wouldn't be much to bite," Isis quipped, exchange winks with Madame Patricia. "I think I'll have some wine now."

"Yes, do drink up. A woman of such radiant beauty should enjoy the spoils of her company." Ra lifted his drink to Isis. "You're still such a rare specimen to behold, despite your years and child bearing, no less. For you to keep things in such tight quarters is either a testament to hard work or good genes. It's no wonder Amun carried such lust for you, given his own wife's... let's just say 'weathered' appearance. If the space between her thighs is as loose as the skin on her hips and belly, then I can't blame Amun for looking elsewhere."

"I too shall be fit after bearing a son, much like our recently deposed queen," Hathor laughed, rubbing Ra's arm.

"That remains to be seen." Ra sliced through a chunk of meat and chewed it in an exaggerated fashion. "The blood of your mother courses through your veins. A popular human saying suggests that looking at one's mother-in-law shows one's wife's future."

Hathor laughed nervously. "Well, surely some of hers is stress-induced..."

"Whatever the cause, Isis sits before us with beauty still unmatched by many stars, even young ones." Ra glanced at Hathor. Her lips shut and her eyes cast down. "Osiris must've counted himself lucky to be the first to lay with her."

"It was I who was lucky to have known the love of such a man. For him to fill me with a presence never rivaled to even half the worth was truly a gift." Isis drank her wine while Amun turned pink. "This is good."

"It seems the festivities become livelier." Ra tapped his chalice and the butler poured more wine into it.

"Food." Hapy drooled over his placemat and repeatedly banged his fork on the plate. He cackled. "Food for mouth."

"Yes, it is. Please be quiet," Sekhmet whispered.

"Food for mouth," Hapy yelled, growing louder the more his mother trembled.

"Can you shut that retarded twit up, dammit?" Amun threw his napkin on the table and stood from his seat. He lunged for Hapy—his wife trying to get between them—and grabbed his son by the shirt. He scooped the food and forced it into Hapy's mouth. "Food for mouth. Now chew and shut up. Next time I'll leave you with Tawaret and the servants and you can eat their mush. Pathetic moron."

"I'll not have you treat my brother as such," Hathor said, squinting at her father. Her lips pursed and she breathed through her nose. "You don't have to love him, think fondly of him, or even speak to him with respect, but I'll draw the line at cruelty."

Amun opened his mouth in shock, red in the face. Ra returned Amun's agitation with a stone cold look and Amun nodded humbly. He spoke with forced contrition. "As you wish, my beautiful daughter."

"So you're collecting special children," Madame Patricia prompted, moving the food around her plate with a fork. "You spoke of prophecies and said there were others?"

"Surely you know the week-of-years is upon us?" Amun asked.

"My words weren't for you," Madame Patricia snapped, "but for our host. Ra, please do share this prophecy."

"It's really the combination of many different prophetic words. It starts with those who shall inherit the Earth after the chosen believers are called home in the rapture. The book speaks of 144,000 people who shall be saved. An insignificant sum, if you stop and think of it." Ra leaned back in his chair and belched. Hathor wiped his mouth dry. "But the words were translated wrong. Wires were crossed when the Father divinely inspired his messenger to deliver the word, or perhaps John wrote them wrong. It wasn't 144,000 thousand shall be saved, but 144,000 people made whole shall save."

"That's quite the misunderstanding," Isis scoffed, rolling her eyes. She swayed in her seat, still drinking her wine. She drunkenly raised her cup. "My glass is empty." A servant quickly filled it.

"It gets more interesting." Ra clapped his hands and a teenage girl was dragged out of line and into the middle of the room. As if routine, Rashini immediately stood and walked to the teenager's position. She touched the girl's face.

"Nothing happens." Madame Patricia shrugged. "I don't get it."

"Child," Ra said with force, pointing at Jaden and then the teenager. "Touch the beaten one."

Jaden looked up at Madame Patricia, frightened. She kissed his forehead and rubbed his cheek. He conceded. Rashini stepped away to give him and the teenager space. Jaden knelt. His fingers caressed the girl's leg. Her wounds healed. The contact of their bodies glowed, turning into a translucent light.

"Made whole, I concluded, means to become one flesh." Ra smiled at his own genius. "In the beginning, he made man and woman to populate. Divine intention not made possible with the union of like genders. For them to equal our power, they need man and woman." Ra waved Jaden away. "Very good, boy, you may stop." Jaden remained touching the teenager. He smiled, glaring at Ra. The Architect stood, agitated. "I said enough."

"Jaden, don't." Madame Patricia rose from her seat. The boy flashed a grin.

Jaden pointed at Ra. In a flash, molten plasma from the sun tore through space and released through his hand. Hathor jumped out of the way. The energy pounded into Ra. That section of the table splintered into a thousand burning shards upon impact. Jaden removed his hand from the teenage girl, watching the smoke clear. When the haze dissipated, Ra stood firmly in place. His beautiful cream skin had cracked, charred in several places. Red lines of magma split his flesh, but otherwise he remained unaffected.

"I am the giver of day. The stars that power angels, give life to the Earth, and imprison Lucifer were built by my hand. Did you really think that would be an effective weapon?" Ra lowered his open palms, directing them toward Jaden. Streams of fire swirled outward and threw Jaden across the room. Ra closed his fists and the fire ceased, but Jaden continued to burn. "You will learn to accept your new position."

"Help!" Jaden's screams eventually ceased. The flames scorched his lungs.

"My boy!" Madame Patricia yelled, running to Jaden's side. Even though they weren't of the same blood, the years spent raising him had imparted a motherly attachment. She removed her long coat and doused the flames. Smoke hissed from his skin. His hair was gone and his flesh oozed. Red heat blisters sprouted up on places that weren't completely burned through. "You cruel and evil monster, he's just a child. You are unaffected by his actions—why did you take it so far?"

"He will learn to fear my hand, much like a dog trained to heed its master." Ra removed his iron mask from his back pocket and placed it over his face. "I will see his wounds tended to. He will be well cared for, but he must obey."

Ra nodded and a couple of men hauled Jaden off. His groans echoed down the hallway until finally he was so far away that they could no longer be heard. Madame Patricia looked over at her onetime lover, wondering how he grew so twisted.

"I fear I no longer have an appetite, but merely desire the taste of wine and women," Ra said, gripping Hathor's dress and pulling her so hard that her dress tore. He smelled her hair. "Have you lain with a man? Tell the truth, I will feel it."

"I've not." Hathor shook, closed her eyes and turned her face. "My chastity is yours, but I wish to keep it until our vows are complete."

"It is tradition," Amun added.

"Tradition?" Ra chuckled, speaking loudly. "There is no real tradition for you angels. There's only the breaking of it for love, greed, and wealth. The very fabric of the Angel-borns' existence was founded on breaking traditions..."

"Hathor is to be your wife and to do as you see fit for years to come," Madame Patricia interrupted Ra. He scowled at her. "Give her this small token. Surely your pleasures will be tenfold when you consummate."

"I have desires that need tending to." Ra gazed at Madame Patricia, presumably remembering the decades they'd spent ravaging each other. She lowered her blouse and moved her hair behind her ear. "You would have us rekindle old flames?" he asked.

"The two of you?" Hathor was shocked. "You were once together?"

"Yes, before the war of pride and creation of man, we Architects had free rein." Ra smiled.

"I would have you again, if you would me." Madame Patricia nodded, hoping to win favor with Ra so that she could personally see to Jaden's injuries.

"The idea holds intrigue, yet I fear beauty has long since fled your face. The familiarity of our union holds little to be discovered." Ra looked at Isis, devouring her with his stare. "The Southern Queen, on the other hand, holds under her blouse treasures worthy of my stature."

Amun begged, "Pardon my saying so..."

"Hold your tongue," Ra interjected. "Do you wish to sway me from familiarizing myself with your sex puppet? You forget your position. She is no longer yours to invade, but mine if I desire." Ra groped Isis. Amun bit his lower lip while looking longingly at her. His wife smiled at his displeasure. Ra continued, "Reserve yourself to your wife before I decide to take her too."

"As you wish," Amun conceded, bowing. Sekhmet winked at Ra. Amun noticed the exchange, snatched her hand, and jerked her along. "We retire to our quarters."

"You will have another woman before our union?" Hathor stuttered. "This used play toy?"

"Used she may be, yet she holds far more appeal than any other I've cast my eyes upon." Ra stared Hathor down. He smelled Isis' skin. "And there's something to be said for the experience of a woman versus the lethargic pillow biting whimpers of a child not yet soiled. Remind yourself, I will have what I want." Ra didn't bother looking at his future consort. Hathor stormed off. Ra helped Isis to her feet and looked at Madame Patricia. "Danu, the largest portion of my heart will always be yours. Tonight, my pleasure is hers. Do not take offense."

"None is had."

"My men will escort you to your room." Ra waved her off and his butlers led her away. He called out, "And if you wish to see the boy, you may do so. Heal his internal wounds, but he will bear the pain and scars upon his flesh as a reminder of his place. Understood?"

It sure was, but she didn't feel like acknowledging it. All she cared to focus on was poor Jaden and how they could possibly get away from Ra.

CHAPTER THIRTY-SIX

Anubis IV

Anubis awoke with no pain. His hand felt fuzzy, though. He made a fist then stretched his fingers. He yawned, surprised his jaw opened without a burn. He rubbed his face firmly. Everything seemed fine.

"I'm healed?" he asked himself in shock.

"Do you know why I spared you?" Shiva asked. Anubis found that baffling. What did Shiva have to gain? He offered Anubis a canister of water, but Anubis refused. He prodded Anubis with the canister until he took it. "Good. You need to replenish your fluids." Shiva examined Anubis. "I think it's important for you to know Lord Vishnu has refused you any care or assistance. What you received was of my own volition."

"You should have let me die." Anubis threw the canister across the room. He rolled onto his side, turning his back to Shiva. "My reason for being is done."

"Or does it temporarily escape you?" Shiva stood at the docking station. His fingers swiped across a light panel and window shields lifted, giving a view out over the magenta skyline of Vishnu's realm. "Swarga Loka," Shiva announced. "No planet is like it."

Out the window, several planets and moons beamed in the daytime sky. The windows dimmed, adjusting to the radiant light pouring into the room.

"Your father and I were close," Shiva admitted, piquing Anubis' interest. "We fought together in the Pride Rebellion, before the brigade realignment and creation of the Corners." Shiva leaned against the window, staring blankly at the rolling hillside of red grass and purple trees. He looked over his shoulder at Anubis. "We were sent on a far-reaching endeavor, hoping to cut off back route supplies for Lucifer's legion. Only a few of us lived. Most were slaughtered. Others tortured and then slaughtered, but not us. We managed to evade capture."

Anubis couldn't tell if Shiva was speaking half-truths, lies, or something else. It didn't matter. He was engaged. Shiva pulled a chair alongside his guest and Anubis sat closer to listen.

"We were surrounded for what seemed like eons, more than enough time for your father and me to get well acquainted. We weren't sure we'd speak again after our rescue, so we bid farewell hoping to one day reconnect and regale one another with our life's stories." There was a hint of pain in Shiva's body language, like a desire left wanting had snuffed out his words.

"When I heard Set was to be a father, I didn't believe it. I couldn't picture such a man shouldering those responsibilities. In truth, Anubis, it was your birth that sparked all this." Shiva tenderly squeezed Anubis' hands. "Your birth breathed life into mere rumors. From then on, Set knew existence for our kind would never be the same. I last saw him at the end of the Last Great War. Every moment of my existence since has guided us to a reunion. Do you understand the meaning of what I say?"

"The words of Vishnu... weren't lies?" Anubis tried to understand exactly what it meant, but his mind refused to piece everything together. He wished Horus were there to explain the situation. That's how he'd been conditioned growing up. "He killed Osiris and let mother die?"

"It was never his intent for Nephtys to perish, though, regrettably, Osiris had to die. For you see, though Osiris made plans to lead your Corner to sanctuary, Set knew it would be nothing more than another tyrant strategizing according to a lie." Shiva led Anubis through the room, knowing Anubis struggled with the thought of Set being a traitor. "Osiris and Zeus were old fashioned. They believed in a hierarchy of all beings, and would have seen you be a lowly servant to their children. Set, on several occasions, tried to appeal to Osiris' more sensible side, but your uncle was far more concerned with keeping you under his foot, jealous you were the first of your kind. So, you see, your father was a hero. Though your path's been long and arduous, it's led us here to this moment.

"You were abandoned by your aunt and cousin. If you follow me, and become like the child I always deserved, you will soon see your father again."

"Vishnu works with my father?" Anubis stared out the window while Shiva rubbed his back in a soothing manner.

"Worry yourself not with questions and politics. Search your feelings and trust my words are true," Shiva whispered.

Anubis felt lethargic again. He was certain Shiva had put something in the canister of water, but he didn't want to believe it. He desired to feel at home the way he never was under Isis.

"You wish to have words?" Shiva asked.

Anubis turned around to find Skanda had entered the room.

"The son you always deserved?" Skanda yelled loud enough for others in nearby suites to hear. "Mother lies in misery while you play host to this creature?"

"We've spoken of this previously." Shiva jerked his son in close, snarling through his teeth. "You'll not question my authority. Know you're lucky I don't take your head."

"Lucky you don't return my adoration?" He tried to pull away, but Shiva's grip grew tighter. "Let me go or else…"

"What?" Shiva sneered. "You'll handle me as well as you did Horus? Please. I'd take your arm with one stroke of the blade then beat you to death with it." He released Skanda. His son stutter-stepped backwards. A crystal with pink light emerged from Shiva's control panel.

"What's that?" Skanda asked.

"Not for you." Shiva snatched the crystal, not bothering to look at Skanda. "If you're worried over your mother's well being, perhaps you should spend the evening with her while I testify to my brigade."

"What are you to do with that ghastly giant?" Skanda pointed at Anubis. "Make him your son?"

"Make him the warrior and servant my own blood will never become." Shiva struck his son's face with all the force he could muster. Skanda hit the smooth floor like a toppled tree. "You're a warrior by birthright only, though you exude none of the fortitude required to truly be one. Learn your place. Now, leave me be."

"As you wish," he replied, wiping blood from his busted lip. His eye swelled and turned purple from the force of the blow. Skanda stumbled to his feet and draped the hood of his cloak over his head to hide his face in shadow.

Shiva inspected the crystal. Anubis wondered who it could be from.

"A moment, please?" Shiva asked, not looking at Anubis. He pointed to another offshoot room. "You'll find appropriate quarters more to your liking."

"What is it?" Anubis gingerly stepped beside Shiva. The Alpha Guardian cast a somber look. "Where does it lead?"

"It doesn't lead anywhere." Shiva waved the crystal. "It carries a message. Only two scenarios could provoke its sender to break radio silence." Shiva put a hand on Anubis' shoulder, staring into his eyes. "What I tell you must never be repeated, lest you find your neck once again at the mercy of my sword."

"Understood," Anubis affirmed.

"Either my alliance is ready for the last piece of the Forge, which seems unlikely given that word of Michael's demise would spread like wildfire, or trouble heads towards Swarga Loka." Shiva brushed the back of his hand along Anubis' face. "Are you with us?"

Anubis stared at his toes. Shiva wasn't such a horrible monster. He commanded a certain control over his people, despite Vishnu's apparent role as master. Even though Shiva seemed ruthless, he was certainly consistent and fair. Plus he was kind, unlike those under Isis.

Anubis wondered why, if his aunt and cousin really loved him, would they allow such atrocities to befall him? No, Horus wasn't to blame. Horus would die for him. Yet Shiva presented a shield he'd never before seen. It was all too appealing.

***

Magenta light blanketed the room, warming his skin. The wounds tended by Shiva were no longer present and scars were absent. The pain felt not long ago was a distant memory. His bare feet padded across the cold, metal floor. He followed the sounds of clashing blades and watched Shiva spar against Khnum and another angel with many spectators.

Anubis did a double take, squinting to make sure that was indeed Khnum. Though his ram's helmet remained the same, his aurascales no longer beamed green with the purity of a Southern starstone. They were orange, reflecting that of the Eastern Corner.

"You two are slow," Shiva grunted, fending off the duo with a pair of swords. He separated the first angel from his weapon by smashing it with the pommel of one of his swords.

Shiva, who stood over six-and-a-half feet tall, moved with the nimble precision of a gymnast. He swung one foot over the other, jumping into a fierce spin. His swords snapped the shaft of Khnum's mallet and forced him to the ground. Shiva stood victorious.

"If you wish to serve under our banner, then you must become a warrior." He joked, "Did you Southern fools rest on your laurels?"

"Khnum filled himself with wine," Anubis said, drawing their attention. Shiva seemed pleased to see him. "You have need for me still?"

"I do." Shiva's aurascales dissipated. He wiped the sweat from his body. "I would see you restored to your former glory."

"That won't take long," Khnum laughed. He stood and cast an aggressive look at Anubis. "He was nothing more than Horus' pet, which afforded him more patience and protection than warranted for a man with his brain. A pet Horus didn't see fit to save."

"My cousin loves me," Anubis yelled, stepping forward with his fists tight. Shiva held a hand up. "I have a place—"

"—Here among us now. Yes, you do." Shiva wrapped his arm around Anubis. "Let us not pretend events unfolded differently. Horus left you behind. I'd make you our equal. Fight under our star and ascend as far as your desires and ability will allow."

"Again, his climb will be hampered by what he lacks between his ears," Khnum added, drawing a laugh from the crowd. "I fear you're wasting time with him. His brain is too shallow to overcome the hardness of his heart. He will not turn from his cousin."

"You presume to tell me how my time is best spent?" Shiva squinted at Khnum. The crowd stepped away from Khnum to not be caught in the crossfire. "Perhaps a contest, to prove one's loyalty and worth?"

"I'm afraid such an endeavor would be foolhardy." Khnum knelt and bowed his head. "You've proven far more skilled and powerful than I could combat."

"That's not quite what I had in mind." Shiva clapped. The doors to his gathering hall opened and a chained Sobek was escorted into the area. His sliced arm had a casing over it where a hand used to be. They removed his shackles and handed him a starstone. "Let's see how worthy and loyal Anubis will be when faced by his former mentor."

"Anubis against a deformed foe, even he could best that." Khnum laughed, as did many others.

"Perhaps a steeper test?" Shiva looked at Anubis and smiled, giving him a gentle nudge forward. "Khnum, take up your sword alongside Sobek. Prove yourself against the grey skinned giant, and he against you. Let your skill be the measuring stick for what lingers in his head. Lest you think that too unfair, given your clear skill advantage?"

Khnum seemed unsure. He slowly grinned, staring holes through Anubis. Khnum stood equidistant from Sobek and Anubis. His aurascales radiated. The ram's helmet and mallet returned with a fiercer glow than ever before.

"How can I defeat their aura?" Sweat ran down the side of Anubis' face. "My starstone escapes me. Even still its radiance lacks when compared."

"I saw the armor you wore in opposition to me." Shiva circled Anubis, examining his muscular frame. "It was found wanting, indeed. Khnum regaled me with stories of your punishment. How you weren't allowed to wear the colors of your people. Instead, past transgressions forced to bear the mark of a jackal made to appear black and grey."

"True." Anubis forced back tears. He wiped the snot from his nose. Khnum chuckled under his breath. Anubis opened his eyes with a focused rage. "I was never allowed to be their equal."

"No longer so." Shiva stepped in front of Anubis and presented a new starstone. "This is yours, if you accept me. Bear the colors of our banner within your aurascales. See a new form for your faceguard, if you so choose. However, if I might make a suggestion…"

"You may." Anubis took the starstone and absorbed its power. Panic overtook Khnum's body language. Aurascales surged over Anubis' body, shining orange with more beauty and magnificence than he'd ever known.

"Wear the face of a jackal as a badge of honor. Let it remind you where you came from, so that you may forever claw yourself a new path and fight to never return to those despicable beginnings." Shiva smacked Anubis on the breast plate. "Remember the pain and mistreatment the jackal stands for. Fight with rage so hot, steel melts in your wake."

Anubis nodded, stepping into the fighter's circle. His silver exoskeleton surged over his face in the image of a jackal. A large curved sword and shield erupted in his grasp. He towered over Khnum and Sobek, standing with concrete resolve.

"I won't fight." Sobek threw his sword to the ground. "I refuse to be your pawn."

"If Khnum takes your life, I will pardon him from this duel and establish him as my second in command," Shiva said. Everyone looked on in shock. "If Sobek kills Khnum and defeats Anubis, I will set him and those under his banner free."

"And what does Anubis gain?" Khnum asked.

"A home and the satisfaction of destroying two figures responsible for his difficult past," Shiva replied, grinning. "Show us your worth."

Khnum attacked. His mallet fell like a meteor. Anubis rolled to the right, avoiding the blow which dented the floor. He sliced at Khnum's feet, missing. His opponent skipped forward and kicked him in the face. Khnum knelt over Anubis, pressing the shaft of his weapon against the Angel-born's neck, choking him. Sobek stood in a ready stance, refusing to grab a weapon. His eyes shifted between Anubis and Khnum.

"I will see the light fade from your eyes," Khnum grunted. His arms quaked as he pressed.

"Not this day." Anubis pushed back, easily lifting Khnum off the ground. He tossed his enemy over his head and rolled to his feet. His sword and shield melded together, forming a double sided battle axe with spear tips at each end of the shaft. The weapon dwarfed Khnum's.

Anubis swung it with one arm and smashed Khnum's shield, splitting it in half and knocking him across the floor.

"You haunt me no more," Anubis yelled, sticking the bottom of the spear-tipped shaft into Khnum's side.

"I yield," Khnum cried as Anubis pulled the weapon from his hip.

"There will be no end to this contest until I give approval," Shiva replied, waving for Anubis to carry on. "I want more."

Anubis nodded and again thrust the pointed tip into Khnum's shoulder blade. He lifted Khnum off the ground with the enemy stuck to the weapon, and held him high in the air at the midnight position. He turned, whipping the shaft towards the ground, channeling all the kinetic energy into Khnum's body as he smashed him into the floor. Shards of slate-grey metal splattered along the ground, falling from Khnum's armor.

"Continue," Shiva called out. His eyes were filled with delight.

Khnum crawled for the exit. His fingers raked across the floor. Those looking on moved from his path, forming two rows to either side.

Anubis stepped with purpose and lifted the man responsible for much of his life's pain by the shoulder plate. Their eyes were level, yet Khnum's feet were at Anubis' knees. Anubis smashed his forehead into Khnum and splintered the ram's helmet.

He tossed his enemy back into the fighter's circle. Anubis swung the axe as hard as he could. Sobek blocked Anubis from taking Khnum's head off with a sword.

"Think of what you do, nephew," Sobek pleaded. Armor didn't cover his face. Tears filled his eyes. "Don't be like them. You were the best of us. You deserved more."

"He knows." Shiva unfolded his arms and stepped toward the circle. He implored, "Remember what they did. Kill them and join me as a son." Shiva lifted his hand to Anubis. "They fear the glory we hold."

"You have family," Sobek grunted, struggling to keep Anubis from Khnum's neck. "You've beaten him and shown you're better. Prove you've the better heart."

"You've made it black!" Anubis yelled.

Anubis lowered his shoulder and knocked Sobek to the floor. He kicked his uncle in the face and stuck a dagger to his gut. Sobek's eyes nearly jumped from their sockets. He pressed his forehead against Anubis' shoulder plate and hugged him.

"Forgive us." Sobek looked up, crying. Blood trickled out of the corner of his mouth. "Forgive me." He conjured a hatchet and raised it over his head. He slung it forward and hit Khnum in the collar.

"Your blood washes the stains from my past." Anubis yanked the knife from Sobek's gut and sliced it across the neck. He stepped on Khnum's chest. "And your blood prepares my soul for the future."

"Please," Khnum stuttered. "Have mercy."

Anubis looked at Shiva. "Do as you see fit," he said.

The beaming jackal eyes turned back to Khnum. Anubis took him by the throat, squeezing the breath from Khnum's lungs.

"Only as much mercy as I was ever granted." Spikes grew from Anubis' knuckles and he beat Khnum relentlessly until the Beta Guardian's face was nothing more than a mangled blob of skin and broken bones. He counted the blows in his head. They totaled three dozen—the number of lashes Khnum had once left on Anubis' back.

Anubis stepped away from the squirming body. His foe was alive, so he counted him spared. His promise of giving Khnum what he once received was kept.

"You've easily proven your worth, Anubis." Shiva applauded. "I fear old Khnum is now nothing more than a redundancy."

Khnum made gargled groans not resembling anything remotely close to coherent thoughts. His fingers and legs twitched randomly.

"Take him to the infirmary," Shiva commanded. "If he lives, see that he's sold on the market. I'm sure many would pay a handsome fee to see a Beta Guardian fight in the arena, wounded though he may be."

Anubis grinned with satisfaction while Khnum was dragged off by the feet. Those who'd previously laughed now stood in fear, shocked at what they'd witnessed. For the first time in his life, Anubis actually felt taller than everyone else.

"Anubis, there is much power within you. Let me give purpose to it," Shiva implored. He wrapped his arm around Anubis' back. "What you lacked in skill you compensated for with tenacity. With my guidance and adoption of my discipline, you can be a great and mighty warrior. Perhaps, one day, head of your own Corner. Would you like that?"

"I," Anubis replied, hesitating. His mind wandered elsewhere. He wasn't sure what to think. Shiva's kind words were well received by his heart, yet a portion of him yearned to be with Isis and Horus, those familiar to him. "I'm not sure."

"Train with me. Submit to my authority, and you'll never give pause to uncertainty again. Women will spread themselves to your desires." Shiva stood in front of Anubis, firmly rubbing his arms and shoulders. "Your father will rejoin us and learn of the man, fighter, and leader his son has become. A reunion far more valuable, and much longer in the making, than returning to be with a cousin and aunt who don't hold you in high regard."

"Yes." Anubis knelt and bowed his head. Shiva placed a hand to his shoulder, smiling with pride. "I submit to you."

344

CHAPTER THIRTY-SEVEN

Madame Patricia III

The star over the realm of Ra never gave way to night. Despite its large and imposing position, the temperature remained steady and inviting. Winds never raised above a gentle breeze. Even though the physical anomalies were alluring and comfortable, Madame Patricia had never been more uneasy.

She stood on a balcony that protruded from the side of a steep cliff. Entrance to the balcony could only be gained by two circular pathways melted with precision into the mountain and carved into long corridors. The mountain disappeared into the sky above her, extending further than she could see. If one squinted they might see the top, but even then they were likely imagining the pinnacle. A sheet of clouds below made it impossible to know if there was a beginning to the mountain. Ra's home seemed like a floating castle.

"I've not been here long, yet already this is my preferred retreat." Hathor entered Madame Patricia's peripheral vision, clothed in delicate night robes. "Though I wonder what's beyond the horizon, and under the clouds, I feel content to gaze at such a brightly burning beauty above."

"Given time, you'll grow tired of just about anything." Madame Patricia kept her face forward, but monitored Hathor out of the corner of her eyes. She didn't trust this Angel-born. Hathor held a sleazy, jealous, and weak disposition: a dangerous concoction. "I suppose you've not experienced many great sights."

"Until just recently, I'd never left the confines of my father's Armada cruiser." Hathor lost her gaze in the star. "All that lined the views of my home were cold, steel walls, black, uneventful skies, and a shattered moon that remained stationary until it turned and battered the planet on which we clung to life."

"I can see how a hole in the side of a mountain could be so entertaining." Maybe the most annoying thing about this kid was that she wasn't playing the game her adult counterparts were. That made her naive or stupid. "It's been a few hours since supper. Aren't you tired?"

"I am. I just couldn't stand another second of Isis' incessant moaning through the walls." Hathor looked at Madame Patricia, who returned the gaze. "Will I be as such when Ra takes me for the first time?"

"If you know what's good for you." Madame Patricia took Hathor's hand. The unapologetic ignorance Hathor exuded was actually just a beaten in disposition by her father. The young lady seemed confused. "Isis likely puts on a nothing more than a good show. It helps build a man's confidence and makes them more agreeable. While Ra gradually became a better lover over the course of my days with him, I doubt he's turned into an expert since we last parted ways. You could probably learn a few things from Isis."

"Am I beautiful like Isis?" Hathor asked with sincerity.

None were, but that answer wouldn't help Hathor. She analyzed the young lady's features and found them appealing and cute, but nothing that anyone would deem overtly sexy. "You are a lovely young woman, I'm sure both inside and out."

"I fear many wouldn't agree with you." Hathor feigned a smile. "I've made mistakes that I can never overcome."

"We all make mistakes. Eventually we overcome them."

"I'm afraid once you've turned against someone too many times, you prove incapable of loyalty." Hathor stood on her toes and leaned over the railing. She put one foot on the mid-rail. The wind held her robe up. Madame Patricia thought about pulling her back, but maybe if the girl leapt it would provide a decent distraction for her escape.

"You're speaking of a boy." Madame Patricia gazed intently at Hathor's body language. Chastising remarks, or the wrong questions, might encourage her to jump. Not even she was that cruel. "Is he handsome?"

"I know not what you say. I love Ra." Hathor's eyes widened as her second foot stood on the middle rail. She lifted both hands and her breathing quickened. "I have eyes for one only."

"I trust you do." Madame Patricia smirked. "But that man is not Ra, though you fake it well. Do you really love Ra with all your heart, or do you simply play your part like a good child?"

Hathor swayed in a circular motion over the drop off. Her left foot slipped. Was this her chance to escape? Hathor caught herself and went rigid, crying.

"I'm afraid my heart belongs to another who will never see past my misdeeds, or his purpose in life." Hathor stepped down from the rail, wiping her face dry. Obviously she was too weak to end her suffering. "So I'll offer it to Ra. With him, I am no longer under my father's hand. He can't make me do those things anymore, or play his games for power."

"Ra is no less a warden than Amun."

"At least I'm used to it. The job will come with title, cause and power."

"Your only cause will be to bear him a son. When you fail or pass that assignment, Ra will discard you." Madame Patricia stayed an arm's length away from Hathor, despite the latter's body language suggesting that she needed a hug.

"How do you know this?"

"Because it was no different with me," Madame Patricia replied, speaking quietly and calmly. "Keep up spirits. Better days are ahead."

"How are you so certain?" Hathor seemed a little too excited. "What word is there?"

"Only the firsthand account of pieces on a chess board." Madame Patricia walked back into the side of the mountain. It was best to be vague with Hathor until she proved strong enough to form a partnership with.

Isis meandered down the hallway, walking towards a joint connection in the cavern that met up with Madame Patricia's journey. She was covered in only a bed sheet, sweaty and disheveled. A hand print was seared onto the side of her neck. The two ladies exchanged nods. Their eyes did all the talking they needed.

Madame Patricia held no discriminating thoughts towards Isis. The former muse had used what talents she had to gain position, though she was given no real choice in the matter. He may have been a powerful, sadistic, and dangerous man, but at his very core Ra was simple and easy to please. He needed to feel dominant and in control of all things. This was in response to his normally gruesome look and God's oppressive thumb which had left Ra no room to be what he wanted.

"You must have impressed. He lets you walk without chains." Madame Patricia kept her body and focus trained ahead, walking side by side with Isis.

"I'm not without skill." Isis smirked, examining Madame Patricia. "So you, too, are an Architect. I believed my husband crazy when he spoke of such things."

"He wasn't."

"Yes, an answer plainly given by my sight," Isis quipped while wrapping the sheet over her shoulders, chest and around her waist, tying it off. "He said you held the key to all of our freedoms. What did he mean by that?"

"Probably that the Architects would be no more than a symbol to rally more of your kind to his cause." The two approached the dining hall where already the table had been replaced, and the debris created in Jaden and Ra's exchange cleared. Madame Patricia sat, gesturing for Isis to join her. "Only I doubt it would have done any good. The problem with you angels is that you can never unite under a single cause. Not too unlike humans in that regard. You're either busy following a fanatic like Gabriel or heeding Zeus in his explosive endeavors. This was no more evident than in the Pride Rebellion, when Lucifer's small yet focused taskforce nearly decimated the scatter-brained defense helmed by those opposing him. Strict rules and regulations have always been your best leaders. Absent focused purpose, you always end up prisoner, hiding, or dead."

"I know." Her agreement shocked Madame Patricia. "Osiris was a good man, strong, gentle and kind hearted, but he lacked the courage to take up the mantle of leader. That trait I tried hard to forge in my son, may he too rest in peace."

"Your efforts continue to pay dividends." Madame Patricia covered Isis' knee with a hand. The hidden intent in the message was understood as Isis gave a mother's smile. "Past betrothals of pre-birth work in unison, along with the sister of the boy who joined me on my journey here, and the symbol which sparks debate among the stars. He's well assisted, so let's hope he proves the leader you forged him to be."

"He found Death?" Isis asked. "Is he hope or the end?"

"That remains to be seen." Madame Patricia shrugged. "Let's pray for the sake of our intertwined fates that hope joins his cause."

"When women whisper they often conspire," Amun said with a chill in his voice. He walked behind the ladies. Sekhmet followed. Amun's fingers curled around Madame Patricia's earlobe and she slapped him away. He turned his attention to Isis, pulling the sheet from her body. "This is how you were meant to be gazed upon. Do not hide it."

"You wish to have Ra's seconds while you dishonor your wife in her presence?" Madame Patricia stood, slapping Amun's hand. "You heard our host. She's no longer yours to do with as you please."

"And yet how will he come to learn of it lest I tell him of Horus' intention of coming here?" Amun grabbed Madame Patricia's face and lifted her off the ground. "If you wish to keep your secrets, then I will have you both."

"Horus yet lives?" Hathor gasped.

"Try not to sound too excited, my dear. You're to be tied to another." Amun dropped Madame Patricia and lumbered over to his daughter. She cowered in his shadow. His hand slithered over her face and turned her gaze upward. "Remember, you still belong to me. You will give your future husband a good show and continue blessing this family favor. Understood?"

"No." She pulled a knife from inside her robe and plunged it into Amun's stomach. She twisted the blade, pushing him back and over the table. "I will not. Be. YOUR. PUPPET." A vengeful rage seethed from her eyes, her voice shrill.

"You brat." Amun backhanded Hathor. She fell to all fours, still screaming. He pulled the knife from his abdomen. Aurascales surged over his body, sealing the wound. He kicked her onto her back and stood on her throat. "Your place is here."

Madame Patricia commanded the ground. It split open with vines and flung him into the wall. She marched toward Amun, trapping him in a shell of rock constructed from thin air.

"Take the girl and go," she commanded Isis. "Release the children."

The Southern Queen obeyed, taking Hathor by the hand. Amun struggled to break free. A light cannon formed over his arm and he blasted through the stone. Shards of rock hit Madame Patricia's face. Before she could recover, he slung her onto the ground and pinned her hands above her head as he tore at her clothes. Sekhmet continued watching.

"Do something," Madame Patricia begged her.

"There's a reason you are the weaker sex, good for no more than entertainment," Amun taunted, pinning his elbow into her throat. She couldn't breathe. Lightheadedness set in. His facial armor vanished into his shoulder blades. "I'll slice you open and see what powers there are to behold within your gem."

Sekhmet clawed his face, drawing blood. Madame Patricia gasped. Sekhmet stabbed at him with Hathor's knife, but Amun redirected the blade into her diaphragm.

"Don't think I'll shed a tear for you." He lifted her off her feet and slid the knife further up her chest before removing it. She hit the ground, dead. Amun dropped the knife and knelt on Madame Patricia's chest. "You'll replace her."

"No, father." Hathor had returned. She scooped up the knife and sliced it across Amun's throat. His hands clamped around his neck; vermillion gushed between his fingers. The aurascales couldn't react in time. Amun toppled over.

Madame Patricia rolled onto all fours, coughing. "I told you to run."

Hathor sat with her mom's head in her lap. "I couldn't leave with him alive," she sobbed into her mother's chest. She grabbed Sekhmet's starstone. "It felt good, taking his life." Hathor looked at Madame Patricia with snot and tears mixing on her face. "The rage was comforting, filling the numb I've had for so long."

"Indeed." Ra's laugh was muffled by his mask. "Despondent women find solace in like company and rise against tyrannical forces. Sounds like a fairy tale."

"He attacked us first," Hathor said, running to him. "My father was an evil man..."

"Am I any different?" Ra interrupted. "I care not for his life. His voice grated my spine. He was to die shortly, anyway. The gusto of calling us the 'Amun-Ra coalition'—like I would accept second fiddle. No, I care about little mice gathering without my say so."

Madame Patricia began to speak. "We don't mean..."

"Silence." Ra stomped his foot. "Or I'll bend you each over and mount you until you obey, do I make myself clear?"

Hathor went cold, but Madame Patricia burned inside.

He glared at her. "Danu, are we in agreement?"

"We are not," she replied. Hathor looked up in shock. Madame Patricia walked towards Ra. "I don't fear death. So while I yet breathe, I will not live under your foot."

"There are fates worse than death." Ra rubbed his hands together sinisterly.

"Then so be it."

She lunged onto a knee, casting a hand forward. A light erupted from her hand, knocking him to his back. She curled her fingers, commanding the rock to split and rumble. Vines grew through the floor and wrapped around him. New conjured rock and crystals held him down. "You must flee while you have the chance."

"I'll not leave your side," Hathor replied. She clasped Sekhment's starstone. Billions of slate-grey cubes flowed over her body. The aurascales took the form of her mother's faceguard: a green-faced lioness. "If death be on the cards, then so be it."

Bass heavy laughter overtook the realm. "It's been ages since I've been entertained so." Light vanished. The women clung together. The ground rumbled.

The vegetation caught fire. Flames raced towards Madame Patricia and sliced across her face. Ra appeared in a blaze of orange, white and blue.

"I'm not finished." Madame Patricia lunged after Ra. She harnessed the power of their proximity, turning his skin into soil and rock. A crystal spear formed.

She slashed her spear into Ra. He turned to smoke. The weapon passed through. A heat blast flowed from his hands, shoving her into the wall. She pushed a shield forward and dispersed the flames.

Madame Patricia caught Ra off-guard by lopping off his right hand. Magma flowed from the severed limb. She stabbed, but again he turned into smoke, trying to penetrate her lungs. She shifted into a plume of dust, seeping into the cracks of the floor. Ra took a solid form and his hand grew back.

"Where are you, my dear?" Ra asked, looking every which way.

This time, the entire fortress rumbled. Foundations cracked beneath his feet. The mountain was going to come down.

"Hapy!" Hathor called out for her brother.

The floor caved in, swallowing Ra. Hathor teetered on the edge but Madame Patricia pulled her back.

Hathor nodded with appreciation. "This way," she implored.

Madame Patricia steadied the floor beneath them long enough to find Hapy, who was being held captive by Taweret. Her large frame stood between Hathor and Hapy. She tapped her sword against her shield. Madame Patricia waved her hand, turning Taweret's aurascales into dust. Hathor drove her dagger into Taweret's chest and kicked her away.

"Let's go." She took Hapy's hand.

The cave collapsed in front of them. Madame Patricia conjured a hole in the wall, leading to a new exit. The trio stood above the clouds in the dead of night.

"There's no way out." Hathor pulled Hapy's screams into her bosom. The collapsed cave behind Madame Patricia melted through. Ra was coming.

"You have to fly," Madame Patricia insisted.

"I've never used a starstone before," Hathor cried.

"The aurascales will act out of self-preservation. I promise." She pushed the two through the hole and watched them disappear into the clouds.

"Danu," Ra screamed. The rays of light springing from his body evaporated the rock around him.

Madame Patricia squeezed her fist, took a transparent form, and sprinted for her one-time lover. The two merged. Her powers grew exponentially. Before he could regain his senses, she released the fabric holding the mountain together. His fortress crumbled.

CHAPTER THIRTY-EIGHT

Austin V

The announcement of the 11:30 express to Paris echoed through the station. Austin analyzed the board to find the platform they needed. They had just twenty minutes to secure tickets. He kept repeating in his head how horrible the plan was.

"Exchange one heavily populated city for another," he joked. "Great idea." He turned and spotted Harold approaching them. His pupils turned yellow and wolf-like. Grey hairs sprouted from his arms as he took Harold by the trench coat and forced him into the restroom. "What are you doing here?" Austin barked. He tossed Harold to the floor. "The last I saw you, Madame Patricia was kicking you to the curb. Come to sell us out?"

"Would you get your knickers out of a twist?" Harold adjusted his tie. Several men standing at the urinals hurriedly zipped their pants, moving for the exit. "You're making a bloody scene."

"I'm about to make a Jackson Pollock on that wall with your blood." Austin lifted Harold off the ground, his feet dangling. "You've been warned."

Horus pulled Austin back. Harold fell to his knees. Austin struggled to break free. Jarrod stood watch at the door.

"Numerous eyes are upon us," Horus whispered. Austin settled and leaned over a sink to wash his face. Horus helped Harold to his feet. "You missed our last rendezvous."

"I know." Harold nervously rubbed his arm like there was an ache he was trying to relieve. He looked at Jarrod. "Hello mate."

"Eat a dick," Jarrod replied. "How do y'all know each other?"

"I was following a trail of sightings," Horus said. "The Ourea battle brought me to Harold, who told me what I needed to hear." He looked at the descendant. "Why did you miss our last appointment?"

"Apparently I've offended you blokes. Why'm I getting the first?" he asked, standoffish.

"Something doesn't smell right about him." Austin could sense it. It was like each time Harold exhaled his breath was rotten and his blood cold. He couldn't figure it out.

"You don't smell like sunshine and lollipops yourself, mate."

"I asked a question," Horus interjected.

"Right. I got held up. On the news, I saw that fiasco you and mind-freak here put on." Harold pointed at Jarrod. "I figured you lot needed my help."

"Bullshit." That wasn't something only Austin could smell. "He wanted to hand us over to the Assassins. I overheard him arguing with Madame Patricia about it." Austin lunged for Harold. Horus pushed him back with Jarrod's help. "Did you sell out our mission to save Lian's kind?"

"Don't blame me." Harold pointed at Horus, shaking. "This strange fellow here wants to meet where demons gather. How do you know it wasn't him?"

"I'm the only thing keeping Austin from tearing your throat out. You know this, right?" Horus asked.

Harold nodded. "Point taken..."

"Just shift blame," Austin snarled.

"I came upon Madame Patricia at her safe haven, a place she's frequented often when times are troubled. I've joined her from time-to-time." Harold ran his fingers through his reddish hair. "It's true, I didn't trust you fellows. However, I'd never put Madame Patricia or Athena in danger. She sent me here to help."

"She didn't know we were going to be here." Jarrod loosened his grip on Austin. Harold flinched. "She just knew our final destination. How come you're here and not where we're going? In fact, where are we going?"

"Are you guys done urinating?" Athena barged into the restroom. "Our next chance for Paris leaves in fifteen minutes." She saw the awkward scene but ran to Harold all the same. She kissed his cheek. "Where did you go?"

"I was going to say Paris," Harold replied to Jarrod. Sweat ran down his forehead. He hugged Athena back. "I had an argument with Miss. P."

"How many times has she kicked you out again?" Athena looked at him sideways and laughed. "You have to stop being such a—what is the term—knucklehead." She took Harold's hand and acknowledged the others. "Lian is getting impatient. You should get out there."

"Shit." Austin stepped away from Horus and Jarrod, holding his hands up. "Paris right?" He eyed Harold. "Madame Patricia told you that?"

"On my honor." Harold crossed his heart.

"I'm sure." Austin squinted.

They left the restroom. Lian stood with her head cocked sideways and her fists on her hips, tapping her foot. She pointed at her watch.

"Well?" she asked. "Where do we go for the train?"

"Upper level, platform six," Austin replied, recalling the information from the timetable. "We'll need to split up. Lian, Athena and I will secure the tickets. Harold and Horus will take Jarrod to the platform and find a quiet spot to wait for us."

"Sounds like a plan." Jarrod shrugged.

"I'm sorry, but Miss P. was very clear about me not letting Athena outta my sight." Harold took Athena by the hand. "So the four of us will get the tickets."

"Ill advised." Horus pointed at Lian then Jarrod. "Did you not see what she locked away in his mind? He may be harmless now, but the being in his head is far from it. There should be two of us guarding him at all times."

"Listen guys, I'm the most acquainted with human civilization." Austin stepped between them, crossing his arms. "I call the shots. Besides, I trust Jarrod more than I do this fat asshole." He pointed at Harold.

"Not everything has to be a dick measuring contest." Lian stamped her foot. "Seriously, Athena and Harold go with Jarrod. Horus, you come with us. Shit. It's settled."

"What is a dick and how is it measured?" Horus asked. His tone was blunt and naïve, his eyes rigid and curious.

"Your wanker," Harold laughed, patting him on the shoulder. Horus shook his head, not understanding. "The ol' todger. Your kibbles and bits. John Thomas..."

"Wait, I think I know him," Horus interrupted, snapping his fingers. "Patron Saint of the chaste."

"No, you idiot. It's your trouser snake. Prick. Knob. Tally Wacker. Junior down stairs..."

Horus squinted. "What language do you speak?"

"The Queen's, just like everyone else around here. Is it not?" Harold shrugged his shoulders and turned to see the perplexed and blank stares of Jarrod and Athena. "What?"

"You need help." Jarrod walked away.

"Says the schizophrenic with mass homicidal tendencies," Harold scoffed, jogging to keep up with them.

CHAPTER THIRTY-NINE

Lian VII

Lian and Austin stood at a ticket window.

"I'm sorry, but the 11:30 is booked solid," the station clerk responded to Lian. "We do have one leaving in five hours time, but I'm afraid only three seats are available."

"Impossible." Austin rubbed his face. "You mean to tell me that the whole entire train is booked up? Like everyone in London wants to go to Paris?"

"Stupid question," Lian muttered. "They're just two of the most traveled cities in the world, but yeah, it's rare people would go back and forth."

"Less heaping bullshit onto my back, more helping." He squinted at Lian. "Please."

"I'm sorry about my boyfriend." Lian smiled, gently pushing Austin away with her shoulder. She stood on the tip of her toes and leaned over the counter. "Is there some sort of waiting list you can get us on? Maybe some passengers who haven't checked in yet?"

"Let me see," the station clerk cleared her throat and typed on the keyboard with her long, multi-colored acrylic nails. Lian peered inside her mind. *Stupid, obnoxious Americans. Come here like they own the place. I bet they're still boasting about how they saved our arses twice from the Germans.*

"Yup, it was a really big war," Austin said to Horus, who stood stoic and unimpressed. Their ill-timed, coincidental conversation broke

Lian's train of thought. "This whole place would be speaking German if it weren't for us."

"My father was killed several thousand years ago on the day of my birth, helping us flee persecution from the creator who grants you favor. My aunt was decapitated. Countless numbers of my kind were wiped from existence in the largest ethnic cleansing this galaxy has ever seen." Horus yawned, still keeping a straight face. Austin couldn't tell if he was being sarcastic or blunt. "Was it something like that?"

"The Jews had it pretty bad…"

"Shut up." Lian glared at the two.

"I can get you on the waiting list, but there's not much else I can do for today." The woman looked up, but Lian and the others were already gone. "Typical."

Lian marched with her head down and eyes closed. The masses of people barely missed her as she moved through them with ease, sensing their trajectory as they walked by. Horus and Austin sprinted to keep up, bumping into other pedestrians along the way. Lian's mind jumped from person to person trying to find tickets to commandeer.

First, she found a man and his lover on a getaway to Paris while his wife stayed back in Kent with their five children. Lian entered their minds, took their tickets, and then implanted the urge for the man to divorce his wife, giving her everything. "Thank you for the tickets."

"You're just taking their tickets?" Austin was shocked that she would just take from hard working people.

"Just from the assholes who don't deserve it," she replied, giving him the tickets. "Need four more."

"There's a bigger goal to be achieved." Horus took the tickets from Lian when it was obvious Austin wasn't going to, nodding at her. "She does what she must."

Her consciousness sprang out again and her feet followed. She found three friends leaving for a vacation getaway to the 'City of Lights' before travel between borders was halted. They handed her their tickets. "First class. How nice."

"One short," Austin said. "And three more screwed."

"You two find the others and get on the train." Lian insisted, her tone more than signaling her annoyance with her boyfriend. "I'll find a way on."

"No. Not leaving you." Austin stood firm.

"I can make you." She raised an eyebrow, as if wanting him to test her. He lowered his head, steadfastly staring at her. "Fine. That would be wrong. I just need you to trust me."

He leaned into her and whispered, "You're getting mighty liberal with your powers. I don't like where it's taking you."

"It's taking us to Paris… where we need to go. I didn't say a thing when you put us on that rodent infested freight liner. It's time you trust me."

"Come." Horus tugged on Austin. "Let's find the others."

"Don't make me tell you again." Lian didn't blink, which told Austin she meant serious business. He stood tall, shrugging her off, defying her. "Seriously, Austin, I'll just compel you to go."

"Don't stop there." His eyes narrowed. "Just go ahead and wipe everything away. You promised you wouldn't do that to us, your friends. Much less me, the one closest to you."

"You pick now to be self-righteous?" She chuckled, frustrated. "It's not enough that I'm doing this for us, but the fate of the world hangs in the balance and you get stuck on the principles of how it's done?"

"Someone has to. It's what makes us human. It's what separates the good from the bad. You don't fly airplanes into residential apartments just because someone else did it to you. You rise above. Otherwise why stop the genocide of mankind if it has to be corrupt to survive?"

"Because it survives. Seems pretty cut and dry."

"That's Sanderson talking," Austin said. She slapped him. He turned back to her with a shining red handprint on his cheek. "Is that because you copied more of him than you think, or because maybe you were more like him all along than you want to admit? What others do or don't do doesn't matter. What matters is how we conduct ourselves."

"I'm not having this argument now." Lian turned away, scowling. She couldn't believe he would suggest that she was anything like Sanderson, even with his good intentions and change of heart toward the end of his life.

Hershiser, or Elliot, or Beelzebub, whoever the hell he was, didn't leave her any other choice when it came to Paula. Lian had hidden what she'd done from everyone, but it ate her up nonetheless. If she hadn't put the bullet through Paula's head, then Ra would have another gifted in his possession. That was far worse. Right?

Lian refused to believe that she had behaved like Sanderson. Taking tickets from people who didn't really need them didn't mean she was like him, either. She was certain that, if given the choice between a vacation or humankind's survival, those people would've taken the selfless option. Wouldn't they? That was a stupid argument.

"That's fine. We'll continue this later," Austin said, following Horus. "But make me or our friends do anything against our will, for whatever reason, and I'm done with you."

Lian looked over her shoulder. Austin and Horus were gone. She glanced at the board and panic struck her. She was running low on time.

Last call for the 11:30 to Paris, Gare du Nord, the loudspeaker boasted.

Lian hunched against the wall. *Maybe Austin's right.* A tear dripped down her cheek. She supposed the line between her morals and Sanderson's was more blurred than she cared for. It scared her that maybe it was like that before copying his mind. An old lady touched her shoulder.

"Pardon me, dear, but are you OK?" the lady's voice croaked. Lian's head turned up. The woman shook like an earthquake was destroying the city. She reached into her purse and removed a handkerchief for Lian. "Here, dry your tears, sweetheart."

"Thanks." Lian took the cloth and wiped her face.

"Did you lose your family?" the old woman asked.

Lian smiled, thinking about the fantastic times she had with her parents while young. Yet her new family waited at the train platform. They made living worthwhile. Austin's words struck her heart. Even though he'd lost everything, he remained true to his principles.

However, he was never a slave and prisoner like Lian. A part of his argument was valid, but sacrifices had to be made to ensure the legacy of those she loved. Lian couldn't let anything get in the way of their mission, or the wellbeing of her family. For that reason, she knew Sanderson's method was also right.

"I haven't yet," she replied. "Where ya headed?"

"Paris, though I'm afraid I'm running a bit behind."

Lian momentarily thought about compelling the woman to hand over her pass. As if needing to clear her own conscience, she wanted to know why the woman traveled.

"Do you have family there, or just leisure?" Lian asked.

"My husband passed on several years ago. He wanted his remains spread on the Seine." The woman smiled, beaming with joy and flush in the cheeks while recalling a fonder time in her life. "It was where we honeymooned sixty-plus years ago. I've been meaning to make this journey for some time, but it can't wait any longer."

The old lady struggled to hold back her emotions. Lian heard them. She closed her eyes and poked inside the woman's mind to find out what they were. The woman had recently received a terminal prognosis from the doctor. This would indeed be her last chance to carry out her husband wishes. Lian opened her eyes, compelling the woman to remove the ticket from her bag.

Lian's hand hesitated. *Can I do this?* The clock ticked to 11:30 and Lian made up her mind. She took the woman's bag and first class ticket and sent the old lady on her way.

While sprinting, Lian removed a few items from the woman's purse and placed them into her own backpack, discarded the purse, and rounded a corner to find the conductor and Austin waiting.

"Where'd you find it?" Austin asked.

"I bartered for it." Lian showed the conductor her ticket and stepped aboard the train.

"With what?" he pushed.

Lian shoved forward, staring at her feet, and spoke where Austin couldn't hear.

"My soul."

CHAPTER FORTY

The Observer

The bullet train zipped through the French countryside. Flat clouds blanketed the faded wheat fields. Small villages popped up sporadically along the rolling hills. Lines of ancient stone walls zigzagged through the crops and alongside the tracks.

Lian turned her focus back to her cup of espresso. Across from Lian sat Athena with Harold to her right. Austin flanked Lian to the left. His untrusting gaze was fixed on Harold. She attempted to speak but instead dumped more sugar into her cup.

"Could it be any smaller?" she asked sarcastically. "Look at the size of this thing. It cost nearly five dollars."

"Five quid." Harold corrected her. "That's well more than five measly dollars."

"Makes me feel a lot better." Lian took a sip and jolted in her seat.

"Packs a punch don't it?" Harold laughed. "Unlike that watery shit you yanks try and pass off." Harold noticed Austin's eyes narrow further. "Care to join me for a drink in the dining car? It's only two testicles for a pint nowadays. A real bargain."

Austin crossed his arms and leaned back. It was obvious he wasn't budging. Harold stood and Austin snatched his wrist.

"Where ya going?" Austin's question sounded more like a strong suggestion to sit down.

"I'm gonna drain me-self then get a pint of bitters." Harold tried to pull his arm away, but Austin's hand grew tighter. "Come now doggy, let's not make a scene." Austin let go and Harold adjusted his sleeves. "Very well, old chap."

"I can't sit here." Austin rubbed his head feverishly, messing up his hair. "You girls hold down the fort."

"OK." Athena nodded.

"We need to talk." Lian reached for Austin but was too late. She smiled awkwardly at Athena who gazed back with excitement. "Ever been to Paris?"

"I've only been to earth four times my whole life." Athena was giddy. "Have you?"

"No." Lian set the cup of brew to the side. "Well, this conversation was delightful. Please excuse me."

"I would like to remedy whatever hostility there is between our groups," Athena said as she stepped in front of Lian. "We've not been on the same page since Harold and I arrived at the shipwreck to save you."

"Save us?" Lian laughed. "If I remember correctly, Jarrod was kicking your ass before I stopped him."

"The voice inside his head would have surely butchered the three of you if not for our intervention." Athena crossed her arms. "Have I caused you offense?"

"Just… shut up." Lian stormed off to find Austin, passing Jarrod and Horus as they napped. She pushed Jarrod's shoulder. "We gotta talk."

"What about?" he yawned.

Lian glared at Horus, who was now awake, and tapped her foot.

"I think I shall go for a walk," Horus whispered.

"That'd be great. Thanks." She flashed a closed-lipped, wrinkled-faced smile as he left.

"OK, what's with the 'tude?" Jarrod stretched, popping his joints.

"Am I a bitch?"

366

"Sorta." He grinned. The answer just seemed to anger her more. "That's, uh, not a bad thing... World needs bitches."

"So I'm a bitch for doing what's needed?" She became rather animated. Curious eyes swiveled in her direction.

"Look, you asked and used the term... I... Not going to win this debate, am I?"

"Not funny."

"It is." He squeezed her knee. "What's really going on?"

"I forced some people to give me their tickets unwillingly." She plopped her forehead against the window and sighed.

"That's not that bad..."

"One of them was an old widow hoping to spread the remains of her husband in Paris."

"That's a little more..."

"I shot Paula in the head to keep Ra from getting her."

Jarrod bit his knuckles and nodded. "Give me a moment to digest."

"Yeah. I'm a bitch." She slid down in the chair.

"Not the approach I'd have taken." Jarrod took a moment to soak in her body language. He wrapped his arm around her. "You're wondering if the ends justify the means."

"Do they?" she asked, desperate.

"That's a case by case basis, I suppose..."

"Do they?" Her voice was firm this time.

Jarrod hunched over—averted his eyes—rubbing his hands raw. "Context is all I can say. I know you, Lian. Whatever your situation when inside Paula... there must've been no other way. There's no telling if she was even going to live if you let her go. In that light, you did what had to be done to keep someone evil from taking advantage."

"And in another light?" she said with a lump in her throat.

"Don't concern yourself with option B..."

You're going to answer this. "Jarrod?"

"Any other light would be artificial. What matters is what happened and not what could. We can't rewrite history." He squeezed her hand. "My words or beliefs can't change the way you feel about something. The only person who can justify the means by the ends is you."

"And that means…"

"I… I can't say for sure." His apprehensive tone said he was mulling over the possibilities. "Make sure her death isn't for nothing."

"I need to find Austin," she surmised.

Jarrod exhaled. "Thank god."

As Lian passed through the train on the way to the dining car, Horus and Athena watched her vanish through the door. Horus, leaning down in his seat, appeared relieved Lian didn't stop.

"Do arguments make you uncomfortable?" Athena asked, propping her head up with her hands. Horus flashed a perplexed look. "A great look of relief washed over you when she passed."

"I'm no stranger to intense debates and squabbling among peers. A woman's emotional wrath is another thing altogether." He smiled, nodding. "I'd sooner face a thousand enemies."

"Been scorned before?" she giggled, leaning back in her seat. "I've never been intertwined with another."

"I've not been so much spurned as I've avoided a suckling trap." He leaned forward, speaking in low tones. "There've been plenty in the past seeking my courtship. I found the distraction cost dearly when a pound of flesh was taken from my cousin. I needed to remain focused. Complete what my father never could. That is what my life has been built for, not sexual games."

"Perhaps you never found the time for love because you were swarmed by girls." Athena smiled. "A true gentleman and warrior such as you needs a woman."

"My mother would like you," Horus chuckled, staring out of the window. His face turned solemn.

"It's a shame the events that welcomed us into existence unfolded the way they did." Athena cupped her palm over his hand. Horus kept his eyes fixed elsewhere. "Do you wonder what it would have been like? I have fleeting glimpses of my mother's warmth and the rumbling tone with which my father would sing me to sleep."

"I never had the privilege to hear my father's words. I've only been regaled with tales of his moral compass and steadfast leadership." Horus pulled his hand back gently. His lips quivered but his speech didn't. "I regret the horrible things I'd say about him when I was younger. I must've seemed like an entitled brat. I was angry that everyone else had experienced who my father was and that he didn't try harder to ensure I could know him firsthand."

His hands matched the tremor of his face. "Now that our people have fallen under my watch, I too share in his failures. The faults I cursed in my father course through my blood as well. At least the great Osiris saw to the survival of his loved ones. All I did was watch them perish."

"Then clear it from the mind and steel your resolve," Athena said. Her voice was firm, yet gentle and encouraging. "When this is over, we shall see your mother returned to your arms, and the rendezvous refused by the Last Great War shall finally come to fruition."

Lian passed through the gangway and stood silently in line for the toilet. It was currently occupied. Austin made his way back in her direction. His firm jaw and narrowed eyes said what his mind screamed. The man occupying the restroom exited and Lian pulled Austin in as soon as he arrived.

"Why are we in here?" He asked. Lian tore his shirt open, ran her fingers through his hair, and kissed him. Austin pulled back. "That's not why I came..."

"I know." She pulled him towards her and jumped onto the sink, wrapping her legs around his hips. His hands warmed her body, swaddling her. Suddenly, he jerked back. "What's wrong?" she asked.

"Are you making me do this because you knew what I was coming to talk about?" Sweat ran down his sculpted back. His arms bulged with power as he held her up. His lips suggested they wanted to continue.

"Why would you ask that?" She saw mistrust in his eyes. "I didn't pull you in here to distract you from your thoughts."

"But you kicked the tires in my head anyway?" He turned her chin up to stare in her eyes. She closed them and nodded. He stepped back. "Just more games with you."

"It's not…"

"Save it." His fingers covered her lips before stroking her cheek and brushing some hair behind her ears. "This is us now. I'm not just concerned about you relying too much on your powers and forcing people to do your bidding so you can get what you want easier. I'm worried I won't know when we're real. Is this real?"

"You kissed me first." She grabbed his hands. Her head pressed against his chest. "Your passion saved me from Maya's spell. That's not something I thought of. You did."

"And what would you do to keep from losing that?" Austin glared at his reflection. His arms hung limp at his sides and not around her.

"Anything."

"That's what I'm worried about." His fingers clamped around her shoulders. They connected gazes. "Some things are more important than the individual…"

"There's nothing more important." Lian suppressed a frustrated chuckle, rubbing her face.

"At the risk of corrupting something pure, just to make sure it stays intact?" Austin leaned over her shoulder, breathing down her neck. "We're wasting time right now. I don't trust Harold…"

"I know." She rolled her eyes, squinting at him through the mirror.

"Because you read my thoughts?"

"Because you wear your heart on your sleeve." Lian pushed out of the restroom.

"Hey, what were you two doing in there?" The conductor said, trying to grab Lian's arm. "That's not permitted. Save it for a hotel..."

"Shut up." Lian waved her hand in the man's face. He stumbled about and went on with his business. She marched towards the dining car. "Keep up, Austin."

"Again, another unnecessary intervention of your powers. There's nothing he could've done to us." Austin shrugged, irritated. He kept close to Lian's heels. "Walking fast, aren't we?"

"You're worried about whether or not we can trust Harold. We're gonna find out."

"You've acted strange since we failed to rescue Paula. Why?" he asked.

She lowered her head and pushed through the crowd like a fullback. "I'm just mad they were able to capture her."

"Yeah, but we'll save her eventually." His misinformed words made her face twitch.

She turned and put a hand to his chest with her eyes fixed on his feet. "Look, I..." He tried to get her to look at him, but she shrugged it off. "Maybe we need some space."

"What aren't you telling me?"

"I'm just tired of disappointing you," she said. "You're not in the best state right now to deal with Harold. Let me prime the pump. Get inside his mind. Figure out what's really going on. He'll shut off if you come out guns blazing."

"He's got powers too..."

"I know." She pushed Austin back. "I'll handle myself."

"Ten minutes," he insisted.

"Fifteen."

"Fine."

Harold sat alone at the bar, rubbing his left arm feverishly. He pulled his sleeve up, staring at the rotting, black veins moving through the flesh. His pale hand had a slight bluish hue.

Something to take the edge off would be appropriate, he thought. Harold nodded at the bartender. "A dram of Scotch if ya wouldn't mine, me-lady."

She slid a child's glass in front of him and poured a quick drop into it. He scooped it up and slammed it back. *Not quite there.* "How 'bout a few fingers' worth this time. Let's not bother with the cheap stuff either. I want something old enough to be Prime Minister."

While the bartender turned away, he reached into his coat and pulled out a crystal. He fumbled and it landed on the floor. The barkeep poured a larger glass and he quickly downed it, nodding for another. She obliged. Harold hunched over and clasped the crystal tightly just as Lian made her way through the dining car. He took the glass and downed it again. His fingers motioned for a refill. "Keep 'em coming, lass."

"Care to buy me something?" Lian leaned against the bar. He swirled the remaining dash of Scotch around in his glass before finishing it. "That looked good."

"Did it now?" He smiled. The lady put two glasses in front of them. Harold gave one to Lian. "It's the good stuff. I never have it less than thirty years old."

"Never?" Lian raised an eyebrow, speaking with a sexy rasp. Harold adjusted in his seat. "Some things aren't meant to linger in the bottle for long."

"Is that so? How would you know?"

"My surrogate father taught me all I needed to know about Scotch and cigars."

"Perhaps I should try uncorking a bit sooner." Harold loosened his tie and undid a few buttons. A spider web of black veins surged through his skin under his shirt. He noticed Lian's gaze linger there a

372

little longer than normal and covered it up. "I thought you had a fella that looked after your... desires."

"He's presently indisposed to render those services." She grinned, sipping from the glass. She coughed and her eyes immediately watered. "It's... so smooth."

"Is it?" Harold laughed. He wiggled his nose and Lian robotically finished the glass with a disgusted hack. "Paris, the city of love. It's magnificent this time of year. The crowds are lighter after the holidays, yet the ambience and cheer of the decorations still lingers. Have you ever wanted to ice skate on the Eifel Tower?"

"Can you?" Her eyes widened. She reached behind the bar and grabbed a bottle of rum. The bartender went to stop her but Harold waved her off. Lian filled her glass to the brim. She chugged. Her speech slurred. "You're lyin' to me."

"You're just about ready, aren't you?" Harold asked, laughing. His hand went up her leg, exploring her body. "Yes, nice and primed."

"Hey now," Lian said, unable to keep from laughing. "I didn't say you... could put your hand there."

"You didn't say I couldn't, either." He laughed and so did she. He gazed at her mouth and suddenly her voice muted. "Look there, you're now the perfect woman."

Austin passed through the gangway into the dining car. Several standing cocktail tables and a few intimate booths littered the space between Austin and the bar. Lian sat next to Harold, wobbling around in her seat like a drowsy mummy.

"What is she doing?" Austin wondered.

Harold noticed Austin, so he pulled his hand from Lian's inner-thigh. He snapped his fingers and Lian opened her mouth, vomiting on the floor. She fell onto all fours.

Harold laughed. "I told the lady it was good stuff."

"Are you alright?" Austin knelt, grabbing her face.

"Get the child outa here. She's causing a scene," Harold grumbled, speaking into his glass. Austin grabbed Harold by the trench coat and shoved him into a booth. The half-breed laughed at Austin's fury. "I'm trembling."

"You should be." Austin leaned over Harold. His nostrils flared when he breathed in. "You trying to get her sick?"

"She's an adult playing an adult game to get adult company. She knew what she wanted." Harold rubbed his hand in Austin's face. "Give 'er a sniff."

Austin bent Harold's arm back, nearly snapping it. The crystal rolled out of Harold's sleeve and onto the floor, bouncing off Austin's foot and over to Lian.

"What's this?" Lian caressed the edges, looking at the pink storm inside.

"How about we ask Horus and Athena about it?" Austin suggested.

"I wouldn't do that, mate." Harold wriggled out of his coat, exposing his sickly limbs. "Give the crystal back now."

"Who's gonna stop us?" Austin shook his head, grinning. "You?"

"In a roundabout way." Harold nodded and his eyes sparkled with orange energy. "Yeah." The passengers and staff in the dining car stood at attention. Their snarling gazes fixed on Austin with glazed-over eyes. Harold clapped and the passengers attacked. "I've a few tricks up me sleeve yet."

Austin shoved Lian toward the exit. She put the crystal into a pocket. He elbowed the first passenger and kicked the second in the sternum, sending him backwards into the next three. The bartender broke a bottle over his head and stabbed him in the back. Austin grabbed her by the shirt and threw her over his shoulder.

Harold lunged into a step, planting his front foot firmly. His hands came together, forming a diamond. A shockwave of sound rippled through the train car, shattering glasses and windows. Austin and the others lifted off the ground. He tumbled headfirst into a booth. The crystal rolled out of Lian's pocket during the commotion and was sucked into Harold's palm.

"You changelings are always so small-minded and predictable." Harold pressed his thumb into the crystal. It roared with pink light and hovered in place. He spoke over the rift. "But you hero types are even worse. Do you even know what you're fighting for?"

The passengers piled onto Austin, punching and kicking him. His face turned into a snarling snout, and his eyes grew fierce. Gray hairs sprouted from his body as his skin ruptured from his enormous muscles. Austin broke free and jumped at Harold.

Harold swiped with his hands. A sound wave tore the sides off the train car and threw passengers outside. The force of the wind from the speeding train ripped anything not bolted down from the dining car and onto the tracks. Austin dug into the floor, holding Lian. Harold pulled himself over the bar. The Assassins emerged from the pink light and the rift closed behind them.

"I wanted subtle," Set yelled, looking over his shoulder at Harold.

"My apologies," Harold replied, holding his hands together, as if praying. "But my blood is literally curdling. It hurts."

"As will your asshole if we don't complete our mission because of your incompetence." Set pushed his hand into Sif's back and pressed her forward. "Let's go."

The train jostled, causing those around Jarrod to stir. He looked out the window, spotting passengers skidding across the ground with chairs, tables and other debris. He shot from his seat.

"My friends!" he yelled, running through the crowd towards the source of commotion. People screamed and flooded the aisle. They ran towards the back of the train, against Jarrod. "Everyone, out of my way."

Is it my turn to play? Ryan taunted. The hairs on Jarrod's arms straightened.

Jarrod wiped the sweat from his face. "No. It can't be. You're locked up."

The train shook again. The horde was thrown and knocked him onto his back. He rolled into a seat and cradled himself in the fetal position until the wave of fleeing people had passed. Slowly, he stood.

Horus extended his hand. "We must go."

Jarrod looked behind Horus. Set approached. A crossbow took shape over his hand and light crystallized.

"Is that an Assassin?"

Horus wrapped his arms around Jarrod, encompassing him into the aurascales. The crossbow erupted, blasting them from the train.

They hit the ground and bounced to a stop, tumbling through the eight track grid. Set burst out the top of the train, ripping away the back three train cars. The rear cars turned sideways, unhinged from the tracks, and barreled into the wheat fields.

Jarrod sprinted toward a road down a long slope. Set, stalking his prey from the sky, soared toward his target. The aurascales around Horus repaired their damage and the hawk mask took form. His weapon of choice sizzled into his grasp.

Set landed in front of Jarrod. Dirt kicked up. Set put his fist to Jarrod's chin. Two blades shot along his jaw line, shaving whiskers. The third prodded under his mouth. Set remained still.

"What're ya waitin' for?" Jarrod asked. He grabbed Set's wrist. "Do it." He shook the Assassin, but Set remained stoic. "KILL. ME."

Horus chopped. Set parried left and spun into his own attack. His sword caught Horus along the ribs. The prince's aurascales sliced open and resealed.

"Your moves are telegraphed. Obviously taught by a lesser fighter," Set taunted, kneeing Horus in the face. "The energy of your star is familiar." Set evaded a stab, spun, and elbowed Horus in the back of the head. "Your colors hail from the Southern Corner, but your faceguard is unfamiliar." Three jagged blades shot out from his forearm. Set drove them into Horus' shin. "Who are you?" he grunted. "My sweet nephew?"

376

Jarrod's heel caught Set between the shoulder blades, pushing him away from Horus. The ground rumbled. A local commuter train swiped into Set like a wrecking ball and tossed him several yards. The train screeched to a halt. The passengers pressed their faces to the windows and watched the action unfold, recording the events.

"Can you fly us back to our train?" Jarrod helped Horus stand. His wounded compatriot draped his arm over Jarrod's shoulders. The steel tracks vibrated. Another bullet train headed their way. "Anytime you're ready."

Horus' wings expanded, ready for flight. Before he could lift off, three jagged spears stabbed into his armor, latching hold. Set circled above. His wrist blades had dislodged from their holders and penetrated Horus' armor. Attached to them was a long wire which retracted and yanked Horus off the ground.

Jarrod leapt out of the bullet train's path with no time to spare. The drag created by the speeding locomotive sucked him along the ground like a soda can. He grabbed for anything to stop with. His nails ripped from their fingers. Finally, he slammed gut first into a signal light.

"The smell of Osiris is on you." The chrome armor vanished from Set's face. He tied the wire around Horus' neck like a noose and hooked it to the speeding train. "Another time I'll slay you like I did him." The train sped off over the horizon, dragging Horus with it. Set lowered to the ground, grinning.

Jarrod stumbled and eventually fell into a crawl. The people on the train continued to snap pictures, in awe of Set's wings as they crawled back into the aurascales.

"Don't leave on my account." Set stood in Jarrod's way. "I must admit, I'm underwhelmed. I thought you'd be... less like Azrael. I definitely figured you'd be more of a challenge. Someone worthy of my skills and blade."

"Get it over with." Jarrod rolled onto his back, revealing his battered and bruised condition. "You'd be doing the world a favor."

"I don't do favors." Set ran his hand along Jarrod's chin in a provocative and exotic fashion. *Maybe more attractive than I thought, given your bloodied state.* "I do myself favors."

He grabbed Jarrod by the hair and dragged him toward the stalled commuter train. A crossbow manifested over his forearm. Scintillating green light crystallized into an arrow and propelled out. The side of the train car split open. Several passengers were instantly vaporized.

"No." Jarrod reached for the people as if he could save them.

Set grinned and repeated the process until the whole side of the train car had disintegrated. The passengers still alive clung to their seats with their heads pressed down to shield their eyes. The souls of those departed lingered in the air, their blue haze visible only to the angel and clone.

"Enough." Jarrod struggled to free himself from Set's grasp, but it was futile.

"Only when you stop me." Set kicked the side of Jarrod's leg and snapped the tibia. Jarrod collapsed, writhing in pain. "That should keep you there until you decided to heal yourself and stop me."

"Why?" Jarrod cried.

Who cares why? Ryan spoke up.

"Build the mental wall, Jarrod," he said to himself.

Fight or flight has kicked in. I'm not going anywhere. Ryan responded.

"Crawl back where you came from." Jarrod slapped himself, sweating profusely.

Set lifted an old woman. His sword swiped down her gut, spilling her insides in front of her grandchildren. The more souls available for the taking, the more Jarrod's skin illuminated. Cold sweats soaked him.

"This does nothing for you?" Set squinted. He snatched a young boy, holding the edge of the blade to his neck. "I was told you were Death incarnate, yet you cower like a school girl, letting these innocent people die. They're gone already. I know you see their souls. Take them for your own and give me a good match."

He has a point. We can take him.

"I let you out of the cage and you won't go back," Jarrod whispered, spitting blood. He looked at the ground, shaking his head as if willing himself into defiance. A blue glow spiraled through his temple and spurted from his eyes.

"Speak up coward, I hear you not," Set yelled, dragging the blade across the boy's throat. The blood seeped slowly at first, but turned into a flash flood. The eight year old hit the ground with his blank eyes looking towards Jarrod. "Some prophecy. It seems we missed the mark again. I'll finish you now."

Dammit, you coward, he'll kill us both! Ryan yelled in a panic.

"It is what it is." Jarrod nodded, breathing with relief.

Set pulled Jarrod to his feet. It was then he spotted a pale bluish hue in Jarrod's skin. The eyes were bloodshot with repressed desire. Set tossed Jarrod to the ground.

"You almost fooled me." Set turned away. "I slaughtered more than I had to because you let me. You'd do well to remember that."

He's right, Ryan taunted.

"Shut up!" Jarrod screamed.

"You just let them die." Set rubbed the blood from his chin. He scratched the back of his head, deep in thought. "You are a dark messiah, aren't you? Clearly you've never been properly motivated. I'll get to your real potential. You shall see." Set vanished in a sparkle of pink light.

Athena and Sif sparred a few train cars back from the dining car. Two daggers twirled in Sif's hands. Spikes protruded from her knuckles. Jab-jab-cross, Athena's depowered armor dented along the chest and back. Sif kicked Athena onto her stomach and lunged with her daggers. Hermes stopped her.

"What are you doing?" Sif asked.

379

"Choosing my own place, for once." Hermes soared through the top of the car, pushing Sif. "I know you fight in fear."

"I fear nothing." Sif drove both elbows into the base of Hermes' skull and they crashed a good distance from the now stopped train.

Athena sprinted in their direction. The two Assassins fought against each other. The clang of their blades echoed through the field.

Hermes struck. "I fight for loyalty, Sif…"

She deflected his sword and shoved a shield into his chin. "Then why do you turn against us?"

"You know as well I do there's never been an 'us'." He rolled across the ground. Her sword barely missed his head. He punched her chin and lunged for her heart. "You still fight for love."

"Love of Father." She caught his hands and pushed the blade away. Her weapon tapped his throat.

Hermes looked at Athena, raising a hand for her to stop. "For Thor and your son," Sif gasped, pulling the blade away. "We can stop Set. I know you didn't kill Thor. You just took his head when you found him. It was all too easy for the Archangels to fill in the blanks."

"You know nothing," she sobbed.

"He knows more than we'd like to admit." Set appeared and Athena hid in the crops. Set pushed Sif aside. Hermes attacked. Set evaded him and jammed the wrist blades into Hermes' gut. "I told you where defiance would lead. You had only to trust." Set knelt and laid Hermes' head on the ground.

"Did you kill him?" Hermes asked. "Did you stop fate like I know you desire?"

"I prefer permanent solutions." Set caressed Hermes' cheek, twisting the blades further. Blood trickled from Hermes' mouth. "I intended only to test him. The real thing is yet to come."

"I hope you die…" Hermes wailed.

Set nodded. "All will in due time." He stood and took Sif by the hand. The female Assassin dried her tears as they vanished into pink light.

Athena slid to Hermes' side, distraught.

"I've often wondered how you've grown." He grimaced. "As a baby you looked like Hera, but now I see your father written… in… your… eyes."

"Don't talk," she cried. "Your armor will heal you."

"Not… from this." He leaned into her lap. Austin, who was dragging an unconscious Harold by the feet, and Lian stood behind Athena. Hermes cupped her hands. Inside their grasp a purple flicker ignited. Aurascales drained from his body and formed into an egg shape. "As an Angel-born, you've no star of your own to shield and protect you. Take this and with it accomplish the great things you were born for."

"No. I won't." Athena shoved it back into his chest. He wiped the tears from her eyes and sang the melody her mother would when she was an infant. As his grip on the starstone weakened, so too did the force of his words. The slate-gray egg rolled out of his grasp and over to Horus' landing feet. Athena sobbed. "I wish I was never born. My life has caused nothing but pain to all I've ever loved."

"'Tis love which makes pain worth bearing." Horus laid the starstone in her lap. "For existence isn't worth creation without love, and love itself cannot be without sorrow. We honor those who came before us by completing the visions they set forth. Otherwise, we doom ourselves to extinction without purpose."

Jarrod stepped away from the group. Stress lines blanketed his face. "Those are wise words."

"They're not mine," Horus replied. "There my uncle's. The one who didn't just try to kill us."

I know our purpose, Jarrod, Ryan whispered so as to not let Lian hear. *Do you?*

382

CHAPTER FORTY-ONE

Jarrod VII

After arriving in Paris, Lian commandeered an apartment with a central location for their base of operations. The television reflected across Jarrod's face while the others argued in the kitchen several feet away. Harold was tied to a chair in the middle of their circle.

"I'll enter his mind," Lian said. "Find out what's going on."

"No, we saw how that worked on the train," Austin protested.

"I'm adept at information extraction," Horus said. "It'll be seamless."

"This is my friend," Athena argued. "We do not know if he is himself."

"What's wrong with his skin?" Lian asked.

"He smells rotten," Austin said, gagging. "Seriously, like he's decaying."

"You're all fools," Harold said with a groan. "My joints are stiffening."

"What's wrong with your soul?" Horus examined him closer.

"He's dead," Jarrod said, listening to the wiser voices in his mind. "I was too self-absorbed earlier to pick up on it. Harold's soul is trapped inside his decomposing body."

"Harold?" Athena whimpered, covering her mouth. "Can you fix him?"

"Set's counting on it," Harold chuckled. "He wants Jarrod to consume more souls and unleash the freak, be it mine, an innocent civilian's, or, more likely, one of his friends'."

"We're all here." Austin clutched Harold's throat. "You gonna bring them back?"

Harold squeaked something, but Austin's grip snuffed it out. Horus pulled Austin's hand away.

"Speak," Horus insisted.

"It wasn't me they followed." Harold stared at Horus. "It was the crystal you left behind. It's attracted to your starstone." He laughed at the worried expression Horus gave. "Get over yourself. The crystal is broken, but they know where you're headed. I'm sure they're in the city by now."

"Do they know why?" Horus asked.

"They haven't the foggiest."

Lian furrowed her brow. "He's hiding something." Austin rolled his eyes. Lian huffed. "What do you expect?"

"For you to listen," Austin replied.

"This is taking too long." She slapped Harold. "Out with it."

"I'm not hiding anything, you just haven't asked the right questions," he laughed.

Athena laid a hand on his knee. "Please."

"Oh, don't give me them puppy-dog eyes." Harold swayed, stamping his foot. "Fine." He looked over to Jarrod. "Did you forget someone, ol' blue eyes?"

Jarrod took a second to think about what he meant. It couldn't be. She left well before Horus even got there. Jarrod sprang from the couch, lifted Harold with one arm, and slammed him into the wall. The plaster caved in and splintered. Harold was beside himself with laughter.

"How?" Jarrod reared back and slammed Harold into the wall again, breaking studs. "TELL ME."

"Who's he talking about?" Horus stood to Jarrod's right.

"Anyone else concerned he's about to blow his lid?" Austin asked.

"I'm in control," Jarrod snarled. He spun and slammed Harold onto the floor. The table and chairs jumped from the vibration.

Lian gasped. "They've got Claire…"

"She went back for you." Harold couldn't budge Jarrod's grip. The fading soul inside him longed to be absorbed. Jarrod considered it. "You've no idea how much I hurt."

"I can imagine." Jarrod squeezed, breaking Harold's skin. It would be easy. Kill Harold and see his memories firsthand. The more difficult, and right, thing to do was to back away. Despite the craving, he did.

"They were able to track Horus' movements. They must've scoured your hideout moments after you'd left. That's when Claire arrived." Harold sat up, rubbing his neck. "They'd already killed me. But they returned me. I was in… this light with souls everywhere. They plucked me from oblivion and shoved me back. This isn't how it's supposed to be."

"I've heard of this," Horus said. "Sobek taught me. A soul must be supported by a living shell. The degenerative process of death corrodes the soul, making it no longer itself."

"Demons occupy dead bodies all the time." Athena helped Harold over to a chair and dabbed his neck with a washcloth.

"Demons are a different breed." Horus patted Athena on the back "The other side of the soul coin, if you will."

"Set didn't kill me," Jarrod divulged. "He had a chance. I begged him to. He wanted me to absorb the souls of the innocent civilians… to goad me into what he called a 'worthy' fight."

"Claire's as safe as she'll ever be until they find you, mate," Harold reassured him. He tried to stand, but his hips were locked in place. "Rigor mortis's been delayed long enough, it seems." A pale blue shine washed through his cheeks, showcasing his gooey black veins. "Set me free. Please."

Athena conjured a dagger and put it against his throat. "It will be over soon."

"No." Jarrod pulled her away. She struggled but Horus steadied them both. "You let him go and I can't promise I won't snatch him. And if I don't snatch him, they'll be attracted to the soul or absorb him into that light he talked about. Either way, he's theirs."

"You're gonna leave me in 'ere?" Harold drooled and hacked.

"Yeah." Jarrod stood over him. "Depending on how long you've been dead, you've got some time. It's gonna be excruciating, but seeing as they've enabled your body to keep going, it's the safest place to store your soul for the time being."

"You twat." Harold spit on Jarrod's face. "Y'know you want to devour me."

"I do." Jarrod nodded. "But I won't." He stepped toward the back of the room. The words of his mom, stressing that the world would have to deal with whatever he'd become, looped in his head. What would he become? "I need some fresh air."

Jarrod stood out on the third floor balcony. Morning arrived and his stomach was in knots. He kept repeating Claire's name, over and over. She loved him too much. There was no way she'd really leave him behind. The noble thing was to encourage her to live a normal life, but maybe the right thing was to support her choice: him. Though they weren't visible, the bells of Notre Dame made themselves known as they chimed seven times. Jarrod knew the Assassins lingered somewhere just around the corner.

After about half an hour of solitude, the sun stretched its coral fingers through the close-knit pedestrian streets of the Latin Quarter. The smell of hot and fresh pastries danced its way up to him from the bakery across the street where the baker's wife and triplet toddlers had the first pick of the morning batch.

"Care to know what we decided?" Austin asked, opening the window to step out onto the balcony. He leaned against the railing with his back to the street.

"Claire's safe as long as they don't find me. I'm riding the bench." Jarrod continued staring at the three kids, all curly blonde girls, stuffing their faces with éclairs just inside the shop window. "You gonna be at the museum before opening?"

"That's the plan." Austin shook the morning chill from his arms. "You remember a few years back, we had that stopover in Stuttgart on our way for deployment in Kabul?"

Jarrod nodded with a slight grin. He remembered. They'd landed in the middle of the night with just three hours to prep for the next leg. Jarrod had insisted they take in some sights, as if there would be something worth doing at two in the morning.

Jarrod laughed. "The major and those two hookers in the alleyway behind the pub." He slapped Austin's arm. "I won't say that sight didn't have its perks, such as less mop duty, but I don't completely agree that our troop saw significantly more patrol time, either. His wife was a babe too, and those skanks... woof. What was he thinking?"

"You just had to take a picture," Austin laughed. "What possessed you to do that?"

"I had to have something to remember the occasion by." Jarrod leaned forward and rested his arms on his knees.

Austin's grip wrung out the tension along Jarrod's spine. What loomed ahead came back into focus. He couldn't shake the feeling that Ryan's odd silence meant something.

"And here we are. The most traveled-to tourist destination and we're just stopping by on the way to something even bigger than before." Every moment that saw his friends in their predicament had been triggered by him. If only he'd made different choices along the way, maybe they wouldn't have been sucked into this. "What I wouldn't give for y'all to see the world from atop the Eifel Tower like every other tourist. Instead you're doing this, with what seems like the fate of mankind once again in the balance. At least we got to stop and briefly take in the sights and smells."

"You didn't mention a key part." Austin sat.

"That would be?" Jarrod tilted his head, looking at his life-long friend.

"When my life was darkest and we'd spend days baking in the Afghan sun…" Austin paused, choked up. "You said 'if you don't take a break, I don't take a break. That's how it's been for both of us since before I can remember'."

"I did." Jarrod nodded. He covered his face. "And I'm sorry you feel compelled to return the favor."

"Compelled? Hardly. I do this willingly." Austin moved for the window and opened it. "I used to take your devil-may-care attitude as arrogant. But that was never the case, was it?"

Jarrod shrugged.

Austin ruffled Jarrod's hair. "You'd leap without looking because that's what we needed. If you weren't putting things in motion, none of us would've lived long enough to be here, so to say you deny us a normal life is absurd. The only reason we get to wake up to the chorus of bells from Notre Dame is you."

"Be careful out there. I promised I'd look out for you." Jarrod sat up, his face now dry. He ached to come clean about a secret he'd longed silenced. "I never told you that I'm the reason you never said goodbye to your parents. I hid your phone as a joke. Your father screaming your name has haunted me ever since."

"You think you're the only one who ever made a promise?" Austin asked. "Aunt Liv asked the same thing of me. Oddly enough, it's like she could see the future."

"She could," Jarrod quipped under his breath.

"She told me, before shipping to basic, a day like this would come. I thought she spoke in generalities, but she meant today. There would come a time when I would have to force you to act against everyone else's best interests and protect you from yourself." He knelt, turning Jarrod's head up to make eye contact. "Let someone else be the hero today. We all know the guy you are inside. If we lose you, the real you, then Heaven can't help us."

"Just remember," Jarrod replied, firmly clasping his friend's wrist, "there's no real me without the rest of you."

"You don't have to convince me to come back in one piece," Austin laughed. "I want to live." Austin moved inside to bid farewell to Lian before leaving with Horus.

"We will make quick work of our mission and return promptly," Horus said to Jarrod, leaning against the inside wall. "Do you still wish to be left in isolation after I uncover the chariot? You would be of much better use to the cause if you were in control of your powers, rather than left on a planet to die alone."

"I'm not sure there is any controlling them." Jarrod turned his attention back to the three small girls. "The best thing for your cause is not me."

"So be it." Horus left.

The bells sang once again, declaring that yet another hour was upon them.

390

CHAPTER FORTY-TWO

Set V

Hundreds of recently deceased souls wandered aimlessly. The burning train cars still housed several screaming voices. As the yelp of a woman ceased, one more soul manifested. This mess would be difficult to clean up, and harder still to explain. It was all part of the plan.

A rift zipped through space-time and Raphael emerged with several of his most trusted direct reports. Uriel was among them. Raphael looked displeased, which was understandable, but amusing nonetheless.

"This is low profile?" he asked with a pug-faced scowl.

"I don't show up at your job and tell you how to do it."

"And you further insult me by talking back." Raphael acted like he was going to slap Set. They both knew better, which probably left Raphael feeling jilted further. "Did you at least kill him?"

Set shook his head. "Before you spout off again, I know my theory will work."

"How are we supposed to clean this up without Michael being drawn to the numbers?" Raphael grumbled. "A soul spilled here or there is understandable, but this many will heighten his urge."

"Did you bring the Light?" Set asked, motioning with his head for Raphael to follow. Sif and Raphael's lieutenants tagged along, but were halted by Set's ominous frown.

"Indeed." Raphael unhinged a pentagon-shaped artifact from his aurascales. Inside was a radiating blue sphere. A key to the Light of Souls had been forged. One had to be dumb to not be attracted to its power. Raphael held it away. "Like I'd give it to you."

"Are we not partners?"

"Please," Raphael laughed. "This is merely an alliance of convenience. Don't act like I know not of your true intentions."

"My loyalty to Lucifer has never faltered."

"I'm no fool." Raphael walked circles around Set. "Neither side was ever appealing to you. Tell me why you had me construct this and we'll go from there."

Not getting his hands on the Light's key posed a problem. Set would need it to complete his mission. Nevertheless, emotional beings like Raphael could be tipped one direction or another by subtle suggestions.

"Activate it," Set insisted. Raphael was skeptical. "Seriously. Just briefly, though."

"It's encoded to my print." Raphael grinned. "Lest you get any funny ideas." He pressed his thumb against the blue core. The pentagon opened along several slits. The souls wandering aimlessly were drawn like moths to the flame. Once touching it, they fused into the artifact. Raphael was in awe. The souls vanished and the pentagon sealed. "A portable key. How did you know?"

"Schematics I'd examined before the Light of Soul's construction. With that, we can reap the dead." Set nodded for Sif to approach. "Now Michael won't be drawn to the chaos we inflict, unless he's watching or called."

"How interesting." Raphael reattached the pentagon key to his aurascales and removed another device. He wiggled it in front of the Assassins. "Do you know what this is? I had the idea when booting Gabriel from Heaven." Set and Sif both shook their heads. "Oh, Istheal?"

A cupid, one of Raphael's recently trained henchmen, marched over and stood at attention. "Yes, sir?"

"Nothing. Just wanted your assistance in a demonstration." Raphael squeezed the device and Istheal collapsed into the fetal position. His agonized scream boiled Set's blood. Istheal's aurascales were ripped from his flesh and vanished. "At any moment, I can sever your bond with the Deliverance. You'd be less than human."

"The reason behind the display of power escapes me." Set remained calm in order to chafe Raphael's pride. He knew full-well the message Raphael intended.

"Don't!" Raphael yelled, shaking from trying to hold back his anger. He took a deep breath. "Don't mock... me."

"I would never," Set proclaimed with satirical reverence.

A few angels chuckled but quickly went silent in response to Raphael's cold grunts. He put the Deliverance remote under Set's nose. "I wouldn't hesitate."

"I wouldn't either... if I were in your wise and clearly more powerful and enviable shoes." Set remained calm with his hands folded behind his back.

"Why didn't you kill Death?" Raphael placed the Deliverance remote into his armor and paced. "Is he more powerful than we thought?"

"I've taken certain assurances that he won't be a problem." Set nodded at Sif again. She opened a rift and vanished.

Raphael said, "I don't understand...."

"Just a moment." Set held a finger up. Sif reemerged, this time holding a human woman. Set revealed his prize. "Behold, the instrument with which Death will be brought to his knees."

"A girl?" Raphael scoffed.

"Not just any. One close to Death's heart." Set cupped Claire's chin. "The half-blood you allowed me to revive told us as much."

"If he's telling the truth," Raphael countered.

"For a chance to live again and be made whole, few would gamble," Set assured Raphael and the others. "Death was able to slay Hermes. I'll need some men…"

"You ask too much," Raphael interrupted. He pulled on Claire's hair, looking her over. "It can't be done. You'll have to make do."

"I know their destination, but not their exact location. If you want him found quickly, you'll give me the boots on the ground."

"And what, you'll create a bigger scene?" Rahael refused. "I know better than to give you an army."

Uriel chimed in. "Gabriel's men need a new leader, do they not?" Raphael and Set both turned his direction.

"As if I trust you any more than Set." Raphael leaned in to Uriel's face. "Tell me why you'd go?"

"We're rebuilding against the tyranny of those who've betrayed us. That's why you constructed a key for the Light of Souls, no?" Uriel took Raphael by the shoulders. "The messengers are eager to atone for the sins of your commander. Send us. I'll lead with Set as my adviser."

"He has a point." Set nodded. "What'll it be?"

Raphael squinted at Uriel and the Assassins. Set waited anxiously for the answer at the tip of Raphael's tongue. His lips opened.

CHAPTER FORTY-THREE

Austin VI

Austin followed a tour group through the Louvre's Egyptian exhibit. It was a French speaking tour, but he hopped along for the journey hoping to fit in. He pulled Horus with him before the group left them behind.

"C'mon, keep up." He snapped his fingers. "I don't want to get separated. I need you to keep the Assassins from killing me."

"Fear not for your life." Horus scanned the space around them. "As soon as we find the chariot, we'll be on our way."

"What exactly will it look like?" Austin walked up to an egg-shaped carving with three curved lines in it. "This seems familiar."

"This is tribute art to our starstones." Horus touched the carving. "The lines represent the triple helix of an angel's DNA."

"I'm pretty sure that should mean something." Austin noticed the tour guide getting riled up. "I think you should stop touching it."

"Indeed." Horus placed his hands in his coat.

"You know, I'd like to pretend what this dude is saying is hitting home, but I got nothing. Even if I could speak French, he talks too damn fast." Austin saw a statue of a bird's head on a human body. "Hey look, that's you."

"I'm sure." Horus didn't bother looking. When he walked by the statue, a green light scanned him. The floor rumbled and lights flickered. Display cases and exhibits fell over. The monitor on Horus' left wrist lit up.

395

"Does Paris get earthquakes?" Austin turned but Horus was gone. "Dude, seriously?" The tour guide funneled everyone towards the exits. Austin moved counter to the flow, searching for Horus. He finally found him. "What gives?" The quake stopped.

"I was drawn to this." Horus stared at an artifact. "Sorry for leaving you."

"Yeah, no problem." Austin leaned against a large stone sarcophagus. "Just give me some warning next time."

"Je suis désolé, Vous devez quitter les lieux. Vous ne pouvez rester ici." The guide tapped Austin's shoulder.

Austin glanced briefly at the guide before speaking to Horus. "What does he want?"

"Says we must leave." Horus meticulously inspected the artifacts and pressed his nose against the security glass. "How curious. Could it be?"

"What's that?" Austin held a finger up in response to the guide, acknowledging him with butchered French. "Uno momentum."

"I speak English." The Frenchman attempted to shove Austin along but he didn't budge. The guide pushed with all his might, but it was like Austin was weighed down with cement blocks. He stepped back, scratching his head.

A razor thin blade materialized in Horus' hand and he cut a hole in the exhibit large enough for his hand to fit through.

"Non, non." The guide scooted over to Horus, wearing a stern look. "It is not possible to touch the exhibits."

"What do you mean?" The artifact floated in place, glowing green. Horus scooped it up. "It quite clearly is possible."

"I think he means you're not allowed to." Austin rubbed his face in a nervous manner. "We're so gonna get caught."

"You must now put it back." The guide extended his hand, palm up.

The artifact disintegrated, swirled in the air, and latched onto the back of Horus' head. He grimaced, hunching over as his aurascales

396

formed involuntarily. His helmet took shape and his wings expanded. Everything in the exhibit came to life, glowing and floating, breaking through layers of rock and centuries of dirt. The rectangular stone sarcophagus behind Austin decompressed with a hiss. He turned around and large seams opened up as it rearranged, emitting a funky odor.

"That's ripe." Austin held his nose shut.

The guide took three steps back, scanning Horus and the large statue to Horus' left of a man with a bird face. "Mon Dieu," he exclaimed, flashing the Sign of the Cross as he ran away.

"Now I get what he's sayin'." Austin smirked, smugly pointing at the guide. "It roughly translates to 'you look like that freaking statue'."

"I don't," Horus huffed. He looked at the statue and his shoulders sank. "Just barely, perhaps." He brushed past Austin. "A strange path is illuminated in my faceguard."

The cameras in the corners of each room focused on them as they wandered through the exhibit. Austin couldn't help but notice the hallways were cleared of people.

"It's not a chariot." Horus held his right hand up and several artifacts broke through their cases and assembled around his body in random sections. The pieces of metal clicked into place to the chorus of whistling zips and clanking. The artifacts glowed and lifted Horus further off the ground, making his armor taller and larger as he walked.

"What is it?" Austin remained still while Horus meandered, watching the pieces adhere and build around the aurascales.

The alarms rang, making it impossible to hear anything else. The flashing lights were just as obtrusive. Austin watched the tourists gather in the Cour Carrée and flee while security directed them.

"Evacuating already? Seems a bit excessive, don't ya think?" Austin wondered aloud. Two vessels resembling the one Horus had used to find them—and a bit larger—lowered from the clouds and hovered over the Louvre. Austin's eyes widened and his breathing stopped. "Oh. Maybe not." He noticed Horus was gone. "Damn it, not again."

A sense that time was running out gripped him. Did Horus see the spaceships and abandon him? Who were they? The museum seemed never-ending as he searched. He slipped and landed on his back, staring up at a hole in the ceiling which led to the next floor. The ground and his breath were frozen, as if all heat had been sucked from the air.

"Arrêter." Twelve policemen in riot gear swarmed. Half slowly collapsed toward him. The others took defensive positions behind columns and half-walls.

"Relax." Austin knelt and placed both hands behind his head. There had to be an escape route. The urge to shift gnawed at him. Vibrations in the floor warned of reinforcements approaching.

He steadied his breathing. The scent of those most afraid entered his nose like an ocean current pushing his mind to those ready to piss themselves. He listened for those most calm. They'd have to be the first to go. The time to act was now.

He swiped the zip-ties off the two policemen closest to him and bound them together. To his six, a dagger swung for his kidney. A quick slap dislodged the weapon. The officer's momentum carried forward. Austin flipped him onto the floor. Palm-strike. Palm-strike. Out cold.

Austin rolled right. Bullets ricocheted, spraying dust. He leapt steps up the wall and pushed off into roundhouse. He grabbed the next assailant by the gear, tossing him through a window. Sliding between the bound policemen, he used them as a shield. The other members of task force wouldn't open fire.

A radio on one of their lapels went off. Agitated and frightened, they barked at each other so fast it sounded like one long word.

"What are y'all waitin' for?" Austin crouched, pulling the policemen together. Every time a rifleman adjusted aim, Austin moved his prisoners into the line of fire. The door fifty yards down the hall was the only way out.

An officer sprang forward. Austin ripped the rifle away and swiped the blunt end off the SWAT member's mask, cracking it. A front-kick knocked the air from another officer's lungs. Austin released several key shots, not harming any of the men. When they dove for cover, he vanished.

Austin's massive paws scraped across the marble floor as he ran for an exit. His heavy panting was rhythmic and soothing. He rounded a corner. Two riflemen drew their weapons. He leapt, shifted back into human form, and tackled the two, knocking both unconscious.

Abrupt gunfire prompted cover. The sirens cut off.

"I can hear myself think again," he panted heavily.

The shots were aimed away from him, probably at Horus. He peeked around the corner, noticing three men with large wings and red aurascales marching through the halls. They were a blur in pink haze. The French taskforce unloaded at point blank, not landing a single round.

In a larger flash of pink, the human fighters froze in place. Austin recognized the two Assassins who emerged from the vapor trail with Claire in tow. He quickly pulled his head back.

Winged shadows moved his direction until Set's command halted their course. They turned back. What had alerted them to here? It dawned on him. When Horus was scanned, activating angelic technology, the Assassins had their beacon.

"We're looking to give a push," Set ordered. "The one we're looking for is close."

"Jarrod," Austin whispered. He crawled, with his head down, until his eyes hovered over a pair of silver boots. As his focus moved up the female body, the yellow aurascales shifted.

"The cat and her mouse." Two short swords crackled into Sif's hands.

"Tom never catches Jerry," Austin snarled.

He morphed into wolf form and slashed. Sif evaded the strikes and easily tossed him through a display case. Glass shards stuck in his back. She skipped once and kicked his midsection. He lifted through a window into the courtyard and barreled along the concrete.

Sif landed in front of him, cracking the cement. Five more angels lowered in from the sky with their crossbows fixed on Austin. Sif halted their descent, twirling a blade as she stalked Austin. He tried standing but collapsed under his own weight. He slowly shed his wolf skin, trying to pull the shards from his shoulder blades.

"I'm not here to kill you," she said.

"Could've fooled me." Austin grimaced, pulling himself onto a stone bench.

"I enjoy this no more than you."

"Yeah?" He threw the broken glass at her feet. "Jab those into your spine and get back to me."

"I've a job to do."

"We all have jobs." His anger flared, clearly visible through his furious gaze. The rage numbed his pain. "I was a soldier once. When we blindly follow the lies, we're complicit."

"The difference between you and I is choice." Sif reappeared behind Austin and lifted him. "You've my sympathies. I once knew how free will tasted. The smell lingers with me still. You and I, though, are pawns." Her sword poked against his belly. "Forgive me."

CHAPTER FORTY-FOUR

Horus V

The aurascales' augmentation was complete. Horus estimated an additional metric ton of armor had fused to his exo-suit. His joints zipped-and-whizzed with a mechanical tune while moving. The suit stood almost four meters tall.

Initiating defensive measures.

The suit prompted him. It'd never spoken before. The technology bonded seamlessly with his, but was beyond anything he'd ever studied. How could something so ancient be light-years ahead of modern systems? Before his thoughts had finished, it responded to his questions.

System: HALOGUARD. Design year G.C. 75m., Operation assignment: T-GCK., Pilot: Osiris.

What was G.C. 75m.? That didn't fit any celestial time measurement he knew. That could be anything. Maybe the future? Impossible.

Recommendation: evasive maneuvers.

The HALOGUARD pulled the video feed from the Louvre security system. Two angels—advancing to his six—displayed in a HUD projection. The HALOGUARD rotated, sucking warmth from the surrounding air. The right arm shifted into a cannon, releasing a super-heated plasma blast. The assailants' red aurascales flickered, with several sections melting away.

A magnetic pulse pushed the HALOGUARD inches from the floor and propelled it forward. Fizzing over his hands were energy blades constructed of a combination of light, heat from the surrounding air, and power from his starstone, held together by electromagnetic fields. The result was that putting them to use felt like slicing through water vapor. Both angels toppled over, severed at the waist.

Energy weapons—unnecessary. Power conservation in effect.

The energy blades dissipated and the magnetic lift ceased. Each step rumbled like an elephant herd. This battle-armor had once belonged to his father and must have been attracted to the power core of Horus' starstone, which was probably why it had remained idle all these years.

Was this how Osiris earned his legend? Sobek would encourage Horus to fight at his best in the hopes of earning the mantle his father built. Though further exploration of the HALOGUARD's systems and history was warranted, more important business demanded his immediate attention. Heaven had found them. It was likely something to do with the HALOGUARD's activation. Finding Austin took top priority.

If the HALOGUARD was able to sense the other angels advancing, perhaps it had a lock on their power signature. Horus wondered why it indentified angels under Gabriel's banner as threats. Given the timeline Horus had been taught, the HALOGUARD must have predated The Last Great war. Gabriel and Osiris would've been allies. No matter.

"Can you lock onto similar power signatures?" Horus asked, barely able to believe he was talking to his armor.

Scan radius specifications?

"How about anything close enough to deliver offensive strikes," he replied. "Start with closest and work further out."

Initiating...

Recommend threat level prioritization.

Continue?

"Aren't those two the same thing?" He wondered aloud. "Fine."

Scanning...

A map of the world displayed in his HUD. A list of adversarial targets formed. The HALOGUARD pegged several Armada Cruisers hovering fifteen kilometers from the earth's atmosphere, cloaked to human scanning, as Horus' prime threat.

Omega-level 8: 3 targets.

Recommend power shutdown to avoid detection.

"What are three Armada Cruisers doing in orbit?"

It was highly unorthodox for the angels to be in such close proximity to the planet. Something didn't feel right. Each cruiser had the ability to wipe the entire city from existence. Evidently the HALOGUARD's logical reasoning didn't understand Heaven's desire to limit collateral damage to humans. Unless it had that ability, in which case the answer was all the more terrifying. Either way, there wasn't much Horus could do about it. If the cruisers decided to annihilate the city then so be it.

"Limit range to five cubed kilometers."

Reorganizing.

Top threat:

Unknown – unknown

Unknown Omega-level

Legion head: unknown

"What in the world is that?" It displayed an icon less than a kilometer south-east of his location. The energy readings stumped the HALOGUARD. It was obviously something too new to be in the database. "Scan known targets."

Set – War Captain.

Alpha-level: 5

Legion head: Lucifer

Sif – Primary Defense

Beta-level: 7

Legion head: Thor

"That's enough." It was as he expected. The Assassins were at the top, though seeing his Uncle Set listed under Lucifer's command was a bit of a shock. Obviously, Set had a knack for ditching alliances at opportune times. Several other targets registering in the lower Gamma levels were also listed. "Display location."

The HUD adjusted. It displayed a 3D rendering of the Louvre with color-coded dots representing each target and their threat level. Three lower level threats headed his way.

The HALOGUARD plunged through the wall. It leaned forward, generating magnetic force shields. An angel manifested a bow, pulled back on the shimmering string, and released a crystallized arrow. The arrow shattered into dust upon impact. Horus plowed into the angel and crushed it through the wall and into the street.

The road along the Seine was void of traffic. Local authorities were already rerouting motorists. Human officials wisely sat on the sideline. Horus' armor registered mounting human forces at the edge of the city with an evacuation protocol already in effect. Radio transmissions were relayed into his faceguard, giving him up-to-the-second information on their plans. They kept repeating that it wouldn't be another London or Moscow.

A chariot swung around the north corner of the building. His suit alerted him of a charge. Wings expanded at his back. Automatic evasive operations kicked in. The armor turned rigid, forcing his arms and legs to the midnight and six positions. Boosters at his feet and the small of his back propelled him just as an energy blast from the chariot pulverized a crater into the concrete.

Aero-mode initiated.

Within seconds, he shot through cirrus clouds. The blue of the sky slowly darkened. "Adjust course." Outside noise came to a halt. The suit compensated for a lack of air pressure. "Locate offending aircraft. Draw it out of the city."

Affirmative.

The jets cut off. Top heavy, Horus swung around and fell headfirst back toward the city. Tiny propellers along his abdomen straightened his course. The main thrusters reengaged. The HUD expanded to the entire city. A small cluster of blue, yellow and red dots appeared. One was black. The majority clustered near the Louvre. The black one was furthest out. The red one—Set—had separated from the others and was drawing nearer to the black speck.

Horus soared past the museum. Windows and glass within earshot of his suit shattered as he passed. Both chariots chased after him.

He zigzagged less than a meter from the road. The HALOGUARD navigated turns with pinpoint accuracy. The chariots couldn't execute the same moves. They lifted above the buildings. Horus aimed north, passing the city's highest elevated point. He flew by a golf course and hovered over a nearby park and grasslands.

Horus landed, digging into the dirt. He jumped back to level ground just as the chariots honed in. Two turrets on his shoulders materialized and unleashed a swarm of crystallized arrows, shredding the chariots in several places. His arms morphed into cannons, this time drawing in cold from the air. Two charges released, setting the grass around him ablaze. The chariots froze and crashed, breaking apart. The angels inside were incapacitated.

Threat neutralized.

Recommendation: Final Blow

"No," Horus refused, not wishing to kill the angels for just following orders. They were unconscious, and he planned on being long gone before they woke up. "Head back. Eliminate Alpha and Beta level targets with extreme prejudice."

Affirmative.

At the HALOGUARD's recommendation, Horus made a beeline for Sif as she was the lesser target. She was west of the Louvre commanding a few angels. The armor listed their names. One of them was Gabriel's right hand man, Uriel.

Horus crashed into the middle of the group. The stone ground rippled and finally exploded. An energy wave released on impact, disrupting some of their aurascales. None of them would be able to fly for a short time.

Sif stood. A shield formed over her left arm, a sword in her right hand. They engaged.

Small propellers forced air through the HALOGUARD, sliding Horus left. Sif struck the ground. Horus swiped his plasma blade across her shield. A glowing cut seared through her metal. The top half of her shield fell and reabsorbed into her aurascales.

Sif lunged. Horus' long reach kept her at bay. His left claw snatched her, pinning her arms down. Horus aimed at two angels on his right flank. The shoulder cannons unleashed a flurry at them. Multi-dozens of green, hard-light projectiles cut through them. The HALOGUARD rotated, lifting Sif over top, and slammed her into the ground.

"Stop," an angel in red urged. HUD indicated it was Uriel. "You know not what you do."

"That right?" Magnetic pulses forced Horus forward. He kicked Uriel, sending him barreling through the pyramid.

Beta-Level Threat engaging.

Sif sliced through Horus' wings. She ran up his back, flipped over his front, and dragged him into the group by the shoulders. Horus toppled over. Sif spun her sword in hand and drove it into Horus. The magnetic shields diffused her blade.

"Sif," Uriel called out. "Move back."

The HALOGUARD's boosters initiated. Horus flew into Sif and Uriel, plowing them through the Louvre's roof. Horus halted midair, and the angels tumbled helplessly to the ground. He lowered slowly to their position. HUD warned of the proximity threat of the Omega-Level target. Sif was out cold. Somehow, Uriel remained conscious.

"You've left me no choice." Uriel scooted away from Horus as his energy blade formed. The glow of Horus' blade illuminated Uriel's unmasked and scared face. "I must call him. I must have the faith that Gabriel displayed."

"Call who?" Horus asked.

"If you will not see that I am an ally, then you must be stopped by any means," Uriel replied, moving to his knees. A shrieking vibration rattled through Horus' skull. Uriel was glowing. After a few seconds, it subsided. "It's done. Michael comes."

408

CHAPTER FORTY-FIVE

Lian VIII

It was nerve-wracking having no control over the day's outcome. Being cooped up with a rotting asshole, a blunt, non-metaphor understanding blonde, and a ticking time bomb wasn't exactly Lian's idea of the best way to spend the day. Thoughts of Austin and his well-being—how far along in the mission was he, did he remember to blend in—kept her brain alert. There wasn't any downtime, which was downright tiring. To cap it off, no one felt like talking, as if self-regulated to their own corners.

Athena kept staring at Jarrod. *Enough already*. The guy's heart was clearly elsewhere. *Talk about pining for what you can't have.*

Harold smacked kisses in Lian's direction. "Care for a stiffy?" he crudely joked.

"I prefer my men soft after they've been hard, not perpetually stiff."

"Touché," he conceded. "But you can end me. Admit it. It'd feel good, no? You're not like the other blokes, are ya? I've seen you work. Heard from the demons 'bout what ya did to that little girlie you lot was tryin-a save." He faked a chill. "Cold."

"That's enough." She shuffled a deck of cards. Was he right? *No.* In her head, she kicked the wall. Paula was doomed either way. It was mercy.

"Bet ya tryin to convince yourself it was merciful, no?" Harold hunched over and grunted. His skin was an almost-translucent baby blue. His eyes were stained green and black veins littered his flesh. "It's no use fightin' what ya are."

She fumbled with the cards and they spilled across the floor. "What are you?" She glared at him. "A walking corpse of doucheness? You know what your problem is?"

"I'm sure your 'bout to tell me," he laughed. Lian grabbed a butcher's knife and sprang toward Harold. Jarrod grabbed her wrist before she could slit Harold's throat, pulling her back. Harold mocked, "Can't get no satisfaction, can ya…"

Jarrod punched him and knocked out several teeth. Harold rolled over, unconscious.

"What the hell were you going to do?" Jarrod chastised.

Lian hung her head. "Just going to scare him."

"I'm sure." He folded his arms.

"What do you expect, huh?" She threw the knife onto the table. "He's right about me. I was tired of hearing it."

"I know prophecies, and I'm pretty sure that one is self-fulfilling." He laid a hand on her shoulder, but she shrugged it off. It wasn't time to be sentimental. "Talk to me."

"Just… mind your own business." Lian scooped up the cards and shuffled through them again. He sat across from her. "Seriously."

"I am." He nodded, tapping the table for some cards. Lian stacked them in the middle. "You know how to play bridge? My Aunt Liv… I mean, mom taught me."

"Sanderson taught me." Lian took the first card and discarded the second. They took turns selecting a hand. "He said he used to play it all the time when he was younger. Never knew it was with his wife. Couldn't quite picture him married."

"You never peeked?" Jarrod sounded surprised.

"That's what you think of me?" She took offense. Everyone assumed she was just a snoop. "Believe it or not, there was a time when I rarely liked to use my powers. I was obsessed with being normal…"

"I know that."

"Yeah, and I respect people's privacy. I respected Sanderson's… most of the time."

"What changed?" he asked.

Lian slapped the cards onto the table. Athena jumped from her seat.

Lian growled under her breath. "Results, Jarrod. That's what really matters. Isn't it? Isn't that why you leap without looking? Isn't that why you're content to run off, or drive away the people closest to you? Results?"

"I could be mistaken…"

"Oh, so you're the only one who gets to act that way. Right? That's good to know." She drew the next card and continued with the game. "I know what matters to me. I know where I want my head to lay at night. You said yourself, only the individual can justify the means. That couldn't be truer, because the ends are different for everyone. Means create the ends. That's the point. I see it now. Sanderson's end was a peaceful life with him and his wife. But you, a young and untamed *you*, stood in his way. He thought getting rid of you would be the correct means, but that wouldn't have delivered the end he wanted."

"So how do you go about choosing the correct means?"

"Sometimes nature delivers only one option. The only way to keep your end possible."

"Is that what happened with Paula? You had only one option?" He folded his cards into his lap and stared at her until she looked back. "You absolutely couldn't let her go?"

"I'm on a learning curve." She poked her head. "I'm enlightened now. Maybe I should've done things differently, but I know what it's like to be someone's lab rat. I was one for ten years. TEN, Jarrod. Prodded and scanned and showered with a hose. My developing, naked body was inspected routinely by men who I could hear in their thoughts would've loved to have shoved themselves inside parts of me that shouldn't be invaded. I had my first period on an examination table with nothing on but a paper gown." Lian rested her head in her hands. Her chest seized with memories. No one would ever get it. "I did Paula a favor and I'd do it again. Don't argue ends and means with me."

"Now you know why I push y'all away."

What the hell was that supposed to mean? She snarled at him.

He smirked and stared into nothingness. "Your end to all this is close. The reason it continues is because of me. If I were removed from the equation, then you wouldn't have to keep going. Austin wouldn't be out there right now, away from you. Who knows, if I was never created, maybe your father wouldn't have gotten involved with Sanderson and Elliot and you never would've been the subject of creepy men's rape fantasies."

"Then I'd never have met Austin," she said softly.

"Exactly." Jarrod leaned back, as if showcasing his point. "The means do matter in that they determine the ends you're allowed. So the individual can justify them if they get the conclusion they want, but that means it's at the expense of someone else's end." Jarrod moved around the table and offered a hand. "Terrorists despise America for supporting an ideal that's counter to their means and disrupts their ends. They set out to tell the world this and they choose to fly airplanes into skyscrapers. Their message was delivered, their ends achieved, and their means justified."

She could see where he was going with it, but he kept pushing.

"But so many fathers were silenced that day, and the ends they'd planned with their wives and kids were destroyed along with it. To those who remained, the terrorists' means weren't justified. So we strike back and the cycle continues. That's what I am, Lian." He rubbed her face and kissed her forehead. "I'm the motor of this cycle. Set has to kill me. I see it."

"If that's what you want, then go." She took his hand and rubbed her face against it. Fighting was getting old. Would the fighting ever stop? Or would Jarrod's end just bring a new war? "You don't really believe that, do you?"

"Did you see that?" Athena asked. Her face was glued to the window. "That giant angel-buster just threw Sif and another angel to the ground."

Austin's whimpering thoughts dashed through Lian's brain. *He's got Claire here. You can't tell Jarrod.*

"Back away from the window," she implored, pulling Athena to her back. A car door sliced through the apartment and stuck in the wall.

"How'd you know?" Jarrod crawled to Lian, gently brushing the glass off her face. Several abrasions and cuts stuck her. "You'll be fine."

"It's Austin," she panted. "Set has him." Athena and Jarrod writhed in pain, covering their ears as if a loud noise was pumping right next to them. "Are you OK?"

The moment passed. Athena sat up on her knees. "It was a call," she said, breathing heavily. Her purple aurascales spread across her body. The metallic faceguard covered her head. Her voiced became robotic. "Get Jarrod out of here. I'll hold off Set."

"A call?" Lian asked. What did that mean? "A call for who?"

Athena stepped toward the hole in the apartment. Her wings expanded. She looked back at Lian. "Michael comes."

414

CHAPTER FORTY-SIX

Set VI

The changeling would lead Set to where he needed to go. He was counting on Sif not having the fortitude to kill him as instructed. Since Hermes' death, Sif had been on edge. Set knew her real motivations for joining the Assassins had nothing to do with atoning for sins against Father and everything to do with protecting her child. Set traded in secrets. They were the most valuable commodities in creation; not souls, starstones, or the key to the Light of Souls.

The changeling, who he knew to be Austin, stopped and looked over his shoulder at Set who followed in the air. His shirt was soaked with crimson. He stumbled and fell over, splashing into a fountain. The water turned red.

Set pulled Austin out of the water, Austin coughing up the liquid. Set's facial armor retracted and he laid the bleeding changeling down. He knelt, examining the wounds.

"Why didn't you just let me drown?" Austin asked, weakly trying to push Set away.

"I need you to die with him watching." Set hovered his fist over a few gushing wounds. A laser shot out from over his wrists, sealing the gashes shut. He held his hand over Austin's mouth, muting the screams. "That will prevent the major cuts from bleeding you dry. Your advanced healing should catch up soon."

"You found us when Horus was scanned, didn't you?" Austin eyes grew too heavy to keep open. Set slapped him awake.

"Indeed." Set yanked Austin to his knees by the hair. "You'll take me to the one known as Death; Jarrod."

"You keep calling him death. I don't get it."

"Death is a moniker, not a figurative call-sign for a state of being." Set stood and looked at the Fountain of Saint-Michel. He smirked with contempt. "This is not at all how that happened. It's funny how the memories of war are skewed when written by the victors. As if the line that separates good from evil is so easily defined. Just look at how legend and myth remember me. Pretending I'm chaos, a betrayer, a murderer, a jealous sycophant with my own ends in mind. History was written prematurely."

"Why would I take you to him?"

"Because I'll kill your female friend." Set dragged Austin through the streets. The Parisian police force formed a perimeter, blocking his path towards the Latin Quarter. They opened fire. His wings surrounded them both. "We both know Jarrod would trade his life for hers. The question you must ask is: would you?"

Set flapped his wings open. A shockwave of air shoved the police back. Following the gale-force wind was a flurry of soaring daggers with deadly precision. Those not behind cover were sliced to pieces.

"Allow me to carry you." Set tossed Austin over the shoulder. With a single flap of the wings, they were soaring over the maze of streets. Set shook Austin awake. "I know we're close. What'll it be?"

Austin pointed at a third floor apartment opposite a bakery. "There." He grimaced.

Set landed forcefully. Several cars in close proximity jumped. He discarded Austin and ripped a door from a nearby vehicle. He looked to Austin for affirmation. "It's that one, right? If it isn't, I'll kill her slowly."

"It is." Austin nodded.

Set reared back, seeing Athena's platinum hair, her focus turned elsewhere. "Let's see if I can bowl a strike." He threw the door and it smashed through the window, puncturing a large hole into the wall. He'd missed. "You warned your psychic friend, didn't you?" Set stomped on Austin's chest. His wrist blades elongated. "Big mistake."

A screeching vibration caught his head. He fell to his knees, squeezing his skull. Uriel had called for Michael. A little sooner than anticipated, but no matter. That just meant the timetable was moved up.

The call subsided. Austin attempted to crawl away. Set picked him up by the back of the neck and flew to the top of the building. He dropped Austin from a distance he knew would break a few bones. Austin bounced on the roof top. Set landed hard, driving a fist into Austin's diaphragm.

"Finding it hard to breathe?" His wrist blades slid out. "Just wait."

Athena smashed into Set, driving him through the building and into the road, creating a ditch in the pavement across the city block. Her wings flapped, lifting them off the ground. She spun like a tornado, launching him. Set crashed through one end of a building and out the opposite side, scattering brick, steel, beds, and more across the road like an erupting volcano. He bounced off the street and rolled to a stop.

His aurascales worked to repair. "Didn't see that coming." Set looked around, dizzy, but couldn't find her. "Where are you, little girl?"

"How about this?" Athena yelled at the top of her lungs. "This is for Hermes."

She landed on top of him like a missile. The force shoved them both through the ground and into the subway. Athena's attacks were berserk. Spikes grew from her knuckles, tearing away at his armor. She shoved his helmet into the wall and repeated the process several times, eventually puncturing a water pipe. Athena threw Set into the opposite wall and conjured a sword.

"How is that for a girl?" She tightened her grip on the sword.

"Glorious," Set coughed, falling forward onto his knees, "but it was not enough."

Athena swiped. Set rolled forward. She missed. He sprang to his feet, jumped off the wall, and rotated into a spinning kick. Athena's faceguard shifted, rippling from the impact. He punched her into the wall, pinning her there. Set's blades protruded over his hands.

A headlight washed over him, dragging an empty train behind it. He pulled her from the wall and elbowed her head. He flew through the hole above just as the train hit her.

"Now, where was I?" Set stumbled, regaining his balance. A mass of super-chilled air froze his aurascales. Horus crashed in front of him. Set recognized Osiris' HALOGUARD. "That's where it went. Doesn't quite fit you."

Horus kicked his uncle—breaking the ice—into the river. Set tried to fly, but his aurascales were out of sync. He crawled up the banks to Athena's waiting feet.

"You again," he sighed.

Athena's sword tapped his chin. She swung for his neck. He rolled forward, kick-jumped to his feet, and knocked her into the water. Horus landed behind him. His claw snared Set and he tossed him up through the bridge.

Set landed and again skidded to a stop. Athena soared from the river and flew toward Set, sword first. He jump-kicked, swiping her face with his foot. She rolled to a halt. He tried summoning his wrist-blades, but his aurascales still wouldn't conjure weapons or wings—a result of the HALOGUARD's frozen weapon.

Athena's sword was at his feet. He picked it up spun to his six, slicing Horus' HALOGUARD. He severed one claw, but the sword dematerialized in his grasp and moved back into Athena's. Set slid between Horus' large, spread legs. Athena sprinted, leapt off Horus' shoulder, and smashed into Set, stabbing her sword through his shoulder. She twisted.

Set screamed, "You bitch!" His faceguard rammed hers, splitting her helmet. He rammed her once again and she let go. He yanked her sword from his shoulder and drove it through her knee, pinning her to the bridge. His wrist blades formed. "Finally." Set backhanded and split her faceguard open, gashing her cheek. He took off before killing her, not wanting to deal with Horus' HALOGUARD.

"Kill him," Athena yelled to Horus.

Set glanced back, seeing Horus lift off. He cut down to the streets, flying between buildings. The HALOGUARD was faster. Set chucked an idle car but Horus blew it to pieces.

"You're ruining everything, just like your father." Set evaded a swipe of Horus' energy blade but not a kick. He crashed through a bank window. Glass fell from him like rain as he pushed to his feet. "Think, nephew. Try to see the bigger picture."

"You murdered him." Horus stormed into the building and crushed Set through the wall and out the other side.

"I do what's necessary. He never did." Set clung to Horus' armor and was then thrown like a rag doll. His head throbbed. "He isn't the saint everyone remembers." Set's aurascales were scathed and his exo-armor shredded. "Your HALOGUARD is evidence of that." He propped against a light pole and wheezed.

"What do you mean?"

"Osiris was a bad man, just like the rest of us." A static charge assembled into a broad sword. "Search the database. When you see it, you'll know."

"Liar." Horus charged forward, cutting Set's blade in two and crushing Set into the street with a HALOGUARD claw. "Your words may end up being true, but you'll die none the less."

A battle chariot de-cloaked behind Horus and discharged several energy blasts. Horus bounced down the street, his armor splintering. The chariot did it again. It released several crystallized arrows from a turret underneath. The HALOGUARD's Magnetic shields diffused some of the blasts, but not the full force. The armor splintered.

Set pulled Horus from the broken HALOGUARD with one arm. His faceguard dispersed so he could get a clean look at Horus' naked face. "You resemble your mother more than your father. That's probably why you've shown more tenacity than Osiris, but not his skill in a fight."

Horus gingerly punched at Set, but his uncle twisted the blow and turned him around. Set's arm curled around Horus' neck and removed Osiris' piece of the forge. His wrist blades elongated.

"If you can't see the truth, you've no use for these." Set dragged a blade across Horus' right eye and split it in half. His nephew fell in agony. He was tempted to end Horus, but the Jarrod issue could wait no longer. "We'll finish this one day."

Set flew back to the roof where Austin was slowly waking and the chariots followed. The back hatch of one of the crafts hissed open. Raphael stepped out with a few angels and the human girl in tow. He seemed none too happy with the damage to the city, or the fact Michael had been alerted to the situation. His arrival was surely imminent.

"Claire," Austin said, lunging for the human woman.

"You took longer than I expected," Set chuckled, pulling Austin away from Raphael.

"Too much collateral damage." The angels around Raphael remained stoic in their aurascales while he spoke. "It's obvious you can't get the job done."

"I'm working on it." Set's aurascales grew additional plating, anticipating a fight. "It's almost done."

"If you wanted that, it would've been so by now." Raphael nodded. The angels took offensive positions, amusing Set. "I've longed to wipe that smile from your face."

"You could never stomach a little urgency." Set monitored his perimeter. "When the pressure is on, Raphael collapses. What are you going to tell Michael?"

"You betrayed us and let Gabriel take the fall."

"And what, you'll just wait around for Lucifer to free himself?" Set laughed. "There's a thought. Loyalty means nothing to you."

"Says the one with no intention of honoring our alliance."

"What are these?" Set asked, pointing at the other angels. "Cherubs? Please. They may be clothed as guardians, but they'll never be that. Just as you'll never truly be an Archangel. You'll always be the sniveling coward who had to lie his way to the top, never really able to handle confrontation or get bloody. When that time comes, you remain flaccid and unable to perform. That's why I had to finish Osiris."

Austin wobbled to his feet but Set pushed him down near the edge of the roof.

"Austin!" Claire cried.

Set looked at her. "If you've no intention of keeping with the plan, then why did you bring her?" He stepped away from Austin, leaving him exposed after seeing Lian and Jarrod watching the action from across the street. There was one last chance to coax the beast. "That's right. You're a coward. We just had that conversation. You can't finish the job."

"Be quiet," Raphael ordered.

"Make me."

The two exchanged blows and when it was obvious Set was going to win, the other four angels stepped in. Set drove his wrist blades up through the jaw of one angel and sliced another's throat. Raphael rammed a bostaff into Set's back, releasing a surge of sparkling purple electricity. Set fell to his knees.

"Am I still weak?" Raphael barked.

Set screamed in agony. "Yes."

Raphael pulled away. "If that's the way you want to play it." He detached the remote to the Deliverance. His thumb slid across the remote. Set collapsed onto his face. His aurascales tore from his body, ripping apart his skin. "It stings, doesn't it?"

Set curled into the fetal position, naked and whimpering. A necessary pain to get what he wanted: Raphael thinking he was in control.

Austin stared at Set's raw flesh and exposed bone. Their eyes connected. Set provoked, "The changeling and girl yet live. Coward."

"You can let us go," Austin pleaded.

Raphael lifted him by the throat. "Shut up." He looked at Set when the Assassin gargled something unintelligible. "I can't hear you," Raphael said.

"Pissing your pants?" Set burst with laughter.

Raphael put Austin down. Set could tell he was squirming at the thought of killing Austin. One more nudge should do it.

"Look at your leader," Set said to the other angels. "He's incapable."

There was an eerie calm for a few seconds. Raphael nodded. "OK." He shoved Austin over the side. "See, I don't care."

Claire screamed and was restrained by the other angels. Her muted cries were overtaken by others from across the street. The changeling was dead, but would it be enough to stir a response?

CHAPTER FORTY-SEVEN

Jarrod VIII

Numbness and silence, that's all there was. Twenty years of brotherhood extinguished like a pistol bolt to the head. Anger bubbled through next. It wasn't aimed at the perpetrators, but inward. Jarrod tormented himself because he should've fought to leave. He'd allowed himself a dash of hope and with that Austin met his demise.

His best friend laid sprawled out over the street in a puddle of his own blood, and there'd be no healing this time. He knew it because Austin's soul lingered severed from his body. The powerful lure of Austin's soul coaxed a blue shine from Jarrod's skin.

Lian's cries slowly came into focus. "Damn you." She tried clawing her way out of Jarrod's clutches. "No... No... NO!"

Jarrod stared at the shimmering static of Austin's bluish essence. He effortlessly curled Lian into his body and yanked her away from the hole in the side of the building. They plowed into the outer hallway.

Lian slapped him. "Snap out of it." It did little to deliver her desired effect. "What are you going to do about it?"

Everything. Maybe nothing. The plan hadn't quite been pieced together. He knew what he wanted to do. Rip them limb-from-limb and devour whatever it was that made them tick. Grow more powerful and feared than any being in creation. DESTROY EVERYONE AND EVERYTHING UNTIL IT WAS ALL JUST AS NUMB AND SILENT AS HIM.

But that'd be easy, and wrong, and that wasn't what life was about or what Austin would've wanted. It hurt to fight against it. Not just some pussy ass, don't harm a fly Buddhist shit. It literally fucking burned like pressing your face into boiling grease.

He felt the aurascales moving. Jarrod turned away from Lian. *Get a grip.* He pulled his hair, railing against his inner force. The hallways lights flickered in response to his surging power.

"When are you going to fight, Jarrod?" she asked.

"I am fighting it!" he yelled. The walls cracked down the hallway, knocking Lian to her feet when the jagged lines passed. "You think this is easy?" Jarrod stood. Her soul flared beneath her flesh the more afraid she became. "I told you all what I was and none of you listened. Why. Won't. You. LISTEN?"

Jarrod punched the wall and pulled his hand from the plaster.

"Leave me, Lian, if you know what's best for you. Before you end up like Austin, Sanderson, my mom, and all the rest. Go now. Please."

Face it Jarrod, we need each other, Ryan said. The urge to feed on souls subsided with his gentle voice. *I can be what you fear. You don't have to do it alone.*

"No," Jarrod replied. "You're wrong."

"Is he?" Lian asked, standing behind Jarrod. She knelt and hugged him. "I understand it."

I know you can hear me, Lian.

"Shut up," Jarrod ordered.

Ryan didn't care. *Jarrod is good. You know this. It pains him to do what's needed. I've seen you work. We're alike, Lian.*

"No, we aren't." She squeezed Jarrod harder, crying into his back. "I don't want to kill people."

You think I do? I'm needed, Lian.

"Lian, you need to go," Jarrod urged. It was coming together: Set's reason for letting him live, Ryan's eerie suggestions, and Lian's ability and desires. His mother's words about the world coping. This was what she meant. "Don't listen to him."

Jarrod won't give you Austin back, but I will. Those words pulled air from her lungs like a vacuum. It was out there and there was no taking it back. Lian jumped away, no longer crying. She understood the message. Jarrod looked at her, concerned. She wiped the tears away, oddly calm. *Yes, Lian, Jarrod is stronger with me. This wall, it's cracking. I'll be out eventually, but not soon enough to help Austin. Think about where you want to lay your head. Help me.*

"Don't." Jarrod ran away, but it was a dead end. Lian calmly followed. He went to burst through the wall, but a crippling pain shot up his spine. Ryan paralyzed him. "Please, Lian."

It's gonna happen eventually, Lian. You can't fight fate, but you can choose how to get there. FREE ME.

His pain subsided. She knelt by his side, holding his face. "Jarrod," she said calmly and kissed his cheek. "I love you like a brother." Her tears flowed again. He shook his head, struggling. Her eyes turned back and her hair rose to static.

The numbness was replaced with chilled spikes stabbing through his muscle and bone. Darkness overtook the light. It was as if he was being shoved into a box. The aurascales controlled his body. The ghoulish, skeletal face of his helmet emerged.

Do you feel it? Ryan asked. *What it's like to be subordinate?*

Jarrod's eyes opened, but it wasn't him moving the body. It was as if he watched remotely, with goggles relaying live feed. He tried moving his arms and legs. Nothing responded.

"Jarrod?" Lian asked. Her voice seemed to echo through an empty hall.

"I'm here," he yelled. She couldn't hear him.

I'm alright, Ryan responded. Lian sighed with relief. *I'm intact.*

"That's a lie," Jarrod protested. "That's not me."

***

Two more angels attacked. Ryan stabbed through the first's heart and cut the second's throat. Before the angels' lives completely halted, he stood over them and drained their auras, just as he'd done to the fifteen previous.

Invincible. Nothing could stop the juggernaut he'd become. Every time he drained an angel of what they were, he obtained their skills, memories, and power. It was all he'd ever dreamed of.

"We need reinforcements!" Raphael yelled. The chariot he'd piloted had crashed when Ryan broke through it to free Claire, allowing her to return to Lian unharmed. The real target was what Raphael carried. It was something powerful. An unlimited source of power, souls, and light. It sang to Ryan like a Siren on the ocean. "You." Raphael trembled as Ryan approached.

"Me," Ryan laughed.

Stop, please. No more, Jarrod pleaded. Ryan tuned him out.

"You're Raphael, correct?" Ryan asked, shredding the chariot in half with his bare hands. It was fun, the ease of it all. "What is it I'm drawn to about you? I see inside your aura, but it's cowardly and frail compared to what I can taste at the tip of my tongue. What is it?"

"The Light of Souls," Set replied. Ryan turned around, unable to keep from noticing Set's pecker dangling free in the wind.

"Would you cover yourself?" Ryan averted his eyes, turning back to Raphael. "The Light of Souls." He sifted through the memories of every angel he'd just consumed. "Yes. You have the key to the light."

"Set, what are you doing?" Raphael crawled over broken glass and stumbled to his feet. He manifested a sword and shield. "You fool. You'd give him the light?"

"What did you think this was all about?" It noticeably pained Set to walk. "Killing Death would only delay the end. Freeing him and making him more powerful than we can imagine leads to more possibilities."

"You orchestrated this?" Ryan looked back at Set, impressed. "Why, thank you."

"Much obliged." Set bowed.

Ryan turned back just in time to dodge Raphael's sword. He slid to the right, then left and right again. Raphael's sword stuck into the faded limestone brick building and Ryan took him by the throat.

"The key," Ryan insisted. Raphael shook his head no. "Now's not the time to grow a spine."

"It's the perfect time," Raphael grunted. Ryan slammed him into the ground. The remote to the Deliverance bounced out of Raphael's grasp.

Set stepped toward it, drawing a snarl from Ryan. "May I have that?" he asked politely, pointing at the remote. Ryan nodded. "Thank you." He scooped it up and stood by Ryan. "I'll need one more thing."

"What?" Ryan barked.

"His thumb."

Ryan stepped on Raphael's neck. "Which one?"

Set shrugged. "For the life of me, I can't remember." Ryan severed both of Raphael's hands and then pinned him to the ground through the gut. He placed both hands to the sides of Raphael's face and drained his aura. Raphael's body turned to ash and his starstone fused together.

Set swiped Raphael's thumb across the remote and his aurascales returned, healing his wounds. Soon he was covered with the green sentient armor which sprouted a silver exoskeleton.

"Where's the key to the light?" Ryan asked, pushing Set to the ground. "I can't find it on him."

"It should've detached from his aurascales when you killed him." Set crawled backwards. Ryan moved so quickly, he was a blur. He appeared behind Set. "It should be there."

"Find it." Ryan shoved Set into Raphael's ashy corpse and starstone. The Assassin worked feverishly to find the key. His hands fumbled. "I'm growing impatient."

"Imagine my sentiment," Michael said. Both Set and Ryan turned around. The Archangel leader stood with brilliant, unblemished armor, his eagle faceguard almost translucent. "Set, what've you done?"

"Shit, time ran out." Set hung his head and stood. He stepped equidistant from Ryan and Michael. "What no one else had the courage to do."

"It wasn't time, you fool!" Michael yelled.

"Did I tell you to stop looking for the key?" Ryan asked Set, snapping his fingers. "Find it, dog."

"You don't get it, do you boy?" Set kept stepping back. "You're done for."

"So are you," Michael added.

"There's no beating him." Set nodded Michael's direction. "You're as good as dead. We'll wait for the next chance at the prophecy."

"We'll see about that," Ryan growled.

Stop, Jarrod urged. *Rethink this.*

Ryan lunged for Michael and Set leapt out of the way. Ryan cracked Michael across the face, followed with a blow to the midsection, and finished with a jumping butterfly kick. Michael soared down the end of the street and crushed the side of a car.

Ryan looked at Set, laughing, "You were saying?"

"How stupid you are." Set pointed behind Ryan.

Ryan spun around and was met by a soaring Michael. In a matter of seconds the Archangel pushed Ryan outside the city limits. Reality seemed to flicker and vibrate. They moved so fast, up and down had no meaning. Their collision created a noise twice as loud as a sonic boom. Ryan came to when Michael—still flying—pushed his head into the ground and repeatedly pummeled his face.

Michael stopped, flew straight up, and slung Ryan back to the ground. Ryan crashed, puncturing a crater into the dirt, creating a rippling wave of earth. He tried pushing up, but Michael was too fast, shoving him back down.

"This was not our time," Michael said, kicking Ryan onto his back. His blade light sizzled into form. "Father said I would know it when the right one came for me. Yet I look at you and I see it not."

"More gibberish," Ryan growled. "I'm going to enjoy draining your aura and ripping your head off."

Michael sliced and missed. Ryan rolled between his foes legs and swiped his feet out from under him. It was his turn to deliver punishment. He made it count. Blue fames fueled by souls consumed his fists as he tore into Michael. Ryan channeled all his kinetic energy into a rotating jump punch which snapped into Michael's chest and sent him blowing through an abandoned, medieval stone church. The overgrown wheat fields which surrounded the area bowed to the wind caused by the blow.

Michael steadied himself midflight, flapped his wings and zipped forward. Ryan sprinted with all he could muster into a collision course. His body was consumed with flaring blue light. Their impact rumbled through the earth. What followed was darkness.

Is this it? Jarrod said. The show broadcast to him was gone. There were no sounds, no smells, no tingling sensation where his hands used to be. Just emptiness. *Did Michael win?*

"Hardly." Ryan opened his eyes. The show flickered until the signal strength returned. The air around him was cluttered with a dust cloud. A mild breeze blew an opening for him, allowing stray rays of sunlight to penetrate the brown haze.

Ryan stumbled over towards the church. The ground around it had cracked open, rupturing its foundation. The steeple had toppled over in the commotion. He rummaged through the debris as the haze blew away. When everything cleared up, he spotted Michael at a farm across the fields, kneeling over the dead and taking their souls. A pink light popped over Michael and released him to Ryan's six. Ryan turned and noticed the bruising on Michael's had face cleared.

"More needlessly killed." Michael stood completely still. "We'll have to reset the clock. Precious time has been wasted because of you and Set."

"I knocked you down." Ryan shook. Even Jarrod could feel his sense of panic. "No way you got up before me."

"You're mistaken." Michael stepped casually toward Ryan. "I never fell and never will."

The battle resumed. For every blow Ryan landed, Michael succeeded him by four. Ryan pulled from the memories of other angels, trying to learn Michael's moves, but his tactics and style were ever flowing, as if he were able to channel himself into someone completely different every fight, sometimes mid-fight.

Ryan went into defensive mode. He pulled his hands up to his face to protect his head at the expense of his torso. It was a swap Michael seemed fine to accept. Cross after hook, followed by palm strikes and elbows. The Archangel leader was a machine. His blows were so hard that Jarrod could feel them. Ryan's ribs had cracked several punches ago. Now his lungs were punctured.

Michael kicked his heel into Ryan's chest, sending him over a mile through the air, crushing his sternum. Ryan crashed, sticking into the rocky ground. Meteors were tossed into the sky by the impact.

Finally, it's over, Jarrod sighed.

"No," Ryan sobbed, crawling from the crater. Michael's shadow slid over him. He pulled his arms over his head and cradled himself in the fetal position.

You're afraid to die.

"We all are," Ryan cried, pounding the dirt. "I deserved a life."

I know.

"You took that from me. From us. What we could've been."

Let it go, Ryan. Death isn't something to be afraid of.

"You won't lecture me." The energy of the lives he'd devoured healed his body. Ryan mustered all the strength he had left and sprinted up the crater. Wings took shape and he flew as fast as he could back towards Paris. He sensed the power of every soul and aura he'd absorbed drain from his body as blood slowly dripped from his mouth.

Where are you going? Anxiety swelled through Jarrod. *Leave them alone. Enough have died.*

"I need more power. I'll take Lian first," Ryan laughed. He landed unceremoniously on his shoulder mere feet from Raphael's destroyed chariot. "Then I'll slowly skin Claire alive. I won't kill her, though."

"Jarrod, are you OK?" Claire asked, running out into the street with Lian trying to pull her back. "Listen to me, Jarrod. I know you're in there."

"Come back, Claire," Lian implored.

"But I won't end her there, Jarrod." Ryan cracked his knuckles and lumbered toward Claire and Lian. "I'll let her suffer while I absorb the city and kill Michael. Then I'll make her beg."

"I can see you've exhausted the power inside you." Michael landed gracefully between Ryan and Claire with his sword of pure light in hand. He walked to Ryan. "It is unfortunate that their souls may not be returned to their resting place, but necessary for your defeat. Though I see there are two within you, at home as they should be, which is curious."

"That's Jarrod," Lian yelled, running to Michael's side. "He's in there. He can take control."

"No matter who lingers inside, they're too dangerous to live." Michael reared back and attacked but his blade was stopped by Set's. "What is this?"

"My last effort." Set slashed Michael across the ribs. He tossed the key to the Light of Souls over to Ryan. "For both our sakes, I hope this works." Set dove for cover.

Every soul ever collected flowed into Ryan's body like a black hole. His wounds healed, his armor glistened, his skin turned blue. The light was blinding. He crumpled to a knee, feeling stronger than ever before. Souls young and old, wise and ambitious, voices all stirring.

431

Ones he recognized, like Austin, his parents, and presidents he'd read about, and families obscure and never known.

What's going on?

Jarrod could hear Ryan's voice assimilate among the others. Soon, his own thoughts joined the tide. They all became one. They became something else. They all became Death.

He caught Michael's light sword and crushed it in his hand. The energy from the Light of Souls formed a protective barrier. He hooked a fist across Michael's face, shattering the eagle helmet. The Archangel flipped backwards and landed on his stomach.

"I am what you waited for," he said.

Michael nodded. "Yes." He knelt, wiping the blood from his lips. "But I must try anyway."

"Stop, Jarrod." Claire ran over to him and wrapped her arms around him. "Look at me." Her hands trembled when taking his. "Remember what we are."

There were too many voices. It was hard to focus on one that should take control. It was like there wasn't a Jarrod or a Ryan. They were one again. Memories once erased from his childhood were clear as day. The other voices railed against them.

"Stand away," Jarrod said, momentarily breaking through the power that was his fate: Death. It was short lived.

Michael reengaged and Death held up a hand. A powerful entity lingered inside the Archangel leader. It wasn't a soul, nor was it angel. It was both, just like both halves of Ryan and Jarrod were intended to be. A deep understanding formed between the two. The four horsemen referred to the four who needed to perish in order to prepare for the final battle. Michael would be the first.

The power that fueled Michael rushed into Death and his flesh turned to ash, leaving only bone. Michael's starstone and aurascales fused onto Death. His black exoskeleton armor turned white, but the aurascales remained pale blue.

"It worked," Set whispered, still audible to Death. He sat up straight. "Are you going to kill me?"

Death shook his head. "Only those who are needed to complete what is necessary." Wings of radiant white spike-like armor expanded and he slowly lifted into the air. Claire took his hand and tried pulling him back to the street. He halted, looking down at her.

"Jarrod?" she whimpered, putting her forehead to his knuckles. "For me, please. We can go home. It can stop when you say it."

Death yanked his hand back. "The one you seek is no longer present." He looked away, hearing a faint voice inside his consciousness try and break free from the others. "Let it be consolation enough that he knows you were right."

Death bolted into the sky and vanished with a crack of pink energy.

434

CHAPTER FORTY-EIGHT

The Observer

Set marched somewhat untriumphantly over to Michael's remains. The Armada cruisers that had previously been suspended in outer space descended over the city. The other angels surrounded him and their dead leader in shock. He knelt by the skeletal remnants and sifted through them, snapping the necklace that Michael used to wear off. At the end of the necklace was a jagged piece of a larger artifact.

"His piece of the Forge." Set merged the fractured piece with the one he'd taken from Horus, and Gabriel's which he retrieved from Raphael. He tucked the now larger piece into his aurascales and stepped away from the dead Archangel leader. He looked over to Lian and Claire, nodding at them. His business in their lives was done. There was a sliver of remorse which wiggled its way into his heart for all the pain he'd caused them, but he quelled it just like he did all the others.

"I'm sure we'll cross paths again." He nodded.

"Count on it." Lian squinted at him.

"What happened?" Chamuel asked, alarmed. "Raphael is dead. So many are dead. Is that…"

"Yes, it's Michael," Set interrupted him, comforting Chamuel with a warm hug. "We must leave and reorganize."

Chamuel glared at Lian and Claire. "What of them?" He lunged but Set restrained him.

"They're not to blame." Set yanked Chamuel back.

"What do we do now?" Chamuel asked with lost eyes. "Our enemies will find out. We're weak."

"We regroup," Set said. The two angels soared toward the Armada cruiser. "We redefine what an enemy is and prepare for what's to come."

"What is to come?" Chamuel asked, clearly lost. "Who will lead us now?"

Set bit back a smile. "I will," he said, displaying Michael's piece of the Forge. "Michael wished for us to reassemble the Forge. It's the only way to defeat what's been unleashed."

***

Lian watched the large spacecrafts vanish from the sky. In all the commotion, she hadn't gotten to truly grieve for Austin. She knelt beside his dead body, crying. She should've known Ryan wouldn't keep his word. Her happy ending had been altered. A new one would need to be forged, but not now. For now, she wished to lament her losses. Tomorrow, she'd do what she'd always done: pick up and start again. It was a cold way of shutting out the pain, but it worked.

Sif and an unfamiliar angel assisted Horus and Athena over to Claire and Lian.

"They're friends," Horus reassured them. A cloth wrapped around his eye was soaked through with blood. "You've met Sif. This gentleman is Uriel."

"My deepest condolences for the day's events." Uriel bowed. "I bear the shame of Heaven's failure."

"We all do," Lian replied, returning to Austin's side.

His body was cold. She stepped away, not wanting to remember him like that, but when she closed her eyes his scent and warmth eluded her. *Another crippling blow.*

She imagined Sanderson's hand upon her shoulder. For a brief second, she swore he was somehow speaking to her from beyond the grave.

"Are you injured, my friend?" Athena asked Claire, hobbling over to her with Uriel's assistance. "I'm relieved to see you alive."

"I don't feel alive," Claire replied.

"We must go," Sif insisted. "Protocol dictates that Heaven organize clean up, but in the wake of Michael's demise we don't want to wait around for whatever comes next."

"Where do we go?" Uriel asked. "Earth has plunged into the start of tribulation. Heaven offers no shelter. The stars even less."

"I know of a place," Sif assured them. "If only you'd all trust me."

"I do," Horus said.

Athena, Claire, and Uriel added affirmations of their own. They waited for Lian. But what was trust, anymore? Maybe Jarrod was right, and the only way to stop the wheel from turning was to jump from it. Then again, the fact that one's end was always altered by someone else's means meant that she'd never really be off the wheel. What mattered now, what Austin would want, was for her to find her new end, her new goal, her new home, and fight for it.

She stood, placing a hand into Claire's. "I trust you."

***

The city slept well at night, for it knew not what was to come with sunrise. The wind howled like all the voices of oblivion inside his mind. It was like omnipotent power replaced his blood. An instantaneous link with those recently expired. They sought him out, drawn to what he possessed: answers.

They weren't good answers. Downright horrible, but anything was better than aimlessly venturing across earth without form. Death was a welcome change of scenery.

As if plucked from the aether, or vibrations through space-time, a subconscious urge alerted him to when tragedy loomed. Tomorrow, this city would tear itself to shreds as a disease rampaged through it and those with means procured cures, stomping on those less fortunate. The desperate would sink into the depths of depravity to escape Death's awaiting fingers. Like the ten plagues of Egypt, a massacre on the scale of what awaited tomorrow transcended reality and beckoned him.

"We can change it." A voice railed against the others, like it didn't want to belong.

There would be no changing it. This was what needed to be. To feast and grow stronger, allow fate and time to perform their duties, until the time came to defeat one of the others, just as he'd done with Michael.

Who was Claire and why did Death hzold affections for her over the many awaiting his embrace?

"There's always a way. Different paths can lead to where we need to go."

Maybe so. But tomorrow, this city dies.

EPILOGUE

The radio hummed an old-timey, banjo led composition. The speakers on the passenger side of the cobalt blue pickup were completely shot and only emitted a static clicking sound—on beat, no less. Mrs. Rigby adjusted her silver-dollar-sized bifocals and immediately placed her lace covered palms back to the ten-and-two position. She hunched forward, able to see the full gauntlet of stars because the lights of Polokwane, South Africa, had long since faded from the rear-view mirror. Even though her truck puttered along a dirt road in the middle of nowhere, twenty miles under the speed limit, she was well aware of events elsewhere in the world.

The past year and a half had been a trying time on her faith, and her church. Friends and kids she'd seen grow up, worshiping the Lord in their small, close knit community, had suddenly abandoned the word. Some of them turned into radical militants, preparing for a 'war of the worlds'. Others started their own fanatical religion, coordinating mass suicides, self-mutilating protests, and worst of all, in her opinion, human sacrifices to the new gods. Mrs. Rigby, however, remained steadfast, holding closely to the promise her God provided of a life ever after. It'd be a time when she could reunite with her late husband, gone ten years the coming June.

She tapped the brakes and pulled the truck into her bumpy driveway. The house sat about a football pitch's length off the road. The brakes squealed as the car stuttered to a stop. Her white border collie greeted her with a sniff of the hands and a wag of the tail. Mrs. Rigby snapped off a piece of jerky, which her parish priest made himself, and tossed it to the dog, Parker. She grabbed the paper bag of leftovers from her church dinner—barely a handful had attended the gathering—and headed up the steps of her front porch while Parker danced around at her feet.

"Old boy, you're going to make me fall," she said in a shaky voice. Parker sat, looked up at her, and tilted his head to the right. She put the sack down on the kitchen counter and acknowledged him. "It's too late for that. It's almost bedtime."

Parker swatted his paw at her hand.

"I said no. I'm tired and it's late."

Parker groaned and laid flat, resting the underside of his head on his front paws. His eyes remained fixed upon Mrs. Rigby.

She spent the next half hour catching up on the housework she'd neglected all weekend. The dishes were washed, the floors were swept, and Parker's nap mat was scrubbed clean. Soon, she found herself with her feet up, dressed in a nightgown, reading a book about strengthening one's faith, while the TV created some ambient noise.

... Devastating gun fights, explosions and mass displacement of the civilian population ruled the night in suburban Virginia and Maryland as battle lines from Manassas to Baltimore surrounded the American capital. There's been no word on if Vice President Paulson, the remaining chiefs of staff, and members of congress who were left in Washington have escaped the wrath of the raging infected. President Cascade released a statement from an undisclosed location earlier this morning, encouraging the citizens of the United States, and the rest of the world, to remain calm during these trying times. As the rate of infection of this horrific disease grows, and cities all over the world prepare for mass inoculations in an event that is being labeled "Sundown", protestors and advocates...

"That's enough nonsense," she said, clicking the TV off with her remote. She looked at Parker, but he kept his head on the floor and moaned. "The Lord won't let this go on for much longer. He'll be back for us."

Parker sat up, rigid. His tail swept the floor, excitedly.

"I'm sure you're welcome too." Her long fingers ran through Parker's coat. "You like that, don't you?"

The wind picked up, pressing against the window screens. It swam through the bushes, causing the prickly leaves to brush against the side of the house. The trees and bushes rustled, and the collection of wind chimes on the back porch started singing. Parker stood on all fours, his body straight and his tail stiff as a board. He growled as the lights flickered and then went off.

"I've got some candles somewhere," Mrs. Rigby said, feeling her way through the living room. Several knocking sounds tumbled down the roof. She quickly knelt, feeling her heart jolt. She laughed it off, looking over at Parker who remained completely still.

She peaked through the curtains. The Red Maple next to her barn looked like it was trying to do the limbo. Parker barked, and his agitation rubbed off on her. He continued to get louder.

"I really wish you wouldn't get loud if there's nothing out there." Her hands trembled.

The wind huffed like an asthmatic. Parker moved to the door and scratched feverishly at its base. Mrs. Rigby sat under the window, her back pressed firmly against the white panel wall. Her left hand searched for a candle and matches while her eyes remained fixed on Parker. Finally, she found a large candle. She struck the match and illuminated her small living room.

"Parker, what is it?" she asked quietly, her voice straining. Her aching bones twitched as a voice in her head called into question everything she believed in. She tried to bury her thoughts and prayers into God's word, but at this very moment she found herself believing in the scared ramblings of former church members, and news reports about aliens, monsters and infectious diseases.

Where is Christ in the world today? she thought, closing her eyes with her chin pressed into her folded hands. *Father, I'm alone and scared. If you're not bringing me to be with my Roland, show me what you'd have me do, Lord.* Parker continued to howl in tune with the wind. Her eyes briefly snapped open. She wished he'd be quiet, but she was unable to speak. *Give me a purpose. I don't know how I can help fix this lost, sick world. But I'll do it. Give me a sign. Send your angels to protect me.*

The windows shattered and the door swung open, throwing chairs, tables, and other furniture around the room. Mrs. Rigby fell flat onto the floor, pulling a blanket over her face. Through a fold in the blanket, she watched Parker rush outside. The sound of his barking grew fainter as he ran into the wind.

"Parker, no!" she cried, stretching her fingers towards the door and then slowly dragging them back across the hardwood floor.

High pitched squealing pinched her hearing aids and suffocated any other noise. A bright flash of light erupted and imposed itself on her vision until all that was left for her to see was thick pink flares. When the flash disappeared, the wind stopped and her hearing aids adjusted. Serenity returned to the night.

The air chilled, yet everything seemed to be as it should. With a rug wrapped around her shoulders, she ventured onto the back porch. The tree next to the barn had crashed right through it. A flashlight from an overturned coffee table rolled to her feet.

"Parker?" she yelled, scanning the cornfield a few yards from her back porch. She heard him bark in reply. "Parker, baby, stay where ya are. Mama's coming to get you."

She walked by the destroyed barn and grabbed a shovel that had been thrown into her yard. The rows of corn towered over her, but she waded through them nonetheless whistling for Parker. He didn't come running like normal, instead howling as if trapped. Her foot caught the edge of a drop off and she tumbled into a circular crater deep and wide enough to be a pool.

Parker licked her face as her blurry sight slowly came into focus. To her left, steam hissed away from a shining red and silver armored figure. It wasn't heat that gave off steam. The stranger's frigid nature permeated the air and kissed her skin.

Mrs. Rigby clenched her shovel and walked around the tall figure, whose silver plated armor was rigid and boxy. She swore the red parts underneath the silver portion watched her as she moved. The figure's helmet mimicked the look of a tiger.

Suddenly, the armor retracted, folding into itself until it formed a large, slate-grey egg, leaving the blonde man naked. The stone floated into the air and stopped. The bottom of the stone split open and a white beam shot out. It pierced through the man's back, causing him to wake and scream. Light emanated from his eyes, mouth, fingers and ears, until finally the stone vanished into thin air.

The man grimaced, grabbing his ribs as he shrieked in pain. He cried out, speaking in hundreds of different languages. Some of them Mrs. Rigby recognized, others seemed to be little more than random whistling sounds. The man sighed, his body finally relaxing. She shone her flashlight across his face. His blue eyes turned in her direction and she fell in shock.

"Bùyào pà," he said in some Asian sounding tongue she didn't understand.

"I'm sorry." Her body trembled as she pulled the shovel up to her face. "English. Afrikaans?"

"Inglés? Un momento, por favor," he replied. He squinted, as if trying to get it right. "Est-ce qu'il?"

"No. Sounded like French there. Were you a part of what happened in Paris?"

"Ich versuche zu erinnern." He grabbed his head, rubbed his temples, and then hit the ground. He roared with frustration and tried again. "Where am I?"

"Polokwane," she replied. "Who are you?"

"I am Gabriel, the messenger of God."

"Oh, that's nice." Her eyes rolled back and she fainted.

Thank You

Without the following, this novel would not have come to fruition or been its absolute possible best. I am deeply thankful for their assistance, support, feedback, comments and help. Thank you for believing in me and casting your strength upon my back to help prop me up. I am nothing but the shell of an aspiring artist and author. Because of you I evolved into something greater.

My wife, for the hours of reading with me looking over her shoulder, the many more to come, being a loving, wonderful mother to our two children and keeping track of the funds. You're my PIC, my one and only, my best friend and I'd be hopelessly lost without you.

My parents, for their annoying support, love and affection and for always telling people I'm writer, which made me work harder so I didn't look like a wanna-be-shlub when those they told looked me up.

Clare Kauter, for meticulously inspecting 120+K words for consistencies, tone shifts, correct spelling and punctuation, verb usage, and making suggestions and being all around awesome.

My BETAs, Michael, Ginette and Gretchen for putting up with my endless emails and questions. For sometimes giving way-too-brutal of opinions and saying more than "I liked it" when you found scenes that worked.

Jamie Nobel, for awesome artwork which brought my vision to life and told the novel's story without having to crack a book. You delivered that Mona Lisa.

Seth Small and Josh Johnson, for your amazing work on the book trailer and theme song respectively. You're masters of constructive criticism and refining work.

To my translators, Noe, Ginette, Ike, Olga and Chrisje.

About the Author

So, you made it. Congratulations. Was it because you really liked it, or because you know me personally and don't want to look like a douche who didn't care enough to support a friend? That's OK. You actually cracked the book. You've already done better than about 95% of my other friends—especially the ones who create shitty indie films and beg me to spend $5 to go see it, and then are somehow absent when asked to reciprocate the favor. But I'm not bitter.

You may have noticed my growing, and successful, use of the em dash in this novel. I know. I was so excited to show off my skillz using keyboard shortcuts. Did it improve your opinion of me?

You may be surprised to find out—or incredibly thankful, depending on your opinion of this book—that Artificial Light was actually intended to be much longer. However, in order to try and keep it in-line with series norms (novel, novella, novel...) I decided to cut about 25k words and expand on that to make the next installment. Those of you deeply depressed fan favorite Oreios didn't make it into the main portion of this novel (and not just the After Credits...oops, I let it slip) will be pleased to learn he makes it back for a very interesting adventure in the next book. If you were hoping to find out immediately what happens with Jarrod, Lian and the rest, you'll have to hold on. Depending on how things shake up, I have the new Oreios and Zeus buddy novel to get out, a dystopian thriller featuring Gabriel and then a horror novella set to destroy Manassas Virginia—because fuck that place and their shitty roads and traffic.

You can plainly see that this royally screws up my intended novel-novella-novel outline. Whatever. As long as you're entertained, and the series doesn't seem needlessly bloated to try and coax out more sales, who cares? It's not like I'm giving you 18 novels of school lessons and fights with the same reoccurring villain who shall not be named or maybe I should because it'd help my sales. The point is, my first novel didn't come out in 1996 and you're not still waiting for the 6th installment…or maybe that too would help my sales. Fuck.

My whole goal is to create an intriguing universe and explore all aspects of it to give you, ~~my friends and family guilt tripped into buying this book~~ the loyal reader, a comprehensive outlook on everything that's happened in the plot so that when the final end comes you know all the little quirks and what's at stake. When I'm done with this series I want to be done. I don't want to go and create a second shared world series about where to find hiding monsters, under a different pen name, and then divulge it was me all along and that yes it shares a world with Jarrod and Oreios all in the name of boosting sales…unless it would help sell more books. Dammit.

To end it all, I had a lot of fun writing this book. It was more challenging than I'd hoped, but it took many different forms and I'm very confident in the end product. I wrote a large portion of it while in the hospital with my wife as she recovered from giving birth to our gigantic baby boy and his 98 percentile sized head. The really gory and bloody parts in this novel had real-world inspiration. Yeah…

Thanks again to all of you. If you're a continued fan of this series, you've my upmost gratitude. If you're new to the world of E.o.A, I hope you check out the previous books even though you know Sanderson dies. But it's still good!

After Credits

Windswept sand permeated the cracks along the walls and roof, replenishing his form. The rumble of spectators, cheering for the release of Loki's next prized fighter, caused the ground beneath him to rattle.

"Y—Mir. Y—Mir," they chanted in sync.

Oreios had heard stories. A frozen giant with a literal axe to grind, Ymir was a ferocious warrior from realms unknown. The legends were supposed to be myth. Of course, most of the things in his life were *supposed* to be myth. Oreios, however, knew they were all too real.

A pod-drone lowered into sight, beaming a search light over him through the window. "Away," he huffed, waving the drone off. The lens in the middle of the spherical pod elongated, presumably focusing on him for the entertainment of those at home. "Seriously."

Oreios clenched a fist. The sand in the air formed jagged spikes and sliced into the turbines on each side of the pod-drone. The flying camera sputtered about and finally fell, bouncing off the ground. The sand seeped out of the pod through the cracks along the baseboards and rejoined with Oreios' frame.

The floor bounced again. It was a heftier thud and obviously not caused by the crowd. The vibration through his feet quickened and grew stronger. He peered through the door, into the fake alley made to look like something resembling urban life on earth, and watched the lifeless corpses of the other gladiators fly through the air.

A fellow fighter stabbed Oreios through the shoulder blade. The weapon pierced through his chest. "Found you," the man boasted.

Oreios yanked the spear through his chest and out of the other gladiators' grasp. A slow trickle of dirt wept from the gash before it sealed. He swiped the blunt end of the spear off the Centaur's face, knocking him cold.

"Quiet, you fucking idiot." He knelt, pressing against the wall as a shadow fell over the room. The streetlights were blocked out by an enormous figure. His hands froze against the wall behind him. Ice swirls formed along the floor, latching onto this pants and shoes. *Ymir,* he thought.

Did the frost giant see him? Could he smell the body odor of the Centaur Oreios had just cold-cocked?

Ymir's plodding footsteps headed away, growing fainter each second. The Centaur, in a daze, groaned loudly as he woke. The giant's steps halted. The Centaur spit out a few teeth and griped.

"My mouth."

"Seriously, shut up." Thunder in the walls jolted him. His body turned as loose and thin as possible, pressing into the walls.

A gigantic, translucent hand of ice bashed through the ceiling to the high pitched, feminine screams of the Centaur. The gladiator wailed like a dying pig, pleading to be spared. Oreios felt a miniscule sense of relief and quietly made his escape, crawling towards the back door.

"The Ourea," the Centaur sobbed. Suddenly, the ruckus caused by Ymir halted. His attention must've been snared. "He's in there."

"Damn it." Oreios jumped into a full-on sprint just as Ymir burst into the building, discarding the Centaur's ripped off head

Made in the USA
Charleston, SC
16 February 2016